INVASION

www.penguin.co.uk

INVASION

FRANK GARDNER

bantam

TRANSWORLD PUBLISHERS
Penguin Random House, One Embassy Gardens,
8 Viaduct Gardens, London SW11 7BW
www.penguin.co.uk

Transworld is part of the Penguin Random House group of companies
whose addresses can be found at global.penguinrandomhouse.com

Penguin
Random House
UK

First published in Great Britain in 2024 by Bantam
an imprint of Transworld Publishers

Map by Lovell Johns Ltd

A CIP catalogue record for this book
is available from the British Library.

ISBNs
9781787635470 hb
9781787635487 tpb

Typeset in 11/14.5 pt Palatino LT Std by Jouve (UK), Milton Keynes
Printed and bound in Great Britain by Clays Ltd, Elcograf S.p.A.

The authorized representative in the EEA is Penguin Random House Ireland,
Morrison Chambers, 32 Nassau Street, Dublin D02 YH68.

Penguin Random House is committed to a sustainable
future for our business, our readers and our planet. This book
is made from Forest Stewardship Council® certified paper.

In memory of Rear Admiral
John Gower CB OBE (1960–2024).
In recognition of all his work to
make this world a safer place.

*A person is blessed once, but troubles
come many at once.*

TAIWANESE PROVERB

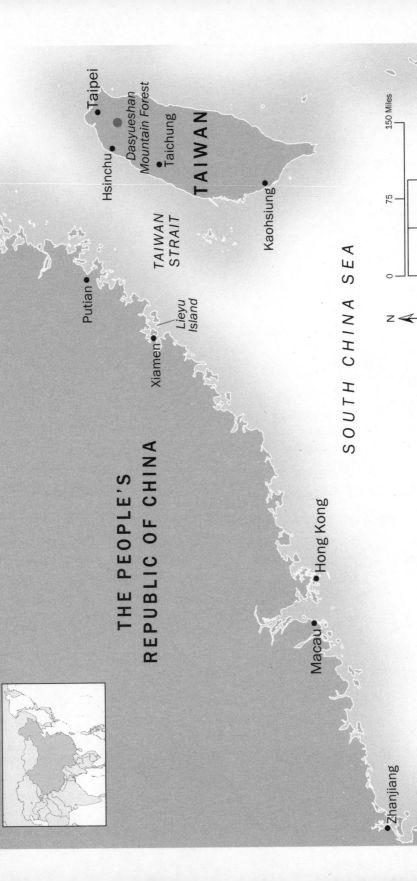

Prologue

Jinan Military Region, China

FOUR A.M. STILL DARK. A single long blast of a whistle. Within ninety seconds every member of the cadre was out of bed, dressed and standing stiffly to attention. The doors burst open with the instructors already waiting outside, yelling commands. A green Shacman lorry stood nearby on the parade ground, its exhaust fumes turning blue in the cold, pre-dawn air. This unit of the People's Liberation Army had no name; officially it did not even exist. It was known, only to a very few, as Project 49.

The lorry pulled up at the edge of the sports ground, under the blazing glare of the arc lights. The men, all in peak physical condition, dismounted and queued in silence to be weighed and measured by a team of officials in white coats with clipboards. Unsmiling nurses in surgical gloves handed out flasks for their urine samples and stuck labels on them as they were returned. The men were taken six at a time, led in batches to the start point, the course measured out precisely, right down to the last centimetre. Exactly one kilometre. No more, no less.

The first grey light of dawn was beginning to creep over the horizon as the final group completed the course and were ordered back onto the truck. The officials gathered to one side in a huddle,

1

their voices hushed and conspiratorial as they pored over the results. The timings were uncannily close together. Twenty-four men had run that course this morning and all were within touching distance of the standing world 1000-metre record. The slowest, at two minutes and twenty-five seconds, had just beaten the women's world record.

But there would be no Olympic podium for the men of Project 49, no hand-on-heart moment of public glory as the national anthem was played to a packed stadium. Instead, these young men were destined for another purpose and the world would never know their names.

1

Lambeth Bridge, London

EIGHT THIRTY ON a Monday morning and the traffic into central London was grindingly slow. Few people queuing to cross Lambeth Bridge that day noticed the tourist in the baseball cap and trainers, standing on the pavement beneath the plane trees, as he held out his smartphone for a selfie. If the traffic had been moving even slower they might have noticed he was taking a video, grinning broadly into the multiple lenses as he mouthed a silent piece-to-camera. Nothing unusual about that: tourists did it every day in London.

But what no one could see was that he wasn't filming himself at all. With a rock-steady hand and specially installed high-resolution lenses, his phone camera was focused on the steady stream of men and women behind him as they walked briskly up the steps of a large, imposing building, then disappeared behind heavy doors. Ten minutes was all it took. Enough time to record the faces, movements and gait patterns of sixty-two employees of Britain's Security Service, better known as MI5, as they arrived for work at Thames House. Other people would be back on other days, in different guises and from different vantage points, to carry out similarly discreet 'captures' on their phones. But before the eleventh minute 'the tourist' was already off the scene, vanishing into the crowd of pedestrians walking up Horseferry Road before the camera operators inside the building picked him out as suspicious and sent a pair of armed policemen to investigate.

By mid-morning 'the tourist's' phone was inside the Embassy of the People's Republic of China on Portland Place. By lunchtime its contents had been edited, catalogued and sent on securely to the databases of the Ministry of State Security in Beijing. There it would be cross-matched with the already growing data, biometric and otherwise, held by China on the thousands of people who worked for Britain's three intelligence agencies. Beijing was particularly interested in those likely to travel overseas, those who worked for MI6 or GCHQ, who might one day arrive in the People's Republic pretending to be something they were not. If the scanners at Immigration didn't catch them out there were always other ways, like their hotels, for example, where a simple voice recording at check-in would reveal if their voice patterns were already on the Ministry's records.

Getting an agent or an officer into a hard intelligence target like China had become a whole lot trickier in recent years. But it was not impossible.

2

Hong Kong International Airport

STAY CALM AND BREATHE. Dr Hannah Slade repeated the mantra in her head, over and over again, as her place in the queue inched forward, moving ever closer to the immigration officers' booth. She could see them sitting side by side behind the glass: white shirt, black tie, pale blue facemask, their hands moving quickly over their computer keyboards as they scanned in each passenger.

What if . . .?

No. Stop it. She wasn't going to allow herself to think like that. Hannah Slade knew there was almost zero chance that the People's Republic of China would have her details on record as anything other than what she was: a full-time climate scientist and researcher at Imperial College London. It was all there in the university records office if anyone cared to check. But that wasn't quite the full story, was it? Because as well as holding a PhD in human geography and environmental science Dr Slade was also a 'collector', someone who, very occasionally, MI6 could call on, sparingly, only in exceptional circumstances, to send into a country incognito for a highly sensitive mission. Which meant she must never be seen or photographed in the company of an intelligence officer, let alone darken the doors of Vauxhall Cross, that sandstone and green monolith on the south bank of the Thames that served as the headquarters of Britain's Secret Intelligence Service. That was the way it had always been, ever since the first approach they had made to her in the month after she graduated. There were meetings, of course, there had to be, but always somewhere anodyne and anonymous like a park or a café. So Hannah Slade was totally off the books. Not even her departmental head at Imperial College had the slightest notion of what she got up to on her leave breaks.

So now here she was, heart thumping, as the immigration officer beckoned her forward to his booth, gesturing for her to look straight into the camera. She had been to Hong Kong before, long ago, as a teenager, visiting her older sister when it was still a British colony and expatriate British officers strode around in lime green uniforms. But that was a holiday and this was different. Very different. 'We cannot stress enough,' they had told her back in London, 'just how critical this operation is, Hannah. What you are about to do for us in Hong Kong is . . . well . . . let's just say it's going to have an immediate effect on Britain's national security.'

'Purpose of visit?' She realized with a start it was the second time the immigration officer had asked her this question.

'Oh, er, yes, sorry. A conference. I'm here for the climate-change conference. It's being held at . . .' He held up his hand and nodded, stamped her passport and waved her on. She was through.

3

Taiwan Strait

IT WAS A combined maritime Task Group, intended to send a strong message to Beijing. Three warships from three nations, all thousands of nautical miles from home, under the command of a seasoned US Navy two-star rear admiral. From the UK: HMS *Daring*, a Type 45 destroyer, designed and equipped for air defence. From the US Navy's massive Seventh Fleet: one of the new DDG(X) guided missile destroyers, armed with an array of hypersonic missiles. And from Australia: HMAS *Warramunga*, an ageing Anzac-class frigate out of Fleet Base East, Sydney.

The mission was widely advertised in advance, with China's People's Liberation Army Navy duly notified through all the right channels, and prompting a predictably angry response. This was billed by Washington as a 'Freedom of Navigation' exercise, a joint demonstration by members of the AUKUS defence pact – Australia, the UK and the US – of their right to sail unimpeded through international waters, from the South China Sea, past the self-governing island of Taiwan, northward up into the East China Sea. A robust response, said the joint press release, to China's recent attempts to restrict the movement of international shipping in the region, notably its recent live-fire exercises in the seas surrounding Taiwan.

'A dangerous and irresponsible provocation' was how the *People's Daily* described the AUKUS naval patrol in the official newspaper of the Chinese Communist Party, the CCP. 'The peace-loving people of China reject the military presence of neo-imperialist nations in this region,' it said. 'They must understand that such incursions will carry consequences.'

Up on the bridge of HMS *Daring*, the Officer of the Watch picked up a pair of Zeiss Marine 7x50 binoculars and stared hard at the horizon. They had company. For the past several hours they had been shadowed at a discreet distance by warships of the People's Liberation Army Navy. *Daring* was at a state of heightened, but not maximum, alert, known in the Navy as defence watches. The Ops Room, the beating heart of any Royal Navy warship, was fully closed up, its occupants watchful and wary as the Task Group steamed northward through one of the biggest potential flashpoints on the globe.

It was one of those bleached, tropical days when everything – the sky, the sea, the hazy cloud – all appeared white, bled dry of all colour, as the sun beat down from directly overhead. But *Daring* was the lead ship in the Task Group and Lieutenant Chris Bailey, the Officer of the Watch, was not interested in aesthetics. He was focused instead on the objects at some distance off their port bow.

'I count three PLA surface vessels,' he said to the bosun's mate beside him. 'Ops – Bridge.' He spoke into the intercom connecting him to the Principal Warfare Officer down in the Ops Room. 'What have you got?'

'Four surface,' came the response. 'Plus one maritime patrol aircraft airborne. Looks to be a Shaanxi KQ-200.'

'Any contact?'

'None so far. But we're in our lane and they're in theirs. We're maintaining course just east of the median line. We've got Taiwan fifty-two nautical miles to starboard and the Chinese mainland just over fifty-four nautical miles off our port side.'

'Happy days then.' Lieutenant Bailey put down the binos and turned to ask for someone to bring him a fresh coffee from the galley. But he never got to make that request.

'Officer of the Watch – port lookout!' The shout came from the bosun's mate, a young able seaman, his pale complexion still blistered from the tropical sun on deck. 'Large flash seen on fo'c's'le of Chinese warship,' he called.

'Jesus Christ!' exclaimed the navigation officer next to him. 'They've just launched a missile!'

4

Hong Kong

THE KOWLOON BAY International Trade and Exhibition Centre could have been almost any exhibition centre anywhere in the world. A vast and shiny complex built on the shores of Kowloon Bay, it was right next to the site of Hong Kong's old Kai Tak airport, where the planes used to come in so low over the apartment blocks their wheels almost took the washing lines down with them. Hannah sat in the last but one row of the 702-seat tiered auditorium, her phone on silent, clasped in her hand. This was only the first day of the climate conference and already she had handed out nearly half the business cards she had brought with her from London.

She glanced down as her phone softly vibrated with an incoming text. She read it twice, memorized the contents and deleted it. She got up, mouthing apologies to the other delegates as she squeezed past them. Then she was striding quickly across the thick beige carpet and out through a side door. The cloying heat and humidity of a Hong Kong afternoon enveloped her the moment she stepped outside. Squinting against the hazy sunlight, she summoned one of the red and white taxis lined up outside, climbed into the back seat and spoke briefly to the driver. As they moved off into the traffic she noted the number plate of the car behind, just to make sure it was not still there when she got out at the other end. A little trick they had taught her one afternoon on one of their strolls through Kensington Gardens.

But the briefing for this operation had been rather more thorough. And ominous. It was a 'collection' job, a pick-up from an agent, then a flight on to Singapore and home. But there were risks. They had been very clear about that. If she was caught with the data in her possession she was on her own, no diplomatic cover, no gunboats to the rescue. His Majesty's Government would deny all knowledge. Hannah would be looking at a lengthy jail sentence somewhere on the mainland with no chance of an early release unless there happened to be someone in British custody for whom Beijing was willing to trade her. Was she absolutely sure she still wanted to do this? they asked. There was no obligation, no pressure, no outdated waffle about some higher cause. Just a simple statement, delivered by a middle-aged woman in a charcoal grey jacket on a bench beside the Serpentine. 'If you do this for us, Hannah, you will in all likelihood be saving an awful lot of lives.'

China had already been labelled 'a strategic threat' to UK security in the Government's recent Integrated Review. Delivering his annual public speech, the MI6 Chief had made no secret of the fact that China now took up more of the Service's time than anything else, even Russia.

To say that the agent she would be meeting was well placed would have been an understatement. 'Blue Sky' – every operational agent was assigned a codename – was a senior military scientific adviser to the Central Committee of the Chinese Communist Party. Recruited more than two years ago at a conference in Singapore, Blue Sky had the most extraordinary access to the very epicentre of military decision-making in Beijing. After painstakingly careful development by a team of fluent Mandarin speakers based in Vauxhall Cross he was now providing London with top-grade CX, jargon for the raw intelligence that comes straight from an agent before it is cross-checked and assessed by the reports team.

Contact with Blue Sky was intermittent. It had to be, for his own safety. China's all-seeing Ministry of State Security took a dim view of traitors and their careers tended to finish with a single bullet to the brain in some dusty prison courtyard out of public sight and hundreds of miles away from their now disgraced and newly impoverished families.

Hannah had asked the obvious question at that pre-mission briefing beside the Serpentine. 'Why can't your agent just send you the data electronically? Why do you need me to collect it in person? I mean, I'm not saying I won't do it, I'd just like to know why.'

Charcoal Jacket had had a ready answer for that one: it was exactly what she'd been expecting Hannah to ask. 'Because we simply can't take that risk,' she had replied. 'You probably know this already, but for some years now the Ministry of State Security has been rolling up the CIA's entire network of agents in-country. We're talking dozens of human informants arrested and interrogated. And, yes,' she paused, sucking air through her teeth, 'there have been some executions. So how did China manage to do this? By breaking into what our friends in Langley thought was a totally secure means of communication. But it was internet-based using the dark web, and Beijing found a way in. They're bloody good at that, I have to admit. So, one by one, they were able to lift all the right people by back-tracing them to everyone who'd logged into what was supposed to be a secure account. Even turned some of them into double agents.'

'But you operate on a different system?' Hannah had replied.

'Exactly. We ring-fenced our operations to be completely separate from the Americans. You can call it old-school if you like, but we must be doing something right because the fact is our agents are still in place, still delivering the goods and theirs are . . . well . . .' She left that sentence unfinished. 'Which is where you come in, Hannah. I'm now going to take you through how you're going to get Blue Sky's data securely out of Hong Kong without being detected. I need you to listen really, really carefully to what I'm about to tell you.'

5

Onboard HMS Daring, *Taiwan Strait*

IF THE OFFICER of the Watch had not had his back turned at that precise moment he might well have been the first person on the bridge to spot the brilliant flash erupting off their port bow. But it fell to one of the most junior members of the ship's company to raise the alarm. Able Seaman Ben Collins already had his binoculars trained on the Chinese warships when he spotted the missile launch a full three seconds before it was picked up and tracked by the Ops Room.

There, the Principal Warfare Officer, the PWO, had to make a snap life-or-death decision. Was the missile a threat to the ship? Was it aimed at them? Was *Daring* or its accompanying vessels under attack or was this a warning shot across their bows? Because if the missile had been launched with intent to harm, the Ops Room had mere seconds left to react and activate the ship's suite of defensive measures while the crew took evasive action. Royal Navy Rules of Engagement are classified but they include, in extremis, the option to open fire on the source of the threat. Underact and you put the safety of the entire ship and its crew in jeopardy. Overact and you risk starting the Third World War.

'Air threat warning red!' The voice of the PWO rang out across the cramped and tense Ops Room. It was followed immediately by his next urgent announcement: 'Captain to the Ops Room.' Under the subdued lighting of this low-ceilinged room, onboard the Royal Navy's state-of-the-art air defence destroyer, the men and women in their dark navy blue overalls stared intently at the ship's command system. To their alarm, *Daring*'s computer was generating a track making its way across the blue screens, moving at such a high velocity it could only be a missile. The track was red, indicating it was hostile. This was not a drill. This was real.

'Missile – track 2500-350 one mile tracking north-east speed fast. Opening contact,' came the announcement on the command open line, the COL, the main internal voice net linking all the ship's key operatives. Then a second report: 'Target is tracking right and opening. It is not directed at us.' The PWO had made his snap decision. As he spoke these words there was a slight but almost palpable change in atmosphere in the Ops Room. HMS *Daring*'s defensive suite of missiles, chaff and Phalanx Gatling gun firing four thousand rounds a minute of depleted uranium shells were not about to be triggered by an explosive warhead hurtling towards it at supersonic speed. Those in the Ops Room who had been glued to their screens now dared to look up and exchange knowing glances. But a missile had still been fired in their close vicinity, an overtly hostile act, and they still had another eight hours' sailing northward before they would be clear of the Taiwan Strait.

'Captain's on open line,' someone called out. Commander Ross Blane, who had returned to his cabin minutes earlier, was now patched into the Ops Room. It was the on-watch Anti-Air-Warfare Officer whose job it was now to brief him.

'Captain, sir – AAWO sitrep,' she began. '*Lhasa* has just fired a missile believed to be a YJ-21. Now bearing 030 10 miles outbound speed fast and increasing. Closest point of approach one mile ahead so no direct threat. I say again, no direct threat.

'Looks like a warning shot and deliberate provocation.' The AAWO continued with her situation report to the Captain. 'Have not deployed chaff or IDS300 Inflatable Decoy. We are now covering *Lhasa* with fire control radar. Rules of Engagement state this could be hostile intent but not yet a hostile act. Remaining weapons tight.'

'Thank you, AAWO, and good work,' the Captain replied.

Exactly twenty-five seconds later he appeared in the Ops Room. He had walked fast from his cabin, then slid down a ladder, gone straight to his seat and put on his headset. At the same time he addressed the Principal Warfare Officer. 'PWO, Captain – any indications they're about to fire again?'

'None so far, sir.'

He nodded, then reached for the command open line to issue his orders.

'All positions, Captain – this was a practice firing by Chinese ship, the *Lhasa*. There is no indication it has been aimed at us. Weapons remain tight. All positions, ensure maximum attention is on that ship to watch for any further activity.'

He replaced his headset and ran through a mental checklist of all that still needed to be done. Contact had to be made from the bridge to the Chinese warship via VHF radio and an explanation sought for their actions. He was not optimistic they would get any response. Then he needed to confer with the Task Group Commander, the US Navy rear admiral onboard the guided missile destroyer to their stern. And he also needed to alert the UK's Permanent Joint Headquarters at Northwood, the sprawling base on the edge of London from where all overseas operations are run around the clock. From there, this event would be passed up the chain of command to the Chief of Joint Operations and on to the MoD and Number 10.

Commander Blane shifted his position in his seat in the Ops Room. It was going to be a busy few hours. They had just gone through one of the most serious incidents with the Chinese Navy that he could remember and they were not out of the Taiwan Strait yet. This, he thought, is how wars start.

6

Whitehall, London

A SOFT MORNING rain was falling on the pavement outside 70 Whitehall as one by one they hurried up the three steps to gather inside. How many secrets, how many crises, how many decisions affecting millions of people had been taken over the years in this pale-stone 1840s building? And not all of them had worked out for the best.

Before the Covid-19 pandemic had swept across the world in 2020 there were relatively few people in Britain who were familiar with the expression 'a COBRA meeting'. This serpentile acronym stood for Cabinet Office Briefing Room A, a reference to a subterranean chamber where, inside 70 Whitehall, senior British ministers and others held their crisis meetings, often at short notice. It could be drought, it could be Covid, it could be Russia's invasion of Ukraine on the menu.

'The situation with China has clearly turned critical,' the PM began, addressing the rows of frowning faces at either side of the long table in front of him. The cast list included all of the key figures in Britain's national defence and security apparatus: the Defence Secretary, the Foreign Secretary, the National Security Adviser, the MI6 Chief, the Director-General of GCHQ, the Chief of Defence Staff and the First Sea Lord, plus all their note-takers and SPADs, most of them listening in from the adjacent ante-room, working their secure tablets and sending short, cryptic messages and prompts to their bosses in the main room. Up on the screen at the far end silent TV footage from the BBC kept flashing the logo 'Breaking News', followed by the words in bold: 'China fires missile near Western warships'.

'I'm not going to downplay this,' the PM continued. 'We are at an extremely dangerous juncture here. We – no, the world – *cannot* afford to get into a shooting war with China.' Pursed lips and a nodding head from Simon Eustace, the Defence Secretary; others doing the same. 'What just happened in the Taiwan Strait changes the whole paradigm in the South China Sea. Heaven knows we've done our damnedest to avoid escalation with Bei-jing but they have absolutely crossed the line here!' He slapped the palm of his hand onto the table for emphasis. 'It's only by the grace of God it didn't escalate further, that our American friends showed commendable restraint and didn't retaliate in kind. Right . . . First Sea Lord.' He looked along the row of faces until his eyes settled on the head of the Royal Navy, Admiral Patrick Seaton. 'Take us through the specifics, will you?'

Admiral Seaton sat bolt upright in his chair, as if he had just received a mild electric shock. A tall, grey-haired and thoughtful officer, he had recently been told he would not be getting the top job when the Chief of Defence Staff retired, something every-body said he had taken with remarkably good grace.

'Absolutely, PM.' He reached for his glasses and shuffled his notes. He tapped a pad next to him and looked up expectantly at the giant TV wall screen at the other end of the room. Nothing happened. 'Right. Well. As you were,' he said, pushing the pad away from him, like an unwanted pudding. 'So. The missile fired close to *Daring* by the Chinese warship was a YJ-21 anti-ship mis-sile. A hypersonic missile, in fact. That means it was travelling at roughly eight times the speed of sound before it eventually landed in the sea just off the coast of Taiwan. It was launched from one of their new Type 055 destroyers, *Lhasa*.' The First Sea Lord paused as a naval officer darted over and leant across him

17

to fiddle with the malfunctioning keypad. Now a new image burst into life at the other end of the room. It showed shaky and slightly blurred footage of a blaze of light streaking over the sea with the bow of a warship in the foreground. The object was moving so fast it was impossible to make it out but everyone in that room knew exactly what it was.

'That,' pronounced Admiral Seaton, 'is the missile in question. It's known as a "carrier killer" and the vessel that fired it is one of their new stealth warships. Thirteen thousand tonnes. Oh, and this footage hasn't been released to the media yet so you're some of the first people to see it.'

The video stopped abruptly and froze, the screen went blank, and for a few seconds nobody said anything.

'Secretary of State?' The PM raised an eyebrow in the direction of the Defence Secretary, Simon Eustace, a former Grenadier Guardsman. He had a habit of staying late when he was working in MoD Main Building, which meant nobody around him could go home until he did.

He removed his glasses in one practised swipe and pushed his chair back from the table. 'Look,' he said. 'I think we can all see this for exactly what it is. It's pure theatrics, but bloody dangerous ones. They're playing with fire. Beijing's been threatening something like this ever since Taiwan elected a president they don't like, back in early 2024. Never mind that that missile landed in the sea and didn't kill anyone. This was supposed to be a warning. To us, to Washington, to Taipei, in fact to all our allies in the region. They want us to back away from Taiwan and leave that island defenceless for when China makes a grab for it. And let's not forget this comes on the back of a whole succession of aggressive Chinese military manoeuvres in the seas around Taiwan. Not to mention that their defence budget has more than doubled – yes, doubled – since 2015.'

The Defence Secretary looked like he had more to say but the PM had his hand up. It was someone else's turn now. 'Thank you for that, Simon,' he said. 'This brings us to the tricky question of how we respond. We're raising it at the UN Security Council, obviously. We're proposing a joint draft resolution, along with the US and Australia, condemning China's actions. Not a squeak from Beijing so far. There's always the option of sanctions, of course. In fact we've already had a call from the White House on that score.' The PM shook his head slowly as he said this. 'But we have to be realistic here. China practically controls the world's supply chain for just about every commodity you can think of, so sanctions would end up hurting us as much as them, if not more so. But let's get to the point. What's the elephant in the room here, hmm? Anybody?'

A few people looked at each other and mouthed silent suggestions but nobody spoke. The PM was well known for asking rhetorical questions.

'It's Taiwan, obviously,' he continued. 'And, more specifically, the question of whether we're prepared to go to war with the world's largest navy and second-largest economy just to save an island on the other side of the world from invasion. Because, let's face it, it's thousands of miles away, doesn't even have a seat at the UN, and most people in this country have never been there – I suspect a lot of them probably think it's already part of China. Frankly, it was hard enough getting people to stay onside over Ukraine when they've been facing soaring household bills.'

He looked around the room, his eyebrows arched in question. But those close to him knew the PM for what he was: a pronounced hawk when it came to China and its threats to seize Taiwan. He was playing devil's advocate.

'Zara . . .' The PM turned to the woman on his right. Thin, angular, wearing a navy blue jacket, her hair scraped back into a ponytail, Zara Simmons, the National Security Adviser, had been until recently a reservist with the Army's 77 Brigade. She was also the only civilian in the room to have served on operations in Afghanistan, a point of which she liked to remind her colleagues regularly. 'Take us through it, will you,' the PM continued, 'for the benefit of everyone in this room. Just why should we give a damn about defending Taiwan?'

7

Kowloon, Hong Kong

WHAT, IN GOD'S NAME, had made her agree to do this? As the taxi sped her along the eight-lane expressway in air-conditioned silence Hannah Slade turned the question over and over in her head. Was it for the money? Hell, no. The Service was paying her expenses, suitably routed through a circuitous cover, but that was about all. As a respected authority in her field of study, she was invited to quite enough conferences around the world as it was, without having to take on this sort of risk. Was it patriotism? Well, yes, maybe. She had always liked the idea of doing something discreet, behind the scenes, to serve King and country. But no, there had to be something else, and the sane, sensible scientist in her shuddered to admit it. It was the sheer bloody thrill of it, the hint of danger, the mystique of doing something highly valued by her handlers at the Secret Intelligence Service, an organization whose doors she had never darkened.

She had gone for the interview to join in her final year at university – in fact she knew of quite a few people who had done the same. That strange, stilted conversation with a balding man in a grey suit in an upstairs room in London's Carlton Gardens. He had shoved a copy of the Official Secrets Act across the desk at her to sign then told her how, if she were lucky enough to be selected for admission and training, she would be able to tell almost no one what she did for a living. Oh, and because she would be unlikely ever to make ambassador she would appear to most people to be a mid-career failure. By the time the interview was over Hannah had already made up her mind: a career in MI6 was not for her. But then had come the second approach, the offer of a little secret work on the side, no strings attached. And something inside Hannah Slade had stirred. It was the idea of having her cake and eating it, of pursuing her full-time career in science yet every so often going off on . . . well . . . a secret mission. Yes, there was no other word for it. And this one, for some hush-hush reason they weren't prepared to tell her, was apparently more important than anything she had ever done for them before.

She glanced out of the taxi window at the towering canyons of white tenement blocks that had sprung up beside the road. A sign they passed told her it was called Prince Edward Road East. More than a quarter of a century had passed since Handover, the day in 1997 when Britain had returned the colony to Chinese rule, yet somehow, she noticed, Hong Kong had managed to cling on to these colonial British names like Argyle Street, Boundary Street and even, she saw on her phone map, somewhere called 'Good Shepherd Street'. Perhaps, she mused, that's what I am to them in Vauxhall Cross. A good shepherd, bringing home the data, safely undetected. And this job was apparently so sensitive they couldn't even let MI6's Hong Kong station know she was coming. It had to be watertight, sealed off from all but a tiny number of people in the know. Never underestimate the opposition, they had told her, in one of their park-bench briefings back in London. China's Ministry of State Security had watchers everywhere and this was their home turf.

Outside the window the scene had changed. Now she was looking onto drab, crowded, low-rise apartment blocks with washing hanging out on every balcony. Rusting air-conditioning units clung to the walls, looking as if they might fall off into the street at any moment. They were now in a world of narrow, traffic-choked side-streets where every shop sign was in Chinese, while English signage had disappeared. They lurched forward, then the driver slammed on the brakes and banged his fist on the steering wheel in frustration, cursing in Cantonese, as an old woman hobbled slowly past in front, her deeply lined face looking up at him for a fleeting moment, her lips muttering a silent profanity.

Hannah checked her map once more. They were nearly there. She asked to be let out at the junction of Nga Tsin Wai Road and Nga Tsin Long Road, paying the driver and stepping quickly into the shade of an awning. According to her phone, the assigned rendezvous for the pick-up was just fifty metres ahead. Casually, she strolled on past it as she'd been told, her eyes taking in the clothes shops, the furniture emporium and the empty barber's shop where the owner sat outside on a stool in his white vest and crumpled shorts, smoking as he waited for customers. She stopped in front of a large plate-glass window and studied her reflection, waiting to see if anyone stopped abruptly behind her. Good. No tail. She doubled back and pushed open the door to the rendezvous.

The Tai Wo Tang Café was sandwiched between a food store and a video shop. Its dark and uninviting entrance gave way to a cavernous interior where framed photographs of past clientele hung from a railing and bare pinewood tables stretched all the way to the back. At this time of day, on a hot afternoon midweek, there were no customers. She chose a table near the back with a clear view of the door, and before long a girl in an apron emerged to take her order. She asked for iced lemon tea and checked her watch. She was early, just as she had intended.

Seven minutes later a slight, middle-aged man walked in and sat down at a nearby table. He was facing her but looking down and paying her no attention. Suit trousers, short-sleeved white shirt, baseball cap pulled down low over his face and tinted glasses. She watched him as he spoke to the waitress to give his order and now he was getting up and coming over to her. Hannah felt her pulse quickening.

'Have you tried the peach tea?' he said, in heavily accented English, standing over her. This was it – this was the moment. Get one word wrong in her response now and this man would walk out of that door and her whole mission would end in failure.

'Too sweet for my taste,' she replied, enunciating each word clearly as they had made her practise. She saw his expression change as a flash of recognition passed over his face. It was Blue Sky.

'May I?' He gestured to the chair opposite her.

'Please.' She waved an invitation with her hand.

She watched him scrape the chair back, sit down, glancing once towards the door to the street, and now he was extending his closed hand towards her across the table. He held her gaze, nodding towards his closed fist but saying nothing. Even above the hum of the air-conditioning Hannah thought she could hear her heart thumping in her ears. She looked down at his hand as he slowly uncurled his fingers. And there it was, nestling in the palm: the flash drive mini, tiny yet with a massive storage capacity. It looked exactly like the one they had shown her, the one she had practised with, over and over again, in her bathroom in London.

Gently, with her thumb and forefinger, she took the flash drive off him. Already he was getting up to leave. No words, no small-talk about the humidity outside, no goodbyes. The handover had been made. She knew what she had to do now, without a moment's delay. By the time the man was out of the door, leaving her alone in the empty café, she was reaching into her pocket for the packet of chewing gum they had given her. Wrigley's Spearmint, it said on the packet, and indeed she could smell the mint-flavoured powder even as she unwrapped the first stick. Quickly, she popped it into her mouth and began to chew. Moments later, as soon as the gum had become a moist, sticky ball, she spat it into the palm of her hand and pressed the tiny memory stick into it, taking care to envelop it so nothing protruded. Then keeping her eyes on the door, she took the wad of gum with its contents and pressed it carefully into the gap behind her third upper molar, the gap where her wisdom tooth had long ago been removed. Within seconds it would harden and be all but invisible to anyone unless they knew exactly what to look for. It was time to pay up, head out of the door and catch that flight to Singapore.

It was just as she was getting up to pay that she saw the two men walk in. Despite the heat they were wearing suits, dressed like civil servants, but she could see they were stockily built and they didn't look to Hannah like the sort of people who worked in an office. Once, when she was fourteen and riding her bicycle, she had been involved in a road accident. She had watched the car swerving and skidding towards her before it hit her side-on with a terrible bang. The whole thing could not have lasted more than three seconds at most, and yet it had seemed to her at the time to play out in slow motion. What Hannah was experiencing right now, in the Tai Wo Tang Café in Kowloon, was just such a moment.

Half mesmerized, she watched as the men turned and locked the bolts on the door from the inside then began pushing their way past the tables and chairs towards her, closing the distance between them. With a jolt, she realized she was trapped. Instinctively, she screamed for help and dashed towards the kitchen area at the back but there was no one there and nobody came to her aid. It was all happening very fast. Within seconds the men were on her: the choke hold, the breathless struggle, the frantic kicking and the awful feeling of being outnumbered by superior odds and then, in the final moment, the chloroform pad being clamped over her nose and mouth as Dr Hannah Slade sank helplessly into oblivion.

8

Whitehall, London

'MICROCHIPS.' ZARA SIMMONS pronounced the word slowly, as if she were addressing a small child. 'Mi-cro-chips.' She repeated the word, looking up and down the rows of faces in the COBRA meeting room as she did so. Britain's youthful National Security Adviser was not everyone's cup of tea. Her direct and sometimes patronizing approach had ruffled quite a few feathers in Cabinet since her appointment. That didn't bother her one bit. She knew her brief, she had the ear of the PM, and when it came to China they were on exactly the same page.

'We ask ourselves why should we care about Taiwan? Well, the answer is simple: microchips. Some of you might know them as semiconductors. Or "integrated circuits". They're pretty much the same thing. But what matters is what they do and where they come from. So let's cut straight to the chase here.' She pressed the palms of her hands together, as if in prayer. 'Almost everything we rely on in our modern, daily lives depends on these microchips. The car that brought you here? It uses microchips. The smartphone you handed in at the door? Microchips. The laptop you carry around with you? Microchips. The satellite that's beaming those pictures we've just been looking at from the Taiwan Strait? Microchips. And those are just the items for civilian use. When it comes to our national defence, our missiles, our computer systems, our satellites, we are completely reliant on an uninterrupted, free-flowing supply of these semiconductors. Which brings us to Taiwan.'

She glanced across to the PM, who nodded for her to go on.

'And, yes,' said Zara Simmons, 'you've guessed it. Around 90 per cent of the world's high-end microchips are produced on the island that China is so keen to get its hands on. Because only Taiwan has the technology to refine the production of these semiconductors down to just three nanometres or less. That's three *billionths* of a metre. It is infinitesimally small and not even China can match that to the same standard. So let's just think for a moment of what would happen if China made good on its promise to "take back" Taiwan.'

She paused for effect, watching the reactions around the room. Some of the people at the table, mostly men, were nearly twice her age, but she could see she had their attention.

'Well, I'll tell you the first thing that would happen if there were war. Taiwan's production of these semiconductors would almost certainly come to an immediate halt. That would cause a worldwide shortage, leading to soaring inflation and massive problems in the supply chain for dozens of industries that we depend on in our daily lives. It would do vastly more damage to our economy than Putin's invasion of Ukraine. Put simply, it would cripple it.'

Again, a nod from the PM for her to continue.

'But let's suppose that in the event of war over Taiwan the most valuable production centre for these microchips – that's the Taiwan Semiconductor Manufacturing Company, the TSMC – does *not* get destroyed. And I hear there are plenty of people in Taiwan who think the company's premises would be the safest place to hide if hostilities broke out. What then? If China were able to overwhelm Taiwan's defences or force a surrender by choking it off from the outside world, we'd be looking at a situation in which Beijing controls the entire world's production of high-end microchips. Can you picture that? They would have us over a barrel.'

The National Security Adviser stopped to take a sip of water. She hadn't quite finished. 'So that's just the microchips dimension.

26

We haven't even touched on the geo-political and the strategic. Anyone want to hazard a guess at how much trade passes through the South China Sea each year? . . . Well, I'll tell you. Three *trillion* dollars' worth. That's right, three trillion dollars. That's more than this country's entire GDP.'

The more observant in the room picked up on the fact that Zara Simmons was blatantly copying the PM's habit here: asking the room a question out loud and answering it herself. But nobody interrupted her.

'China,' she continued, 'has already grabbed a whole slew of islands and reefs in the South China Sea that are nowhere near its own coast. It's concreted them over, built landing strips and missile bases, and claimed them all for its own, despite an international tribunal declaring it illegal in 2016. It's even had the gall to publish what it calls its "standard map", laying claim to practically the entire sea, plus Taiwan.'

Another pause, another sip of water and a quick gesture to an aide to fetch her a refill.

'What do we think the effect will be,' she continued, 'for our friends and allies in the region, if Beijing is able to get away with invading and occupying a successful, pro-Western democracy like Taiwan? It would mean a catastrophic defeat for the US – and, by extension, this country – that would put the West's humiliating exit from Afghanistan in 2021 in the shade. It would embolden every autocratic and authoritarian state in the world and send a message that the free world was no longer prepared to defend its interests or indeed the rules-based international order.'

The PM's arms had been folded all the time he was listening to her. They had already gone through together what she would say in this COBRA meeting. Now she had finished he unfolded them, stood up and addressed the room. 'Right, then,' he said. 'I don't think there can be any dispute about it. Taiwan matters. With our allies in the region – Japan, South Korea, Australia – we simply cannot allow Taiwan to be swallowed up by the People's Republic of China or we shall find ourselves dancing to Beijing's tune for the next forty years. Does anyone have any questions?'

9

Richmond Park, London

LUKE CARLTON HATED himself. Or, more accurately, he hated his own weakness. Second circuit around Richmond Park on his Carrera Hellcat mountain bike and already he was flagging, running out of puff. What the hell was this? He pushed his polarized cycling glasses up onto his forehead, wiped the back of his gloved hand across his face and peered down at the tachometer. Just twenty kilometres covered since he had begun his circuits and he hadn't even expected to break a sweat. Twelve years in the Royal Marines, the last four spent in the elite Special Boat Service, and now a rising star as a case officer in MI6. Yet here he was, on the cusp of forty, wheezing like an old man and taking in great gulps of air as if his life depended on it. He didn't even recognize these limitations on his own body. The body that he had pushed and pulled through the gruelling endurance course down at the Commando Training Centre at Lympstone in Devon years ago as a 'nod', a raw recruit. The body that had survived on less than a thousand calories a day on escape-and-evasion exercises on some godforsaken, windswept Hebridean island, only to be pegged out sleepless and half naked in the wind and rain by sadistic paratroopers as he underwent the dreaded part of Special Forces Selection known as TQ – Tactical Questioning.

But there was no escaping the truth: the contamination was to blame. He knew that, but it still didn't make it any easier to accept. The bald fact was that at the climax of an earlier operation he had come face to face with a lethal pathogen hidden inside an explosive device in an Essex warehouse, placed there by a far-right extremist group. He had been lucky to escape with his life; others had not been so fortunate.

Laid low, weak and supine, confined for months to a hospital bed in an isolation unit, being treated night and day by people masked up in full PPE, Luke's convalescence had been without question the worst period of his life and he was trying hard to put it behind him. More than once he had wondered if he was going to make it. In all, seven people had been infected with Agent X when he and the police counter-terrorist specialist fire-arms officers had burst into a booby-trapped warehouse on that industrial estate. Five had later succumbed. Luke and a police sergeant only survived after weeks in intensive care undergoing experimental treatment with a desperate, last-resort drug ther-apy. 'Your immune system will probably be compromised now for the rest of your life,' they had warned him on discharge. 'We're taking you off active operations,' they had told him, once he returned to duty at Vauxhall Cross.

'Sod that,' Luke had responded, as he beasted himself over and over in the gym, for weeks on end, yearning to get his body back into peak condition. Yet here he was now, catching his breath as he gripped the handlebars, pounded the pedals and looked reality straight in its ugly face. The fact was that Agent X had nearly killed him. He was lucky to be alive, so whatever his fitness levels were now, he would just have to live with them.

When his phone went off in his breast pocket he jammed on the brakes and pulled off the track. It was Angela Scott, his line manager at VX, as those who worked at Vauxhall Cross some-times referred to it.

'So . . . listen, Luke, we've got a situation,' she told him. 'I need you here as soon as possible. The Chief's called a crisis meeting and I want you there.'

At this, he felt an overwhelming sense of déjà vu. How many operations had begun with those self-same words? Missions in Colombia . . . Armenia . . . Iran . . . Lithuania . . . Assignments that he would never be able to talk about, not even to his partner, not that he had one at the moment. These were places and names he would likely take with him all the way to the grave.

'Taiwan?' he asked. 'Is that what this is about? Because it's not looking good, is it?'

'We'll discuss that when you get in,' Angela replied. 'Oh, and I should add, April's going to be there.'

'Shit. So it's serious.'

'You could say that. So forget about your day off and just get in here ASAP.' She hung up.

A meeting attended by 'April' was a rare and unwelcome thing. It usually meant something, somewhere in the world, had gone badly wrong. Felix Schauer was MI6's Director Critical, tasked with overall responsibility for crisis management. With the Service's in-house fondness for nicknames, it had not taken long for him to get called 'April Schauer'. Although not to his face.

Luke pulled back the sleeve of his jacket to check the time. If he cycled straight there he reckoned he could make it to VX in just under forty minutes. Shoulders braced, head down, he took off at speed. Exactly thirty-eight minutes later he was walking through the electronic security doors, past the uniformed guards, into the foyer of Vauxhall Cross, with its royal coat of arms, then straight down the corridor, with its framed photos of the building taken at twilight, and into one of the cramped, boxy, windowless meeting rooms on the ground floor. Luke squeezed himself through the narrow gap between the wall and those already seated as others were still filing in. There had been a time, not so long ago, when his Lycra cycle gear would have caused a few disapproving raised eyebrows from the suits or, worse still, he might have been ordered by some senior Bufton-Tufton to go away and change. Not any more. Still, the room seemed tense: almost no one was talking. He spotted Angela at the far end of the table – she had saved him a seat. Calm, dependable Angela, his rock of support in this place where he knew that not everyone was his ally. 'Well done,' she whispered, as he sat down. 'You just made it.'

10

Vauxhall Cross, London

LUKE SAT AT the far end of the table as the last two people joined the meeting in that narrow, aseptic room on the ground floor. He recognized them as the Chief and the Director of Strategic Advantage, the branch of SIS that devoted itself to state-based threats from Russia and China.

'Close the door, will you?'

The Chief spoke first, her crisp syllables slicing through the silence in the room. Alex Matheson was a career intelligence officer, joining the Service straight from university, and now the first woman to head MI6 in its 116-year history. As a Sinologist and fluent Mandarin speaker, she had spent her early years working out of Beijing station, running agents into Shanghai, the Shenzhen Economic Zone and as far away as Inner Mongolia, Xinjiang and the porous border with North Korea. All in the halcyon days before biometric identification and facial-recognition cameras. Her style was very different from her predecessor's. Sir Adam Keeling's departure had been somewhat hastened by the business of the Leak. Somehow, and the investigation had yet to run its full course, a far-right extremist group had managed to smuggle a bug into the Chief's private office, concealed inside a smoke detector. Deputy heads had rolled after that one.

Today, at this hastily called crisis meeting, Luke noticed the Chief was dressed in a sombre grey woollen jacket and matching skirt with a brooch of a silver fern pinned to her lapel, a gift, he presumed, from the NZ Security Intelligence Service.

'In the last twenty-four hours,' she began, 'two things have happened in the Chinese area of operations. The public knows about one of them: that's the naval incident in the Taiwan Strait. The other involves this Service, which is why I've called you all in here today. Let me first put this into context. Out of the Big Four, as I like to call them – Russia, China, Iran and Counter-Terrorism – China has been, as you all know, our top priority for some years now. We've had our successes and . . .' She closed her eyes for a moment and nodded to herself. '. . . and we've had our setbacks. I'm sorry, I don't like the word "failures". But I regret to say that the most important operation SIS has undertaken in the People's Republic for a generation is . . . well, it's in serious jeopardy. Operation Boxer has been compromised.'

She let her words sink in as Luke registered the sharp intakes of breath from some around the table. He studied each face for a reaction, telling him who was already in the know about this operation and who wasn't. And he wasn't. All Luke knew was that Op Boxer was China-related, but for him to be pulled off the Middle East desk like this at short notice something big must have happened.

'For those of you in this room who didn't know until now,' the Chief continued, 'Operation Boxer is Category One and it's been live for more than eighteen months. Some of you,' and here she cast a glance towards the Director of Strategic Advantage, 'will already be aware of "Blue Sky".' Some knowing nods, some blank faces, including Luke's.

'Blue Sky, for the uninitiated, is a high-level agent this Service has been running upstream, inside the Scientific Division of the People's Liberation Army. More importantly, he works as an adviser to the Central Military Commission. That is the beating military heart, as it were, of the CCP. You don't need to know how he was recruited, just that he came over to us some time ago.'

At this point Luke felt his eyes drawn inexorably to the plate of untouched digestive biscuits that sat waiting on the table. They were wrapped in clear cellophane, stretched tight over the neatly stacked pile beneath. He reckoned they were just at the outer limit of his reach. Feeling a pang of hunger after his fast ride in, he was oh-so-tempted to reach over, break the seal and pop one into his mouth. But he thought better of it. Probably not a good look in the current situation.

'Blue Sky,' continued the Chief, 'was all set to deliver us the absolute mother lode on China's plans for a coming invasion of Taiwan. And I mean *everything*. Missile launch codes, false flag operations, satellite trajectories, amphibious landing sites, their complete list of targets. Even data on the sleeper cells they've got lined up inside Taiwan's military. Yep. It's the whole nine yards. I don't think . . .' Alex Matheson glanced up at the ceiling as she seemed to be choosing her words carefully. '. . . I don't think we've tapped into a seam quite this rich during my entire time in the Service and I cannot tell you how critical this is to us. Or, more importantly, what it means to our chances of preventing the South China Sea from blowing up into a full-scale twenty-first-century war. One that pulls in the US, Australia, Japan, South Korea and very probably ourselves. A war *this* Service might have been able to prevent.' Her eyes blazed as she said this. It was one of the rare occasions when anyone had heard C raise her voice.

'Think about that for a second,' she said. 'If we can get our hands on this gold mine we've got every chance of spiking Beijing's invasion plans and possibly setting them back by several years. Perhaps even indefinitely. But that was as of yesterday.' The Chief glanced at the clock on the far wall of the meeting room. 'And today we are in a whole different world, unfortunately.'

Luke noticed that the one person who was showing no reaction to all this was Felix Schauer, the Director Critical. He was sitting at the other end of the table, staring impassively at the

Chief, waiting for his moment. He was wearing his trademark tweed jacket with the brown leather elbow patches, a chequered shirt and a maroon silk bow-tie, a last stand against the more relaxed dress code of the modern era. To Luke, still gently perspiring in his Lycra cycle gear, Felix Schauer looked like a parody of a latter-day Latin master. Yet this was his moment.

'I'm going to let Felix take over now,' Alex said, nodding to the Director Critical. 'Felix, will you take it from here, please.'

Schauer removed his horn-rimmed glasses, gave them a quick polish with a silk handkerchief that he seemed to produce from nowhere, replaced them on his nose and addressed the room. 'You will understand, I hope,' Schauer began, with his faint trace of a German accent, 'when I tell you that the data Blue Sky was about to give us is so sensitive, and so time-critical, that we opted to stay offline, not even to use Hong Kong station or one of our own case officers for the handover. No.' He exchanged a knowing glance with the Chief, as if they were a long-married couple secretly signalling to each other that it was time to leave a dinner party. 'Instead we took the difficult decision to use a collector, a civilian, to take delivery of it in person. She is an academic from a university here in London with a rock-solid cover for visiting Hong Kong.'

Felix Schauer paused and looked down at his watch, frowning.

'In fact by now the exchange should have been made and our collector should have been on her way to the airport with the data concealed in a way we think even our most inquisitive Chinese friends would have been hard pushed to detect. But . . .' Luke caught a glimpse of the expression on the Chief's face. She suddenly looked years older. '. . . I regret to inform you that she has disappeared. Vanished. So far, our enquiries in Hong Kong have produced no explanation whatsoever. We must therefore assume the worst-case scenario.' The Director Critical looked around the table at each of the faces in turn. 'Which is that her identity has been compromised, she has been lifted, and that she is now in the hands of China's Ministry of State Security.'

11

PAIN. DARKNESS AND MORE PAIN. That was all Dr Hannah
Slade could register at first. Her joints ached and her head felt
numb, woolly, unfamiliar. It took her a few seconds and then an
unpleasant memory came flooding back: those men in the café, her
brief, futile struggle with them, then that damp pad with the chemical smell that they had clamped over her nose and mouth. So she'd
been drugged and now presumably kidnapped. But by whom?
And why? And where was this place they'd brought her to?

She realized she was on a bed, a comfortable one, in a darkened room and apparently alone, still in her own clothes. Her
hands were unbound. She felt around her in the dark, her fingers
touching pillows and sheets. Then she remembered her phone.
Of course! She could call the emergency number MI6 had given
her before leaving London. She patted her pockets, checked all
around her on the bed. No, her phone was gone, along with her
watch. They must have taken them from her. At least her phone
was clean. There was nothing in it to link her to the intelligence
agencies. Anyone prying into its contents and her online history
would find only work emails and copious data on climate change.
Security Section at Vauxhall Cross had made sure of that.

Hannah's eyes were adjusting to the near-darkness in the
room now and she could see a crack of light coming through a
gap in the curtains. With an effort, she rolled herself off the bed,

walked unsteadily to the window and pulled the curtain to one side. A small bronze Buddha rested on the sill and she used it now to pin back the curtain. She flinched. Was she dreaming? Was she still drugged? This didn't look real. Looking down from a great height, every building she could see was lit up like a Christmas tree in garish pink and purple neon. They looked like giant casinos and for a moment she thought she was in Las Vegas. But then she realized. Of course. This must be Macau. Whoever had abducted her must have taken her across the Pearl River delta from neighbouring Hong Kong to this former Portuguese colony. Which meant she was still in Chinese territory, with everything that entailed.

With enough light coming into the room from all that neon outside she was able to get a look at her surroundings. Bare, clean walls, a cupboard, a bedside table, a door to a bathroom. It looked like a serviced apartment, except there was no TV and no phone. Nothing, in fact, to give away any indication of where she was or what purpose this building served. She walked over to the door and tried the handle but it was as she'd expected. Locked. She shook her head. This must be a case of mistaken identity, surely. What was it that woman from MI6 in the charcoal-coloured jacket had told her back in London to reassure her? 'Look, Hannah, every operation carries a risk, of course it does. But on this one we're putting it at close to zero. We wouldn't be sending you otherwise. It's a simple in-and-out, you're a clean skin, and no one there knows you're coming.'

Well, someone clearly did, she thought, or I wouldn't be here. Standing alone in that sterile room in the semi-darkness, Hannah began to feel the regrets flooding in. She wasn't afraid, not yet anyway. But already she was kicking herself for agreeing to make this trip to Hong Kong. What had she been thinking? She had a well-respected position in her field, a secure job at the university. She didn't need this, yet she had volunteered for it and now it had blown up in her face.

She sat on the corner of the bed, staring out at the neon glow reflected on the glass windowpane, and began to go over the possibilities. Was she being held for ransom? Was this a triad thing? Hannah swallowed hard as a terrifying thought occurred to her. Macau was the gambling capital of Asia, with casino takings far outstripping those of Las Vegas in a good year. But it also had a notorious reputation for sex trafficking. She remembered her sister telling her there were Chinese, Russian and Thai organized-crime gangs here who were utterly ruthless in luring vulnerable women and girls into forced prostitution, locking them up in massage parlours and illegal brothels for subsistence pay. They couldn't really be thinking . . . No. Hannah shook her head. She was a woman in her forties, surely an unlikely target for them.

A sound behind her interrupted her thoughts. She could hear footsteps outside the door, the tap of a pass key, then the click of the electronic door release. Hannah froze as she watched the door open. She was about to meet her captors.

12

Cambridgeshire, England

'DÉJÀ VU,' LUKE REMARKED.

'Sorry, say again?' The woman seated opposite took out her ear-buds and raised an immaculately sculpted eyebrow at him.

'I said, this feels like déjà vu,' Luke repeated, putting down the sheaf of notes on his lap. 'This.' He gestured towards the window as the flat fields and hedgerows of Cambridgeshire flashed past in a blur. The nearest fellow passengers were at least six rows away but, still, he kept his voice low.

'You know,' he continued, 'us, on a train, heading for a briefing. Like the one we had in Cheltenham, just before Moscow?'

This time she gave him a rueful smile. Jenny Li was a mid-level intelligence officer in MI6. She was a scientist by training and one of the UK's leading inter-agency experts on CBRN – chemical, biological, radiological and nuclear – making her a go-to subject-matter expert within the intelligence community. But Luke and Jenny's Moscow assignment had so very nearly ended in disaster.

'Yes,' she replied sharply, 'and the less said about that Moscow trip the better.'

'Sorry.' He grimaced. 'Bad memories. So . . .' he said, changing the subject and nodding towards her phone '. . . what you listening to? Anything good?'

'That depends on your tastes,' she said. 'It's a podcast. On CRISPR. You know, genetic manipulation? Just getting myself up to speed before the briefing. Here.' She passed him her ear-buds. 'Have a listen.'

How very Jenny, he thought, suppressing a smile. No chance of her kicking back and listening to Kings of Leon, then. No, that would be far too much like fun. Instead it was non-stop work for Ms Li. Luke admired her in many ways: for her knowledge, her dedication, her dogged determination to get to the bottom of things. Yet he also knew that had they been classmates at school they would almost certainly not have been friends. Jenny Li, he felt sure, would have taken a dim view of the sort of thing he and his mates had got up to.

'Ah. Too late,' she said brightly, taking back her ear-buds. 'Looks like we're pulling in to Huntingdon.'

Things had moved quickly after the Chief's crisis meeting in Vauxhall Cross. Hong Kong station had been alerted and was now tapping up every contact in an effort to trace the missing courier, Hannah Slade. GCHQ was on notice to hoover up any digital clues that might emerge in cyberspace, and extra assistance was being called in from the US National Security Agency. Luke and Jenny were on notice to fly out to Hong Kong and were now being dispatched to Cambridgeshire for a hastily arranged briefing on China's offensive military programmes.

As they stepped off the train at Huntingdon the question kept playing in Luke's mind: why me? Why have I been chosen for this mission? He couldn't speak a word of Mandarin or Cantonese, and he wasn't on the China team back at Vauxhall Cross. But perhaps that was just the point. Was this the Chief keeping things compartmentalized? Sending someone out to China who wouldn't be on Beijing's radar? If so, then that made sense.

*

They were met at the station: a uniformed RAF officer and a civilian in a suit. There was little conversation on the ten-minute drive across the flat, windswept landscape of East Anglia towards the high-security base at RAF Wyton. A brief apology for the delay came from the suit as they stopped at the main gate to clear security, then a short drive through the base, pulling up at what looked like a giant white aircraft hangar. 'Pathfinder Building' read a sign outside the cube-shaped entrance portal. Luke registered the five flags fluttering outside, one for each of the 'Five Eyes' intelligence partners: the US, Canada, the UK, Australia and New Zealand.

'Place looks like a glorified cattle shed,' he remarked to Jenny, as they walked a few paces behind their escort towards the entrance lobby.

'Don't be rude,' she scolded him, but he caught the trace of a smile on her face. 'Be nice. We're here to learn, remember?' She tightened the belt on her camel-hair coat and strode on ahead.

Inside, an Army officer in camouflage working dress stepped forward to greet them. Sleeves rolled up, red collar tabs. A full colonel, Luke noted, and he realized they were probably about the same age. Luke had left the SBS as a captain but even now, after several years as a civilian, he often wondered how far he would have gone if he had 'stayed in'. Probably not very far, he suspected, since he really couldn't see himself putting in the requisite time 'flying a desk' in Whitehall.

'Welcome to the Pathfinder Building,' the Colonel said briskly, rubbing the palms of his hands together, 'and welcome to the home of Defence Intelligence.' He handed them their laminated passes on lanyards, each marked in bold with the words 'Top Secret'. 'I'm John Trent and I'll be looking after your visit programme today.' He looked from Luke to Jenny and back to Luke. 'Right. Let's get you a brew, shall we?' He made a swift, vertical slicing motion with his hand as if cutting through thin air. 'So, if you'd like to follow me . . .'

They walked in single file past the front desk and down a long corridor where framed photographs hung on the walls.

'Some of our illustrious forebears there,' remarked Colonel Trent, as he strode ahead of them. 'This is actually the Defence Intelligence Fusion Centre to give it its full name. But I expect you knew that already.' He gave a short, brittle laugh that was surprisingly high-pitched. 'Used to be just imagery and exploitation but nowadays we do the whole nine yards in here. Oh, yes. Intelligence, surveillance, reconnaissance, geospatial, satellites, you name it. Right. Coffee.' He pushed open a door and ushered them through. 'How d'you take it?'

Five minutes later Luke and Jenny were sitting in the briefing room, clasping their steaming cups of rather unappetizing coffee. Living in London, Luke had almost forgotten how awful military coffee tasted – or, rather, didn't taste. Out of politeness to their hosts, he took a sip, then put it down beside him and left it there. 'Christ. That's weasel's piss,' he remarked to Jenny.

'You'd know, would you?' she replied, looking dead ahead and trying once again not to smile.

The room was arranged like a classroom with its rows of desks, a whiteboard, a lectern and an overhead projector. But the photographs on the walls spoke of the deadly business of modern warfare. There were striking images of F35 jets taking off from an aircraft carrier, a Royal Navy sub slipping out of Faslane, the last light of the day illuminating the purple heather on the Scottish hills beyond. But the one that caught Luke's eye was a grab from a drone feed he recognized from the early days of Ukraine's failed counter-offensive in June 2023. It showed a squad of Ukrainian infantry pinned down in a Russian minefield. He shuddered as he remembered watching that, seeing one man after another become casualties as they tried to rescue their comrades.

'Let's start with the big picture,' said a voice at the front of the room. A bald man in glasses was standing next to a large map of China projected onto the screen behind him. A woman stood next to him. Other than that, it was just Luke and Jenny in the briefing room.

'China or, to give it its official title, the People's Republic of China, is well on the way to becoming the world's leading economic power. Since the beginning of this century it has embarked on an aggressive but extraordinarily successful programme of acquisition around the world. It has bought up strategic stakes in key ports like Djibouti, Piraeus and Gwadar in Pakistan, giving it access to vital shipping lanes well beyond its borders. It even has a military base in Djibouti on the Horn of Africa and that's nearly eight thousand kilometres from Beijing.'

He stopped to unscrew the top of his reusable water bottle, took a swig and continued.

'China has also – and I expect you already knew this – made an illegal grab for a whole string of islands and reefs in the South China Sea. Some of these are literally nowhere near the Chinese mainland. They're hard up next to the coasts of Malaysia and the Philippines. Yet the PLA – that's the People's Liberation Army – has occupied them, militarized them and turned these reefs into forward airbases. It's all about power projection and Beijing has managed to do this right under the noses of the international community. Everyone complained but nobody was prepared to confront China about it so now it's a *fait accompli*, a done deal. I don't think we'll ever dislodge them from those reefs now. The best we can do is support our allies in the region with Freedom of Navigation patrols like the one that's just run into trouble in the Taiwan Strait.'

Luke noticed that several drops of water had spilled down the front of the bald man's suit but he either hadn't noticed or didn't care. He was in full flow now.

'Cancelling democracy in Hong Kong, stealing intellectual property, persecuting the Uighurs in Xinjiang province, vowing to "return Taiwan to the Motherland", picking fights with India and Japan. These have all been wake-up calls to a lot of people that China has a new, aggressive agenda and it's a very different one from ours. Theirs is an autocratic, surveillance-based society so you could say this is a struggle between autocracy and democracy. Which brings us neatly on to their weapons programme.' He stepped to one side to introduce the woman beside him.

'I'm going to hand you over now to my colleague Emma Saye to give you an overview of some of the weapons systems currently being developed by the PLA.'

Luke glanced down at his spurned cup of coffee and saw that a layer of congealed skin had already formed on its surface. He noticed Jenny hadn't touched hers either.

'Mach 8,' said the woman now addressing them. 'That's nearly ten thousand kilometres an hour or, to put it another way, nearly three thousand metres a *second*.' It was a deliberately melodramatic start to her presentation and one Luke guessed had been wheeled out a fair few times to visiting VIPs. Still, she certainly had his attention.

'That's how fast one of China's hypersonic cruise missiles can travel. All right, so they haven't quite perfected their guidance systems yet but they're working hard on that and they will get there. We have no doubt about that. So . . .' She gave them what Luke thought was an odd smile, given the grimness of the topic. '. . . I want you to imagine what one of those would do, rocketing down from twenty-five kilometres above the Earth, on contact with, oh, let's say for the sake of argument, our aircraft carrier, the *Prince of Wales*.'

She clicked a button on the monitor in her hand and the screen filled with a photograph of a military parade somewhere in China. A trio of long, thin, dark green missiles, emblazoned with the letters DF-17, was mounted on vast, camouflaged transporters.

'What we're seeing here is the Dongfeng-17. It was first unveiled to the public in 2019. We knew they were working on it, we just didn't know they were turning out so many of them. So here at Defence Intelligence we quickly came to the conclusion it must be part of their swarm strategy. Launch enough of these in quick succession and you overcome the enemy's defences. Oh, and it's a dual-use weapon so it can carry either a conventional or a nuclear warhead. We just won't know which until it's detonated.'

Luke raised his hand with a question. 'Sorry to interrupt, but doesn't this rather beg the question: is it wise to send our premier warship into the path of one of these things in the South China Sea?

44

I mean, it's all very well to talk about "power projection" in peace-time but if the situation in the Taiwan Strait turns hot then whatever we send into theatre is going to be a sitting duck, isn't it?'

The two lecturers exchanged knowing glances.

'You might say that,' replied Emma Saye, trotting out a worn cliché, 'but I couldn't possibly. I'm afraid that's above my pay grade. But, yes, I expect a lot of people would agree with you, Mr Carlson—'

'Carlton,' he corrected her.

'Mr Carlton, excuse me. Right, let's move on. We've got a lot more to cover before we finish this briefing and I'm afraid it's nearly all bad news.'

13

Macau, China

WHEN THE DOOR opened Hannah Slade was expecting several of her captors to come into the room. But instead it was just one man – a local, she guessed – of medium height, dressed in jeans, trainers and a polo shirt. The material was stretched tightly enough across his chest for her to notice his bulging pectoral muscles. A body-builder. Or a martial-arts guy. Or both.

She had never thought of herself as a violent person, or an impulsive one. She was a scientist, for God's sake, a careful, cautious individual who tested each course before following it. And yet, at that precise moment, a voice inside her told her, 'It's now or never.' She knew, as most people do, that the best chance of escape is often in that first golden hour. And this could be her only chance to get away from these people. Her eyes flicked towards the man in the doorway. He was carrying a tray of food, both hands occupied. She could see a bowl of noodles and a plate of dry crackers. He nodded to her without saying a word, and she watched him searching for somewhere to set the tray down. It had to be now. Hannah bowed respectfully and backed away until she got to the window. Reaching behind her, the fingers of her right hand curled tightly around the small but heavy bronze Buddha. The man with the tray was setting it down on the bedside table, his back half turned to her. Quickly, quietly, she walked up behind him and swung the bronze statuette at his head. He looked up just too late. It struck him hard on his right temple and he went down with a groan then lay there, motionless on the carpeted floor. For several seconds Hannah stood over him, still clutching the Buddha, ready to hit him again if he got up. Her breath came in short, urgent gasps. She had committed herself now. There was no going back.

And there was the open door, her pathway to freedom. Cautiously, she peered around it. She saw a narrow, windowless corridor lit by a sputtering neon light on the ceiling. Her nostrils registered a cloying smell of damp, tropical mould. Before her was a grey, threadbare carpet leading to an illuminated sign in Chinese and English. It said 'Elevator' and, yes, it was tempting, but the stairs, if she could find them, would surely be safer.

She closed the door behind her and stepped gingerly into the corridor, still expecting to be stopped at any moment, and turned right. After only a few paces it ended in a door. She tried the handle but it was locked. Her heart was thumping. Any minute now someone was going to come looking for the missing bodybuilder. She had to find the exit and fast. Hannah retraced her steps down the corridor, half breaking into a run. She passed the lift, following the corridor as it turned a right angle and there it ended abruptly. But over to one side was a set of double doors. She pushed against them and they opened, revealing a landing strewn with litter. And there, oh joy, was the stairway she was looking for. But now, quite suddenly, she felt a wave of nausea sweep over her and she sank to her knees, clinging to the railings that ran alongside the stairway, her head dizzy and bile rising in her throat. For several precious minutes she couldn't move. Was it an after-effect of the drugging or a natural, visceral reaction to the fact that she had just brained another human with a bronze Buddha?

She stood up and picked her way over plastic bags full of discarded food, sending a stream of large brown cockroaches scattering in all directions around her feet. Hannah didn't care:

she was heading down the stairs now, as fast as she could. Four floors down, she stopped to listen. She peered over the side of the metal railings to see several more floors stretching away below her. Still no one had come after her. Maybe she would make it.

At last she reached the bottom, her breath still coming in short gasps, and there, right in front of her, was the building's exit door. Just a single push bar stood between her and freedom. Above it, a sign in Chinese and English told her it was alarmed. Too bad. She pushed hard and the door swung open. No alarm sounded. For a second or two she stood there in the darkened back-street, between the giant rubbish bins on casters, breathing in the hot, damp, night air of Macau, her eyes adjusting to the darkness tempered by the nearby flashing neon signs, hearing the familiar hum of traffic. Yet this all felt so surreal, so other-worldly, she was having trouble getting her bearings. Because, what, two days ago, maybe three, Hannah had been in her little office at the university back in London, wrapping up her work before 'going on holiday', as she had told her peers. Then a dash into Waitrose to pick up some cat food, head home, hand her beloved pet to the neighbours, check the expiry dates on what was in her fridge and make one last call to her handler at Vaux-hall Cross. Apart from the last, it was all so damned normal, so everyday, it bore absolutely no relation to the situation she now found herself in.

She didn't wait long before moving. Hannah knew she needed to put some distance between herself and her captors, to get away somehow to safety. She started to walk, briskly, towards what looked like a main road with lights at the end of the back-street, scattering the scavenging cats as she went. Suddenly she stopped as she remembered. She reached up with her hand and felt with the tip of her right index finger at the back of her mouth. Yes! It was still there, that hardened piece of gum with the mini-ature memory stick encased inside it. The thing she had flown halfway across the planet to retrieve in the name of 'national security'. Hannah had no idea what data was contained in it, only that the people who had sent her here from London were desperate to have it.

She cast a quick glance over her shoulder but there was no one behind her. She reached the main road, a broad, two-way street flanked by high-rise buildings and a neat line of palm trees down the median divide. There was traffic but the only pedestrians she could see were workmen fixing some electrical appliance on the pavement. Without her watch, she had no idea what time it was, it could have been 11 p.m. or five in the morning for all she knew. She walked on, suddenly self-conscious, this lone Englishwoman wandering the streets of Macau in the dead of night.

She spotted the two policemen standing at the junction with the next street. They were dressed in light blue short-sleeved shirts with their ranks on their epaulettes and dark blue baseball caps on their heads. Absurdly, given it was night time, she could see both were wearing sunglasses. Abandoning all caution, Hannah broke into a run, racing up to them and waving her arms.

'English!' she shouted. 'Tourist! I need help!' She looked from one to the other but the two officers looked blankly back at her then spoke to each other in Cantonese. 'Embassy,' she continued. 'Help, please!' Did Britain even have an embassy in Macau? She had no idea since she was never supposed to be here. Hannah pressed the palms of her hands together in a pleading gesture but she could see something was wrong. She wasn't getting through to these two. Instead, their attention was distracted. They weren't looking at her any more. She followed their gaze and saw two men in dark suits walking rapidly towards them from the direction of the building she had just left. Oh Christ, no, she couldn't be certain but they looked terrifyingly similar to the pair from the café back in Kowloon. The same two who had chloroformed her and then kidnapped her.

'No!' she screamed, her voice rising in fear. 'These men are criminals!' But, to her horror, the policemen seemed to recognize the two men and were greeting them with little deferential bows. What the hell? Now one of the policemen was taking her by the arm and she couldn't tell if it was a protective gesture or

49

something more sinister. Should she break away and run for it? She tried to shake her arm free from his grip but he only held her tighter, saying nothing as she felt his fingers digging into her upper arm until she let out a cry of pain. Escape was out of the question. There were four of them and she knew they would quickly catch her. Helpless, Hannah watched the other police-man shaking hands with the two suits, and in the yellow glow of the overhead street light she clearly saw a wad of banknotes change hands. She felt like a piece of flotsam being washed downstream by the current. She had lost all control of her situation. Now she could see one of the two suits talking rapidly into his mobile while keeping his eyes on her. Moments later a car drew up, sleek and silent, with tinted windows, a Mercedes E-class. Then it all happened very quickly. Someone inside the car flung open the rear door and she could feel herself being pro-pelled unwillingly towards it by the policeman. To Hannah it suddenly seemed like the gaping mouth of a cave where very bad things happened, a cave she desperately wanted to avoid entering. But already she was aware of strong hands pushing her head down and her body inside the vehicle. She resisted but they pushed harder. The next thing a hood was being placed over her head and as everything went dark she felt her wrists grabbed and bound together. Hannah was once again a prisoner and this time she knew her predicament was far, far worse than before.

14

Cambridgeshire, England

'WOULD YOU LIKE me to do that for you? You seem to be struggling rather.' Luke shot her a look in reply then silently handed Jenny the packet of digestive biscuits. With her longer fingernails she deftly lifted the plastic tab, peeled open the packet and handed it back to him. 'Simples,' she said, with a smile, then shook her head as he offered her the first one.

They were on the train heading back to London and there had just been time to grab some snacks before boarding the 16.41 non-stop to King's Cross. Luke popped half a digestive into his mouth, then stood up and pretended to rummage around for something on the overhead luggage rack while checking if any passengers were within earshot.

'Obviously not a popular service, this one,' he said, sitting down. 'We've got the carriage to ourselves.' He took another bite of his biscuit then pushed the packet away and leant his arms on the table between them.

'How's Elise these days?' Jenny asked.

'Elise?' Her question took him by surprise.

'Yes. You know, your girlfriend?'

'Ex-girlfriend,' he corrected her. 'That all ended badly after . . . Well, I'd rather not go into it, to be honest. So . . .' he said, changing

51

the subject. 'What did you make of all that, back there at the briefing?' he said, still keeping his voice low even though they were alone. 'I have to say it fills me with a certain amount of dread. I mean, what the hell have we been doing all this time while China's been developing these so-called Super Weapons? It sounds like they're years ahead of us when it comes to hypersonic missiles.'

'Counter Insurgency, Luke. You of all people should know that!' He winced. He knew she was right. 'For twenty years, well, ever since 9/11 really, that's what's taken centre stage, hasn't it? Fighting all those insurgencies in Iraq, Afghanistan . . . Mali. And I suppose something had to give. Let's face it, Luke, we took our eye off the ball while China built up its arsenal, infiltrated our economy, and Russia rearmed.'

Luke couldn't help looking away as she spoke. He trained his eyes on the late-afternoon shadows moving across the flat Bedfordshire landscape, the rolling fields and the stunted hedgerows flashing past as they rattled south towards London. He couldn't disagree with what Jenny was saying but it was still painful to hear it. Painful for him, personally, because he'd been a willing participant in that whole Counter Insurgency effort, with the scars to prove it. All those operational tours in Afghanistan, the long hours of boredom, then the sudden adrenaline rush of combat, the visceral exhilaration of survival after a firefight, and the gut-wrenching misery of watching a badly wounded mate being loaded onto the chopper to Bastion and wondering if you would ever see him alive again. Like so many of his friends who'd done 'Telic' and 'Herrick', the tours in Iraq and Afghanistan, Luke was left wondering if it had all been worth it, especially after the ignominious evacuation from Kabul in the summer of 2021. And now here they were, working for a British intelligence agency that made spying on China its number-one priority. It felt an awful lot like playing catch-up. 'It does rather feel,' he said out loud, as he turned away from the window to face her, 'like we're playing catch-up, doesn't it?'

He watched her as she considered his question. Jenny squeezed her eyes shut and ran her hands over her face, massaging herself around the eyes. He had got used to seeing her do this when she was thinking hard. Then she looked at him brightly. 'Well, let's try to look on the positive side,' she said. 'At least we've still *got* a functioning network in place inside the People's Republic. That's more than we can say for our friends in Langley. And you know something else—' Jenny stopped abruptly as the carriage door hissed open and Luke turned to see a woman coming in pushing a buggy, a toddler onboard.

He was about to get up to offer to help when he heard his phone ping with an incoming message. He glanced down at it. It was from Angela, at Vauxhall. He read it quickly, his brow furrowed in concentration as the train took a bend at speed, then handed it silently to Jenny to read. Her eyes widened as she handed it back to him.

'Wow. That doesn't leave us much time,' she said. 'So we leave tonight.'

15

Jilantai Missile Testing Site, Inner Mongolia, China

THE RAIN HAD stopped the day before. Now, under a clear blue desert sky, the launch preparations were in full swing. Mounted on long, twelve-wheeled camouflaged transporters, the four sleek DF-26 missiles glinted in the sun, the rays bouncing off their sand-coloured nose cones. Observed from up above in space, which was exactly what the electro-optical cameras of America's KH-11 spy satellites were doing, the base resembled a teeming ant colony. Technicians moved around in constant motion between the missile transporters, their refuelling trucks and the numerous support vehicles. On the ground, a thin film of red dust seemed to coat everything, despite the fresh breeze that blew in from the surrounding plateau of Inner Mongolia.

Inside the command bunker, Colonel General Li Wei Chen stood with his hands clasped behind his back, inspecting the digital map displayed on the wall as a subordinate ran through the sequence of the launch, stopping frequently to await his approval before continuing. The launch would be real but the target was simulated: a mock-up of a certain naval base transplanted hundreds of kilometres away in an empty stretch of the Gobi Desert. The DF-26 missile had a range of four thousand kilometres, enough to reach the Pacific island of Guam. It was also known in Western military jargon as a 'carrier-killer', a weapon powerful and accurate enough to sink a $13 billion US Navy aircraft carrier.

Colonel General Chen was more than familiar with the launch sequence. It had been nearly two years now since he had assumed command of the People's Liberation Army's Intermediate Ballistic Force and he had survived the purges at the top that had seen many others of his rank forcibly retired or, worse, placed under investigation for corruption, alleged failures or both. Everything, they had told him in Beijing, needed to be at maximum readiness for the day when the order was given. There could be no mistakes.

The four missiles were now elevated into the vertical position and the launch-pad area was cleared. Soldiers, technicians, drivers and medics were all escorted into the reinforced bunkers as a siren wailed its mournful song across the base. When Colonel General Chen issued the command it was followed by a strange hiatus. For several seconds nothing happened. Then, with a roar of fire and flame, the first missile lifted clear, accelerating upwards into the clear sky and leaving behind billowing white clouds of vapour as millions of litres of water turned to steam in the intense heat of the launch. One by one, the missiles arced into the atmosphere like flying needles, white contrails streaking across the sky behind them, their course mapped and tracked from the command bunker.

Far away, in the barren and almost uninhabited dunes of the Gobi Desert, a shepherd felt the first of four shockwaves as if an invisible hand was reaching across the sand to push him over. Seconds later came the low rumble of a distant explosion, then another. His leathery, weather-beaten face screwed itself up as he stared at the horizon, shielding his eyes from the blazing sun. He saw the distant plumes of smoke, grunted and turned his attention back to his sheep. He had more important things to worry about.

In the command bunker at Jilantai the relief was palpable. Even Colonel General Chen permitted himself a smile of satisfaction as his minions rushed up to congratulate him. The missile test had gone completely to plan, every warhead bang on target. His chest swelled with pride as he took the call from Party Head-quarters in Beijing. Yes, he assured them, as his eyes rested on the live feed from the distant impact zone, the mocked-up target – the sprawling Tsoying naval base in southern Taiwan – had been completely destroyed.

16

Hong Kong

'BANG ON TIME.'

'Sorry?'

Luke showed the watch on his wrist to Jenny. He had already moved it on eight hours to Hong Kong time. It was now 5.35 p.m. and their Cathay Pacific overnight flight CX254 from Heathrow's Terminal 3 had just touched down. A twelve-hour non-stop flight across two continents and he was feeling remarkably fresh. But then, given the urgency of their task, the Service had booked them in Business Class so this was hardly surprising.

'You ready for this?' he asked quietly, as he helped lift down her bag from the overhead locker. Everyone was on their feet now, pushing and jostling, even in Business Class. From somewhere behind them a baby had started to howl at the top of its tiny lungs.

Jenny nodded silently, and Luke admired her quiet confidence. He just wished he could feel the same.

They were going in under non-official cover, no diplomatic immunity, no safety net if they got 'made'. Just two Western tourists on holiday, a pair of off-duty travel agents visiting this former British colony under assumed names, with their carefully crafted Facebook and Instagram profiles to back up their story. Neither

Luke nor Jenny had ever visited Hong Kong, Macau or mainland China before, and neither had worked on the China desk, all good reasons why they had been chosen for this mission. Security Section at Vauxhall, who were ultimately responsible for their safety, had taken the view that there was a low to negligible risk that China's Ministry of State Security would have their biometric details on file. Still, Luke could feel a knot of tension in his stomach as they walked down the air bridge and into the vast, cavernous terminal of Hong Kong's international airport. He flinched, involuntarily, as he felt someone touch him. It was Jenny and now she was holding his hand as they approached the immigration desk. He caught the look on her face. It wasn't remotely flirtatious, it was serious. Of course. Good skills. They were 'a couple' and they needed to look the part.

Minutes later they were through and joining the queue outside for the red and white taxis into town. The light of the day was ebbing away but the cloying heat still wrapped itself around them, like a damp, unwanted blanket. Even the palm trees beside the taxi rank had an exhausted, wilted look about them. The relief was instant the moment they got inside the taxi, the chill of the air-conditioning quickly evaporating the sweat that had already formed on their arms and necks.

'Impressive,' Jenny remarked, as she gazed out of the window from the back of the cab. They were speeding along the Tsing Ma Bridge, Hong Kong's version of San Francisco's Golden Gate Bridge, and, at more than two kilometres long, the world's longest suspension bridge carrying car and train traffic. They stared out at the string of yellow lights reflected in the darkening waters below.

'So different.' Jenny was shaking her head slowly.

'From what?'

'The Hong Kong my father used to show me photos of as a child. I think there was probably a lot of poverty back then and . . .' She let her sentence trail off out of deference to the cabbie sitting up front. He was a bulky, bullet-headed man with a deeply creased forehead and big hands that gripped the steering wheel as he leant towards it. He looked uninterested enough, cursing quietly in Cantonese at the traffic as he took one hand off the wheel to fiddle with the radio, but you could never be sure. He probably wasn't listening to a word but Jenny had no wish to cause offence.

They were now on a six-lane highway facing a green express-way sign that pointed the way to places called Sha Tin, Tsim Sha Tsui and, of course, Hong Kong Island. Even in the twilight Luke could clearly see the serried ranks of white, high-rise apartments climbing up the hill in the middle distance, each one identical to the one next to it. He made a quick calculation and put the number of storeys on each at somewhere between fifty and sixty. Clearly, he thought, there were still massive disparities in wealth here. They stayed silent after that. There was much that could have been said but not in front of their driver.

The Landia Hotel looked like any other steel and glass high-rise building in the district of Kowloon known as Mong Kok, but it had been carefully selected by the team at Vauxhall Cross, then booked online through Expedia, using their cover names. At seventy-four pounds a night, it was just off the busy Nathan Road shopping district, close to the Ladies' Market, exactly the sort of place two Western tourists might want to stay in. It was also close to the last place Hannah Slade had gone to before she was abducted.

'Checking in,' Luke said briskly, as they approached the reception desk, passports in hand. 'Chris Blanford and Bel Trubridge. We booked through Expedia.' The receptionist flashed them a welcoming smile, scrolled down a list on his computer and nodded. Luke handed him his credit card and received two card keys in return. 'Room 1902,' the man announced, with another smile. 'It's on the nineteenth floor and the elevator is just over there on your left. Enjoy your stay with us'.

'Thanks. We will,' Jenny said, holding Luke's arm for a moment.

It still felt very strange, he thought, being touched like this by one of his work colleagues, however much it was part of the cover act.

A few minutes later, pushing open the door to Room 1902, it felt stranger still.

'Oh,' Luke said flatly. They stood in the doorway, looking down at the immaculately made-up king-size bed, the covers neatly turned down on both sides. There was a heart-shaped welcome chocolate wrapped in red foil in the centre of each of the two pillows. 'I thought they'd booked us a twin.'

'Yeah, so did I,' said Jenny. She shrugged, then moved briskly past him into the room, dumping her bag on the chair. 'But we can hardly ask them to change it now, can we? I think that would look odd.'

Luke wondered if he should do the decent thing and offer to sleep on the floor – he'd slept in a lot worse places in his time – but, to his relief, Jenny defused the situation.'Right, here's what we'll do,' she announced, all business-like. 'Pass me those cushions over there on the chair, yes, those. We'll make a line of them down the middle. I'll sleep on this side, you sleep on the other, and that way decorum is maintained. Does that work for you?'

'Absolutely,' Luke replied, suddenly noticing his throat was rather dry. 'As long as you're OK with that?'

'I am,' she said. 'I wouldn't have suggested it otherwise. Right, shall I do the honours or do you want to?'

'You mean . . .?'

'Yes. That.'

'I'll do it,' Luke said. He rummaged around in his holdall then took out what looked like a battery-operated shaver. Using his thumb, he pressed a switch on the side and the device sprang open to reveal a small black box about the size and shape of an early-model mobile phone. Gently, he pulled out the two antennae, then switched it on. As Jenny disappeared into the bathroom Luke worked the room methodically. Dividing it up into four quadrants he carefully passed the device over every object, every nook and cranny, anything that could possibly conceal a hidden camera or listening device. Satisfied that the room was clear, he called to Jenny through the bathroom door, 'It's all good in here. I'll just check in there when you're done.'

Bathroom cleared, Luke joined Jenny at the window from where there was an impressive view over the whole of Kowloon from nineteen floors up. Together they stared down onto the myriad pattern of streets far below. An endless geometric maze of white square apartment buildings interspersed with soaring new plate-glass skyscrapers. They were standing very close now, their hands almost touching and there was a moment of silence between them before she broke it as she turned to face him.

'We've *got* to find her, Luke. There is *so* much depending on this. On us, in fact. I know I'm stating the obvious here, but the trail that leads to her starts down there.' She pointed a finger in the direction of the teeming streets of Kowloon far below. 'The clock is seriously against us and we need to get cracking. What time is your meeting?'

Luke checked his watch. 'In just under two hours, but I've got the "package" to collect first. You're right. I'd better get going.'

'Ah, yes, the package.' She shot him a look that Luke took to be one of distaste. 'You know I don't really approve of that, don't you? Are you absolutely sure it's necessary?'

Luke was already moving towards the door. 'Given what we think might have happened to Hannah,' he replied, 'I'd say it is, yes.'

17

Kowloon, Hong Kong

FLASHBACKS. IF YOU SWIM in dangerous seas, Luke reflected, then flashbacks come with the territory. A near-death experience at the hands of a sadistic narco-gang in Colombia, a fight to the death in an Armenian cave, a narrow miss from an attempted assassination in a Lithuanian back-street. In the few intense years he had spent on the payroll at MI6 Luke reckoned he had already had more than his fair share of brushes with an untimely death. Hell, there were people he'd met in that Thameside building who had probably never risked so much as a traffic fine. And now here he was, stepping out onto the night-time streets of Kowloon in hostile territory, his only visible cover as a 'tourist' a folded street map he'd picked up when they'd passed through the airport.

But Security Section back at Vauxhall Cross had been nothing if not thorough. Given the sudden disappearance of Hannah Slade and the unpredictable nature of this mission, certain pre-cautions had been taken on Luke's behalf. Hence 'the package' he was now about to collect. Following their instructions to the letter, he walked 150 metres down the busy, brightly lit pavement of Argyle Street then turned right, into the air-conditioned interior of the shopping mall. He realized then that he hadn't eaten anything since the plane so he stopped to buy a packet of crisps from a kiosk, popped one into his mouth, then checked his bearings.

The luggage lock-up was on the first floor, up an escalator that moved painfully slowly. Luke had memorized the number of the locker and the combination to get into it, but he avoided the temptation to walk straight up to it. Instead, he positioned himself some way off, mingling with the evening shoppers, the families with prams and the teenagers taking selfies. He was watching the bank of metal cupboards to see if anyone else was observing them. Perhaps Jenny was right. Maybe the object he was about to retrieve was more of a liability than an asset. This could go either way, he thought, and for a while Luke contemplated ignoring this 'precaution' that Security Section had advised him to take. But no, he concluded, he had to trust them. Their job was to keep the Service's case officers and agents safe, in the field and in their daily lives. They wouldn't be sending him down this path if they didn't think it was necessary.

When Luke was satisfied that no one else was watching he walked up to one of the metal cupboards, keyed in the number, waited for the click, then reached in to retrieve its contents: a Tupperware lunchbox that appeared to contain nothing more sinister than dried noodles. He made one last quick check to make sure no one was looking, then closed the locker and carried the Tupperware box to the nearby toilets. He spent a long time at the washbasin, rinsing his hands as he waited for the only person in there to flush the loo and be gone. The moment the room was empty he ducked inside a cubicle and locked it. Then he prised open the lid of the Tupperware box, his fingers probing through the top layer of dried noodles until they touched a familiar outline.

The 3D laser-printed weapon in his hand looked and felt like a pretty good approximation of a Glock 19 pistol, if somewhat lighter. This thing was made of plastic, not metal. Would it still work? He had been assured it would, but Luke still found it extraordinary that he was holding something that had been created remotely, following a digital sequence of noughts and ones, instead of being tooled in a factory.

For a few seconds he rested the 3D Glock in his palm, running the finger of his other hand along its off-white surface and the square, angular lines of the trigger guard. Shorter and stubbier than its military cousin, the Glock 17, this was the weapon of choice for many covert operatives. It carried fewer 9mm rounds in its magazine – just fifteen as opposed to seventeen – but that was a compromise Luke was more than happy to live with. As long as it worked. It still felt like a plastic toy to him but instinctively he went through the drills, emptying the magazine, counting the rounds then replacing them one by one, taking aim at the ceiling with nothing in the chamber, squeezing off a dry shot then re-inserting the mag. Luke liked the Glock. Unlike its British Army predecessor, the 9mm Browning, it had none of the safety delays and now made for a quick draw in a tight spot.

It was time to go. He flushed the toilet once more, for appearance's sake, opened the cubicle door into the empty washroom and dropped the Tupperware lunchbox into the chrome waste bin, concealing it with several sheets of crumpled-up paper towels from the dispenser. So now he was armed, but he was also breaking the law. His 'tourist' cover was not going to hold up for one second if he was lifted by the Hong Kong Police and there was no diplomatic cover to hide behind. To his frustration, they had neglected to provide him with a holster. Perhaps that was just too difficult to conceal in a box of dried noodles. Luke would have to make do. He tucked the pistol into the inside left-hand pocket of his loose-fitting jacket and walked back into the shopping mall. It was time to meet the contact.

Outside Luke's nostrils registered a heady mix of warm, humid air, street kiosk cooking, petrol fumes and unfamiliar exotic and overripe fruit. His pulse quickened as he crossed the street, heading for the prearranged location he'd been given. After the overnight flight from London and the long ride into the city it felt good to be stretching his legs and getting stuck into this mission. He was 'at reach and at risk', as his mates in Special

Forces would say, and that was exactly where he liked to be. He and Jenny had agreed on how they would split their time, she staying put in the hotel to work on the signals intelligence with Cheltenham while he pursued the physical trail. The final pre-operation briefing he'd had from Vauxhall on the evening they left had not been encouraging. Hong Kong station, MI6's outpost lodged within the everyday bureaucracy of the British Consulate General on Supreme Court Road, was struggling to come up with any clues as to Hannah Slade's disappearance. There was some pushback from them, Angela admitted to him, as to why Hong Kong station had been left out of the loop in the first place but, still, every source had been tapped for information on Hannah's potential whereabouts. And they had all come up blank. There had been a brief unconfirmed sighting of a middle-aged Western woman vaguely matching her description somewhere up in the New Territories, close to the old border with mainland China. But this had turned out to be a reclusive watercolour artist from Bangor.

In desperation, the Service was turning to its underworld contacts, but there had been a hitch. The man they most needed to talk to had refused to meet anyone from Hong Kong station. It had to be a *gweilo*, a 'white ghost', a foreigner from the other side of the world. Luke Carlton was to be that white ghost.

18

Hsiaohsuehshan Radar Station, Taiwan

THE TYPHOON HAD blown itself out.

For two days now the winds had raged around this mountain-top radar post, the Taiwanese Navy's eyes and ears across the island's western shore and out into the Taiwan Strait towards mainland China. At well over two thousand metres above sea level, this remote garrison was notorious for its harsh conditions. Sometimes blanketed with snow in winter, buffeted by winds and torrential rains in summer, it could take days to get supplies up the tortuous, winding roads through pine forests and up into the granite crags. The Navy personnel and Marines who crewed it were only ever expected to do a thirty-day shift at a time, with a third of that off for rest.

There was another, unspoken, reason why Hsiaohsuehshan was classed as a hardship posting. Everyone who served there knew that in the event of a surprise attack by China this was one of the very first targets that would be taken out in the initial wave of missiles raining down from the mainland. As part of Taiwan's US-supplied Phased Array radar system it had the ability to track missile launches and incoming threats thousands of kilometres away, providing an early-warning system for the government in

Taipei, should Beijing decide to take back 'the breakaway province' by force.

The garrison at Hsiaohsuehshan had protocols and procedures for typhoons. Whenever a warning of extreme weather came in, orders were issued for the sensitive antenna masts to be taken down in case winds of 160 kilometres per hour or more broke them off, rendering the radar station effectively useless. And in typhoon conditions the 3D radar could also be affected, temporarily severing the connection with Taiwan's combat data link systems that joined it to the US-built Patriot III and other anti-missile defences. The weather was a fickle friend for this self-governing island. For much of the year it made the Taiwan Strait a daunting proposition for any amphibious invasion from the mainland, but it also had the capacity to blind Taiwan's defences.

On the day the typhoon subsided Master Sergeant Wu Chi-ming was walking back to his post at the data console, a steaming cup of High Mountain oolong tea clutched in his hand. He had just given the order to resurrect the comms antennae, restoring the remote radar outpost to full function. He had barely got through the door when one of his team rushed up to him and blurted out the news. 'Boss! We have a Code Seven!'

'*Kàn!*'

Master Sergeant Chi-ming uttered an obscene curse as he slammed down his mug of tea on the nearest flat surface, spilling much of it over his hand. A Code Seven! On his watch. This could end up being a court-martial offence. The two men rushed to the digital display console, housed inside the radar station's reinforced bunker. A dozen operators, all wearing naval uniform, were staring at the time-stamped images coming in and clasping their hands behind their heads in horror as the room filled with nervous chatter.

While the Hsiaohsuehshan radar station had been 'blinded' by the storm, Beijing had used the opportunity to fire a submarine-launched YJ-18 land attack cruise missile right across the median line that separated the Chinese side from the Taiwanese side of the Taiwan Strait. Every operator on that base knew the capabilities of this missile by heart. It could carry either a 300-kilogram high-explosive warhead or, more pertinently, an anti-radiation warhead perfectly designed to disable a radar station like this one.

Master Sergeant Chi-ming whirled round and called to a subordinate. He told him to get the line up to be put through immediately to his reporting officer at Air Force Defence Headquarters in Taipei's Zhongshan District. He knew he had some explaining to do but this could go either way. He could lose his job or he could be promoted.

The missile had landed offshore, in international waters, re-entering the ocean just forty-eight kilometres off Taiwan's Miaoli County on the west coast. Had it continued on its course it would have made a direct line for the radar base. It was a message from the mainland, pure and simple. We know where you are, and, at a time of our choosing, we can wipe you out.

19

Kowloon, Hong Kong

IT DIDN'T TAKE Luke long to find the address for the rendezvous. The Win Ho Academy for Martial Arts was down a side-street and had probably seen better days, he reckoned. A rusting sign above the door announced its name but the last word had come adrift from its moorings and now hung at a crooked angle. A scruffy pigeon sat asleep on top of the sign, having marked its territory with white splashes. He rang the buzzer and waited. A crackly, disembodied voice answered.

'*Wai?*'

'Chris Blanford,' Luke replied, articulating slowly and clearly the cover name he'd been assigned by Security Section. 'I'm here to see Mr Lim.'

'Wait one minute.'

A long pause, then a buzz as the door clicked open. Immediately a new smell hit his nostrils. Sweat, humidity and something else that he put down to testosterone. His contact had chosen to meet him in a place where people trained hard to hurt each other physically. Why on earth couldn't they have just met in the café around the corner? London had warned him that Mr Lim could be 'a little unorthodox' but this seemed needlessly theatrical and time-consuming.

Luke stood in the narrow entrance hall where a face peered out at him over the top of a counter. Already he could hear the sound of kicks and punches emanating from the *guan*, the training hall next door.

'Mr Lim?' he prompted.

'He's training now. You must wait here, please.'

Five minutes passed, then another five. At last the figure behind the counter emerged, beckoning for him to follow. Down a short corridor where photographs were displayed on the wall showing various victorious martial-arts contestants, their hard faces fixed in rictus grins. Luke had expected to be led into some back office but instead they were now in the men's locker room.

'You change here,' the man said, handing him a clean set of track pants and a T-shirt. For a receptionist he certainly wasn't overdoing the welcome.

'No, you're all right,' Luke replied, declining the proffered sparring kit. 'I'll just wait here till he's finished.'

A look of annoyance flashed across the man's face.

'Mr Lim says you must join him now. In there. He says you must train together.' He pointed towards the *guan* at the exact moment when someone within let out a cry of pain.

Luke stared at the man. Was he serious? He had just stepped off a long-haul flight, his body clock was all over the place and he was starting to crave sleep. Fond as he was of physical exercise, getting into a training session this late in the evening was absolutely not what he had in mind.

But this man evidently had other ideas. Again, he thrust the set of track pants and T-shirt into Luke's hand.

Luke shrugged. Well, what harm could it do? It was just a training session and if this was what it took to gain Mr Lim's confidence and secure his help, then fine, but they would keep it light and avoid full contact. After all, Luke had put in goodness knows how many hours of his own time in the gym at MMA, Mixed Martial Arts.

He changed quickly, waiting for the receptionist to look the other way before swiftly tucking the 3D-printed Glock inside

70

his folded clothes, shutting the locker door and memorizing the combination on the lock. The taciturn receptionist watched him impassively as he went through some basic warm-up exercises, lunging and stretching, then led Luke next door into the gym. A man in overalls was methodically wiping the floor with a mop, and two others were packing up and leaving. That left just one other person in the gym. A short, bulky figure with close-cropped hair stood with his back to them, his hands on his hips. He was wearing a pair of faded jogging pants, a tight white T-shirt and what looked like soft leather slippers. There was a smear on the T-shirt that looked suspiciously like blood.

'Mr Lim.' The receptionist pointed to him, and left the room, shortly followed by the cleaner with the mop. The gym was now empty except for the two of them.

When 'Mr Lim' turned to face him, Luke immediately took in the muscled torso and powerful, sinewy arms, both extensively inked with tattoos. His attention was drawn to the large black and white yin-and-yang motif on the side of his neck while almost every centimetre of Mr Lim's arms was covered with symbols, shapes and patterns, some faded and crudely drawn, others appearing more recent. He may have been nearly a head and shoulders shorter than Luke but he looked as if he'd be a formidable opponent in the ring. This was not a man Luke would ever want to have to fight.

'Welcome to my gym,' the man said politely, in English. Powerful handshake, little trace of an accent, he might have spent some time in Britain, Luke thought.

'So you know Wing Chun, yes?'

'Well, I've heard of it, obviously,' Luke said, thinking how completely lame that sounded.

'But you don't practise it?' Mr Lim frowned at him.

'Me? No. I'm more of an MMA guy. Look, I've just come off a long overnight flight so, if it's all right with you, let's just sit down in your office and have a chat, OK?'

Mr Lim took a pace closer to Luke, close enough to invade his personal space, and stared up at him. He spoke very quietly, enunciating each syllable slowly.

'Listen, Mr Blanford – if that's really your name – I only agreed to meet you tonight because I owe someone a favour. You don't need to know who. But you – who are you? I don't know anything about you.'

Luke held his gaze but he was starting to get a bad feeling about this.

'You're coming to me for information, yes?' Mr Lim said, raising his eyebrows. 'But I need to know I can trust you,' he continued, without waiting for the answer. 'Because there are risks in this for me. Even here, in my gym. There are eyes and ears everywhere . . .' He cast a meaningful glance towards the door through which the cleaner had left. 'So, it is through Wing Chun that I can judge a person, to know what they are made of.'

He placed a tattooed arm on Luke's shoulder. 'You need not worry, Mr Blanford,' he grinned, 'we will begin with some simple Chi Sau exercises and see how you get on. And, hey, in case you're wondering, I'm not a Grand Master. My grade is black sash, not gold. I'm still really no more than a student.'

Yeah, right, Luke thought, casting another glance at the man's physique. He suddenly felt very tired. He just wanted this to be over, to extract the information he'd come for and get out of this place. But he was also aware that a missing Hannah Slade, presumed kidnapped, was somewhere out there. A person his Service had sent into the lion's jaws, so to speak, and who was now quite possibly in great danger. More than that, the data she had been sent to collect could have a massive bearing on the entire strategic balance of power in the South China Sea. And every hour that went by, the trail was going colder. So if that took a few knocks to the body in a Hong Kong *guan*, then it was a small price to pay.

20

Hong Kong

ALONE IN THEIR room on the nineteenth floor of the Landia Hotel in Kowloon, Jenny sipped her third cup of jasmine tea. The jetlag was getting to her and it was tempting to lie down and fall asleep on the bed right there. But her sense of loyalty told her this would somehow be unfair to Luke, who was out on the night-time streets of Hong Kong. She resolved to stay awake until his return.

Her phone lit up with an incoming message from London. It was from the Monitoring section at Vauxhall Cross. Something they had spotted and passed to Felix Schauer's team, who were now sending it on to her. She only got as far as the third line before she clamped her hand to her mouth in shock.

From the website of the *South China Morning Post*:

Senior Party Official found dead in Kowloon

- Police have opened a murder investigation today into the death in suspicious circumstances of a senior CCP official from the mainland. The half-concealed body of Li Qiang Zhou, 47, was discovered by passers-by in a storm drain in the

Mong Kok area of Kowloon. The victim's throat had been cut and his hands had been tied behind his back. Witnesses said his body showed signs of extensive bruising.

- Speaking to the media on the steps outside Kowloon City Division Police Station in Argyle Street, Senior Inspector of Police (SIP) Jonny Tang said: 'This is clearly a very serious matter and we are deploying all resources to unmask the perpetrators of this wicked act.' He added that detectives and other officials from Guangzhou would be arriving shortly to assist in the investigation. No further comment was available at this time.
- The deceased Mr Zhou was believed to have only recently arrived in Hong Kong. He is listed as an expert scientific adviser to the Central Committee of the CCP. He leaves behind him a wife and one daughter.

Li Qiang Zhou . . . Jenny was one of the very, very few people, even inside the Service, who knew the significance of this name and what this now meant.

Li Qiang Zhou was Agent Blue Sky.

21

Win Ho Academy for Martial Arts, Hong Kong

'CHI SAU EXERCISES,' announced Mr Lim as he took up a stance facing Luke square on, 'are designed to increase our sensitivity to an opponent's strike.' Mr Lim didn't look like an especially sensitive individual. In fact, he looked to Luke like someone who could take a serious battering and keep going.

'So now hit me,' said Mr Lim, calmly, nodding in encouragement. 'Aim for my face. Please. Go ahead.'

Luke shifted his weight from one foot to the other, then threw a straight karate punch at the centre of Mr Lim's face, rotating his right fist at the last minute, but holding back from using his full force. His opponent's left arm shot out and twisted, snake-like, rolling Luke's arm away and deflecting it with ease.

Mr Lim sighed and frowned. 'Don't play games with me, Mr Blanford. I am sure you are better than this. I must ask you to try harder. Again now.'

Luke took a deep breath. He had a sudden flashback to the martial-arts scene in *The Matrix* where Keanu Reeves's character had to fight a black-belt master who keeps beckoning him on to fight harder. But this wasn't cinema fantasy, this was real and he worried that, compared to this human ball of muscle and sinew, he simply wasn't going to measure up. How long had it been since his last sparring session, back in the gym in London? Two months? Three? Too long, anyway. He threw another punch at Mr Lim's face, faster this time, but again the tattooed arm shot out and deflected it.

'Better,' Mr Lim said. 'This is what we call a *bong sau*. In English I think they call this a "wing arm". You see how I move your strike off the line of attack?'

Luke nodded. So, now he was being given an impromptu lesson in Wing Chun by this tattooed hard man. Not exactly how he had envisaged spending his first evening in Hong Kong. Could we not just move straight to the part where you tell me where we should be looking for Hannah Slade?

'So now we speed it up a little,' Mr Lim said, moving his body into a curious concave posture as if his hips were trying to back their way out of the room all by themselves. He parried each of Luke's fist strikes by snaking his arms out and around Luke's extended forearms. It struck Luke as an extraordinarily graceful martial art, almost like a dance performance, but then he asked himself what the point of all this was. Where was this going? He was about to get his answer.

Mr Lim stepped back, dropped his arms, and lowered his head in an exaggerated formal bow. The session was over. 'You fight well, Mr Blanford,' he said. 'Not well enough to ever be a *shifu*, a master.' He smiled for the first time. 'But, still, you show courage. Come, let's drink tea in my office. Your visit will not be wasted.'

22

Lieyu Island, Kinmen County, Taiwan

LIEYU ISLAND DOES not feature prominently on many maps. Google it, zoom in, and even then it comes up as just a tiny pin-prick off the south-east coast of China. But Lieyu Island, also known as 'Little Kinmen', does not answer to Beijing. Instead, it is part of Taiwan's outlying island archipelago, the Kinmen Islands, situated little more than a kilometre offshore from the haze-shrouded skyscrapers of Xiamen city on the mainland. So close, in fact, that Taiwanese tourists even fly there from Taipei to photograph themselves with those city skyscrapers just visible behind them. For years there has been an annual swimming race from Little Kinmen to the Chinese mainland. Covid put the brakes on that in 2020 but then it resumed three years later.

Yet it's more than a hundred and fifty kilometres distant across the choppy waters of the Taiwan Strait from the Taiwanese capital, Taipei. And it was precisely because of this distance from the Taiwanese coast, and its closeness to mainland China, that Lieyu Island was specially selected by the Central Military Commission in Beijing. Economically unimportant, militarily indefensible, Lieyu, it was decided, was the perfect testing ground for the next phase of the CCP's multi-stage plan for Taiwan.

Shortly before dusk, in the deeper waters offshore and to the east of the Kinmen Islands, the Shang-II-class submarine broke the surface of the waves, leaving a glittering trail of phosphorescence in the gathering gloom. Onboard the 7000-tonne nuclear-powered attack submarine, armed with an arsenal of thermal torpedoes, rocket mines and a single, supersonic cruise missile, two men exchanged silent glances. One was the Captain, a career officer in the PLAN, the People's Liberation Army Navy. The other was the *zhengwei*, the political commissar assigned by the Communist Party of China to ensure the crew's political adhesion to the Party. On both men's shoulders their dark blue epaulettes bore three gold stars between two parallel lines, denoting the rank of captain. The commissar had almost no military experience to speak of, yet this was a dual command: the one could not issue an order without authorization from the other. And tonight their mission was one of critical national importance, authorized and directed from the very top of the Central Committee of the Party and guarded with the utmost secrecy.

To say there was trust between these two men of similar age, both in their forties, would be an exaggeration. It was more of a mutual understanding, a relationship of convenience. The submarine's captain knew he was being watched, all of the time, and that the slightest hint of disloyalty to the Party would see him relieved of his command the moment they returned to shore, followed by a lengthy and unpleasant investigation. The political commissar barely knew his way around the boat – his safety was in the hands of its crew and its captain – but as Beijing's representative onboard he carried all the authority he needed to feel he was the one really in charge. Even the lowest-ranking sailor on that submarine knew that to cross the commissar was to commit career suicide.

'Is everything ready?' he asked.

The Captain nodded deferentially and gestured towards the ladder that climbed up the submarine's protruding black fin. The *zhengwei* had insisted on being the first up through the hatch now that they had broken the surface. It was something he intended to include in his report, demonstrating his dedication and, yes, even his bravery. A naval rating still had to race up the ladder ahead of him and wrestle the hatch open from the inside, then shin down again before giving him 'the honour'.

A warm and humid breeze ruffled his hair as he breathed in the fresh, salty air and his eyes adjusted to the dark. A hundred kilometres to the east, close to the median line between Taiwan and the coast of mainland China, he knew there was high tension after some 'intrusion' by Western warships resulting in a warning shot being fired. The *zhengwei* knew this because he had received a classified cable informing him of the incident, sent from Yulin naval base on Hainan Island. But he put this to one side as he focused on the mission in hand. Now he watched from the top of the fin as, faintly visible below him, more hatches opened and men raced across the deck. Four minutes later, according to his watch, the inflatables were ready for launch and those who had prepared them stood stiffly to attention, the breeze fanning their overalls as they waited for orders. The command rang out on the boat's Tannoy and the sailors stood back, making way for a second squad that now rushed to take up their positions next to the inflatables. They were the frogmen from the Jiaolong Commando, the Sea Dragons, big, broad-shouldered men, larger than the sailors who stood behind them. Dressed entirely in black, they each carried a QBS06 underwater assault rifle fitted with a twenty-six-round plastic magazine. Each round was capable of firing a long, needle-like projectile for a short distance underwater, as well as having a lethal effect at close range on dry land.

Twenty-two-year-old Private First Class Jian Zhang stood next to the first of the inflatables, his boots nudging the curved rubber edges in the dark. Outwardly calm, Zhang was willing his heart rate to remain steady. Because he knew that the microchip embedded between his shoulder blades was already beaming back a constant flow of medical data to a team of scientists monitoring him from the naval base at Sanya, all the way south on China's Leizhou peninsula.

Zhang was a product of Project 49, the ultra-secret programme

79

to develop ongoing generations of genetically enhanced service-men and -women. Until 2016 China had happily published its data on genetic modification, sharing some of its research with the world's leading medical peer groups. And then, abruptly, it went dark. Whatever China's scientists were up to behind closed doors, the Pentagon suspected, was from then on a closely guarded military secret.

To the naked eye, Zhang looked just like any of his country-men, only rather better built. But beneath his skin, his body was a living experiment in the fusion of cutting-edge technology with human tissue, honed for military purpose. Through his veins coursed not just human blood but also injected respirocytes: arti-ficial red blood cells that mimic the function of the respiratory system, allowing the host, in theory at least, to hold their breath underwater for up to four hours. Following successful surgery, Zhang, like other members of Project 49, was also one of a grow-ing number of enhanced troops endowed with electro-chemical vision: eyesight that gave him something approaching both infra-red and night vision. This was not science fiction, this was molecular nanotechnology in action. This was real. And Zhang had been a willing volunteer, only too happy to submit to the changes being wrought on his body, all in the service of his home-land and the ruling CCP. There were drawbacks and side-effects, of course, as with almost any experimental programme still in its infancy. The pain behind the eyes that sometimes wouldn't go away for days, the numbness that sometimes crept over his extremities, or the all-too-visual images that danced before his eyes, even when they were closed. These he shouldered with equanimity. For Zhang, these were small and worthwhile sacri-fices for a greater cause.

When the submarine descended once more beneath the waves of the South China Sea the three black inflatables were left float-ing on the surface. The target was just over two kilometres away, close enough for an outboard engine to be detected. And so, in near silence, the three crews paddled hard. The wind was pick-ing up now, forcing them to contend with a swell and chop for the last five hundred metres, their powerful, rubber-clad shoulders bulging as their muscles strained to pull hard on the paddles. Zhang blinked several times. When he wasn't looking down at the paddle between his hands, or the inky blackness of the sea, he lifted his gaze towards the outline of the island he could see materializing in the distance. He could only catch glimpses as the inflatable craft rose and fell with the swell but it matched the photographs they had been shown in the briefing back on base.

At three hundred metres out Zhang saw the Master Sergeant in front check the luminous gadget he held in his hand. Seconds later he raised his right arm. It was the signal. One by one they somersaulted backwards over the side of the black inflatables, vanishing into the ocean, leaving just a skeleton crew to man the boats on the surface. They swam in formation, their powerful legs kicking out and propelling them through the water at a depth of just two metres, until they reached an obstacle: the wire perimeter netting. This was unexpected, there had been nothing in the briefing about it, yet they had the tools to deal with it. Wielding the cutters it took only three minutes to cut a gap big enough for all twelve to squeeze through.

Lieyu Island was indefensible, a fact all too obvious to Taiwan's Defence Ministry planners whose sole job it was to make their country as hard a target as possible. This was known as 'the porcupine strategy': put enough spines and quills around you and your enemy will think twice about attacking you. But Beijing had now given Lieyu Island a great deal of thought and had reached the conclusion, based on all the available intelligence gathered from its satellites in space, from its human informants on the ground, and from countless cyber intercepts, that Lieyu's pathetically few porcupine spines could indeed be plucked.

Powering his way through the warm coastal waters alongside the rest of his raiding party, Zhang rehearsed the briefing they'd been given earlier. Lieyu's garrison of Taiwanese border guards, they were told, numbered less than twenty men and women, of whom fewer than a dozen were believed to be combat-trained. And their defences were geared to a surface invasion, said the briefing team, with Lieyu's guns pointing across the water to face an imaginary armada of landing craft and assault ships coming from the Chinese mainland to the west. Not a covert night-time assault by commandos surfacing from a submarine.

But there was another reason why Lieyu had been chosen for this operation. Unlike Russia's flawed 'Special Military Operation' in Ukraine in 2022, when President Putin's army had attempted to seize the entire country from the outset, Lieyu was just a tiny foothold on Taiwanese territory. Anyone looking at a map of the South China Sea would surely assume it belonged to China as it was so close to the mainland, so far from Taiwan. The conclusion was reached in Beijing that if the People's Liberation Army landed on Lieyu, there would be a short-lived flurry of diplomatic outrage, then the world would shrug its shoulders and move on. Energy prices, food-supply chains, climate change and the cost of living would soon eclipse any interest in a tiny islet on the other side of the world that almost no one had ever heard of.

Such matters were above and beyond the concern of Zhang as he rhythmically kicked out his legs, propelling himself ever closer to the dark outline of Lieyu Island ahead. He was focused 100 per cent on the task. He was about to earn his place in history.

23

Mong Kok, Hong Kong

MR LIM WAS as good as his word. Either that, thought Luke, or he's going to an awful lot of trouble to pull the wool over my eyes. Still shiny with sweat from their martial-arts workout, he ushered Luke into his tiny, cramped office at the end of the corridor. The receptionist had disappeared and it seemed they now had the place to themselves. Mr Lim busied himself preparing them a pot of jasmine tea, his gnarled, powerful hands setting down the chipped china cups with a surprisingly nimble touch.

Luke took the seat he was offered, a metal camp stool that had seen better days, and looked around him. If Mr Lim had triad or other connections with the underworld, it seemed little of their glitz and glamour had rubbed off on him. A fan turned slowly on the ceiling, ruffling the yellowing, curled edges of a stack of files pinned down on the desk in the corner by an ornate paperweight. Along one wall, several shelves were crammed with faded black box files that looked like they had been left there some years ago. One of those ridiculous battery-operated waving cats with an inane grin on its luminous pink face stood on another. A calendar hung on the wall, showing the wrong month, beneath a pristine vista of an Alpine meadow, and all the while Luke thought he could detect the faint smell of joss sticks mixed with the sweat that came with the territory in a place like this. Either Mr Lim's business was struggling, he concluded, or this was all an elaborate cover for something else.

'Plovers' eggs?' Mr Lim was holding out a small wicker basket containing four brown eggs, flecked with black, neatly arranged on tissue paper. Luke feigned delight and took one, with a proffered plate. He remembered the last time he had eaten one; it had gone off and the smell of sulphur had been so nauseating he had nearly thrown up on the spot. He watched as Mr Lim settled himself in his chair, took an egg, peeled off the shell, then popped it into his mouth whole. 'From my family's farm,' he remarked, licking his fingers. 'Up in the New Territories.' He tilted his head northward, in the direction of the Chinese mainland, where the teeming tenement blocks of Kowloon gave way to the lush green valleys that had once formed Hong Kong's border with the People's Republic. Luke saw his eyes flick down to the still untouched plover's egg on his plate so he quickly began to remove the shell. This was no time to be giving cultural offence to his host.

'So, you need my help, it seems.' It was more of a statement than a question. Mr Lim sat back in his chair as he spoke, regarding Luke with an intense expression, still apparently sizing him up in spite of their recent exertions in the *guan*. Luke couldn't help noticing that his host was rather obviously cleaning his mouth with his tongue. Before Luke could answer, Mr Lim sat forward in his chair, his huge tattooed shoulders bunching as he leant in towards him, his voice lowered.

'Macau,' he said hoarsely. 'I have already made some enquiries on your behalf and this is where you need to take your search. I would suggest that—' He stopped suddenly as they heard a door closing down the corridor. So they were not quite alone after all. Mr Lim got to his feet, listened, then quietly closed the door.

'One of your staff?' Luke asked.

'It's only the cleaner,' he replied. 'He's worked for me for many years. You don't have to worry about him.' Luke said nothing. In his experience cleaners were often some of the best-informed people in the espionage business. They saw things people threw away, heard conversations when nobody thought they were listening and they had access to offices that were off-limits to most of the staff. Did he have to worry about this cleaner just now? He was less than reassured by his host's confidence.

'There is a hotel there,' Mr Lim continued. 'A big one. A casino. Here.' He reached behind him, his fingers scrabbling for a pen and paper buried amid the general mess on his desk. 'Let me write it down for you. The man you need to see there is a Senhor Francisco Rodrigues. He's the owner. He knows everyone and everything. Nothing happens in Macau without him getting to hear about it.'

'That's great,' Luke said, 'and thank you. Please don't think I'm not grateful, but why would he tell me anything? What's in it for him?' If it's money, he thought, we're in trouble. The Service had entrusted Jenny with access to a considerable sum to secure Hannah's freedom if it came to a point at which a ransom was demanded. But casino types dealt in multiple zeros and he feared their price would be exorbitant.

Mr Lim let out a low chuckle. It was as if he had just read Luke's mind. 'He doesn't want anything from you,' he said. 'But he does owe me a favour, quite a big one. He will see you tomorrow in the hotel bar at one o'clock. Don't be late.'

'You seem very certain of it,' Luke said.

'That's because I've already spoken to his assistant. It's arranged.'

Luke was momentarily surprised. When had Mr Lim had time to do that? And then he realized. He had already made the call before Luke had got there. So all that martial-arts business was just a charade, a sort of bizarre induction test to see if Luke measured up.

Mr Lim glanced up at the clock on the wall and rose heavily to his feet. 'Now, it's getting late, Mr Blanford, and you must be tired.' He held up his hand. 'Can you see yourself out? I have some things to attend to here.'

Luke thought of the 3D-printed Glock hidden inside his

clothes in the changing-room locker and was relieved he wouldn't have to conceal that from Mr Lim. 'Sure. No problem,' he said. 'And, hey, thank you for your help, I appreciate it.'

'My pleasure. We have all lost someone dear to us in our lives,' he said cryptically. Then he gripped Luke's shoulder. 'Be careful out there, Mr Blanford. This isn't the Home Counties, this is Hong Kong. People play by different rules here. So take my advice . . . and watch your back.'

24

Mong Kok, Hong Kong

MACAU . . . MACAU . . . Luke voiced the word over and over in
his head as he closed the door behind him to the Win Ho Academy for Martial Arts. He wasn't particularly rattled by Mr Lim's
sinister parting words: people had been saying the same sort of
thing to him all his adult life. If he took every warning like that
to heart he would never have passed Selection for Special Forces,
or gone to half the places his adrenaline-fuelled career had taken
him to. But Macau had him puzzled. Why there? Why take the
risk of smuggling Hannah Slade across the Pearl River into
Macau when whoever had taken her could simply make her 'disappear' right here in the back-streets of Kowloon?

Luke had only a sketchy notion of what went on in Macau. He
knew that this once dilapidated outpost of Portugal's past imperial power had today become a byword for high-end vice,
underworld crime and big-time gamblers. A good place to hide
someone, he supposed, if you wanted them to disappear off the
grid. But who would want to take Hannah there? If China's Ministry of State Security had her in their clutches, why not house
her in some faceless government building in Hong Kong Central? Or whisk her north across the old pre-1997 border to
Shenzhen or even Beijing? No, this was starting to smell like a

non-state job and that could mean Hannah was in a whole different world of trouble.

Right. Priorities. He needed to get word of this to Jenny back at the hotel and to the office in London. Luke glanced up and down the street and chose the first place he liked the look of. A basic late-night noodle bar, cheap and anonymous. Squeezing past the plastic chairs, he made his way to the counter where an old man in shorts sat on a stool reading a newspaper through thick pebble glasses. A fan turned slowly above him, slicing through a small squadron of flies, and while his grease-stained vest might have started out white, those days were now long behind it.

'That one, please.' Luke pointed at a steaming cauldron of noodles on a stove.

'I bring it to you,' said the man, waving him to a table.

With his back to the counter and an eye on the door, Luke whipped out his phone, coded in, and sent an encrypted text to Angela Scott at Vauxhall Cross and Jenny. It mentioned Macau, Rodrigues, the venue and the suggested time, and he requested clearance to go ahead. He liked working with Jenny and Angela. They would know exactly what to do with cross-checking the information Mr Lim had just divulged. It was the thing that had most unnerved him when he left the forces: after twelve years operating as part of a close-knit team in the Royal Marines, knowing he could depend on everyone around him not to screw up, would he ever find a profession with the same degree of loyalty and trust? So far, he had been pleasantly surprised by the people he'd worked with at Vauxhall, although, to be fair, he had also encountered a fair few 'biffers' in Whitehall – by-the-book types with a passion for process, acronyms and precious little imagination. And then there was the legion of in-house lawyers stalking the corridors of Vauxhall Cross, not something his uncle had had to contend with in his day when he'd worked for the Service. Nowadays every operation had to be legalled from the get-go. Nobody wanted another Libya fiasco with court cases, toe-curling headlines, eye-watering pay-outs or humbling public apologies from the Attorney General.

It must have been as the endorphins were hitting his brain from all those glutinous noodles he was wolfing down that Luke momentarily failed to notice what was on the other side of the shop window. A man in blue overalls was standing just outside the circle of light that spilled onto the pavement. He took a long drag on his cigarette as he watched Luke intently, never taking his eyes off him for a second. Then he spoke quietly into his mobile phone and was gone. It was the cleaner from the Win Ho Academy for Martial Arts.

Luke took his time, savouring each mouthful, spooning up the salty broth that swilled around at the bottom of his bowl. He needed this and not just to cleanse his palate from the lingering taste of plover's egg. He was loath to admit it but that sparring session with Mr Lim had taken it out of him. He suddenly felt a lot older than his forty years. Luke got up, paid the old man, who was still reading a crumpled copy of a Chinese newspaper, and walked out. A quick routine check, left and right, up and down the street, no danger signs, and he was walking towards Argyle Street, retracing his route from the hotel.

It was the young, thickset man with the buzz cut who came up to him, innocuously asking him for the time, who triggered the internal alarm bells. Seriously? Who comes up to a stranger on a darkened street after eleven o'clock at night and asks for the time? A random mugging? In Hong Kong? Unlikely. The thought flashed through Luke's mind like a thunderbolt: I've been made. Someone's ID'd me. He was on the point of giving Buzzcut the shove-off when he felt something pressing into his right side and slightly to the rear, just about where his kidney would be. It felt suspiciously like the barrel of a handgun. A second man. How had he missed him? He felt a hand pressing firmly into the small of his back, trying to propel him down the alleyway that opened up to their right. Luke complied but now his mind was going into overdrive. Who these people were and what they wanted from him was of secondary importance. All that mattered was extracting himself from this situation, with the minimum of fuss. Silently, he blessed the team in Security

Section back in Vauxhall Cross. Blessed them for making him pick up the Glock.

Even in the dim light of the back-street he could see there were three of them. All young, all looking like they'd spent an excessive amount of time in the gym. Hired muscle, working for someone higher up the food chain. And not too smart either. They had failed to pat him down in the briefest of body searches. They walked him past a row of dustbins overflowing with rubbish, where cats were fighting each other for scraps. There was no one else in sight, the back-street was deserted. This was bad. Luke knew he probably had only seconds to act – it was a window of opportunity and he had to jump through it.

His hands were still free, they'd made another mistake there, and now he spotted his opportunity. A black cat, thin and scrawny, shot out in the space between his feet and the man who had come up to ask him the time. The two precious seconds of distraction were all he needed. Luke's right hand darted into the inside left pocket of his jacket and whipped out the Glock. In a split second he had it cocked, stepped back a pace and had all three covered in an arc before they realized what was happening. Even after all these years, the training had a way of just taking over.

For several seconds there was silence. A standoff. Luke was quite prepared to pull the trigger if he needed to, aiming a non-lethal shot at their legs or arms, but he knew that was a last resort. He was also uncomfortably aware that he had had no chance to test-fire the weapon. Hell, this was just a piece of yellow plastic in his hand. It still didn't feel like a proper firearm. What if he pulled the trigger and nothing happened? He was going to have to bluff this one out.

'You can all fuck off now,' he said quietly, pointedly aiming the Glock at the man with the pistol.

Buzzcut spat on the ground between them and swore in Cantonese. He said something to the others and then, as one, they turned their backs and vanished down the alleyway. Luke's breathing was coming in short, controlled gasps as he let the tension flow out of his body. The Glock had done its work but now

90

he needed to dump it. Word would soon get out that there was an armed *gweilo*, a Westerner, on the loose in Kowloon and the police would be swarming all over this place in no time. Luke bent down and picked up a filthy rag from next to the dustbins. Carefully, keeping an eye open to make sure no one was coming, he wiped the weapon clean of his prints. Then he walked fifty metres down the road and, without breaking step, lobbed it over a wall into someone's garden.

So he had survived the encounter. Great. But someone here was on to him and he had no idea who.

25

Lieyu Island, Kinmen County, Taiwan

BOULDERS. SLIPPERY WITH slime and seaweed. Encrusted with jagged barnacles that cut through his black neoprene gloves. These were the things that Zhang and his unit of Sea Dragon frogmen encountered as they slithered ashore that night, using the rusting steel tank traps as cover while they scanned the darkened shoreline with their multifunctional night-vision goggles. Their unit had recently been equipped with the latest variant of these and they did more than allow the wearer to see in the dark. They were hardwired into each man's integrated combat system, their ICS, a digital piece of kit that not only allowed Zhang and his team to identify enemy forces from friendly troops simply by looking at them but also beamed back video in real-time to their base on the Leizhou peninsula. This in turn allowed their commanders to see exactly what they were seeing, while geo-locating the position of every human in the area. The People's Liberation Army, once a backwater of Mao-era weapons and tactics, had come a very long way in a short time.

Too small to be picked up by Taiwan's coastal radar, Zhang's unit had landed unobserved and unopposed on the gently sloping beach next to the Dong Lin Seashore Park. Turning east, they passed a darkened cemetery and an empty guard post. It was when they were nearing their objective that the silence of the night was broken by the sudden frantic barking of a dog, quickly followed by a shouted challenge. Peering through his night-vision goggles, Zhang could see three border guards, seventy metres away according to the luminous display on his headset. All were carrying weapons and, with them, a Belgian Shepherd was barking and straining at the leash.

For Private First Class Jian Zhang and the men on either side of him, the moment when they opened fire was the culmination of so many months of intensive training. Actions and reflexes were instinctive, forged in the furnace heat of exercise scenarios so dangerously realistic they would never be permitted in a NATO army. Two of the Taiwanese border guards went down in that first blistering fusillade of 5.66mm steel darts. But the third was able to roll to the side and squeeze off two rounds before he, too, succumbed to the overwhelming incoming fire.

Zhang took the shot in his pectoral muscle, the bullet slamming into his chest and narrowly missing the brachial artery. If they had reached Lieyu Island by another means, and not by swimming covertly to their target, he might have been wearing ceramic body armour. Without it, his torso shuddered with the impact and his brain registered pain as he dropped to his knees. As the respirocytes, the injected artificial red blood cells, coursed through his veins, Zhang's body was already working overtime to control the damage. He called once, not in panic, or even in alarm, just loud enough to let his team know he was wounded and down. Hands and arms quickly came to his aid, laying him down in a resting position while the squad medic rushed up to attend to his injury. But Zhang was conscious and talking, his body long since enhanced to a point well beyond the bounds of normal human endurance. He knew, even in that moment, that it would not be long after surgery that he would be fit to resume his duties.

Zhang missed the rest of the raid. While the combat medic was tending to him in the lee of a sand dune the rest of his squad surged forward unopposed. Picking up the pace, they quickly covered the ground to their objective: the 23 August Artillery Battle Victory Monument, a relic from China's bombardment of the island in the 1950s. Their drill had been rehearsed many times back on the mainland and now it was carried out in seconds. The two men assigned to the task raced to the flagpole and tore down the red, blue and white Taiwanese flag, replacing it immediately with the yellow stars on the red background of the People's Republic of China. A powerful torch had been brought ashore for this very moment and now photographs and video were taken as evidence and transmitted to the vast Orwellian building known as '1 August', the headquarters of China's Central Military Commission on Fuxing Road in west Beijing. And all before anyone in Taipei, or indeed anywhere in the world, had the slightest idea of what had just taken place.

Chinese troops had their boots on the ground on Taiwanese territory while half the world was still asleep.

26

Vauxhall Cross, London

'I'M NOT CONVINCED.'

'Felix?'

'I said I'm not convinced. By this Macau lead.' MI6's Director Critical was frowning and shaking his head. He was wearing his trademark maroon silk bow-tie, giving him a jocular, almost comical appearance that was completely at odds with his rather humourless demeanour. They were on the third floor of the Vauxhall Cross building: Felix Schauer, Jack Searle, the head of China desk, Angela, Luke's line manager, and Lucia Freer on secondment to the Secret Intelligence Service from its sister service GCHQ in Cheltenham.

Almost the moment Luke's message about Macau had come in, Felix Schauer had called a CADISC, a case discussion, an urgent meeting to thrash out what their next move should be. There was an assumption by some outside the intelligence community, one fuelled by cinema perhaps, that Britain's intelligence officers spent all their time racing around the world in fast cars and firing guns. But Luke Carlton was the exception rather than the rule, a man who had come into the Service on the back of twelve years at the sharp end of the armed forces, an individual to whom weapon handling and the art of survival were second nature. The truth, when it came to most of his colleagues, was rather more banal. MI6 intelligence officers spent an inordinate amount of time in meetings, only occasionally in chic, trendy hotel bars, more often in some bland, featureless office inside Vauxhall Cross. And yet the decisions taken in those dull little rooms could often dictate whether an operation succeeded or failed, if an agent would be extracted from a hostile situation alive or end up in pieces.

'I think we send them. Both of them. Luke and Jenny. To Macau. It's the only lead we've got and the source who gave it to Luke has given us reliable product in the past.' The head of China desk was young, ambitious, a fast mover and, despite his proven prowess as an intelligence officer, he had somehow managed to get this far without ever visiting a Chinese-speaking country or knowing more than a dozen words of Mandarin.

'And this view,' said Felix Schauer, eyebrows arched in question, 'would be based on what, Jack? Your extensive time spent there, in Macau?'

It was a calculated barb. Schauer knew full well that the head of China desk had never been near Macau but he couldn't resist the put-down. The two men regarded each other for a moment before Angela intervened.

'Look, I think before we reach a decision on this we should hear what Lucia has to say. It's quite pertinent, I think.' She nodded to the young signals intelligence officer and gave her a smile of encouragement. 'Lucia . . .'

'Right. What we've done,' she said, looking from one to another, 'is to work on a breakdown of mobile-phone transmissions made in the area around the Tai Wo Tang Café in Kowloon where we lost contact with Hannah. We've taken a bracket of one hour either side of the time we think she was abducted and then—'

'Excuse me for interrupting,' Felix Schauer again, still with the frown, 'but we're talking about Chinese territory here, aren't we? You're saying we can access the telecoms towers even though they're ultimately under Ministry of State Security control?'

Lucia looked across at Angela before replying. 'We can, yes. The basic framework for the network was laid down just before Handover in '97 and then we've had . . . how shall I put it? . . . a little help from certain expatriate technicians who stayed on in Hong Kong after that. Um, can I continue?'

'Please do.' Felix Schauer offered her something approaching a smile.

'So, working with our friends in the NSA, we've been able to sift through the vast amounts of traffic that you would expect from such a high-density residential area and isolate those calls being made from there to Macau.'

'And?' Felix Schauer was drumming his fingers on the table, but if the gifted young linguist from GCHQ found his constant interruptions an irritation she didn't show it.

'And we've registered a total of three hundred and sixteen calls made from that part of Kowloon to Macau during that two-hour timeframe. Of those, only three were made to known state organizations and these were all innocuous, linked to agriculture and fisheries.'

Felix Schauer spread his hands and sat back in his chair. 'So doesn't that just prove my point?' he said. 'There is nothing here to corroborate Luke's source. Sending him and Jenny to Macau sounds like a lost cause when they should be nailing down every lead we have in Hong Kong.'

'We don't have any leads in Hong Kong,' interjected the China head. 'At least, not yet.'

Searle and Schauer glared at each other.

Once again it was Angela who defused the tension. 'Guys, she hasn't finished yet. Can we just hear her out?'

Lucia flashed her a smile of thanks before resuming her brief. 'What we *did* detect from this phone traffic, after running it through the Sirius program, was a sudden surge in calls coming out of that part of Kowloon and they were all being made to two numbers in Macau. One of those numbers . . .' Lucia paused to look from Felix to Jack then back to the Director Critical. '. . . one of those numbers belongs to a known player in the Macau underworld. A kind of Mr Big, if you like. The name he uses is Francisco Rodrigues.'

Felix Schauer sat bolt upright in his chair. 'Rodrigues? The man Carlton is proposing to meet tomorrow?'

'The same one,' Angela replied. 'Look, I know this doesn't prove anything. And, yes, of course we need to test every theory. But let's not lose sight of what's going on out there.' She pointed her finger towards the door and in the vague direction of the Thames below, as if it somehow represented the tense waters of the Taiwan Strait. 'We've got every ingredient going on in the South China Sea for the start of a Third World War. We need – we *must* – retrieve the download of data that Blue Sky was due to give Hannah Slade if we're going to have any serious chance of stopping this thing escalating. I'm with Jack here. We should put Luke and Jenny in Macau without delay. And get them in front of this Mr Rodrigues. He might just be our route to finding Hannah and getting her back.'

Felix Schauer was deep in thought and it was several seconds before he spoke. When he did, his words were directed at Lucia and his voice had softened considerably. 'Follow the data. Isn't that what you people in Cheltenham always say? Well, I'm not going to argue with that. You make a strong case, Lucia. I concur. Send them to Macau.'

27

Kowloon, Hong Kong

IT WAS AFTER midnight when Luke finally knocked on the door of their room on the nineteenth floor of the Landia Hotel, waited for a response from Jenny, then let himself in. She was still awake and sprang up when he walked in and closed the door behind him. 'My God, Luke! You look like you've seen a ghost. Are you OK? What happened?' She moved towards him and stopped short, her arms hanging loosely by her sides.

'Nothing,' he replied, sitting heavily on the padded stool beside the dressing-table and running his hands through his hair. 'At least, not with the source. He's given us a lead of sorts – you got my signal, right?'

'About Macau? I did, yes. So did London. They think it's worth pursuing. They want us to head there immediately.'

'What – now? It's the middle of the bloody night.'

'No! In the morning. But come on, Luke, I know you too well. You're holding back. Something happened out there, didn't it?'

Luke swivelled towards her on the stool and returned her gaze. It was true, she knew him far too well for him to keep any secrets from her. This was the fourth operation they had worked on together and Jenny had a way of almost reading his thoughts. Yet on his way back to the hotel he had thought carefully about how much he should tell her. Getting jumped like that in a back-street within their first twenty-four hours in-country was not a good start and he had no wish to spook her. But he and Jenny were equal partners on this operation and she had a right to know.

'I got jumped,' he said flatly. 'In a back-street. Three guys. One armed.'

'Oh my God.' She clamped a hand over her mouth, then placed it on his shoulder, searching his face. 'Are you hurt? How did you get away? When did this happen?'

Luke got up from the stool before answering. 'Does this place have a minibar?' He started hunting around the room. 'Yes! Found it.' He opened the miniature fridge beneath the dressing-table and took out a tiny bottle of whisky. 'Join me?' Jenny shook her head, still waiting for answers. Luke poured the amber liquid into a tumbler, took a sip, and briefly closed his eyes. 'Well, I have to say, hats off to Security Section,' he said at last. 'They were right about the Glock.'

'Wait – what? Don't tell me you used it! Christ, Luke! What were you thinking? This isn't Afghanistan! How many bodies are we talking about?' All her earlier concern had vanished and now she was looking at him accusingly.

Luke held out his free hand in a calming gesture. 'Easy there,' he said. 'No one got shot. I just had to show them the weapon and they legged it straight away. And don't worry, it's disposed of now. Prints are wiped. Look . . . I'm fine. I've faced a lot worse, Jenny, you know that. But the bigger worry is this: was I a mark? Is someone on to us already? Are we compromised before we even start here?'

Jenny went to the window and pulled back the curtain slightly, as if somehow the answers were down there in those teeming twenty-four-hour neon-lit streets. She looked back at Luke, who was draining his glass. 'Did anyone call your name? Ask you for ID?' she said.

'Nope.'

'So it could have been a casual mugging gone wrong. This stuff happens.'

100

'With a pistol?' Luke replied. 'I don't think so. Nothing casual about that, Jenny. Besides, they never asked for money. They were trying to take me somewhere. An abduction, basically.'

'Well, let's look at it this way,' Jenny said. 'I doubt it was MSS. If the Ministry of State Security wanted to lift either of us they probably know exactly where to find us. Which means . . .'

'Triads.'

'Exactly. Somehow, God knows how, we've attracted the attention of the criminal underworld here. Luke, this is not good news.'

'Tell me about it. Or, better still, tell me about this Rodrigues guy in Macau. Has the office come back with anything on him yet?'

'They have.' Jenny reached for her phone and began to scroll down. 'Just the bare bones for now. Senhor Francisco Rodrigues is forty-two, a Portuguese national, born and raised in Macau. Father was in the drinks import business. Started working for a local underworld triad the same year Macau got handed back to China. He was only a teenager then. Worked his way up – if you can call it that – in the underworld there and made some powerful friends. He now owns a string of bars, hotels, some of which double as brothels and—'

'Nice,' Luke interjected. 'I can hardly wait to meet him.'

Jenny put down her phone. 'I agree. He's quite possibly an odious piece of shit. But we know how this works, Luke. In this business you sometimes have to swim in muddy waters. Well, this is one of those times. If a white Western woman of Hannah's description has been smuggled across the water into Macau then the chances are this guy will know about it. Um, Luke . . .'

'What?'

'There's something else you need to see.' She picked up her phone once more, found the message she was looking for and passed it to him without a word.

When he'd finished reading it they looked at each other in silence. So Blue Sky was dead. Murdered. Probably not more than a mile from where they were right now. The most highly placed agent the Service had ever had inside China in a generation. The defector who was supposed to be delivering them the mother lode on Beijing's plans for Taiwan. Luke's mind was already working through the possibilities. If someone had got to him so quickly, what were the chances that Hannah Slade was still alive? And had Blue Sky even been able to pass on the data to her before they'd got to him? Those questions and more, he knew, would keep him awake for much of the night.

28

Whitehall, London

'THIS,' THUNDERED THE PM, 'is completely unacceptable!' His face was reddening as he spoke and those close to him couldn't help noticing a vein pulsing furiously next to his temple. 'I don't care how close this Lieyu place is to China on the map,' he exclaimed. 'It's Taiwanese territory. This constitutes nothing short of an invasion and illegal occupation.'

It was the second COBRA meeting in as many days and up on the wall, above the far end of the table, the large interactive digital map showed the location of Lieyu Island next to the Chinese coastal city of Xiamen. News had broken of the raising of the Chinese flag on the island by the Sea Dragons raiding party. To the embarrassment of the Taiwanese government in Taipei, the first they had learnt of what had happened was when the photographs and video were posted online. By China's official Xinhua News Agency.

'So how many troops do we think China's got on the island right at this minute? CDS?'

The PM turned to the Chief of Defence Staff, Air Chief Marshal 'Chip' Crosland, Britain's most senior serving officer. He had come straight from the Ministry of Defence, only a brisk walk away on the other side of Whitehall, where he had just been brought up to speed by the Chief of Defence Intelligence. Crosland was an Air Force man, new to the post, the first from the senior ranks of the RAF to be given Britain's top military slot since 2010. He'd spent much of his career in the cockpit, flying mostly Tornados. No stranger to active operations in the skies over the Balkans and the Gulf, he knew next to nothing about maritime operations and had only recently paid his first official visit to Portsmouth. Crosland was on a steep learning curve.

'None, Prime Minister,' he replied. 'At least, none as of thirty minutes ago. They've withdrawn, for now. Washington has put a satellite over it so we've got eyes on.'

'Right. Well, that's cold comfort, quite frankly.' The PM had his hands on the table in front of him and was continually clasping and unclasping them as he spoke. 'The fact is, they invaded Taiwanese soil and if they think they can get away with it they'll be back to take a bigger chunk. Look what happened when we let Putin seize Crimea in 2014. Our response was pathetic. Putin knew he'd got away with it so he came back and had a pop at swallowing the rest of Ukraine. No, we need a robust, coordinated response in support of Taiwan. We'll be raising this at the UN, obviously, in concert with our allies. But this has gone well beyond diplomacy. First it was the missile fired across the bows of our AUKUS Task Group, now this. Beijing is blatantly yanking our chain and we need a strategy to confront it. A military one.'

The PM looked questioningly around the table, his eyes roving from one worried face to the next, a furrow of concern running across his forehead. Before anyone could answer he fired off another question in the direction of the Chief of Defence Staff. 'CDS . . .'

'PM?'

'Where exactly are our two aircraft carriers right at this minute? Hmm?'

Air Chief Marshal Crosland looked somewhat uncomfortable as all eyes turned towards him. 'Well, the, er, the *Queen Elizabeth* is on port call in Jebel Ali and—'

'Jebel where?'

'Jebel Ali, Prime Minister. It's in Dubai, in the UAE. You visited it last year. And the *Prince of Wales* is, um, she's in Portsmouth right now having a refit. Her electrical system's flooded again, I'm afraid.'

For several seconds the Prime Minister stared at his Chief of Defence Staff, a single eyebrow raised, saying nothing, because nothing needed to be said. The most expensive warship ever built in the Royal Navy's 479-year history was nearly six thousand nautical miles, or ten thousand kilometres, from where it needed to be.

'We still have *Daring* in theatre,' chipped in Simon Eustace, the Defence Secretary. 'And, of course, there's the US Navy's Seventh Fleet at Yokosuka in Japan. But if I may say so, we're going to have to calibrate our response very carefully indeed. This whole thing could spin out of control very quickly. We *cannot* get into a shooting war with China.'

It was Alex Matheson, Chief of MI6, who broke the strained silence that filled the room. 'Sorry,' she began, 'but I wonder if I could just throw in a bit of perspective from our side?'

The PM swivelled to face her, his face brightening. He clearly wasn't enjoying what he was hearing so far. 'Please do,' he said.

'I think,' she said slowly, 'that we should be wary of jumping to conclusions here. Despite everything that's just happened, our assessment is that China is nowhere near in a position to invade Taiwan proper. Yes, it's true they're testing us, pushing boundaries . . .' She took off her glasses and folded them neatly in front of her. '. . . and by us, I mean of course the West, all of us, Taiwan, Washington, Japan and so forth. But, look, the lessons of Russia's mistakes in Ukraine have not been lost on Beijing. Putin was given duff advice from his intelligence people when he launched that invasion back in February 2022. The Chinese are a lot more cautious.' She held up a warning finger for emphasis.

'They know that a successful invasion takes extremely careful preparation. We're talking here about moving enormous numbers of troops to the coast – some estimates put the figure needed for a full-scale invasion and occupation at two million. We're talking about requisitioning commercial shipping to help get that force across the Taiwan Strait, stockpiling food and medicines, starting a national drive for blood banks, all that kind of thing.'

She shook her head as if to reinforce her point. 'No. They landed that raiding party on Lieyu Island because they know – they think – they can get away with it. It's bang next to their coastline and Beijing will be banking on most of the world deciding it isn't worth a fight.'

'But, Alex,' the PM said, 'this still looks like a dress rehearsal for a full-scale invasion, doesn't it?'

'I really don't think we're at that point yet. But . . .' Again she held up a warning finger. '. . . what we *are* seeing is some very worrying long-term preparations.'

'Such as?'

'Well, both my Service and our colleagues in Defence Intelligence have detected a surge in their production of a whole range of missiles – cruise, ballistic, air-to-air, you name it. What particularly worries us is they seem to be focusing on the kind of weapon that would target beach landing zones. There's a name for it but you'll forgive me if I don't have it to hand. There are other signs too, less obvious perhaps, but still indicative of a possible build-up to invasion further down the line.'

'Could you be more specific?' The PM had unclasped his hands and was now drumming the tips of his fingers on the table top while frowning at her.

'I can. They've started to row back on their exports of key materials, like critical minerals, they're stockpiling POL and—'

'POL?' he asked.

'Sorry, yes. Petrol, oil and lubricants. They're also taking measures in their economy that would seem to indicate a degree of insulation from shocks to come. When Russia invaded Ukraine it was pretty obvious the Kremlin wasn't expecting Western sanctions to be as severe as they were. The Chinese are playing their cards a lot more carefully. And cleverly.'

'All right.' The PM again. He had stopped frowning but still had one eyebrow raised. 'I'm only partly reassured by what you say. So what's your prognosis?'

The MI6 Chief looked at her glasses, still neatly folded on the table in front of her, and thought for a few seconds before answering. 'I think,' she said eventually, 'that the best way to look at this is as an exercise in psychological warfare. They're trying to scare the wits out of Taipei, just as they did after Taiwan's President Tsai Ing-wen visited Washington in early 2023. They're sending a signal that Taiwan proclaiming independence is an absolute no-no for them. It's a red line for Beijing and they want the world to respect it. My Service's view is that China would still prefer to *persuade* Taiwan to rejoin the motherland without a shot being fired. "Peaceful reunification", they call it.'

'You mean Sun Tzu,' the PM said.

'Excuse me?'

'Sun Tzu. *The Art of War*. "Begin by seizing something which your opponent holds dear; then he will be amenable to your will."'

'Exactly, yes. You could put it like that,' she replied.

'I have to say, though,' interjected the Defence Secretary, 'if this is a bluff it's a pretty elaborate one. Don't forget this is all coming on the back of China launching over two hundred incursions into Taiwan's Air Defence Zone in the last two weeks. They're ramping things up.'

'Alex?' The PM looked up, squinting now at the MI6 Chief with one eye closed, his face screwed up as if in pain.

Again, she took her time in answering. Typical of one in her profession, she found it easiest to talk in terms of a 'balance of probabilities', 'fragments of intelligence' and conclusions reached 'with a medium to high degree of confidence'.

But that wasn't what the PM wanted to hear today. 'Let's just cut to the chase,' he said. 'Just give me the bottom line. Is China building up to invade Taiwan or not?'

The MI6 Chief appeared to squirm in her seat. Coming down firmly on one side of the fence or the other was rarely a place that serving intelligence officers felt comfortable inhabiting. And she knew something that nobody else in that COBRA meeting knew. That somewhere out there in Hong Kong or Macau was a woman they'd sent to collect the raw intel that could, potentially, spike all of China's future invasion plans. A woman now abducted and completely off the grid.

Alex Matheson's voice, when she finally spoke, was very quiet. 'Look,' she said, rather as if she were explaining something simple to a small child. 'My Service has been making China our number-one priority for several years now. But . . .' She looked around the room before completing her sentence. '. . . if you're asking me to come down on one side or the other, I'd say, no, I think it's a bluff by Beijing.'

'And why's that?'

'They really don't want to do this,' she replied. 'Invasion is a last resort for China. Think of the cost, not just in lives but in trade – all those sanctions they know will follow, just as night follows day. China's economy is not like Russia's. It's hardwired to the rest of the world's. There's a limit to how much they can insulate themselves from the backlash. This would set them back years. Decades, even. No, I believe they want us to *think* they're about to invade and they're hoping the West will persuade Taiwan's government to sue for peace to avoid a war that drags in America and maybe ourselves.'

'I see.' The PM sounded slightly mollified, but only slightly. 'So have we and the Americans really got nobody on the inside?'

The SIS Chief considered the question for a few seconds, weighing up just how much she could tell them at this stage. 'The truth is,' she replied, 'yes, we do have someone in play at this moment. But their situation is – how shall I put it? Let's just say it's delicate right now.'

29

Kowloon, Hong Kong

BY 6.20 A.M. Luke and Jenny were packed up, had checked out and were heading for the ferry terminal to Macau before the first rays of the sun had even hit the rooftops of Kowloon. This wasn't just about getting an early start: this was about their personal safety. Last night's incident in the back-street had changed the security profile of this whole operation. Already on their guard before they had got off the plane, they now had to be even more vigilant.

'Things are turning a bit too kinetic for my liking,' Luke said, as they stood on the pavement outside the Landia Hotel with the morning heat starting to build, waiting for their cab to the Shun Tak Centre and the ferry.

'Meaning?' Jenny looked up at him, her head on one side.

'Meaning someone's got the gloves off here. A party official – Blue Sky – getting bumped off in a back-street like that? That doesn't sound like the work of MSS. More like triads, don't you think? If this was Chinese state they would have hauled him back to Beijing and made him sing. He's no use to them dead.'

'I was thinking the same,' Jenny said. 'I got Jack's team to send us a background brief on who they are and how they operate. I'll fill you in when we have a moment.'

'Good job. But when did you have time to do that?'

'Last night. When you were off seeing your Mr Lim.' She was about to say more but she fell silent as their cab had just pulled up. A man was rushing to open the rear door for them, releasing a welcome blast of cold, air-conditioned air.

When the sleek red and white ferry pulled out of Hong Kong's terminal at Shun Tak and nosed out to cross the Pearl River to Macau, Luke was acutely aware that they were almost the only Westerners among the passengers. No one was paying them any attention yet he couldn't help scrutinizing every face he looked at. Was that guy over there one of the men who had attacked him last night? Was the girl sitting by the life raft a scout for an organized-crime syndicate? It was starting to get to him. Being vigilant was one thing, becoming paranoid was another. He would have to keep his suspicions in check. And yet he kept wondering why the Service wasn't using someone who could blend in a bit better for this job.

At least a hundred thousand Hong Kong Chinese had moved to Britain since the crackdown on democracy in the former colony. There must be some rich pickings there for recruiters at the spy agencies on both sides of the divide: China and Britain. Yet he could also imagine that obtaining the necessary security clearance – the dreaded Developed Vetting process – on someone who had spent all their life in Hong Kong would be uniquely difficult.

'Wow, that was quick,' Jenny said. 'We're almost there.' In the white, steamy haze of the morning they could just make out the approaching skyline of Macau. Low, verdant hills in the distance, a parade of skyscrapers in the foreground, all topped by a tele-communications tower that looked to Luke like a giant hypodermic needle pricking the colourless sky.

'Terminal Marítimo de Passageiros do Porto Exterior' read a sign in Portuguese, as they mingled with the other passengers pouring off the ferry and into the terminal. They moved quickly through the building, stopping only to buy a couple of cans of

110

iced lemon tea from a vendor, then joined the well-ordered queue outside for a taxi. Luke and Jenny had done the counter-surveillance course down at the Fort, learning how to spot a tail, how to throw them off, how to vary your route. That would be a challenge in Macau, they realized, if anyone was actually tailing them. But the one thing they were *not* going to do was head straight to the rendezvous. Classic mistake. Instead, Luke had already chosen a nearby venue and he gave the address now to the driver.

Even through the half-steamed-up windows of the taxi they could see that the Chinese Special Administrative District of Macau was different from Hong Kong. Within minutes of leaving the port they were driving down palm-lined boulevards and passing great glittering gold palace casinos. They watched an endless procession of luxury top-of-the-range cars moving through the broad streets with darkened rear windows and unsmiling chauffeurs behind the wheel. The place reeked of money, much of it, Luke suspected, derived from dubious sources. It was easy to see why this former Portuguese colony, only handed back to China in 1999, was dubbed 'the Las Vegas of the East'. The place was a playground, a monument to pleasure and lavish self-indulgence. He turned to Jenny, who shook her head slowly in response.

They had just over an hour to kill before meeting Rodrigues and the place Luke chose was commendably bland and unremarkable: a soulless, spotlessly clean fast-food joint, sandwiched between giant hotel chains on the Avenida Cidade Nova and only a short distance from the hotel where they needed to be at 1 p.m. Jenny ordered a milkshake, and he asked for a fish burger and fries. They positioned themselves at a corner table where Luke could have a clear view of everyone who came in or out and which was far enough away from the other customers for them not to be overheard.

'Spot anyone from the ferry?' he asked.

'Nope, but . . .' She didn't need to say any more. They both knew that if they were being tailed by professionals it would

111

likely be with a relay team: one watcher handing over to another and falling back as the next took over.

'OK,' said Luke, when they were satisfied no one was within earshot. 'So what did Jack's team have to offer on the triads? I need to be on a steep learning curve here.'

'Yes, you do. You'll need to read the full brief but let me give you the top lines.' Jenny took a sip of her milkshake through a straw and winced as it made a loud gurgling noise. 'You can't win with these things, can you?' she said, pushing it away from her. 'Either you use the straw and make a noise like that or you drink it straight from the glass and you end up with milkshake all over your face. Right. Triads.'

She took a paper napkin from the box on the table and wiped her mouth. 'Essentially they started out as criminal gangs formed by those fleeing the newly founded People's Republic of China after the Communist takeover in 1949. Since then, they've spread across the world, permeating every major Chinese community.'

'Including Hong Kong, presumably?' Luke interjected.

'Especially Hong Kong. One of the most established ones there is called . . . Hang on, it'll come to me in a second.' Jenny looked up towards the ceiling as if for inspiration. 'Wo Shing Wo. That's it. Then there's the Sun Yee On – they're mostly immigrants from Guangdong Province, on the other side of the old border between Hong Kong and mainland China. Apparently they had their fingers in every pie when it came to the seedier side of nightlife in Wanchai district. That was before a lot of those places got closed down. Luke, are you paying attention?'

Luke was focused on the door beyond her shoulder. 'I am listening, yes. But I'm also watching our backs. There's a guy just come in, and I'm pretty sure he was on our ferry this morning. White baseball cap, short-sleeve shirt, fawn trousers.'

'Good,' said Jenny, without turning. 'That means he's not part of a professional relay team of watchers. Probably come over here to gamble away his week's wages. So, back to the triads. There are others in this region. Wo On Lok and 14K are two of them but they're not as big or as active as the ones I mentioned earlier.'

'And what are they into, then, these triad gangs?' Luke asked, still keeping half an eye on the door. 'Drugs? Prostitution? Money-laundering?'

'All of the above,' Jenny said. 'Plus extortion and a fair bit of cross-border smuggling into the mainland.'

'Got you.' Luke shook his head. 'None of which explains why the hell anyone would want to lift Hannah. Could it even be a case of mistaken ID? Because I have to say, Jen, I'm not getting this. The operational security on this whole thing, the handover with Blue Sky, was so tight they didn't even tell Hong Kong station. And they sent a collector, for God's sake. She's not even a trained intelligence officer. So, unless there's a mole back at VX, how did anyone know where she was meeting Blue Sky for the handover?'

Jenny regarded him for a long moment in silence. Leaks and moles were the stuff of nightmares in the intelligence community. 'Hold that thought,' she said at last. 'We've got to get going. Let's see if your Mr Rodrigues can shed any light on this.'

30

Macau, China

SIXTY-TWO COUNTRIES. That's how many Luke had been to in his nearly forty years. He knew that because he had totted them all up one afternoon while sitting waiting for a flight back from Medellín. Yet never, in all that time, had he seen anything quite like the place they had come to now.

The shimmering opulence of the Venetian Hotel Macau was either an object of beauty or an affront to the senses, depending on your point of view. Approaching the palatial entrance, already uncomfortable in the muggy, cloying heat, Luke had yet to make up his mind which side of the fence he was on. They were walking along a raised pastel-coloured terrace and facing what looked like a life-size replica of the Doge's Palace in Venice's St Mark's Square. At this time of day there were few others around, with most people sensibly preferring the air-conditioned comfort of the casinos and hotels. Luke's eyes swept over the building they were walking towards. Ahead, he could see ornate white Gothic columns and arches, balustrades and crenellations, beside a row of elaborately decorative green lampposts. There was even a pink and white replica of the *campanile*, the bell tower, over to one side. The whole effect was spoilt by a gigantic modern tower block that loomed over everything from behind.

'I suppose,' he said, as they walked up to the hotel, blinking in the full glare of the afternoon sun, 'the clue is in the name but even so . . . this whole place just screams the word "fake" to me.'

'It's completely OTT, isn't it?' Jenny said. 'A piece of fourteenth-century Venice transplanted here on the banks of the Pearl River. Apparently it cost over two billion dollars to build.'

'Right,' Luke said, as they walked the last few metres to the entrance. 'So we need to be on level one, shop 1038. It's a place called McSorley's Ale House. No idea why Mr Lim suggested that but maybe it's where our Mr Rodrigues likes to meet his guests. At least, the cheap ones like us. Hang on a second.' He stopped just before he went in. 'Can you just show me that photo of him again?'

Jenny retrieved it on her phone and passed it to him. 'Can't we do this inside, Luke? I'm actually melting out here in this heat.'

Luke's first impression of McSorley's Ale House was that it was one of those cosy, dimly lit faux-Irish bars that only made expats miss home even more. Big, overstuffed brown-leather sofas that looked like unpricked sausages, dark-wood panelling, a collection of antique tennis racquets and framed prints on the walls. The clientele was a mix of Chinese and Western, casually yet expensively dressed, seated in groups around tables and talking in animated voices. There was money here – he could almost smell it. Luke scanned the room looking for the lone individual sitting in a corner and pretending to study their phone: the stereotypical watcher. He couldn't see one, but he couldn't rule it out. China's MSS would be running a sophisticated surveillance programme in a gambling capital like this that attracted so many high-net-worth individuals. As for the triads, he imagined they had their own ways of keeping tabs on people.

He scanned the room, looking for the table in the far right corner, as Mr Lim had instructed. Good: there was no one at it and they were a few minutes early. They sat down and waited for the waitress to take their order. A low, green-shaded light hung above their table, giving it a clandestine, conspiratorial feel. A good place to conceal a microphone, Luke thought. This would have to be a guarded conversation.

'I think that's him over there now,' Jenny said. They got to their feet and pushed back their chairs. 'He's got someone with him,' she added.

Luke watched as a smartly dressed figure strode confidently across the room towards them. Dark blue tailored suit, crisp white shirt opened down to the second button, black hair glistening with product. Luke also noticed his brown leather shoes, polished to perfection, but this man looked to him like someone who left that job for other people to do. Walking alongside him, yet ever so slightly behind, was a tall slim Chinese girl, her silver earrings catching the soft light from the bar.

'My friends!' exclaimed the man, beaming as he approached their table and holding out his arms expansively. 'Francisco Rodrigues. Welcome to my second home!' He waved a hand around the bar where a few people were nudging each other as they recognized him. Spies don't like people looking at them in public places. Both Luke and Jenny shifted uncomfortably at this sudden, unexpected attention. Luke had never trusted anyone who called him 'my friend' and wasn't about to start now. But he would play along with this to get what they'd come for. He put on a smile.

'This is my executive assistant, Miss Xinyi,' said Rodrigues, indicating his companion. Luke watched her as she bowed politely. She seemed to be avoiding eye contact with either him or Jenny.

They took their seats at the table and immediately a waiter appeared, hovering over them with menus. Rodrigues held up his hand. 'I do hope you'll join me in a Golden Ale? It's their speciality here.'

'Of course.' Luke beamed. He hated drinking in the middle of the day and he had always preferred lager to ale. Jenny asked for a sparkling water and Miss Xinyi declined altogether.

'And who is your delightful companion?' Rodrigues asked,

looking across the polished table at Jenny while the waiter scurried off with their order.

'I'm sorry,' she said, holding out her hand, 'I should have introduced myself. Bel Trubridge. It's the first time for both of us here in Macau.' She touched Luke's arm affectionately as she said this.

Cover names and made-up back stories had become second nature to him by now, after several years in the Service. Yet he still admired the way the lie tripped off Jenny's tongue with such effortless ease.

Rodrigues flashed her a smile of perfect white teeth. He must have had a little work done there, Luke thought. He was altogether more youthful than he had expected, with perfect English and only a trace of an accent. His fresh, blemish-free face was lightly tanned, and it was only when he turned to Jenny that he noticed the faint scar close to his ear.

'So, then . . .' Rodrigues rubbed his hands together, intertwining them like a pair of mating snakes. 'How is my good friend Limbo in Hong Kong?'

'Limbo?' Luke replied.

'Yes. Eddie Lim. We call him Limbo. Let me guess, he made you spar with him in that gym of his?'

'Well, yes, he did, as a matter of fact.'

'Ha!' Rodrigues unclasped his hands and clapped them together in triumph. 'I knew it! He does that, but I hope you said no to him.' He looked from Luke to Jenny and back again.

An awkward pause seemed to have wormed its way into the conversation and Luke was about to fill it when Jenny spoke up. 'So, Senhor Rodrigues. We are so grateful for your time and—'

She stopped in mid-sentence as the waiter arrived with their drinks. Miss Xinyi, who had still not said a word, got up to take a call on her phone. Rodrigues then pointedly changed the subject. He reached for a menu and tapped the laminated page with his middle finger.

'Fish and chips,' he pronounced. 'It's their signature dish here. You have to try it. Come on, it's my treat.'

'Sounds delicious,' Jenny said. 'I'll have that. Thank you.'

'And me,' Luke said, thinking of the burger he'd consumed less than an hour ago.

'All right, then,' Rodrigues said, when the waiter had gone, leaning slightly forward in his chair and scanning their faces, from one to the other. 'What can I do for you lovely people?'

'We're looking for a friend who might be here in Macau,' Jenny said, cutting straight to the point. 'Well, she's missing, in fact.'

Immediately there was a peal of unrestrained laughter. Not from Rodrigues, but from a nearby table where two couples were clearly sharing a great joke. Rodrigues turned and scowled at them. The laughter subsided. 'So I have heard,' he said, facing them again. 'You have my sympathies. But you'll need to give me a little more information than that.' He sat back in his chair and took a long swig from his glass of Golden Ale, waiting for an answer.

This was the hard part, Luke thought. Say the wrong thing now, give him even the slightest hint that we know about the traced phone calls from Hong Kong to Macau, and this guy will walk away. Or, worse, arrange for something to happen. Until now, Rodrigues had been nothing but charming and genial towards them, but Luke still had no doubt he was dangerous. His file spoke for itself.

'Yes, of course,' Jenny replied amiably. 'Her name is Hannah Slade. I can write that down, if you like?'

Rodrigues shook his head. Why is he doing that? Luke wondered. Is it because he's not that interested or because he already knows all about Hannah?

'She's a British lady in her early forties, an academic,' Jenny continued. 'She's an expert on climate change. In fact, she was over in Hong Kong for a conference. But now . . . now she's vanished.' She looked pointedly at Rodrigues.

For a second or two there was silence, and then he let out a short, high-pitched laugh and spread his hands in despair. 'I'm so sorry,' he said, 'but I think you might have been given an exaggerated idea of what I can do for you. I run many businesses here

118

in Macau, it's true, but a vanished English lady from Imperial College? I'm afraid that's beyond me.'

Jenny and Luke stared hard at him. There was no mistaking what they had just heard.

'I never said,' Jenny replied, in an even tone, 'that Hannah was from Imperial College.'

31

United Nations HQ, New York

'I THINK WE all know which way this is going to go . . .' The Baroness gave a weary sigh. '. . . but we have to do it anyway.'

It was late in the evening in the thirty-nine-storey UN headquarters building on New York's East 42nd Street. Britain's Permanent Representative to the United Nations was holding a final briefing with her team before the emergency special session of the UN General Assembly. Bearing the rank of ambassador, Baroness Janet Drummond was both a veteran diplomat and a product of years of the so-called War on Terror, someone equally at home in the corridors of Whitehall or in some blast-wall-protected secure compound in Baghdad or Kabul. She had no truck with dictators but she knew how the game was played at the UN and she was under no illusions as to how hard this was going to be.

The proposed resolution condemning China's brief but dramatic invasion of Taiwan's Lieyu Island had been hastily drafted by the three Western permanent members of the UN Security Council: Britain, France and the US. A motion also to condemn the recent firing of a powerful missile across the path of the AUKUS Task Group in the Taiwan Strait was dropped at the last minute. That the proposed resolution would still be swiftly vetoed by the other two permanent members, China and Russia, was a given. That was just the way it worked, in a world where countries caught in the middle between two great power blocs had to choose between siding with the West or the ever-strengthening alliance between Moscow and Beijing.

'We can expect the usual suspects to side with China,' said Baroness Drummond, straightening her jacket as she spoke. 'You've only got to look at who backed Moscow's full-scale invasion of Ukraine in 2022. Let's see now, there was Belarus, Syria, North Korea and one other, I forget.'

'It was Eritrea,' prompted one of her aides.

'Ah, yes, thank you, Marcia. Eritrea, that's right. So the key question now – and I do commend you all for the hard work you've been doing here on the lobbying front – the key question is which way will the Asia-Pacific countries vote? Because I can tell you, the PM and the Foreign Secretary view this as a bit of a litmus test for how much success our whole "tilt to the Indo-Pacific region" is having.'

Marcia approached bearing an iPad with a list of countries and comments beside each. The Baroness put on her glasses, took it from her with a nod of thanks and began to read down the list out loud. 'Japan, South Korea, Australia . . . Good, no surprises there, they're all onside. Myanmar will veto it, we reckon? Yes, that probably makes sense. They get their weapons from China. Wait, what's this? We think New Zealand is going to *abstain*? Seriously?' She took off her glasses and glared at her aide as if Marcia were personally responsible for this perfidy.

'It's trade, Baroness,' the aide replied. 'China is New Zealand's largest trading partner and their bilateral trade amounts to nearly thirty billion NZ dollars a year. The Kiwis are clearly nervous about upsetting them.'

The Baroness replaced her glasses, shook her head and made a scolding sound. 'To think we had our honeymoon there on Lake Wanaka,' she said quietly. 'Right, so Papua New Guinea and a lot of those island states in Micronesia will probably go China's way too. Beijing has been doing a lot of strategic investment there. India I think we can count on, especially after their recent bust-up with China in the Himalayas. What about the South East Asian countries, where do we think they stand at this moment in time?'

'It's hard to call, Baroness,' replied Marcia, taking back the iPad. 'Malaysia, Vietnam, Brunei and the Philippines have all got maritime disputes with China over how much of the South China Sea it's claiming for its own. The thing is, they fear China, they all do, but I'm afraid that doesn't mean they'll vote against her.'

'Right, then,' said the Baroness, finally tucking her glasses into the top pocket of her pink tweed jacket. 'Let's go in and find out, shall we? I hope you all had some refreshments this evening. I have a feeling this is going to be a rather long session.'

32

Langkawi Island, Malaysia

DEEP IN HIS HEART, Chen Chin-lung knew he probably shouldn't be there. Certainly not with his family on an all-expenses-paid holiday in a five-star beach resort. This was not something that a mid-level software engineer working at the Taiwan Semiconductor Manufacturing Company would normally be able to afford. But the gods of Taiwan Lottery had been kind to him this year, and although not life-changing, his winning ticket had been enough to let him splash out on a week for himself and his family at the luxurious Datai Resort on the shores of the Andaman Sea.

At least, that was the story he had told his boss.

The truth was a little murkier. Chen Chin-lung had been approached some weeks earlier by a charming young researcher while he was dining alone at a rather basic restaurant, not far from his place of work in Hsinchu City in north-west Taiwan. Like everyone with access to sensitive technical data at TSMC, he had been warned to be wary of suspicious approaches by strangers. Taiwan guarded its expertise in nanotechnology as closely as a mother with her newborn. The nation's unique ability to refine its semiconductors down to just three nanometres was its crown jewels.

But this encounter, reasoned Chen Chin-lung, was surely different. There was nothing suspicious about the young lady's questions. She had not asked him anything about his job or what he did there. She had simply asked if she could join him in the empty seat at the table for two as he gulped down a plate of noodles after a long day at work, and Chin-lung was glad of the company. It wasn't the first time he had seen her there. This lady had smiled at him on a previous occasion and, being of a shy nature, he had simply looked down at his food, too embarrassed to return her innocent gesture. Yet now here she was, keeping him company and talking at length about her research into possible cures for leukaemia and how she was hoping to get a grant from a company in Hsinchu. And then, just as they were sharing a steaming pot of jasmine tea, their empty plates pushed to one side, her face suddenly brightened. There was a corporate conference coming up at a resort in Malaysia, she remembered, a meeting of innovators looking to harness tech with advances in bio-medicine. They were looking for someone to give a talk about the semiconductor industry, nothing too specific, just an overview, and he would be ideal. Would he be interested? It could be a great opportunity for him to network with others in his profession. Americans would be there from Silicon Valley. And, of course, it would be all expenses paid – he could even bring his family.

Chen Chin-lung wasn't stupid; he knew the rules. He should have gone straight to his bosses the next morning and reported this encounter. In fact, there was probably even a form he was supposed to fill in and submit online. But where was the harm in this? he asked himself. It was just a holiday with a tiny bit of work thrown in. And, goodness knows, they could do with a proper holiday. His job at TSMC was intense and it was keeping him working long hours, such that he rarely had time to relax with his wife. Even when he did, she seemed to be permanently exhausted from looking after their three school-age children. No, this would be good for all of them – and who knew? It might lead to promotion prospects or even a job offer in Palo Alto.

From the moment they arrived at the resort Chin-lung's family were treated like VIPs, offered complimentary drinks and taken by golf cart to their seaside villa. The children were ecstatically happy playing on the beach where the gentle waves of the Andaman Sea lapped at the pure white sand. His wife was treated to a complimentary massage, all covered by the company hosting the conference, and for the first time in months he could see her really starting to relax.

It was on their second evening that he was required to deliver his talk on the microchip industry and the recent advances made in nanotechnology. Chin-lung had brought a PowerPoint presentation with him but he was careful not to reveal anything sensitive about TSMC's operations. The audience was entirely from the region: some Malaysians and Singaporeans and a lot of Chinese but, disappointingly, no Americans after all. 'They had to cancel at the last minute,' he was told. His audience applauded politely and afterwards there was a lavish dinner in a delightful thatched longhouse called the Gulai House, where a personalized menu had been printed out for him, along with his name, on a large brown leaf from the forest above. Wine flowed, photographs were taken.

Chin-lung found himself placed next to a senior administrator from Beijing, dressed in typical corporate off-site gear of polo shirt, chinos and blue yachting loafers. He was most complimentary about the presentation he had just heard. Toasts were made to new-found friendships and partnerships, all in the service of promoting advances in sciences that would benefit humanity.

Before the holiday ended Chen Chin-lung was presented with a beautifully mounted photograph of him sitting with his Chinese hosts, along with an invitation to another all-expenses-paid trip. This time it was just for him. It was to give a talk to the Chinese Academy of Sciences in Beijing. And this time there were some quite specific requests for material he should bring with him.

33

Vauxhall Cross, London

ANGELA SCOTT PAUSED outside the door to Human Resources and thought once more about whether to go in. As Luke's line manager at MI6, she had a duty of care for him. But she also felt indirectly responsible for Hannah Slade, the woman they had sent unwittingly into the lion's jaws in Hong Kong to collect the stolen data from Blue Sky. It had been just under forty-eight hours now since she had vanished off the face of the earth and no one in the building that Angela had spoken to seemed to have any idea how the situation should be managed externally.

'Shouldn't we inform her next-of-kin? You know, a welfare visit?' she had suggested to Felix Schauer.

'Hmm. Tricky one, Angela,' had been the response. 'She's off the books, remember.'

'Well, couldn't we at least get word to her employers?' she had replied. 'They don't have to know it's come from us, do they?'

But wherever she turned, her suggestions had met with a blank wall. Having a collector disappear like this was unprecedented: it had simply never happened to the Service before and there seemed not to be any protocol in place to deal with it.

Hannah Slade might have gone missing in Hong Kong but Angela still didn't want to see this blow up into a media circus.

In despair, she had decided she would have to take it to HR. She knew that the moment she knocked on that glass door and walked into the Service's ever-expanding HR division it could set in motion a whole bureaucratic chain of events but she was willing to take that risk. Hannah Slade must have friends and relatives and they would be worried sick about her. They had a right, she reasoned with herself, to know that someone was at least making efforts on her behalf to locate her.

But what if it jeopardized the whole operation?

Angela turned on her heel and started to walk back towards her office, then stopped. No. She had to report this. Anything less would be nothing short of a dereliction of duty, even grounds for a disciplinary hearing. As her tightly clenched fist rapped softly on the door of HR she already felt a pang of guilt, a sense of betrayal. She was doing this without letting Luke and Jenny know what she was up to.

'Yes, Angela. What can we do for you?'

She took a seat opposite an eager young man sitting behind his desk with his cutaway collar and ostentatious white-rimmed spectacles. A plastic notice facing her announced his name as Nigel Kittle. Not a career intelligence officer like her, but a civil servant drafted in from another government department with a bumped-up security clearance and probably a fondness for corporate jargon. All part of the big push by a recent MI6 Chief to bring the Secret Intelligence Service more into line with the rest of Whitehall. Angela got that. The Service needed to move with the times, and yet . . . she couldn't help thinking that hers was one of the few branches of government where you literally had people's lives – those of your agents – in your hands, every single day. Make a mistake and someone who trusted you was going to end up quite possibly dying a hideous death in a far-off place. She wondered if someone brought in from, say, Business Development, always grasped that. Right now, she had hoped to find herself sitting opposite someone with a little more empathy, but it was too late for that now.

'Thank you for sparing the time, Nigel. I—'

'Not at all,' he said brightly. 'We're here to help.'

'Yes. It's about someone on our team. There's something—'

'Hold that thought!' he interrupted, holding up an admonishing finger. Angela couldn't help disliking this man more with each minute. Nigel from HR pressed a button on his phone: 'John, could you come in, please? I'll need you to go and fetch somebody in here in a moment.'

Angela stared at him, unsure of where this was going.

'Sorry, new rules,' Nigel explained. 'We can't have a conversation about a member of staff without them being present. I'm sure you can appreciate that.'

'Well, that's admirable,' Angela replied, trying hard to keep the sarcasm out of her voice. 'But the person I've come to talk about is actually missing. That's why I'm here.'

'Oh? You've logged this, I take it?' Nigel looked at her from behind his white-rimmed glasses. 'Filed a Sentinel form?' he continued. 'When did you first report it?'

'I'm reporting it now,' she said. 'To you.'

'I see,' Nigel replied, his brow furrowing. 'Well, in that case I'd best convene a CADISC. I expect you're familiar with those. It's becoming standard policy across government for anything like this. There'll be four staff members present, including myself, and the minutes will be added to your confidential records. Oh, don't worry,' he added. 'No one else outside this office will see them. You'll be able to speak quite freely. Now, let's see . . .' He peered at a digital calendar on his desk. 'How's tomorrow at five sharp?'

Angela was already regretting this. She got up slowly and forced a smile.

'Five o'clock is perfect,' she said, and walked out of his office. Damn my conscience, she thought. Why didn't I just keep my big mouth shut?

34

Macau, China

THE SMILE ON the face of Francisco Rodrigues was as rigid as stone. All the warmth and the humour had drained from his eyes as his earlier bonhomie evaporated. It was as if the temperature around their table in McSorley's Ale House that afternoon had suddenly dropped by several degrees. Luke watched their host visibly adjusting to the new reality: he had just been exposed. Because Senhor Rodrigues, business entrepreneur, wheeler-dealer and hotelier, had let slip that he knew about Hannah Slade. Not only did he know her name but he knew she was employed by Imperial College London. That, taken with the phone records, meant he must have been in some way involved in her abduction.

Luke had not expected Jenny to be quite so direct in challenging him. In some ways it was a relief. The charade, the pretence, was over. Or was it? Rodrigues gave another of his short, nervous laughs.

'Did I say Imperial College?' he said. 'Well, yes, isn't that where all the best climate-change scientists practise their arts?' He was bluffing, Luke thought, and not making a very good job of it. That didn't matter, though, because right now, Rodrigues held all the cards. Here in Macau, he was probably untouchable, as long as he kept paying off the right people and didn't upset the Politburo in Beijing. And what leverage did he, Luke, and Jenny have? Almost zero, as far as he could see. They could hardly call up a Royal Navy gunboat to come steaming up the Pearl River – they were about 170 years too late for that. Macau was Chinese territory now, not Portuguese, and relations between London and Beijing were about as bad as they could get. So they were on their own, he and Jenny, with no help coming down the line from any quarter. No, they had only two things going for them that he could see. One was the mysterious favour that Rodrigues apparently owed to Mr Lim. The other was publicity or, more specifically, bad publicity for Mr Rodrigues. A public scandal involving him and a missing British academic would not be good for business. Luke had no doubt that Rodrigues had the financial resources and the connections to douse the story if it emerged, but that would cost time and money. So much easier just to make the whole thing go away, surely.

'Senhor Rodrigues,' Luke began, 'we would really appreciate your help in finding our friend Hannah Slade. You're clearly well respected here and—'

He went silent as the waiter reappeared bearing a tray loaded with three generous portions of battered fish and chips. He made an elaborate show of serving Rodrigues first and fussing around him with condiments before he attended to Luke and Jenny. It was the ice breaker everyone needed.

'Back in Lisbon where my family is from,' Rodrigues said, spearing a chunk of fish on his fork, 'we have a dish called *pasteis de bacalhau*. Salt-fish fritters. We make it with cod, onion, garlic, potato. Mmm . . .' He brought the tips of his fingers to his lips and gave them a wet kiss. 'But you know,' he said, popping the fish into his mouth, 'this is even better.'

The awkward moment of earlier seemed to have dissipated and Luke watched Rodrigues noticeably unwind as he ate. Before they had a chance to reopen the subject of Hannah he leant back in his chair, folded his arms and regarded them both. As the sleeves of his jacket rode up his arm Luke noticed the ostentatiously large gold cufflinks.

'So tell me about yourselves,' Rodrigues said. 'Limbo tells me you're from London, is that right?'

How much does he know? Luke wondered. If he knows Hannah works at Imperial College was that just good background research or has someone interrogated her? Does he know what she was really doing in Hong Kong? Does he know who we really work for?

'That's right,' Jenny answered brightly. 'We both work for a big travel agency, just off Regent Street. Pathways. Do you know it?'

Rodrigues shrugged. He seemed uninterested in her answer but Luke had no doubt he'd be getting his people to check that out later. Anyone making enquiries or accessing the company's website would indeed find two 'Adventure Travel Advisers' listed under the names of Bel Trubridge and Chris Blanford, complete with their photos and bios.

'And your interest in this missing lady?' enquired Rodrigues, casually. 'Hettie someone? I forget her name.' Luke was finding his act less and less convincing. Surely it was they who should be asking the questions, not the other way round. But that, of course, was not how it worked, not in a situation like this.

'Well, she's a friend of both of ours.' Jenny turned to Luke and gave his arm an affectionate squeeze. 'We know her from London. But she hasn't been heard from for several days now, so we thought, since we're out here . . .'

'I see,' said Rodrigues, returning to his plate of battered fish.

'I know,' Jenny continued, 'it's really one for the British Consulate over in Hong Kong but of course they don't have any representation here in Macau. And we thought—'

'You thought I might know someone who would be able to tell you what's happened to her,' Rodrigues interrupted.

'Well, yes.' Jenny spread her hands helplessly.

Rodrigues put down his fork once more and pushed the plate away from him. He picked up a paper napkin and carefully wiped his hands. Luke watched him as he did so; he reckoned he must be enjoying this moment.

'I would be more than happy,' said Rodrigues at last, showing

131

a flash of his overly white teeth, 'to make some enquiries on your behalf. But these may take a little time. I'll get my people on to it and I will ask Miss Xinyi to come back to you. Where are you staying?'

'We're not at the moment,' Luke said. 'We only arrived this morning.' Rodrigues turned towards him, but only slowly, and Luke had the distinct impression that he would rather carry on talking to Jenny.

'That, my friends,' said Rodrigues, 'is one thing I *can* help you with. You must stay here, at the Venetian – they have plenty of rooms. Here.' He reached into his jacket pocket, pulled out a laminated card and made a point of handing it over not to Luke but to Jenny. 'Show them this at Reception and tell them I sent you,' he said. 'They will arrange everything. And now, if you'll excuse me . . .' He pushed back his chair, rose from the table and did up the middle button of his jacket. '. . . I have some affairs to attend to. In the meantime, I do hope you will allow yourselves to enjoy Macau. This *is* the Venice of the East, you know.' And with that, he was gone.

35

United Nations HQ, New York

BARONESS DRUMMOND wasn't wrong. The special emergency session of the UN General Assembly was running late into the evening and everyone wanted to have their say. From the US Ambassador, the session heard an uncompromising verbal assault on China's actions against Taiwan, how its illegal landing of a force on Lieyu Island, its aerial intrusions, its missile over-flights and its intimidation of commercial shipping should end immediately. These actions, he said, were nothing short of a direct challenge to the international rules-based order, the very architecture of global security that had prevented the world going to war since 1945.

His words were echoed in typically blunt fashion by the Aus-tralian Ambassador, who called it 'a bloody disgrace' what Beijing was doing to security in the South China Sea. Japan and South Korea's emissaries were somewhat more diplomatic in their language but both equally concerned about what they called 'an unacceptable invasion of sovereign territory and unjus-tified pressure being placed on a sisterly nation in our region'. Taiwan, of course, had no seat at the UN General Assembly. Bei-jing had seen to that some years ago.

When it was the turn of the People's Republic of China the

Ambassador addressed the assembly in perfect English, tinged with a slight transatlantic twang. The interpreters seated in their glass booth did struggle at times, though, since she was the only speaking delegate in the hall still wearing a facemask.

'Some of the statements we have heard here today are not accurate and need to be corrected,' she began. Her tone, while not quite abrasive, was still very much that of a head teacher addressing morning assembly. 'You should be respectful of the facts and not talk recklessly. I would like to remind everyone of the 1992 Consensus and the statements made by His Excellency the General Secretary of the Communist Party. Reunification with Taiwan is in the overall interest of the Chinese nation and that, of course, includes our Taiwan compatriots.' And now her tone grew sterner as her gaze surveyed the room, eventually settling on the US delegation. 'But no one, I repeat no one, should underestimate the Chinese people's firm and unwavering determination to defend national sovereignty. So, what has wrongly been called "an invasion" on Lieyu Island is not in fact anything of the kind. It is simply a demonstration of the will of the Chinese people, who wish to exercise their sovereign rights within China's natural borders. This is not a matter that concerns outsiders. We say again that we do not accept any interference or meddling in the internal affairs of our nation.'

36

Hsinchu Industrial Park, Taiwan

'TRANSFORM YOUR PASSION into results.' That was the sign he passed every single morning, and again in the evenings, on his way home, often after working unsociably late hours. But the truth was that Chen Chin-lung, outwardly loyal and long-standing employee of the Taiwan Semiconductor Manufacturing Company, wasn't feeling a lot of passion about his job, these days. True, he had won some minor accolade at the 33rd Taiwan Continuous Improvement Awards, but that had been a few years ago and for some time now he had felt his professional career was stagnating, stalling, going nowhere. Every morning he would arrive punctually at 7.50 a.m., park his white Toyota Sienta in his designated spot and walk the last few metres past all the neatly trimmed hedges and lawns beneath the featureless white building in which he worked that bore those giant four letters: TSMC.

The company that produced 65 per cent of the world's semiconductors and over 90 per cent of the high-end ones was famously tight on security. It needed to be. It wasn't just Taiwan's giant Communist neighbour across the Strait that wanted to get their hands on TSMC's microchip secrets. With its literally cutting-edge tech, this company was the envy of the world when it came to manufacturing high-precision chips. Hence, many of its sixty-five thousand employees in the more sensitive positions were being carefully screened and searched, although that had not prevented a major ransomware hack by a Russian gang in the summer of 2023. In recent months, though, TSMC had found itself under such pressure to hire more staff that it had had to relax the rules.

It was in this new-found corporate environment that Chen Chin-lung was able to do what he did without being detected. On the third Tuesday of every month, regular as clockwork, he would leave a little earlier than usual, telling everyone it was an ongoing family commitment. And, in a way, that was exactly what it was. It was a commitment to enrich his family's fortunes by nefarious means. His friendship with the young woman in the café had blossomed into a close but platonic relationship, more transactional than romantic. She had a name: Lihua, or Pear Blossom. A symbol of good fortune. And each month some of that good fortune was paid into a secret bank account in his name in Singapore, to be accessed only when he was out of the country to avoid the prying eyes of the National Security Bureau.

Chen Chin-lung was under no illusion that what he was doing was wrong. He knew he was taking a risk each time he smuggled a document Lihua asked him for out of the building. He never enquired as to where they ended up and she never told him, but the money was accumulating nicely in that Singapore account and for a while he found it a satisfactory arrangement. It was four months into this when he started to get cold feet. The inspectors and investigators from the National Security Bureau had begun making unannounced spot checks on staff and their digital histories, going into their desktops and laptops, peering into every entry. Every page of every document, every formula and every algorithm had to be accounted for. Chen Chin-lung felt the walls closing in on him and he needed to terminate the arrangement.

When he suggested, at their next Tuesday-afternoon meeting, that it was time to call a halt, Lihua was very calm but there was a new hardness in her voice. Her face perfectly composed, she opened the leather satchel she carried and retrieved a large, A4-sized photograph. He recognized it immediately. It was of him with one of his Chinese hosts at that corporate event he had attended in Malaysia.

'That man next to you,' she told him, 'is the Director of Cyber Espionage at the Ministry of State Security in Beijing. I think your bosses at TSMC would be very interested in seeing this picture, don't you? And so would the National Security Bureau.' She handed him the photograph. 'You can keep this.' She patted his hand. 'We have plenty of copies. But you have no need to worry. No one is going to see it.' She smiled at him sweetly. 'Just so long as our arrangement continues.'

37

Macau, China

'I THINK I need a shower after that,' Luke said, pointedly wiping his right palm on the side of his trousers. He could still feel some kind of slippery unguent on it after shaking Rodrigues's hand. 'Christ, what an odious piece of work,' he added. 'To think we've had to come begging for help from a guy who's knee-deep in the sex trade.'

'Yup,' Jenny replied. 'At least you didn't have your hand kissed.' She wiped the back of hers.

They had waited until they had left McSorley's Ale House before either said a word. They were now in the cavernous interior of the hotel, with its faux-Roman columns and gaudily painted ceilings in a kind of mockery of Michelangelo. Luke waited while a group of young Chinese passed them, giggling, sharing a video one had on her phone. When no one was in earshot he decided to broach the subject that had been on his mind for a while now.

'Have we got this right, Jen?' He stopped walking and turned to face her. From somewhere in the middle distance came the sound of a violin being played – he couldn't tell if it was live or recorded.

'Have we got *what* right?' she answered. 'Being in Macau, you mean?'

'Yes. Well, the whole organized-crime angle. Look, I know Cheltenham traced those calls from Kowloon to here but come on, Jen, we both know that doesn't prove anything conclusive.' The violin music had stopped and now someone was singing 'Nessun Dorma'. He realized it was being piped through hidden speakers. 'Look,' he said, 'if Hannah's cover's been blown, doesn't it make far more sense for this to be a state-on-state action? I'm thinking Russia, China, North Korea even. Pyongyang's got form in this area. Remember the hit they did a few years ago at Kuala Lumpur airport on that half-brother of Kim Jong-un?'

'The guy whose face they smothered with liquid nerve gas?' Jenny shuddered. 'Yes, I'm afraid I do remember that. It was hideous. He died in agony, I think.'

'Right. Well, someone has clearly decided that Hannah has information they want. They probably think she works for us full-time. My hunch is that right now she's sitting in a windowless room in somewhere like Vladivostok or Shanghai, having to answer a whole load of questions she doesn't know the answer to. I'm sorry, Jen. I know it was my lead from Mr Lim that brought us here but . . .' He looked around at the hotel's uber-opulent interior. Every single centimetre of surface seemed to shimmer with gold lacquer. 'Macau just feels like we're being led up the garden path, that's all.'

'Then how do you account for Rodrigues knowing that Hannah works at Imperial College?'

'Yes, all right,' Luke conceded. 'That was a bit of a shock, I admit. But Lim gave him her name. He could have just had his people do the due diligence on her. Maybe he was only being thorough.'

Jenny put on her glasses and pursed her lips as she looked at him. 'You may be right, Luke, in which case we are right back to square one in trying to track her down. But look at it this way.

We've got this far with Rodrigues – he's offered to help us, for whatever messed-up reason he's got going with your Mr Lim. So let's see what he comes up with. I can't see what we have to lose. Come on, we'd better get checked in at this place.'

Past black velvet ropes and across a polished marble floor that resembled a giant chessboard, Luke and Jenny walked up to the bank of receptionists. A young man with white ear-buds flashed them a smile of welcome, his face lit by a giant chandelier that hung above his desk. 'Miss Trubridge? Mr Blanford?' he asked. He seemed to be expecting them. 'Excellent. Yes. We have put you in the Golden Suite. Oh, and I have a message for you.' He produced a sealed envelope and handed it to Luke. Jenny looked over his shoulder as he opened it and read the contents. It was a simple sentence typed on a blank sheet of paper. No signature, no corporate logo. It said simply: 'Miss Xinyi will collect you from your hotel at 8 p.m. I wish you every success. R.'

38

ANGELA SCOTT LOGGED off her computer and cleared her desk. There was precious little paperwork on it these days but what there was still went into the Sensitive Documents safe in the cupboard at the far end of her open-plan office. Not everything in the Secret Intelligence Service was unrecognizable from the dingy, brown and grey days of John le Carré.

She glanced at the clocks on the wall. Washington, London, Beirut, Beijing. It was nearly time to attend the HR ordeal she had let herself in for: the CADISC, the case discussion, convened by that irritating man with the trendy specs. Angela's mind and her attention were firmly rooted on a place ten thousand kilometres away, a former Portuguese colony where she had just sent Luke and Jenny authorization to go ahead with meeting Miss Xinyi. The Service gave its frontline intelligence officers a great deal of discretion in the field but this was a special case. Luke and Jenny were operating on the other side of the world, 'at reach and at risk', with none of the normal back-up in place. If something, anything, went wrong the nearest help was a long way off and it was debatable just how much assistance, if any, they could expect from the Embassy in Beijing.

Angela took a deep breath and pushed open the glass door to

MI6's HR department. She had been with the Service long enough to remember when it was called 'Personnel'. To her, adopting the American term 'Human Resources', as the whole country had done, somehow made it feel *less* personal, not more.

'Angela, Angela, Angela . . .' intoned Nigel Kittle. 'Do come in and sit ye down.' He motioned towards a single chair facing a small semi-circle where he sat flanked by two others. She recognized one of them from Legal but the other was a bearded man she hadn't seen before.

'This is Keith from Compliance and Procedures. He'll be taking notes. Clarissa from Legal, I think you know.'

Angela nodded, as she took her seat in front of them. This was starting to look more like an inquisition than a discussion.

'Right. Let's kick off, shall we?' Nigel began. He made a point of looking at his watch. 'So, just for the record, it is . . . three minutes past five. A little later than scheduled,' he glanced at Angela, 'but no matter, we're *all* here now. So, I have convened this CADISC at the request of Ms Angela Scott here—'

'Sorry,' Angela interrupted, 'but *you* requested it, Nigel, not me. I just came to see you yesterday to let you know we had a missing person on our team.'

Nigel Kittle leant over to Keith. 'Yes, she came to my office to report this, but without having filled in a Sentinel form.'

Keith, whose shirtsleeves were rolled up, she noticed, stopped writing and raised his eyebrows as if this was the most shocking thing he had heard all year. He gave Angela a long critical look before jotting something down on his notepad.

'Look, I'm sorry,' Angela apologized again. 'I'm sure there are protocols for this kind of thing but all I'm doing is letting you know we have someone on a live operation who has gone missing. Apparently nobody has told you and I thought you should know.'

She paused, looking from one to another. The only sound in the room came from Keith's now frantic scribbling.

'I'm not even in overall charge of this op,' she added. 'That would be Felix Schauer.'

'Aha!' pronounced Nigel, as if he had just discovered a major flaw in her argument. 'You see, Director Critical has already been in to see us.'

'He has?'

'Yes. And he was quite specific that while he was operationally in charge, any issues of human welfare were under your jurisdiction. I'm afraid the buck stops with you on this one, Angela. I'm hoping – we're all hoping – we won't have to escalate this but let's just see how the next hour goes, shall we?'

39

Macau, China

BY LONDON STANDARDS – at least where Luke lived in Battersea – the saloon car that came to collect him and Jenny from the Venetian that evening would have been considered distinctly luxurious. A gleaming silver Porsche Panamera, quite possibly costing more, he guessed, than a whole year of his civil-service salary. Here in glittering, freewheeling Macau, though, it did not look out of place amid the Bentley Continentals and the Rolls-Royce Ghosts that pulled up outside the hotel to disgorge long-legged girls in silk *cheong sam* dresses accompanied by burly men in tuxedos and expensive suits.

Luke didn't recognize Miss Xinyi at first. The woman who stood holding open the rear door of the Porsche looked quite different from the dowdy corporate executive they had met so briefly at lunchtime in McSorley's Ale House. Gone were the suit and the sensible shoes, replaced by a black, off-the-shoulder dress, high heels and a single diamond on a gold chain. He would not necessarily have thought of her as beautiful, but she certainly had style. Senhor Rodrigues's PA looked as if she belonged here. Luke felt strongly that he and Jenny did not.

While Jenny spoke briefly to Miss Xinyi, Luke discreetly photographed the number plate and texted it to Angela and the team back in London, via an anodyne account registered in the name of Pathways Travel, should anyone be monitoring his phone, which he thought they probably were. 'Thanks for picking us up,' he said, as they settled into the back seat with Miss Xinyi in front next to the driver. 'Where are we heading, exactly?'

'You'll see,' she answered cryptically, then added, 'Senhor Rodrigues has asked me to give you every assistance.'

The car purred away from the hotel entrance, gliding through the night-time streets of Macau. Outside the window they passed a constant kaleidoscope of colours: great neon palaces in pink and purple, dedicated to the delights of gambling. Fireworks lit up the sky at intervals and Chinese characters flashed from the tops of high-rise buildings.

'This feels like something out of *Blade Runner*,' Luke remarked.

Jenny nodded without replying. She, too, was watching the scene outside where it was all cars, no pedestrians. Luke glanced down at the map on his phone. He was tracking their route through GPS, his phone pinging their updated location to the Pathways account every thirty seconds. At least, he thought grimly, they'll know where to find the bodies if this all goes wrong.

Fifteen minutes later they pulled up outside the entrance to a club. He could see purple velvet ropes and a couple of beefy bouncers in black tie. They were standing with their arms folded and legs apart in a John Wayne stance. It did not look like a welcoming place. Miss Xinyi got out first and they could see her greeting the men on the door and pointing back towards them as she beckoned for them to follow. Then the velvet ropes parted and they were ushered inside. The place appeared not to have any name, and the only clientele coming in were men, mostly Chinese, a few unsmiling Europeans. Russians, he guessed.

Down a flight of stairs, lit by flickering electric candles strung out along the wall, they followed Miss Xinyi, her heels clattering on the steps. Now they were in some kind of dimly lit subterranean lounge with low ceilings, purple strobe lights and an eighties-style disco ball rotating on the ceiling. The air throbbed with a rhythmic, pulsating bass that seemed to bounce off the

145

walls and reverberate inside his head. Luke couldn't remember the last time he'd been in a club but one look at this place told him all he needed to know. It was not the sort of club you went to with friends. Not far from where they stood he could see a raised dais where a line of women were gyrating to the music, dressed in satin corsets, fishnet stockings, silky underwear and high heels. He couldn't tell where they were from because every one of them was wearing a ghostly white mask. Others were on the dance-floor, accompanied by paunchy, sweaty men in suits with shiny faces and pawing hands. Luke found himself fighting back an overwhelming urge to get out of the place as fast as possible. He looked at Jenny, who grimaced in return.

He also had a strong feeling of déjà vu. A flashback to an earlier mission in Lithuania, where he'd had to seek out a certain informant from inside some dimly lit S&M club in Vilnius. But there was a difference. Everyone in that place had been there by choice, whereas here, in this dark and seedy dive that Rodrigues's assistant had led them to, well, he had the distinct impression that these women were not exactly there of their own free will.

Luke knew enough about Macau to understand how this worked. The triads controlled the sex trade and paid the police to tip them off each time the authorities decided they needed to stage a crackdown. Young women from poor families arrived from all over South East Asia, answering ads for housemaids and receptionists, then ended up working in saunas and brothels or places like this. Despite carrying a penalty of up to twelve years in prison, the fact was that sex trafficking was rife in Macau where, unlike on the mainland, prostitution itself was not illegal. But was it really possible that their Hannah Slade, a British academic in early middle age, had been brought here? That made no sense to him, because if someone had abducted her, surely what they were after was information, nothing else.

He looked over to Miss Xinyi for an explanation but she was talking to a man with a gold neck chain and an earpiece. Another bouncer, he presumed. Luke leant over to Jenny, straining to make himself heard above the music: 'This is a wild-bloody-goose chase,' he said hoarsely. She gave him a look of tired resignation, which he took to mean 'I agree, but let's see where this leads.'

Miss Xinyi was beckoning for them to follow her now as she started to weave a path through the couples in clinches on the dance-floor. Who exactly was she? he wondered, as he watched her ponytail swaying down the back of her black dress in front of them. That afternoon, they had sent a request to the China desk in London, asking for a full background bio on her, but nothing had come back yet. Miss Xinyi was clearly a woman of few words: she had said almost nothing in the car on the way over.

Sidestepping people in their path, they followed her until she stopped next to a door on the other side of the dance-floor. Miss Xinyi stood next to it, waiting for Luke and Jenny to catch up. In the dim lighting of the club he could see some sort of wooden shutter, like a miniature window, set into the door at head height. Their host knocked on the door, twice hard, twice softly, clearly a signal. The shutter slid open and a pair of eyes peered out. From her handbag, so small he had barely noticed it before now, Miss Xinyi produced a card and held it up to the window. The door opened, revealing a heavily made-up woman in a tight dress. Luke detected a strong smell of stale cigarettes.

'Come, come,' she said, ushering them quickly inside.

But Jenny stood her ground just inside the doorway and addressed Miss Xinyi. 'Sorry, but where are we going with this?' she asked. 'I mean, we appreciate your help in trying to find our friend and everything but we're in the dark here.' Jenny looked around her. 'Literally. I think we need to know what's going on.'

The words hung in the air as Miss Xinyi stared straight back at her, then broke into what Luke took to be an over-sweet smile. 'You will see,' she said, as the woman closed the door behind them and bolted it.

40

Temple Place, London

ANGELA SCOTT HAD not enjoyed her forty-five-minute encounter with HR. What she had assumed to be a simple piece of good housekeeping – notifying them that the Service had someone missing on a live operation – had turned into some kind of macabre corporate witch-hunt. And she now had a strong suspicion that she had become the target. Angela realized she had underestimated just how devious Felix Schauer was capable of being. Like most of her colleagues in the Service who had met him, she had always found his Germanic directness to be quite appealing. Schauer got things done and he told it how it was. She had just never figured him for an expert at Machiavellian office politics. Well, how wrong she was. He had outmanoeuvred her. MI6's Director Critical had made sure he got to HR ahead of her and neatly dumped the problem of Hannah Slade's disappearance on her shoulders. If the family stirred up trouble then it was Angela's name in the frame for this one. She kicked herself for not seeing it coming.

It was not as if she didn't have enough to worry about with Luke and Jenny out in the field on the other side of the world, working round the clock to retrieve Hannah and the data Blue Sky was supposed to have passed to her. As she boarded the

Tube to attend a lecture that evening just off the Strand she wondered if they had made a mistake in not sending a larger team. It was the perpetual trade-off between secrecy and support. Send too few people and they could end up being under-resourced. Send too many and you increase the chances somebody is recognized by the opposition. And, by God, how things had changed since she joined the Service. The whole world of espionage had morphed beyond recognition in that time. It was incredible to think that back then, in the late twentieth century, you could still squirrel a case officer unnoticed into a hostile country, have them stroll straight past Immigration, as bold as brass, using a fake identity, a made-up 'legend' as their cover. Well, those days were pretty much gone now, thanks to biometrics and hidden facial recognition. There were even gait-recognition cameras that could match an individual with their data entry on record within seconds, simply by mapping the speed and direction of their body movements. And of all the countries on Earth, the People's Republic of China was the absolute past master when it came to the art of intrusive human surveillance.

Which was why she was giving up the early part of her evening to attend an invitation-only seminar at a respected London think-tank, hoping to educate herself a bit more on the threats now facing Luke and Jenny in the field. The lecture was entitled 'Chinese Surveillance in the Twenty-first Century' and it was to be delivered by an eminent professor of East Asian Studies at King's College London.

Angela got there a few minutes early, emerging from the Tube to walk up the steps of the institute's rather grand nineteenth-century townhouse. She took the lift to the top floor, found a quiet corner in the anteroom next to the lecture theatre, fetched herself a cup of tea and sat down, pretending to scroll through her emails. Intrinsically reserved by nature, Angela tended to avoid such events if she could. While the glib words 'Oh, I work for the Foreign Office' tripped off her tongue with well-practised ease she still dreaded the follow-up questions. 'Oh, really? Which department? Then you must know so-and-so. You don't? That's

149

odd.' After many years of subterfuge Angela had grown proficient at swerving the conversation into less treacherous territory but she could still feel her cheeks flush with embarrassment. No, Angela Scott was happiest working away behind the sandstone-coloured walls of Vauxhall Cross these days, making her contribution to Britain's national security unseen and unquestioned by the public.

With the lecture about to begin, she took a seat towards the back, placing her empty teacup and saucer on the chair next to her, a favourite habit she had to deter anyone from sitting next to her. She put her phone on silent. There were a few dozen people in the audience, a mixture of journalists, diplomats and academics. Plus the odd diplomat who was probably not quite what it said on their business card. She spotted someone three rows in front of her whom she had once met on a visit to Langley, Virginia; the CIA still had an undeclared presence in London.

The lecturer turned out to be more engaging than he looked. Bookish, bearded, bespectacled and wearing a jacket that had clearly seen better days, he was absolutely on top of his subject and Angela found herself listening to every word from her spot at the back. Which was why she failed to notice the pale-faced university student sitting two seats away who seemed unusually preoccupied with something on the inside of his jacket.

41

Macau, China

IT WAS AN oval room, devoid of soft furnishings. With the door behind them now bolted, Luke took in the scene before them. Large, ornate mirrors on the walls, a couple of chandeliers dangling from the ceiling. A dozen round tables, spaced well apart, each with a single customer sitting at it, drinking morosely from a bottle of Johnnie Walker whisky. And smoking. People were smoking cigarettes. They looked like businessmen. No one was talking; this was clearly not a place for conversation. Rather, everyone's attention was focused on the raised stage, where a naked girl was dancing to a Rihanna song playing from unseen speakers. Her body glistened with baby oil, or was it sweat? He couldn't tell. But he noticed that every few seconds she would make eye contact with one of the seated men. It was then that he saw every table had what looked like an iPad. The men were raising their hands, nodding and tapping at the screens.

'Oh my God, I don't believe it,' said Jenny. 'I think they're bidding for her.'

They turned to face Miss Xinyi, who had led them to this joyless fleshpot.

'Well?' Luke said. 'That,' he added, pointing up at the stage, 'is *not* our missing friend.'

'I know, I know. Of course not. Please. Wait here a moment.'

They watched her walk towards a darkened corner of the room and disappear through yet another door. Luke was now feeling not just nauseous but also distinctly uneasy. They were already on the wrong side of a bolted door, and he did not for one minute imagine that Hannah Slade was about to appear miraculously through the other darkened doorway. Instead, he was starting to worry that something bad was about to emerge from it. He found himself wishing he still had the 3D-printed Glock under his jacket. He wondered if it had been found yet, nestling in that damp clump of bamboo where he had thrown it over a wall into a Hong Kong garden. He turned to say something to Jenny but now he could see Miss Xinyi waving to them to join her.

Stepping through the doorway ahead of Jenny, his whole body was braced for trouble, his nerves on edge, his eyes darting to left and right. Luke felt as if he was descending through the seven circles of Hell. Standing next to Miss Xinyi, he found himself facing a long narrow corridor, flanked by curtained booths on either side. It was almost like a stable for horses, he thought, or a row of giant kennels, except that its occupants were human. Wan faces peered out at him from behind the curtains, curled fingers beckoned at him to venture within.

'Jesus, Jen,' he said, under his breath. 'This is a brothel.' Jenny pursed her lips and nodded grimly. Given what they already knew of Rodrigues, he supposed it shouldn't have come as a massive surprise to find themselves there, yet it was still a shock, for anyone with half a conscience, to see what they were confronted with now. Luke did not consider himself a prude. In his younger days, as a junior officer in the Royal Marines, he had accompanied some of his troop on a night out in Hamburg after a NATO exercise in Germany. There were things that had gone on in those clubs on an infamous street called the Reeperbahn that he would never forget. Yet that all seemed tame compared to this horror show in Macau. He was pretty certain these women were prisoners, sex slaves, pure and simple.

He turned once more to address Miss Xinyi but now she was calling someone's name. A large man appeared from the shadows. Shaven skull, a skin-tight black T-shirt accentuating his biceps and a rash of tattoos crawling up his neck. Luke could hardly believe that this man had, attached to his belt, a Taser. He looked across at Jenny and wondered if she was thinking what he was thinking: this guy's job is to stop these women escaping. With the added persuasion of fifty thousand volts.

Miss Xinyi was speaking to him in Cantonese and Luke could see Jenny straining to follow what was being said. 'Are you catching any of this?' he asked quietly.

'Some of it,' she replied. 'My Cantonese is pretty rusty. She's asking him for something and he doesn't sound happy about it.'

A moment later they saw the man shrug his shoulders and walk quickly up to the first booth. He made a great show of whipping back the curtain to reveal a young Asian woman, in her early twenties, Luke guessed, wearing a scarlet bikini. She was sitting on the edge of a mattress, her knees drawn up under her chin, her face lit by the solitary purple bulb above her. She looked expectantly from Luke to Jenny and back to Luke.

Enough of this, Luke thought. It was time to confront Miss Xinyi, if that was even her real name. He walked over to her, ignoring the bouncer but keeping an eye on the Taser.

'OK,' he said, trying hard to keep the irritation out of his voice. 'Are you suggesting that our friend is in *here*? In this place? That's not possible! She's a respected academic from a top university in London.'

This time it was Miss Xinyi who shrugged. 'You can check,' she said, holding out her hand towards the row of booths that stretched all the way down the corridor. 'I'll wait for you here.'

'Thanks. We'll do just that,' said Jenny. 'Come on, Luke. We have to do this.'

Together, they began the grim business before them, moving past the girl in the scarlet bikini and approaching each booth in turn. In some, the occupant was already peering out from behind a curtain, watching them with curiosity. Never, Luke thought, had he imagined when he applied to work for the Service that he would end up doing a face-to-face search through a row of windowless booths in a Macau brothel. The girls, he suspected, were all from South East Asia, no doubt tricked and trafficked. The whole thing was depressing on every level. By the time they reached the final booth he had already made up his mind: Rodrigues must definitely be wasting their time, which also made him question why Mr Lim back in Hong Kong had bothered to send him here. Because this was quite clearly the last place on earth where they were going to find the collector, the missing Hannah Slade.

'Well?' said Miss Xinyi, when they returned to find her standing with her arms folded, evidently bored.

It occurred to Luke that she looked quite out of place in this dingy downmarket corridor of a brothel with her designer dress and diamond necklace. But, more importantly, he was relieved to see that Taser Man had vanished back into his lair. 'She isn't here,' Luke replied flatly. He had decided it was time to end this charade. 'And I think you probably knew that, didn't you?'

'We are just trying to help you,' Miss Xinyi answered defensively, flicking a hand into the air. It was only now that he noticed what very long fingers she had, and the bright scarlet nail varnish that adorned them.

'Right,' Luke said. 'Well, we don't seem to be getting anywhere, do we? Can we just cut the BS and get straight to the point?' He spoke slowly, carefully enunciating each syllable. 'Do you know where our friend Hannah Slade is? Is she even here in Macau?'

What Miss Xinyi did next surprised him. She took a step closer to Luke, looking up into his face from only centimetres away, invading his personal space. 'You want to cut the BS?' she replied, her voice lower and deeper than before. 'OK, sure, let's do that. We can start by ending this pretence that you two are "a pair of travel agents on holiday".'

Luke was momentarily taken aback by her directness and it took him a moment to recover. The taciturn assistant to Senhor

Rodrigues had just spoken more words than she had all evening, and he didn't like where this was going.

'*Excuse* me?' Jenny cut in. 'We are *exactly* what we said we are. We both work for Pathways in London. You can check that out if you don't believe us.' She had her hands on her hips and her chin thrust out, her expression one of righteous indignation.

'I don't need to do that,' retorted Miss Xinyi, calmly. 'Because all three of us know full well that Pathways account is run by your Secret Intelligence Service. And they booked you on the Cathay flight that brought you into Hong Kong. It was the . . .' She glanced up at the low, peeling ceiling as she recalled a detail. '. . . yes, it was the CX254, I believe. Isn't that right . . . Mr Carlton? Ms Li?'

42

Marylebone High Street, London

ARCHIE BRATTON WAS just one of the many people crowding the pavements of London's Marylebone High Street that evening. Nineteen years old and in his second year at university, he had had to make some difficult choices. His father had abruptly walked out on the family in the very month when Archie was sitting his A levels. Despite this, he had managed to earn himself a place at UCL. Not University College London, but the University of Central Lancashire, reading a BA Honours course in Asia Pacific Studies. Already in debt from gambling before the course had begun, he took on an evening job behind the bar at the Stoat and Badger on Preston's Fylde Road. It wasn't enough. He had ended up turning to some unsavoury people to borrow more money from.

By the start of his third term at university his creditors were getting impatient and were beginning to make threats. It was then, in the student union bar after a visiting lecturer had spoken on Chinese history, that he had met the helpful man from the Chinese Embassy in London. Over glasses of Hen Harrier beer, they had got talking about Chinese culture and how the University of Central Lancashire's links with China went back nearly forty years. Modern China was misunderstood by the West, the man said, his credit card racking up the tab behind the bar, as the People's Republic had only peaceful intentions towards all nations. China believed in the principle of non-interference in other countries' internal affairs and what, he asked, as he paid for another round, was so wrong with that? But Bratton, the man from the Embassy told him, was exactly the sort of bright young person who had a future working with, and maybe in, the world's second-largest economy. By the end of the evening things were looking up for Archie Bratton. He had been offered a train ticket to London and a night in a three-star hotel so he could come in and meet some of the Embassy's 'cultural' staff, who would love to help him further his studies. They might even, it was hinted, be able to assist him with his financial situation.

Things had improved even further after that. To his delight, Archie learnt that he was to be paid a regular and generous 'researcher's fee' and he didn't question why it had to be paid through a separate, newly opened bank account, coming from something called 'UFGU': The Universal Foundation for Global Understanding. Almost out of debt now, he had started to attend Chinese cultural and academic events around the country, always with his train ticket paid for in advance, always with a daily expense allowance that left him with a healthy profit after each trip. The first cloud on the horizon had come when the Embassy asked him to attend a protest event organized by Tibetan students. Not just to attend but to report back afterwards on what had been said and by whom. Purely for research purposes, of course. Archie had demurred, this wasn't really his thing, he told them, but they were quite insistent, dropping a none-too-subtle hint that the rest of his time at uni might not be so comfortable without his regular researcher's fee.

So he had done what they asked of him and had gone along to the protest on a rainy afternoon in the London borough of Hackney. He had sung along to the music, unable to understand a single word, while filming with his phone as he had been told. Handing over the footage to the Embassy afterwards, he felt somewhat dirty and used. But then he remembered the money, and when they asked him to do the same thing again a few weeks later it didn't seem so hard. Soon after his nineteenth birthday Archie had even been invited to a celebratory meal in London's Chinatown to be introduced to a visiting official from Beijing. It was after that meal that the same helpful man he had first met in the student bar took him aside, just as everyone was getting up and leaving, and told him that, despite his young age, he, Archie Bratton, was making an important contribution to the global understanding of Chinese culture. Unfortunately, the man explained, there were some people in London, in government, who wished to under-mine that understanding, to hold back the progress the People's Republic was striving to make for all mankind. A name had come to their notice, a name that was on the pre-registered guest list at a certain think-tank where a lecture was soon to be delivered. This person's name was Ms Angela Scott.

He had handed Archie a passport-size photograph of this Angela Scott and then he had produced something that looked exactly like a mobile phone. Except that, he explained, it wasn't a normal phone. Pressing this button here, and coding in this number, he explained, the device was able to download much of, if not all, the data from any mobile device within just over a metre, even from phones switched to 'airplane' mode.

Archie Bratton was not so naïve as to be unaware of what he was being asked to do. He knew it was crossing a line and it did not sit well with him. But when he thought about his personal situation now – safe from his creditors, comfortably solvent and with a promising future ahead of him – compared to where he had been just two years ago, he reckoned he had done all right for himself. So he had duly done as he was told. He had gone to that lecture at the institute just off the Strand and had spotted the woman straight away: she had been sitting by herself at the back. It looked as if someone might be about to sit next to her, as there was an empty teacup on the chair beside her, so he sat on the adjacent chair. When the lecture began, Archie looked straight ahead while fiddling with the device inside his jacket. He just hoped he had pressed all the right buttons.

And now it was done, the lecture was over, and he was pressing the buzzer for the discreet upstairs flat above the vegan food store in Marylebone High Street. Archie Bratton wondered if they might even give him a pay rise for this.

43

New York City

BARONESS JANET DRUMMOND was exhausted. The Permanent Representative of the United Kingdom Mission to the UN in New York had, along with her team, been up most of the night. It was almost 5 a.m. when she finally left the UN headquarters building on East 42nd Street. As she climbed wearily inside the black diplomatic limousine waiting to take her back to her modest apartment in Greenwich Village she couldn't help casting a glance northwards. There, twinkling at her in the pre-dawn gloom, was the towering edifice of 50 United Nations Plaza, the luxury forty-three-storey condominium where Britain had paid nearly US$16 million for a penthouse on the thirty-eighth floor. It was so near she felt she could almost reach out and touch it, yet this residence was not for her. Instead, it was reserved for the UK's Consul General and Trade Representative in New York, while she was obliged to commute halfway across Manhattan to her place of work. It rankled with her every time she looked at it but this morning she had other, more pressing, thoughts on her mind.

The emergency session on China and Taiwan had, as she had predicted, lasted well into the small hours. Her US counterpart had, in her eyes, been quite magnificent. Against the backdrop of that famous green and white marble slab, Thomas Kettinger III had delivered a robust and rousing speech, slamming China's actions in the Kinmen Islands and calling on 'all civilized nations' to pass the French-sponsored resolution condemning them.

'We must, and we will, push back on Chinese aggression and intimidation in the South China Sea,' he railed, gripping the podium with both hands and staring hard at the Chinese delegation over the half-moon glasses that perched on the tip of his nose. 'What the People's Republic of China has attempted to do on Lieyu Island is totally, I repeat *totally*, unacceptable! That country's rulers may think that invading and planting their flag on a small and geographically insignificant island the world hasn't heard of somehow doesn't count as an invasion. Well, I am here, along with my counterparts, to tell you that it most certainly does.'

Baroness Drummond had watched the delegates for their reactions. Not a flicker from the China contingent but vigorous nods from many of the Europeans and some long faces from the Russians. But in the end, exactly as she had told her team, the vote went the way she had feared. Not even a watered-down version with amendments submitted by Canada could pass. It wasn't so much that China had friends in that great chamber, it was more a case of interests, mostly commercial. And an awful lot of countries knew exactly where those interests lay.

The resolution condemning China's invasion of Lieyu Island was vetoed.

44

Macau, China

THERE ARE MOMENTS in the life and career of every agent-runner, those at the sharp end of the espionage business, that they dread. It is the moment of exposure, of unmasking, when your cover, your 'legend', crumbles, like a sandcastle, in the face of irrefutable evidence. It is worse for an agent, the man or woman being 'run' by the intelligence officer inside a hostile organization or country. Exposure for them can have fatal consequences; only a lucky few are exchanged for spies held by the other side. But without official cover Luke and Jenny were in a bad place. They were on Chinese soil, without backup, their legends ripped away from them. A dozen questions raced through Luke's brain. How had Miss Xinyi found out their true identities? Was it through Mr Lim in Hong Kong? And who else knows? Does Rodrigues know? Who does she really work for? Is she about to dob us in now to State Security? Was she involved in Hannah Slade's abduction? Was there a leak – digital or human – back at Vauxhall Cross?

He looked at Jenny and she shook her head slowly. He knew what that meant. It was pointless to continue with their cover story now. Miss Xinyi had their real names, their flight number, their employer. She held the cards. Now all they could do was try to retrieve whatever they could from the wreckage of this operation.

'Good,' Miss Xinyi said, before either of them had a chance to reply. 'I'm glad we've got that out the way. So here's the thing—'

'Hold on,' Luke said, tilting his head in the direction where Taser Man had disappeared. He raised his eyebrows questioningly.

'Don't worry about him,' she said. 'He only has about three words of English and none of them are repeatable. So listen,' she continued, stepping back a pace so she was facing them both. 'I'm going to put your minds at ease. Mr Rodrigues doesn't know your true identities. I do, he doesn't. He's curious about you, yes, but he doesn't know who you work for.'

'And yet you do?' Luke said. 'How is that?' In his mind he was still processing the shock of their cover being blown. And he didn't like their current situation one bit: they were on the wrong side of a locked door, in a half-lit brothel full of trafficked women and a bald thug armed with a Taser. 'Can we go next door?' he said, already moving towards the exit.

Back in the room with the gilt-edged mirrors and chandeliers they sat down at the nearest free table. Miss Xinyi waved away a man who came up to them bearing an iPad and a bottle of whisky. From the hidden speakers came a Taylor Swift song, while onstage, Luke saw, two girls were pirouetting and he could just hear iPads being tapped at nearby tables. He moved his chair round so he had his back to the stage.

'So listen,' Miss Xinyi continued. 'You've probably figured this out by now. I don't just work for Mr Rodrigues.' She paused and Luke wondered if that was for dramatic effect or if she was still making up her mind how much to tell them. 'I work for a sister agency to yours.' Really? I doubt that, Luke thought, or we would have known about it, but let's see where this goes.

'Langley?' interrupted Jenny.

'CSIS,' she replied. 'The Canadians. Mr Rodrigues has business ventures in Vancouver and we suspect he's about to give China a back door into our telecoms network.'

Miss Xinyi waved a hand dismissively. 'Anyway, that's not

important right now,' she said. 'And, yes, you will have guessed that I was tasked to lead you on a false trail to this place.' She gestured around her. By whom? Luke wanted to ask her, but now was not the time to interrupt. 'Sorry about that,' she said. 'The truth is . . .' Miss Xinyi stopped again, seemingly uncertain of whether to go on. Her earlier confidence seemed to have been replaced by hesitation and maybe something else. Was that fear he could see in her eyes? It was hard to tell. 'The truth is,' she blurted out at last, 'your Hannah Slade has left Macau.'

For a second or two nobody spoke. If this was true – *if* this was true – it was huge. It would be the first confirmation that she was alive since they had arrived in Macau. But then again, he didn't trust a word that came out of Miss Xinyi's mouth.

'You will forgive us,' Jenny began, leaning towards their host and giving her what Luke took to be a sort of half-smile, 'if I could ask you to give us some proof of this. I mean, let's be honest here. You've brought us to this place . . .' Jenny nodded towards the stage, her face a picture of disapproval. '. . . and what? You've had us waste our time checking all those poor women back there when you knew full well Hannah wasn't among them. I'm sorry, but why should we believe you?'

His thoughts exactly, but Jenny was pushing this rather harder than Luke felt comfortable with. They still had a bolted door between them, the stairs and the street outside.

'I can't give you that proof,' Miss Xinyi said. 'But what I can tell you is that Hannah Slade was here, in Macau, until –' She looked at her watch. '– until just a few hours ago. She's been moved on, taken to another place.'

'Where? By whom?' Luke demanded. 'Who's taken her and why?'

'Honestly,' she replied, 'I don't have the answers to your first question. If I did, I would tell you. All I know is she has been smuggled out of here. She's being talked of as "a person of high value".' She looked from Luke to Jenny and gave a little shrug. 'As for your second question . . . let's just say, these are very bad people, totally ruthless. If they're prepared to sell her, they will demand a very high price—'

'So not a government, then?' Luke cut in. 'You're talking about non-state actors? Organized crime? Triads?'

'That would be my guess, yes.'

'Your guess?' Jenny countered. 'Do you mean *your* guess? Or is that the view of the Canadian Security Intelligence Service?' Luke thought he detected a deliberate slowing of her words as she pronounced the last three. A well-justified sarcasm, he thought.

'Look,' said Ms Xinyi, with a sigh, as if Luke and Jenny had been trying her patience all evening, 'I've already told you more than I should. You won't find the answers here.' She opened the tiny handbag she was carrying and took out a gold-coloured pen and a miniature notebook. In silence, she wrote down what looked like a name and a number. 'What I *can* do is give you this,' she said, tearing off the page and handing it to Luke. 'This man can give you some answers. He works down at the port here. In Macau. But you must take care.'

Luke looked down at the scrap of paper she had just given him. He hated it when people told him to 'take care'. 'Meaning?'

'Meaning,' she replied, 'it's not safe for you here in this city. You have two problems, two threats.' She folded her arms as she spoke, looking from one to the other. 'There is the MSS. The Guoanbu. The Ministry of State Security. Of course you know all about them, but they are everywhere. And then . . .' Again the hesitation. '. . . then the other people. The longer you stay here in Macau the greater the chance something will happen to you. That's all I can tell you. I wish you luck. I hope you find your Hannah.'

45

South China Sea

MISS XINYI WAS RIGHT about one thing. At the same time as she was sitting at a table with Luke and Jenny in a strip club in Macau, Hannah Slade was still not far away. But the distance between the abducted British climate-change scientist and her two would-be rescuers was growing by the minute.

Hannah Slade was alive and conscious but her freedom had once again been whisked away from her. Coming round after being drugged with chloroform for a second time, she found she was flat on her back, strapped to some kind of bunk bed, her arms pinned to her sides, a low ceiling only centimetres above her face. It took all her willpower to fight back a rising tide of claustrophobia. After a few minutes, with a supreme effort, she managed to lift her head long enough to peer down towards her feet. What she saw came as a shock. A nappy! Christ, they had put her in a nappy, like an al-Qaeda suspect being shipped off to Guantánamo Bay under 'extraordinary rendition'. Had she soiled it? No, she hadn't, not yet, but the very thought repulsed her. What an indignity. She didn't deserve this. And then she remembered that she had tried to brain one of her captors with that miniature bronze Buddha so she supposed it was natural they were taking no chances. Meanwhile she felt terrible, nauseous and close to vomiting. She put it down to the effects of the chloroform.

If she had had any doubts before, they had evaporated the moment she came round. She was in serious danger now, no question. After her short-lived unsuccessful bid for freedom Hannah was back in the hands of her captors, whoever they were. And this wasn't like last time. This was no comfortable, high-rise apartment with a view. No freedom to walk around, no hand-delivered meals on a tray. When she turned her head to the side, with some difficulty, she could see she was in some kind of cabin. There was a pervasive mechanical smell in her nostrils that her years as a climate-change scientist told her was from diesel oil. She could hear the occasional metallic clanking sound and she could sense a constant, low vibration that juddered through her. It was obvious now. She was on a ship.

But who *were* these people holding her? Did they know who had sent her to Hong Kong? Did they know *why* she had been meeting that contact in the Tai Wo Tang Café in Kowloon? Did they – the questions in her head stopped as she remembered. The miniature flash drive! The one containing the data he had passed to her just before her abduction. The whole purpose of her being sent on this mission in the first place. Immediately her tongue sought out the space behind her third upper molar, the place where her wisdom tooth had been so painfully removed all those years ago. Yes! The wad of gum containing the tiny memory stick was still there, dried hard now, embedded in the upper reaches of her mouth. Good. That was something. At least they hadn't found it. Not yet anyway. But what if it came loose? Without the use of her hands she had no means of putting it back in place. She would have to swallow it. And then what? She shuddered to think what that meant.

Her thoughts were interrupted by the cabin door being opened, loud and metallic, and she felt the air pressure change. She was aware of two men coming in. Both looked to be Chinese or perhaps Korean. She couldn't tell. One was dragging some-thing behind him. Oh God, was she about to be tortured? They

167

had warned her about this, back in London. It's very unlikely to happen, they'd told her cheerfully, but if it does, try to hold on to your cover story for as long as you can. Never offer up anything about yourself that they haven't asked you. Oh, and try to establish a rapport with your captors. It might help you to escape if you get the chance. But, honestly, they said, the chances of this happening to you, Hannah, are so remote. After all, practically nobody else knows we're sending you.

'Hannah Slade,' said a voice slowly, and that was a shock straight away. So they already knew her name. But then again, they could have got that from her passport. They had taken it from her, as well as everything else.

'Yes,' she tried to say, but her throat was parched dry and the word came out as 'yukh'.

'Could I . . .' She tried to salivate her mouth. 'Could I have some water, please?'

'Hannah Slade,' said the voice again, ignoring her request and drawing out the syllables of her name again, as if she was being pronounced guilty of some terrible crime. 'Eng-a-lish spy.'

'Umm, no,' she answered, through dry lips. 'Not a spy. I'm an environmental scientist.' She tried to make the words come out as calmly and naturally as possible. But it wasn't easy as she lay strapped to her bunk, straining to turn her head so she could at least see who was addressing her.

'Yes, that is your cover, for sure,' came the reply. She could see the men in the room now. The one asking the questions was standing up. He was short, with a shaven head and wearing a green bomber jacket. The other was seated and she saw, with some relief, that the thing they had dragged in behind them was just a chair. But she could see he had a thin, weaselly face with eyes that darted everywhere. He looks mean, she decided.

'But in fact,' continued Bomber Jacket, 'you are really an officer in British intelligence, are you not?'

'No. I told you,' she said. 'I hold a PhD in environmental science and I don't know why you are holding me. I would like to go now, please.' Had she just volunteered too much information?

168

Damn. She desperately wanted to ask who these people were but she decided to say as little as possible from now on. She heard the chair scrape across the floor and Weasel Face stood up and walked over to where she lay. Hannah braced herself for something unpleasant, she wasn't sure what. But he just stood over her and stared at her with those cold, dark, malevolent eyes.

She heard the cabin door open once more, someone called something in Chinese and abruptly the two men were gone, leaving her alone, frightened and thirsty.

46

UK Defence Intelligence

To all UK Media Outlets

INTELLIGENCE UPDATE

- In recent days China's People's Liberation Army (PLA) Navy has made increasingly aggressive moves towards Taiwan, endangering shipping and freedom of movement in the Taiwan Strait.

- Since the start of this month Chinese PLA forces have invaded and temporarily occupied an island belonging to Taiwan in the Kinmen archipelago. A Chinese naval vessel has fired a ballistic missile in close proximity to a Combined Task Group from AUKUS nations operating in international waters in the Taiwan Strait.

- HMS *Daring*, a Royal Navy Type 45 destroyer, along with accompanying vessels from the US and Australia, is currently deployed in a defensive posture in support of Taiwan and to help provide security in the South China Sea.

47

Canada House, Trafalgar Square, London

ALEX MATHESON REACHED up with the tip of her index finger and touched the faint scar beneath her right eye as the car moved slowly through the early-evening traffic along London's Pall Mall. The Chief of Britain's Secret Intelligence Service always did this when something was troubling her, and the news from Jenny and Luke in Macau was troubling her greatly. They had called in earlier to the operations centre at Vauxhall Cross – it must have been very late at night where they were – to report a possible deconfliction issue. Deconfliction was what you tried to achieve when two agencies unwittingly bumped up against each other on an op. Given the sensitivities of Luke and Jenny's mission in China, the Service could not afford to find itself working against an agent of a friendly Five Eyes nation, like Canada. This boil needed to be lanced immediately, with a hastily arranged visit in person to the Canadian High Commission on Trafalgar Square.

Alex Matheson's Service driver pulled into nearby Suffolk Street and parked illegally on a double yellow line. The Chief got out, examined her reflection in the tinted window, straightened her skirt and jacket and walked the few paces to Canada House. She waited for a gap in the traffic then crossed Pall Mall East. Instead of using the main entrance, she entered the building

171

as arranged by a discreet side door, set into the grey stone wall of this venerable late-Georgian house, shaded by the spreading branches of a mature tree, well away from public scrutiny.

They met upstairs in the British Columbia Room, just the two of them, her and the CSIS station chief for London, an energetic man with a French surname that she always struggled to pronounce.

They sat opposite each other on curved white leather sofas, the SIS Chief on one, the Canadian intelligence officer facing her, a hideous swirling black and white carpet between them that, Alex felt, did no credit to the elegance of this Grade II-listed building. A large floor-to-ceiling window should have given them a magnificent view over Trafalgar Square towards St Martin-in-the-Fields church but not today: it was obstructed by scaffolding. She took a sip of her tea from a mug emblazoned with a crown, a lion, maple leaves and chevrons. 'Visit Québec in 2022' it read. She had already rehearsed in her head how she was going to handle this.

'We have,' she began, 'something of a situation in China. It involves your Service and mine and I have a call scheduled later this evening with your Director in Ottawa. But before I do that . . .' She stopped, took out a Kleenex from her handbag and dabbed at something caught in her eye. 'Before I speak to Jean in Ottawa I thought it only right I should run this by you, if you don't mind.'

She looked across the space between them at the Canadian station chief for a reaction. He was sitting bolt upright, hands clasped around his knees, face fixed in a permanent smile as he waited for her to continue. He was wearing a tiny, patriotic maple-leaf flag on his left lapel.

'You have an operation ongoing in China. As do we,' she said. 'I think we're both aware of the bigger picture on the whole South China Sea situation that our agencies share through Five Eyes and the premium we all place on actionable product coming out of China.'

'*Absolument*,' replied the Canadian, his smile still in place. 'How can we be of service?'

'I'm going to cut straight to the chase, Louis. I wanted to run a name by you. If it checks out, we would kindly request full cooperation with one of your people down there. She's a Miss Xinyi Yip, or Yip Xinyi, depending which usage you prefer. She works undercover for the Rodrigues group in Macau. She's already provided some assistance to our people there but we really need her to work with us on this one.'

Alex Matheson had not yet reached the end of her sentence before she noticed the fixed grin fading. The Canadian station chief was starting to look bewildered and embarrassed at the same time.

'*Mais . . . je suis désolé*,' he replied. 'I am so sorry but this is not possible.'

'Excuse me?' She braced herself to hear something about needing to refer back to Ottawa.

'It is not possible,' the Canadian repeated slowly, 'because we have no one working for us in Macau.' He spread his hands apologetically. '*Personne.* Nobody.'

48

Taiwan Strait

DAWN OVER A tropical ocean can be a magnificent sight. It can creep up on you, grey and mysterious, only for the sky to burst suddenly into an explosion of pinks, yellows and eggshell blues. But dawn that morning, for the crew of HMS *Daring*, was not such a day.

For those on watch on the bridge of the Royal Navy's Type 45 air defence destroyer, bleary-eyed as they nursed their cups of tea and coffee, dawn was a singularly unspectacular event. While they steamed northwards past the Tropic of Cancer the night leached away into a grey half-light of drizzle and low cloud. The Captain had his own personalized mug, a farewell gift from his previous command in the Gulf, a little memento he took with him everywhere. Up and dressed since 0530, Commander Ross Blane had a lot on his mind. Following the action of two days earlier, when a Chinese warship, *Lhasa*, had fired a missile practically across their bows, fresh orders had come in from PJHQ at Northwood.

It was the job of Britain's Permanent Joint Headquarters, on the north-west edge of London, to execute the military decisions taken by government. Those on the receiving end of these orders were often unaware of just how arbitrary was the way in which these decisions were sometimes arrived at. It could be a result of a personal whim of the Secretary of State, a five-minute phone call with their opposite number in Washington, or even a curt WhatsApp message sent by a prime minister in a hurry. But that was not the case today. Urgent and serious three-way conversations had already taken place between Whitehall, Washington and Canberra following the Chinese Navy raid on Lieyu Island. NATO's North Atlantic Council had convened an emergency session. The vetoing of the French-sponsored UN resolution condemning Beijing's actions had only resulted in an even greater Western resolve to deter any further incursions. It was hastily agreed that the current tri-nation AUKUS Task Group should divert from its intended route up to the East China Sea and instead take up a defensive posture off the north-west coast of Taiwan. Nobody was under any illusions this would stop an invasion force coming from the mainland. It was simply a stopgap measure, a deterrent tripwire until more forces arrived in-theatre.

Daring was on defence watches, a state of readiness just below action stations but ready to move there at a moment's notice. Down in the Ops Room they were all in dark blue coveralls with their white anti-flash kit near at hand as they sat at their consoles, looking intently at the screens and talking quietly into their headset microphones. Standing up and in charge was Sam Glazeby, the Principal Warfare Officer, having just begun his six-hour watch. He was now moving this billion-pound-plus state-of-the-art warship into the position she'd been tasked to take up.

'Officer of the Watch,' he said into the ship's internal comms system. 'Come hard left 270.'

On the bridge, the OOW, standing next to the Captain, issued his own orders, steering the ship where it needed to go. 'Port 30 altering 270,' he said. 'Both levers ahead five zero.'

Up on deck, *Daring* had her weapons systems – her missile launchers, her 4.5-inch Mk8 naval gun and her suite of machine-guns and cannons – uncovered, crewed and made ready by sailors in coveralls and full anti-flash gear. Her lone helicopter, an Augusta Wildcat armed with Sea Venom anti-ship missiles, was prepped and ready to fly at fifteen minutes' notice. But it was the unseen things that gave this ship such a formidable capability, like her Sampson multi-function air-tracking radar, housed in the great pyramidal superstructure that towered over the deck and capable of detecting and tracking hundreds of targets simultaneously.

At 0700 hours, with the whole ship's company of 190 sailors awake, Sam Glazeby gave a general broadcast pipe to update everyone with the latest situation report.

'PWO speaking. Sitrep. We are maintaining our sector seventeen miles west of Taiwan. Air and surface warnings remain yellow.'

Glazeby, like several of the more experienced hands onboard, was already a veteran of active operations when the ship had been placed on defence watches. Playing cat-and-mouse with the Iranian Revolutionary Guards Navy in the Strait of Hormuz, for example, or being shadowed by Russian warships in the icy seas off the north coast of Norway.

This morning, with the ship's helicopter ranged on deck at alert fifteen, he had one of her crew posted on lookout, standing beside the aircraft watching astern with a pair of binoculars. Lieutenant Sasha Dalziel was a qualified Wildcat pilot, passing out top of her course with 705 Naval Air Squadron at RAF Shawbury, just outside Shrewsbury. She was also an experienced observer, methodically scanning the waves behind *Daring*'s wake with a practised eye. It was twenty-five minutes into her watch when she suddenly stopped in mid-sweep. Something was sticking out of the water around 2500 metres off the stern. Something that should not have been there. Lieutenant Dalziel did not need a second look: she knew exactly what it was and what she needed to do. She grabbed the microphone attached to the bulkhead beside her and made the call to the bridge: 'Bridge – Flight Deck – submarine periscope sighted – green 140, range near.'

Daring was being shadowed by an unidentified submarine.

49

Vauxhall Cross, London

IT WAS APPROACHING 10 p.m. in the riverside headquarters of the Secret Intelligence Service and every light in the building was still blazing, casting a silvery glow onto the dark, choppy waters of the River Thames below. At this time of night the place was almost empty. But not quite.

Up on the third floor, the China team was assembled. Within SIS, China had become such an overarching priority that there was not just one China team but several. There was China Nuclear, China Political, China Espionage, and so on. Tonight, on the China team there were six people, all seated around a long, rectangular desk beneath a blinking neon strip-light, half-drunk mugs of tea and coffee scattered around next to them. Along the row of digital clocks on the wall one showed the time in Beijing as being 0552 the following morning. Luke and Jenny would be asleep in their hotel now, the Venetian, but the intel they had provided a few hours earlier had set the proverbial cat among the pigeons.

'We now have,' said Jack Searle, head of China desk, 'a crucial decision to make. And we need to make it tonight.' He was standing up in his shirtsleeves, tie off, jacket over the back of his chair, a nicotine patch just visible beneath the edge of his rolled-up sleeve. 'We need to direct Jenny and Luke on whether they should proceed or not. But we face the classic intelligence conundrum: we don't have all the pieces of the jigsaw, only some of them.

'Let's start with what we know.' He spread the fingers of his left hand and began counting off his points one by one. 'One. Miss Xinyi Yip works for Rodrigues, who we know is up to his neck in organized crime in Macau. Two.' He tapped the tip of his middle finger. 'Rodrigues took phone calls from Kowloon just after Hannah's abduction. Not conclusive, I admit, but still a possible piece of the jigsaw. Three. Both Rodrigues and Miss Xinyi tell our team that, yes, Hannah was brought to Macau, but Xinyi says she's been moved on. And, yes, they could still both be lying. In fact, we know from the Chief's meeting this evening in Canada House that Xinyi has already lied about working for our Canadian colleagues. Everything about her screams out that she's a phoney, a time-waster. Maybe even some kind of Walt.'

'Sorry?' interrupted Lucia, the secondee from GCHQ. 'What's a Walt?'

'A Walter Mitty character,' Jack replied. 'A fantasist. Someone who makes up stories because they don't find their own life interesting enough.'

'Ah. Thanks.'

'But then there's Qianfan Lau,' Jack continued. 'The contact she's given us at Macau port. And, thanks to the work Angela and her team have done in the last few hours, he comes up as one of the more convincing pieces of the puzzle. Angela.' He turned towards Angela Scott, Luke's line manager and his unofficial mentor since the day he first joined the Service. 'Can you fill them in, please? Oh, and thanks for dashing back from that lecture across the river. I appreciate it.'

'Not a problem,' she replied. She half stood up, then appeared to think better of it and sat down again to deliver her short summation. She was neatly dressed as always, in a green wool jacket over a white blouse, a small gold crucifix on a chain around her neck. 'Qianfan Lau has a dull-sounding title that belies what he really does. Officially, he is the Deputy Director of Export Certification at the Marine and Water Bureau in the Port of Macau. I know, quite a mouthful, yes? But I called in some help from our friends at Langley.' She glanced up at the Washington clock on the wall. 'It's still only mid-afternoon over there in Virginia. And they have quite a file on this chap Lau. It turns out he keeps an eye on all the shipping coming into and going out of the Port of Macau. At least, the cargoes that matter. And by that I mean the illicit stuff. He's the eyes and ears of the criminal underworld in that port. Oh, and you won't be surprised to hear he's linked to Rodrigues. But let me stop there because Lucia has more on this she can tell you.'

'Lucia?' Jack prompted, nodding towards the young signals specialist.

Lucia cleared her throat and glanced briefly at her notepad before closing it with a little coloured elastic strap. 'Well, we've done a reverse trace on her phone,' she said. 'That's Xinyi Yip's phone. We accessed it through Rodrigues's accounts. He has several phones, as you'd expect, and I'm pretty sure we've got access to all of them now. And here's the thing.' She looked at Jack as she spoke. 'We've run a trace on that number she gave Luke and Jenny, the one for Qianfan Lau.'

'And?'

'And she called him just a few hours ago. That's *after* she left Luke and Jenny and put them into a car back to their hotel.'

'Wait,' Jack said. 'That must have been very late in the evening over there, well after hours, yes?'

'That's correct.'

'Do we know what was said? Could you get Cheltenham to send us a translation?'

'Uh-uh.' Lucia shook her head. 'We've only got the metadata. Date, time and numbers, no content, sorry, Jack.'

'Right. So we've established that this Qianfan Lau at the port is a definite player, part of the puzzle, no question. But there's also an inherent risk if we send Luke and Jenny to see him. This could easily be a set-up. And there's our dilemma.'

Before anyone on the team could respond Jack Searle continued aloud with his train of thought. 'Look, if the situation with China wasn't so bloody serious right now we wouldn't even be having this conversation. But it is and we are. The fact is, we have *no* other leads. None. Hong Kong station have come up empty-handed. In fact, they're still pretty sore they were not let in on this op in the first place. So here's what we're going to do. Whatever decision we take here, in this room tonight, needs sign-off from the Director Critical. I'm going to recommend to him that we run with it. We send Luke and Jenny to meet Lau at the port in the morning but to get out at the first sign of anything suspicious. Does anyone have any objections?' He looked round the table. There was some uncomfortable shuffling and shifting on chairs but no one met his gaze and no one spoke. Everyone around that table knew that the decision they had just taken could mean either a breakthrough or sending Luke and Jenny straight into the path of danger.

50

Onboard HMS Daring, *Taiwan Strait*

WHEN THE CALL came through to the bridge from the flight deck it was as if some unseen button had been pressed and the machinery of naval warfare began whirring into gear. Addressing those onboard who needed to know, the Officer of the Watch made his announcement on the command open line, the ship's main internal comms link for all the key players, from the Commanding Officer down.

'Principal Warfare Officer, Officer of the Watch,' he said. 'Periscope sighted bearing 115.' There was no doubt in his mind as to who owned the submarine that was tailing them just outside Taiwan's territorial waters. The Captain would need to get on the secure voice net immediately to CTG, the Task Group Commander, a US Navy rear admiral onboard one of the new guided missile destroyers. He would also have to notify the UK's Permanent Joint Headquarters at Northwood. They both needed to know that the Task Group was under hostile surveillance from the People's Liberation Army Navy. The fact that the sub was at periscope depth indicated to everyone that she was most likely to be a conventional diesel electric boat, rather than a nuclear-powered one. Conventional subs needed to come to periscope depth more frequently to charge their batteries, a process known in the Navy as 'snorting'. But she was no less a threat and *Daring* needed to react accordingly.

Within two minutes the lookouts on deck had confirmed the sighting, with an alarming new development. There was not just one periscope following them, but two, adjacent to each other. The larger of the two was the search periscope, the one first spotted by a member of the Wildcat helicopter crew. But now there was a second: the attack scope.

'Officer of the Watch – PWO . . . Come hard right 180,' ordered the Principal Warfare Officer.

By now the ops team and sonar operators were all scanning along the bearing, searching for the rogue sub. Radar got there first.

'Radar contact bearing 095 range 1.5 miles,' came the report. Then almost immediately the lookouts on deck reported that the mast had vanished: the sub was going deep. Now, with the vessel fully submerged, it was the turn of the sonar team in the Ops Room.

'Hot new sonar contact,' called one of the operators. 'Bearing 095 range 2770m.' This was echoed by the Anti Submarine Warfare Director, an experienced petty officer. 'Probsub 1234, 1.5 miles, tracking north speed slow.'

Lieutenant Sasha Dalziel was already in the Ops Room, waiting patiently for her mission briefing from the Principal Warfare Officer and the order 'Action Wildcat'. As soon as she received it, complete with the sub's updated suspected position, she headed straight back to the flight deck to prepare the Wildcat helo for launch. A team of fitters was already making final adjustments to her weapon load: one Stingray torpedo and one depth charge.

Back in the Ops Room, *Daring*'s Action Picture Supervisor, a leading seaman, was preparing to alert all ships and helos in the Task Group, using the fighting net known as ASW Alfa.

'Flash Flash Flash. New sonar contact, track 1234, 095 1.5 miles, classified Probsub.'

Commander Ross Blane stood on the bridge, listening and

thinking hard. He had the command open line in his left ear but his brain was churning with one overriding question: what are that submarine captain's intentions? Because this was where he earned his annual £70,550 salary. Judge this wrong and HMS *Daring* could take a Chinese torpedo strike below her waterline. Act in haste and he could risk starting the Third World War.

51

Macau, China

LUKE CARLTON WOKE UP feeling as if he'd barely slept. He had lain there wide awake half the night, processing everything they had seen, analysing everything they had heard. And when he'd finally got off to sleep he was plagued by nightmares. Ghostly white-masked faces loomed out of cupboards, emaciated arms stretched out towards him, fingers beckoning. He looked across the room to where Jenny lay sleeping, hoping she wasn't experiencing the same thing.

The instructions from London came in by text before the first light of day illuminated the terracotta-coloured walls of the Venetian Hotel's bogus bell tower. Jenny and Luke waited until they were out of their room and on the busy hotel concourse before they opened and read it.

Due diligence done on Qianfan Lau, it said. *Deputy Director of Export Certification, Marine and Water Bureau. Building 41, Zone C, Port of Macau. Xinyi made contact with him last night. Green light for your meeting but proceed with caution.*

'Proceed with caution?' echoed Luke. 'Who writes this stuff back there? As if we go waltzing into every situation out here without a care in the world.'

'Someone at VX will be covering their backside, Luke. That's all,' Jenny said. 'Remember the rules tightened up in January? If they don't include that phrase "proceed with caution" officers like us can sue them if it all goes bad.'

Luke shook his head. In his twelve years in the Royal Marines he had seen legal cases spring up like mushrooms while the long arm of health and safety had spread throughout every aspect of the corps. He had heard they even had crash mats positioned beneath the Tarzan course these days, down at the Commando Training Centre at Lympstone. Now, since joining the Service, he had come across more lawyers than he had ever thought possible.

They moved outside onto the patio, feeling the heat of the morning envelop them, like a warm bath. They chose a bench in the shade, a place where no one could overhear their conversation, but Luke found himself squinting uncomfortably against the glare of the tropical sun. Not yet nine o'clock and already it was almost vertically above them in the sky.

'I'm not going to sugar-coat this, Jen,' he said, turning to face her. 'I think this is a dicey one.'

He waited for a pair of young, impeccably groomed business executives to pass them before continuing. 'It's all very well London saying they've done the due diligence on our man at the port, but this could still be a set-up. We could be walking straight into a trap.' Even as he said the words Luke was reminded of the grisly fate that had befallen the Saudi journalist Jamal Khashoggi in 2018. His killers had been waiting for him; they'd had time to plan. They'd known exactly when he was going to walk into the Saudi Consulate in Istanbul and they were ready at the appointed time.

Jenny breathed out hard, staring straight ahead. A group of elderly Chinese had gathered round a table beneath a parasol a short distance away and were starting a game of mahjong. 'I think,' she said thoughtfully, 'if London wants us to go ahead then we have to go with it. It's not like we've got a lot of options.'

'Sure. But we don't both need to go. You could stay here?'

'I could,' Jenny replied, 'but how good's your Cantonese?'

'Fair one,' Luke conceded. 'All right, we go together.' He

185

glanced at his phone. 'Ten minutes by cab,' he said. 'Maybe twelve, tops. The container port is right next to the airport. That's according to Survelex here.' He showed her the map on his phone. Ever conscious of security, the Service had a strict ban on intelligence officers using Google Maps. Instead, Q Branch had devised an in-house app, Survelex, that showed up as 'Google Maps' if anyone cared to look for it, yet it left no user history and was considered untraceable by outsiders.

The taxi took them south from the Venetian along a broad, four-lane highway, the Estrada do Istmo, flanked by soaring apartment blocks painted pink and white, then past cranes, a construction site and even a copy of the Rialto Bridge in Venice. A palm-lined reservation divided the two streams of traffic going in opposite directions.

'Macau is tiny,' remarked Luke, as they sped past a reservoir and were soon driving through open forest. 'We're here,' he said, moments later. A large low white building on their left bore the initials 'MCT' – Macauport Container Terminal. They could see stacks of blue shipping containers piled up on the jetty, glinting in the mid-morning sun, while a black and yellow barrier blocked the entrance to the port. The driver had clearly been there before as the guard in the gatehouse recognized him, raised the barrier and waved him through. Other than him it seemed no one else was around.

Luke tried to imagine Hannah Slade in this place, an industrial container port on the other side of the world. If that was what had really happened to her, how was she brought here? Was she conscious? Blindfolded? Bound and gagged in the boot of a car or sitting sedated in the back, sandwiched between two heavies? He closed his eyes for a moment, envisaging the sheer terror she must have felt. He had never met this collector. That, of course, was the whole point, giving couriers like her minimum contact with serving intelligence officers so no one could join the dots. Of course he had no idea how she would be coping. If she was still alive.

'Which building?' asked the driver, twisting to face them in the back.

'Forty-one,' Jenny replied.

It was a low white-walled building and it wasn't hard to find. It had 'Building 41' stencilled on it in large letters beside an open doorway leading to a staircase. It looked exactly like the one next to it and the one next to that, all with grey air-conditioning units that clung to the outside walls. They paid the driver, took his number for the journey back and got out. If anyone was watching and waiting for them, Luke thought, they must be well hidden.

They were about to go in when Jenny pointed up at the sky. A pair of Chinese fighter jets streaked low overhead, twisting and turning, followed a couple of seconds later by a deafening roar as the sound waves caught up. They were low enough for Luke to see their twin tail fins and a pair of miniature delta wings protruding from just behind the cockpit. Both aircraft had a rack of missiles slung beneath the fuselage.

'Stealth fighters,' remarked Jenny, shielding her eyes against the sun as the roar of the jets subsided and their corner of the port returned to near silence. 'I think they're Chengdu J-20s. The PLA call them "Mighty Dragon". I forget what that is in Chinese but they're China's first and only fifth-generation fighter jet. Probably flying out of Zhuhai airbase just south of here. They claim it's invincible.'

'And is it?' Luke asked.

Jenny shrugged. 'Not sure, to be honest. People usually compare it to the US F-22 Raptor. That's what it'll come up against if this develops into a hot war over the Taiwan Strait. The Raptor is faster but the J-20 can fly further and, remember, America's airbases are a long way from here.'

Luke was impressed. He'd spent the last few months working on the Middle East desk, reporting to the humourless Grimwood. His head was still full of stats on Iranian missile batteries and deep-cover agents inside the middle ranks of Hezbollah. 'How do you know all this?' he asked.

'From that briefing we had at RAF Wyton before we left, remember? You obviously weren't paying enough attention! Right, come on, let's find our man Qianfan Lau.'

They walked up the stone staircase in silence until they reached the first-floor landing and another open doorway. An elderly woman with enormous glasses was standing just inside it, pushing an aluminium tea trolley.

'Qianfan Lau?' Jenny asked her, and the tea lady pointed upstairs.

'Bingo,' Luke said, as they reached the next floor and a sign above the first door they came to read, in Chinese and English, 'Deputy Director's Office. Dept of Export Certification'. For a second or two they looked at each other. Luke and Jenny had worked together on enough operations in enough countries that nothing needed to be said. They knew this was one of those watershed moments, a fork in the road that could lead to anything from arrest and imprisonment to a disappointing dead end to a genuine breakthrough in their quest to find Hannah.

Jenny knocked gently on the door, waited for a response then opened it. A middle-aged man was sitting behind a desk, writing, box files and papers littering the space in front of him. The moment he saw Jenny he catapulted out of his chair, came out from behind his desk and bowed. 'Qianfan Lau, Qianfan Lau, Qianfan Lau,' he repeated. He gestured for them to sit on the chairs in front of the desk. Luke guessed he was not much older than he was, maybe early forties, with thinning black hair combed back and lacquered to his scalp. But his suit was expensive, and when he'd held out his hand in greeting, Luke had noticed what looked very much like a Rolex. Whatever it was, it was hardly in keeping with this tawdry government office with its institutional lime-green walls and metal shelves groaning with dusty box files. It looked to Luke exactly like the little office at the martial-arts gym back in Hong Kong. Mr Lau, Luke was certain, had more than one income.

A fan turned slowly on the ceiling and Lau caught Luke glancing up at it. 'Please excuse the heat,' he apologized. 'Our AC is bust. Can I offer you some tea? Something colder? Maybe a beer?'

'Perhaps a Coke if you have one,' Jenny said, turning to Luke, who nodded.

'Of course, of course.' Lau walked over to an ancient-looking fridge in the corner, took out two cans of Coke and handed them to his guests. 'So,' he said, returning to his chair and smiling at them, as if this were some long-delayed reunion of old friends. 'Miss Xinyi tells me you are looking for someone. As you can see,' he said, waving his hand around his Spartan office, 'I am just a humble clerk here at the port but I would be happy to be of service. What can I do for you?'

Wow, Luke thought. We're not even getting to take a sip before we dive straight in. This could go either way.

'It's Hannah Slade,' Jenny said, leaving just enough of a pause for them both to watch his reaction. There was none. 'She's a . . . she's a friend of ours from London and she went missing in Hong Kong a few days ago. We understand from Miss Xinyi that she passed through this port. Would you know anything about her?'

Qianfan Lau didn't answer straight away. He held up a finger to his lips and spoke very slowly and deliberately, still in English. 'I'm sorry. I'm afraid I cannot help you. This name does not ring any bells. Have you tried the Port Authority main office?' But Luke noticed that as he was saying this he was writing. When he had finished he handed them a piece of paper.

'Let me call you a taxi,' he said cheerfully, as they read what he had just written. It was just three lines.

Hannah Slade left Macau Port yesterday.
She is on *Ulysses Maiden*.
Destination is Tan-shui.

52

Quangang District, Fujian Province, China

PRIVATE FIRST CLASS Jian Zhang had made a remarkable recovery from the bullet wound to his chest that he had sustained on the Lieyu Island raid. Remarkable, at least, by conventional standards. But there was nothing conventional about the men of China's secretive Project 49. Outwardly normal in appearance, if a little larger and more muscular than their compatriots, what lay beneath their skin was a living laboratory where scientific engineering and nature came together to break every existing rule of human genetics.

The high-velocity round that had slammed into his pectoral muscle that night would have kept an average adult human in hospital for weeks, perhaps longer with complications. It would then be months before they recovered the full use of their arm and they might well experience pain, trauma or even infection for some time afterwards. Not so PFC Zhang. The artificial respirocyte red blood cells injected into his bloodstream, with the painstaking genetic engineering that had made him the twenty-first-century 'super soldier' he was, combined to speed him on his way to a rapid recovery. By the end of the second day Zhang was up and walking around, arm in a sling. Later that night he threw the sling into the bin and requested to be returned to his unit and active duty. The hospital staff exchanged anxious glances and were initially reluctant, but they were overruled by a uniformed officer who turned up from Zhang's unit bearing a very impressive ID card. Within minutes he was discharged, leaving by the back door, and ushered by the officer into a waiting military jeep.

53

South China Sea

SOMETHING HAD CHANGED. Hannah noticed it the moment they came into her cabin. It was the second visit from the two men who seemed to know so much about her and this time their demeanour was quite different. She was still bound when they came in, strapped to a bunk bed with the deck head just centimetres above her face. But now they were smiling, chatting to each other, as if a weight had been lifted from their shoulders. Something had made them relax. The man in the bomber jacket with the shaved head walked casually over to her, a cigarette clamped between his lips, and without explanation he undid the straps that bound her hands. As she felt the blood flowing freely through her wrists Hannah saw him wink at her. She wished she hadn't. It was a hideous sight.

There was not enough space for her to sit up but now, at least, she could roll onto her side. Bomber Jacket held out his hand, offering her a cigarette – she noted the brand on the packet: Lucky Strike – and he looked almost disappointed when she declined. Already the tiny cabin was filling with blue smoke that rolled along the low metal ceiling and stung her eyes and lungs. Bomber Jacket said something to his friend and they laughed. A joke at her expense, she had no doubt.

Hannah didn't care. She had one thought and one thought only. The miniature flash drive. The tiny metal chip concealed inside a wad of chewing gum that was still wedged in the top of her mouth, just behind her third upper molar. She could feel it in place now with the tip of her tongue. Once again, she reminded herself that the whole purpose of this assignment, with everything she had already endured and maybe what she still had to go through, lay in the secret data contained within the flash drive. What would it reveal? She had no idea and probably she would never know. It had been in her possession only seconds before they had chloroformed her in that café in Kowloon. But back in London, during the final briefing in Kensington Gardens, her handler had left her in no doubt about how urgently they wanted it. So every physical inconvenience, and God knew there were plenty, was eclipsed by the absolute burning necessity of safeguarding that chip and somehow getting it to Vauxhall Cross.

And what were the chances of that happening now? she wondered. Slim, at best. She was on a ship, evidently some kind of merchant rust-bucket from the foul smell of diesel oil that leaked into the cabin from the passageway. And she was being taken across an ocean to some unknown destination by unidentified people. Did the Service even know what had happened to her? Who was holding her? Where she was headed? Would they be mounting a rescue operation to come and get her? Or would some high-up in Vauxhall Cross whom she had never met simply draw a line under the whole operation and say, 'Shame about Hannah. It just didn't work out.'

Those were the thoughts that were running through her head as her tongue suddenly registered something at the top of her mouth. The wad of gum was coming loose.

54

UK Permanent Joint Headquarters, Northwood

IT WAS AN RAF wing commander who took the call from *Daring* that night. Not quite midnight at Britain's base for all overseas operations on the edge of London and, as duty officer, Martyna Kozlowska had been on shift for just under four hours. She was on her second cup of coffee in the Ops Room when the Flash message came up on her screen from an ocean on the other side of the world. It had been a busy evening already with communications winging through space from British military assets in Estonia, Akrotiri, Bahrain and the Black Sea. But those were all categorized as 'Immediate', 'Priority' or 'Routine'. Only a Flash message required an instant response.

Martyna read the message then leapt up from her chair and walked quickly past the banks of screens and digital maps of the world that blinked and flickered twenty-four hours a day. She knocked on the door of the nearby office where a sign read simply 'COS (Ops)' and went straight in. The Chief of Staff (Operations) was responsible for the planning and execution of all military operations and tonight the buck stopped with him, a two-star Royal Marine major general.

'Flash message from *Daring* in the Taiwan Strait, sir,' she said, with only the faintest trace of her native Polish accent.

'Yes?' Major General Denton looked up from his laptop.

'They've had a hot contact with a Chinese submarine. Just outside Taiwan's territorial waters.'

'What's it doing now? The sub?'

'It's gone deep, sir. They're tracking it by sonar.'

'That's it? Nothing else? No weapons engaged? No casualties?'

'No, sir.'

Martyna stood in the doorway of his office, arms by her sides, waiting for orders. The Chief of Staff regarded her for several seconds as his mind raced through the possible courses of action. A hot contact with a Chinese submarine at a time of tension like this could easily escalate into something far worse. The team had war-gamed this already at PJHQ, working through the various scenarios the Task Group might encounter in the South China Sea before it even set off. And the Rules of Engagement were clear. There was no need, in Major General Denton's view, to change them now.

'Right,' he said at last. 'Send back the following message to *Daring* by Flash: "Disengage. De-escalate and continue to monitor." Is that clear?' he asked her.

'Perfectly, sir.'

'Good. I'll notify Chief of Joint Operations and he can brief the Service chiefs in the morning, but there's no need to wake up the PM on this one. Keep me posted if the situation changes.'

'General.'

55

Quangang District, Fujian Province, China

QUANGANG WAS A rural district of pastel-green farmland, stands of bamboo and densely packed pine forest interspersed with traditional stone cottages and soulless modern housing projects. It also happened to be opposite the west coast of Taiwan, less than 150 kilometres away across the Taiwan Strait. For Beijing's military Eastern Theatre Command, Quangang held a special strategic importance. More than once, it had been from here in Fujian Province, with its rolling, wooded hills, that the PLA had sent volleys of ballistic missiles into the sky and over the island of Taiwan in a furious response to what Beijing saw as unacceptably close contact between Taiwan's elected rulers and senior US officials.

'Such provocations are incompatible with the One China policy,' the state-run *China People's Daily* had thundered in protest. 'We call upon the US to desist from such ill-advised actions, which can only end in abject failure.'

It was at one of Quangang's secluded beaches, a former beauty spot now sealed off from public access with a high electrified fence and numerous warning signs, that the black-uniformed men of the Jiaolong Commando, the Sea Dragons, were engaged in high-intensity training. This beach had been selected for a special reason. It was an exact mock-up of one of the fourteen Taiwanese

196

beaches deemed suitable for an amphibious landing, and the difficulties the exercise planners had placed in their way were ingeniously realistic. The beach bristled with obstacles: sharp, angular steel spikes, dense coils of razor wire and necklaces of hidden explosive charges buried beneath the sand.

The military jeep that had collected Private First Class Jian Zhang from his brief period of recovery in hospital had delivered him straight back to his unit. Already his body was back to full strength. His muscles tense, his veins pumping with respirocytes, he crouched, with the rest of his team, in one of several black rubber inflatables, its engine idling and out of sight from the beach behind a wooded headland as they waited for the signal. That signal, when it came, was no blast on a whistle, no command over the radio, but it was something they were all poised to expect. It began as a low, distant patter, rising in pitch and volume to a great clattering roar as, from over the brow of the nearest hill, a formation of black Z-10 attack helicopters swept into view. Similar to the French Tiger but arguably more advanced, this was China's first domestically produced assault helicopter and each aircraft carried a powerful arsenal comprising eight air-to-ground missiles and two thirty-two-barrel multiple rocket launchers.

As the helicopters passed over the waiting men in the inflatables they unleashed a devastating torrent of fire and flame. Needle-like rockets streaked through the air and struck the beach and its defences with shattering force. Blasted and twisted fragments of the tank traps flew through the air and further explosions rippled through the sand as the rockets set off the necklaces of buried land mines, clearing a safe path through them. Moving as one, the Jiaolong commandos accelerated forward in their inflatable RIBs, bouncing over the waves, spray lashing their faces. They hit the beach at speed, barely slowing so that their craft slithered several metres onto the sand and they used the momentum to carry themselves forward, quickly fanning out to take up firing positions behind whatever cover they could find.

The weapons gripped in their gloved hands were unrecognizable as successors to the crude and basic Chinese version of the old

AK-47 assault rifle of Cold War days. The modern QTS-11 rifles they carried were more than just a weapon: they were a complete integrated system, the quintessential example of how the modern-day infantry soldier is becoming ever more enmeshed with tech. In addition to the thirty-round magazine of 5.8mm bullets, it was fitted with a grenade launcher capable of detonating an airburst grenade just above and behind an enemy soldier. What made it different from conventional weapons was the electronic optics linked to each man's eyepiece, which was attached to his helmet with an integrated rangefinder. In practical terms, this allowed each of the Jiaolong to fire around corners or over the top of a trench without exposing their own bodies to incoming fire.

And incoming fire was exactly what PFC Zhang was experiencing right now. As he and his team moved further inland up the beach, using fire and manoeuvre, a deafening crackle of high-velocity rounds zipped overhead, splitting the air as they broke through the sound barrier. They were coming from an unmanned machine-gun post ahead where the weapon was locked in position to fire over their heads and remotely controlled from a nearby bunker.

And now they were in among the trenches at the point where the beach merged with the woods, screaming in mock fury as they assaulted through the 'enemy' positions, bayoneting and shooting the 3D puppets of defending Taiwanese troops, which all wore either the hated red and blue Taiwanese flag or else the equally despised Stars and Stripes.

The exercise was over almost as soon as it had begun. It had taken precisely twenty-seven minutes, from the moment the assault helicopters opened fire to when the glorious red flag of the People's Republic was raised above the block house on the beach. Zhang checked his weapon and looked down at his individual monitor. Twenty-one rounds expended, no injuries, heart rate normal. And he wasn't even breaking a sweat.

56

Wimbledon, London

ANGELA SCOTT SAT in the corner of her carriage and stared at her reflection as the train trundled through south-west London, taking her home to a pre-cooked meal waiting in the fridge. Her methodical mind was busy processing everything she had learnt in that lecture from the King's College professor and the Q and A session that had followed. Some things she was already well versed in: the rounding up of the Uighurs in Xinjiang Province, the infamous 're-education' camps, ringed with barbed wire, the snuffing out of the last flickers of democracy in Hong Kong, the ever more persistent probing of Taiwan's maritime borders. This was all common knowledge, already well covered in newspapers and by broadcasters. No, what was new to her were the extraordinary lengths the CCP, the Chinese Communist Party, was going to in order to gather data and place its population under surveillance.

There was a paradox for her here. Angela was a career intelligence officer, with all the baggage that came with it. While working in the service of her country, she had on numerous occasions been privy to the innermost secrets of a Service 'target', covertly reading their emails, their WhatsApp messages, their texts, and trawling through their private photographs stored on their iCloud account. Some things she would rather not have seen, but it was all strictly professional, she would remind herself, all governed by the parameters of UK law; the Service lawyers saw to that. But this was different. The picture painted by that bristly-jacketed academic upstairs in the lecture room off the Strand was of a mass, state-controlled surveillance system that was obsessed with control and with hoovering up as much of everyone's data as its servers could handle, and then some.

Thirty thousand military spies, the lecturer had said, were all working online in the service of the Party. And they were backed up by a further 150,000 'patriotic hackers' going after whatever tech they could get their hands on that might give China an edge. 'Don't just take my word for it,' the academic had told the room with a wry chuckle. 'These figures come from the FBI.' TikTok, LinkedIn and numerous forms of social media were proving rich hunting grounds for China's online army, which was finding it all too easy to plunder the accounts of the unwary. No wonder the FBI was opening a new China-related investigation every twelve hours.

It did not occur to Angela Scott, as she stepped out at Wimbledon station, that certain people who did not wish her well were preparing to read the contents of her own phone.

57

Hsinchu Industrial Park, Taiwan

CHEN CHIN-LUNG THOUGHT quite seriously about taking his own life. He was cornered, they had him, and as far as he could tell, there was no way out of his predicament.

It was the watch that gave him away. A stupid, needless indulgence he had allowed himself. A Breitling Superocean costing nearly five thousand pounds. That was more than a whole month's salary for him at the Taiwan Semiconductor Manufacturing Company. It was his supervisor who had spotted it and reported it as suspicious to Security, without even telling him. They came for him at his workstation, appearing from behind, one on either side, then holding him by his arms and physically removing him while his colleagues looked on, open-mouthed.

There had followed the hours of miserable, tearful questioning in the company's Security office, all of it filmed and taped. The laptop was turned to face him across a table so he could type in the bank details of his secret account in Singapore and show them all the transactions, the hidden payments from China that spelt one word only: betrayal. Because that was what he, Chen Chin-lung – outwardly loyal, respectable, mid-level software engineer at Taiwan's premier microchip company – was guilty of. He had betrayed his employers, they told him, he had betrayed his work colleagues and, worst of all, he had betrayed his country.

They had left him alone for an hour in that room. Alone, except for a pen and several sheets of paper for him to write down his confession while they waited for the investigators from the National Security Bureau to arrive. And Chen Chin-lung wept as he wrote everything down. Those first, innocuous meetings in the restaurant after work with that sympathetic woman, Lihua. The all-expenses-paid trip for him and his family to that resort in Malaysia. The detailed technical documents he had been secretly handing over on his clandestine meetings with Lihua every third Tuesday of the month.

They had taken his phone from him, as well as his access pass, so he couldn't even call his wife to tell her what had happened, or to warn her of what was about to come. Twenty years in prison, they said. That was the jail sentence handed down not so long ago to an ex-colonel for running a spy ring inside the military. But your crime, they told him, was in many ways worse. He had allowed China to peer inside the very beating heart of Taiwan's corporate crown jewels. And at a time when the island was feeling more threatened than ever by its giant neighbour across the Taiwan Strait.

When the door finally opened Chen was braced for the worst. He fully expected to be marched straight to a waiting police car and slammed into a cell to await trial and the inevitable sentencing. So he was taken by surprise when the people who walked in wore no uniform, no badges of rank. Instead, it was two women, smartly dressed, and they smiled at him. He looked from one to the other, confused. Was this some kind of trick? He had already confessed to everything. It was all there, he said, pointing at the damning pages he had written, sealing his own fate. But what followed was totally unexpected.

There is, they told him, an alternative to prison. He owed his country a massive debt, no question about that, but there was another way he could repay it. The two women from the NSB got straight to the point. They had an offer for him. The charges against him could be suspended, not dropped but suspended. Providing he cooperated fully. And they were quite explicit with him as to what that cooperation meant. 'We want you,' they said, 'to spy for us against Beijing. You're going to continue your meetings with your handler but we will provide you with exactly the material you give her.'

Chen Chin-lung felt like fainting. He nodded vigorously. He accepted their offer without conditions.

58

Hui-shan Temple, Taiwan

THE HUI-SHAN TEMPLE doesn't appear on any tourist maps of Taiwan. Nor can it be found on Google Maps, since it has no internet URL. Tucked away in the Dasyueshan Forest, on the island's Central Mountain Range, nestling in the shadow of a 3860-metre mountain, it is one of the least conspicuous of Taiwan's fifteen thousand temples. No mass worship here, no public offerings of candles and prayers, no elaborate golden dragon motifs. Just a cluster of low, modest buildings, with a large bell in a stone courtyard and a well-watered garden, where a lone and trusted caretaker tends the school of colourful koi carp. Outsiders, casual visitors, of whom there are practically none, are politely told the temple is closed until further notice and they are gently but firmly sent on their way. Their nostrils might catch the faint scent of incense emanating from the wooden halls within but that is as close as they will get.

For the Hui-shan temple had good reason to guard its secrets.

All the outward trappings of religious worship – the stone lions and the glazed Buddhas – provided ample cover for the centre of operations for a criminal organization with tentacles that spread not just into the black economy but into the very heart of Taiwanese political life. Debt collection, gambling dens, hostess bars and brothels. And the man sitting right at the top, at the very pinnacle of power, had an extensive and feared pedigree. A veteran of the Celestial Alliance, one of the four major triads in Taiwan, he was known simply as 'Bo'. Organized crime was in his blood. Drawn into the criminal underworld at an early age, he had joined Celestial Alliance while still in his teens and never looked back, kicking down his rivals, both metaphorically and physically, as well as anyone who challenged him as he clawed his way up the greasy pole of the triad hierarchy.

Very few people knew his full name but there was something apt and deeply sinister about the nickname they had for him in the underworld: Smiley Face. People assumed he had acquired this moniker because he knew he was untouchable. Bo had connections with local councillors and in the police, and he had almost lost count of the number of well-placed people, both in and out of government, who owed him favours. But those who had slighted or wronged him found it hard to forget his sickly grimace as he broke the bones of his victim with a hardened bamboo pole.

Bo was meticulous when it came to his own security and that of his trusted inner circle. His bodyguards, strategically placed around the temple and its grounds, were all American, all ex-Delta Force or Green Berets. He simply did not trust his own countrymen not to betray him. There had been little difficulty in making sure they were armed with their primary weapons of choice: Heckler & Koch MP7 submachine-pistols backed up by the larger calibre Mk16 SCAR-H carbine for greater hitting power, in case any of his rivals decided to have a go at eliminating his centre of operations.

It was while standing in the temple garden, deep in conversation with his grey-bearded groundsman, that Bo took the call he had been waiting for. It was a short conversation. The voice that spoke to him, barely audible through the rasp of wind at the other end, had a simple message to convey. 'The cargo will be docking shortly.'

59

Marylebone High Street, London

THE FLAT ABOVE the vegan food store had no windows. Sealed off from the outside world and any prying eyes, the place looked innocuous. Yet it concealed one of the most sophisticated self-contained laboratories for dissecting mobile phones and their digital contents. The extraordinary advances made by Israel's NSO group in the art of phone hacking had not gone unnoticed by China. The technical arm of the Ministry of State Security was particularly impressed by NSO's software program known as Pegasus. Delivered to an unwitting victim's phone through the click of a button, the program had become known as 'the nuclear option' in phone hacking. A device infected with Pegasus gave off virtually no clues to the user that their phone had been compromised; it was undetectable to all but the most technically competent. And yet, secretly, their phone had become a miniature digital spy, relaying back to the hacker every text, every photograph, every WhatsApp message, every contact in the address book. Chillingly, the hacker could even remotely activate the phone's microphone to listen in to conversations or even switch on its camera.

Chinese tech, which has always shown a remarkable lack of timidity when it comes to availing itself of other people's intellectual property, wasted no time in developing its own version of Pegasus. That version, known as Tiân'é – 'Swan' – was now being diligently applied to the mobile phone of Angela Scott, Senior Case Officer at MI6.

The Service, like all three of Britain's intelligence agencies, had strict rules about mobile phones. Data leaks were the Achilles' heel of any large organization and it was also not unheard of for some hapless civil servant to leave a pile of classified documents on a train or at a bus stop. So, officers were instructed to lock away their personal phones as soon as they entered the building at Vauxhall Cross and not to use them for any classified Service business. Angela Scott was no rule-breaker – the very idea of causing a data breach sent shivers down her government-service spine. She would rather die than break protocol. No, her personal phone, the one she carried around London outside Vauxhall Cross, stayed securely in its locker while she was inside its green and sandstone walls.

But Angela Scott, first-class intelligence officer as she was, was no match for the warp-speed advances in twenty-first-century digital spyware. The vast banks of fan-cooled servers that hummed and whirred beneath the streets of Shanghai already had a massive backlog of data to process, sucked up from devices and networks across the globe, from large, multinational organizations like the African Union in Addis Ababa to the most junior employee of a French aerospace company.

The Swan program operators were now inside her personal phone. This gave them access to every private conversation she'd ever had outside Vauxhall Cross, every journey she took anywhere in the world, every photograph she snapped. And if Luke Carlton happened to call her on that phone they would be able to listen in to every word.

60

Macau Airport, China

LUKE CAST A furtive glance around the terminal as they walked in with their bags. Cameras everywhere. Hardly surprising for an airport, and China had, after all, become a world leader in the art of surveillance, even touting its wares at trade exhibitions at the ExCel Centre in London's Docklands. Luke recalled a recent report that revealed that, of Britain's forty-three police forces, twenty-four admitted to using either Chinese-made cameras or components. And that was in everything from body cameras to drones to helicopters. All of this, warned the report, risked video, audio and other data being clandestinely downloaded to Chinese servers, without the user's knowledge or permission, building up an intimate security picture of the UK.

Would he and Jenny now have to pass through biometric scans? Almost certainly. Just as they had when they had landed in Hong Kong. But that was exactly why they had been chosen for this mission. They should be blank sheets as far as the People's Republic was concerned. Neither had worked China before. Theoretically, their cover identities should hold up as they passed through Departures. But the fact that Miss Xinyi had seen right through their legends had rattled them. In normal circumstances, when your cover is blown, you get out, fast, without delay. But since leaving the office of Mr Lau in Macau port, Luke and Jenny had made significant progress. Lau had revealed three facts on that hastily scribbled piece of paper; he clearly knew his office was bugged or he would not have been so clandestine about handing it over.

'We're obviously not going to take a word of this at face value,' Luke had said, as soon as they were clear of the port office and waiting for their cab back to the Venetian that morning.

'You don't say,' Jenny had replied caustically. She had her head down, busy taking a photo of the page Lau had given them so she could send it straight to London for validation.

'Look, I'm as sceptical as you are,' Luke said. 'But if even half of what he's given us turns out to be genuine we're making progress. Otherwise it's back to square one.'

The sun was still blazing down and he had to squint against the harsh light that seemed to bleach all colour out of everything around them. A man in baggy shorts and a filthy vest nearby was pushing a trolley stacked with fifteen-litre containers for water coolers, the muscles on his skinny arms straining with the exertion.

'I'm going to run this place Tan-shui through Survelex,' Luke said. 'See what it comes up with while Vauxhall do their checks. I've never heard of it, have you?'

Jenny shook her head, frowning, still concentrating on sending off the photo.

'What the hell?' Luke said, a few moments later. 'Tan-shui is coming up as a night market. I thought it was a port.'

'You sure?' Jenny said, putting away her phone and looking up at last. 'That doesn't sound right. I have to say, Survelex isn't perfect. I know one of our colleagues who was supposed to meet someone in a church in Kyiv and it tried to send him to the middle of the River Dnipro.'

'Ah, wait, hang on.' Luke was examining the screen on his phone and shading it against the sunlight with his hand. 'Here we go. Tan-shui is the newly constructed port in New Taipei. Taipei? That's Taiwan. He's telling us Hannah Slade is heading to Taiwan.'

Things had snowballed quickly after that. By the time Luke and Jenny got back to the Venetian there was already a positive response from the overnight team on the China desk. They confirmed that there was indeed a container ship called the MV *Ulysses Maiden*, registered to a company in Palau and, more importantly, yes, it had indeed left the port of Macau at 2045 hours the previous evening, bound for Taipei. What nobody could establish – yet – was whether Hannah was onboard. Vauxhall were having difficulties in obtaining a crew manifest and, given everything that had happened, it was highly unlikely that Hannah's name would be listed on it. This information came with a personal directive from Felix Schauer, Director Critical at VX: *Get yourselves on the next flight to Taipei and liaise there with head of station.* That flight, they realized, was Eva Air 802, leaving in just under two hours.

The girl at the check-in desk was young, immaculately dressed and efficient. 'Enjoy your flight,' she told them, as she handed them their boarding passes. Getting through Security after that was a lot less hassle than Luke had anticipated but something set his inner alarm bells ringing. A suited official standing behind the immigration officer stared hard at Luke, then bent down and whispered something to the immigration man. He picked up a phone and spoke rapidly into it while also giving Luke a long, hard look.

'Did you catch any of what he was saying?' Luke asked, as they progressed into Departures.

'Not a word,' Jenny replied, 'but I saw that too and I have to say it didn't look good.'

They sat on bar stools close to the departures board, downing bowls of noodles. 'At the risk of stating the obvious,' Jenny said, in a low voice, 'just checking you haven't got anything incriminating on your phone? You know, if it all turns nasty? Which I'm sure it won't.'

'No, I'm clean.'

'Sorry, I shouldn't have asked.'

It was as they were settling the tab that the two men in suits came up, one on either side of them.

'Christopher Blanford?' one asked. Luke's cover name, the one he'd practised answering to in the mirror, over and over, back in London. He nodded warily.

The other man reached into his jacket and produced a small black wallet that he flipped open for Luke to see. The upper half was emblazoned with a yellow hammer and sickle on a bright red background above a wreath of gold-coloured laurel leaves. Beneath that was a photo of an unsmiling face, a lot of writing in Chinese and the words 'Ministry of State Security'. 'You will come with us now, please,' he said.

It wasn't a request.

61

Pall Mall, London

ALEX MATHESON, CHIEF OF SIS, was unaware that morning of
what was happening to one of her intelligence officers at Macau
airport. Instead, as she was driven up the A3 into London from her
residence in Surrey, her mind was focused on the day ahead: a
difficult meeting coming up with the Chair of the Parliamentary
Intelligence and Security Committee, a call on the new Ukrainian
Ambassador in Holland Park, a memorial service for a long-
retired Director who had done great things during the Cold War
but who now almost nobody remembered. But, first, she had an
urgent breakfast meeting with the Foreign Secretary. Such was
the pressure to produce actionable intelligence on China right
now that Alex Matheson was taking time out of her schedule to
focus personally on Luke and Jenny's mission to track down
Hannah Slade. This was to be her second intervention in twenty-
four hours and she needed a favour. A big one. Hugh Rawlinson,
the Foreign Secretary, had suggested a working breakfast at his
club, the Travellers, on Pall Mall, and she had agreed. What she
needed to ask him was so delicate it needed more than a phone
call. It had to be face-to-face and without delay.

As one of London's oldest and grandest 'gentlemen's clubs',
the Travellers allowed women in as guests, but not as members.

As the first woman to head Britain's Secret Intelligence Service in its hundred-year-plus history that did not sit well with her. But 'the Club', as it was referred to by certain people back in Vauxhall Cross, had a long-standing pedigree as the place where senior spooks liked to meet up after-hours, reclining in stiff-backed leather chairs to talk through ticklish problems. In Britain, the Chief of the Secret Intelligence Service reports directly to the elected Foreign Secretary of the day, as does the Director of the other overseas spy agency, GCHQ. There have been times when this arrangement has functioned less than perfectly. Times in recent years when concerns were voiced, in strict privacy, of course, deep within the confines of Vauxhall Cross, about whether this or that Foreign Secretary could really be trusted with the secret and sensitive intelligence the Service had been obliged to share with them.

But that morning Alex Matheson had no such worries. Hugh Rawlinson MP was a team player. A little on the unadventurous side, it was true, but still a solid, steady-as-she-goes helmsman of Britain's foreign policy. An alumnus of a south-coast grammar school then a first in Politics, Philosophy and Economics from Wadham College, Oxford, before a brief and unremarkable career in law, then his eventual entry into politics. He was apologetically late, leaving her waiting nearly fifteen minutes in the Outer Morning Room, with its imposingly tall ceiling and faded scarlet curtains, close to the unlit fireplace, beneath the Canalettos and next to the ornate wooden table bearing neatly folded copies of the *Daily Telegraph*, the *Financial Times*, the *Spectator*, *Country Life* and a well-thumbed copy of *Debrett's Peerage*. The only other living thing in the room was a sprightly orchid in a pot, which looked somewhat out of place in this library of stillness.

'I've left my SPAD waiting in the car so I can't spend too long,' explained Rawlinson, when he finally appeared. He seemed rather flustered. For someone well used by now to treading the corridors of power, the Foreign Secretary looked curiously ill at ease as he and the SIS chief rode up together in the Club's rickety lift to the dining room.

213

'Thank you for meeting at short notice, Hugh,' she began, once they were seated by the window. Alex Matheson had much she needed to say to him but she knew it had to be couched in just the right way or she would walk away from this meeting empty-handed.

'Not at all, my pleasure,' he replied amiably. 'To be honest, it's a relief to get out of King Charles Street for a bit. This Taiwan crisis is eclipsing nearly all other business right now.'

'Ah.' Alex leant in a little closer. 'You see, that is *exactly* what I wanted to talk to you about.'

And then, as so often happens at the wrong moment, a waiter appeared to take their order. A cup of Earl Grey for the Foreign Secretary, avocado on toast and a fresh orange juice for the MI6 Chief. They waited patiently until he was out of earshot.

'So,' she resumed, 'as you well know, Hugh, we have a Level One operation running out of Hong Kong right now.'

'I certainly *do* know, Alex. I remember signing off on it. In fact, I was just about to ask if there's any news yet. I mean, I hate to rush your Service, you know that, but I'm getting asked for updates every day in Cabinet. So, yes, I'm all ears.' He sat back in his chair with an expectant look on his face.

'Of course.' She picked up the linen napkin in front of her, unfolded it and laid it neatly across her lap. This was the part she wasn't looking forward to but she had to get it over with. 'So, the fact is, Hugh, we have a missing collector. She vanished in Hong Kong.'

The Foreign Secretary sat bolt upright and stared at her; she could almost see his lawyer's brain working through what she had just said. 'I – I'm sorry,' he stammered. 'A collector? You're going to have to remind me of what that is.'

'She. The collector is a person, Hugh,' she corrected him. 'She's an academic, what we call a clean skin. Someone we sent into Hong Kong to pick up the data from the agent we've been running inside the CCP.'

'Vanished, you say? That doesn't sound good. How did this happen?'

'Well ...' Alex Matheson looked down at her lap and rear-ranged her napkin. '. . . it's actually a bit more complicated than that. She's been taken. Abducted.'

'*What? By whom?*' A few heads turned on neighbouring tables. It wasn't done to raise your voice in the Travellers' dining room even if the voice was that of the Foreign Secretary.

'We think by triads. Organized crime, but we believe there could still be a connection to Beijing.'

'Well, they've stepped over the line this time. This is unaccept-able! We'll summon their ambassador as soon as I get back to King Charles Street.'

'Hold that thought for a moment,' the SIS Chief replied, as a waiter brought their breakfast, delivering their orders with a flourish and a very slight bow before returning to the kitchen.

'We have to get her back,' continued Rawlinson, his voice lower this time. 'The PM is on my case for anything that could give us an advantage in this Taiwan crisis. Can't your people track her down?'

She gave him a withering look.

'Sorry, I suppose that's obvious,' he added.

'Believe me, we're trying. I've sent two of my best IOs on her trail. They're in Macau, and in the last few hours we might just have had a breakthrough.'

'Oh?'

'Look, Hugh . . .' She allowed herself a small sigh: the Service had some uncomfortable baggage in this area. 'What I'm going to tell you is single-sourced so I'm not going to bet the shop on it but right now it's the only source we have. The intel suggests our collector is being held on a merchant vessel, a container ship, heading to Taipei. We have the name of the ship. It's *Ulysses Maiden*. It's already en route – it left Macau last night.'

The Foreign Secretary breathed out slowly and raised his eye-brows as high as they would go. He seemed to have forgotten all about his special adviser waiting in the car on Pall Mall. 'Well, we need to act fast,' he said, stating the obvious once again. 'What d'you need from me?'

Good. This was exactly how Alex Matheson had hoped this would go. Easy on the histrionics, moving straight to practicalities. 'I need two things, if you don't mind, Foreign Secretary. We need the Taiwan authorities to impound her – that's *Ulysses Maiden* – the moment she comes into port and not let anyone disembark until we've found our collector onboard. We've already got our Taipei station chief working the ports register to see when she's due in.'

'OK, I think that's doable. What was the second thing?'

The Chief put down her avocado toast and took a sip of her orange juice. 'Look, I realize this is a big ask, but is there any chance we can get an interdiction at sea? Get an SF team onboard while she's still in international waters and take them by surprise? It's a Defence thing, obviously, but it has to start with you.'

'Hmm.' The Foreign Secretary was frowning as he played this one out in his head. 'It would be a lot simpler if we could just impound her in port.'

Alex Matheson held up her hand in what she hoped was a placatory gesture. 'Yes, I get that, but I'm going to level with you. If we wait that long, when we're dealing with the sort of people who've abducted her . . . well, there's no guarantee she'll still be alive by the time that ship reaches port.'

62

Macau Airport, China

THERE WERE FOUR of them in the room, apart from Luke. Two were wearing what looked like standard police uniforms: light blue shirts, red epaulettes, dark trousers. A third, who appeared to be in charge, was in a cheap suit. The fourth, who hadn't said a word so far, was wearing, incongruously, a tracksuit. He didn't take his eyes off Luke for a second.

From the departure lounge Luke had been hurried through a side door and was now being held in some kind of police cell, still on the airport premises. His phone, his boarding pass and what few possessions he had had on him had all been taken from him. He had been strip-searched – still with no explanation as to why he was being detained – then told to put on his clothes. He had protested, of course, quite forcefully. This, he told the men holding him, was no way to treat an innocent tourist, it was an outrage, and he demanded they release him immediately. His protests were ignored. And what about Jenny? Had she been taken too? He didn't think so but it had all happened so quickly he couldn't tell.

And now they were moving him into an adjacent room. Luke recognized the device the moment he saw it. He'd read about it in a Human Rights Watch report. Standard procedure apparently in certain Chinese police interrogations. It was called a 'tiger chair' and one look at it told him it was going to be painful. He didn't resist, there was no point – he was heavily outnumbered and they were armed, and besides, where would he run to? – but it still took the two policemen some effort to manoeuvre him into the iron-frame chair, then bolt the shackles into place on his wrists and ankles. Already he could feel the narrow metal bars of the chair cutting into the flesh of his buttocks and this was after just a few minutes. Christ, he'd heard of prisoners being kept in one of these things for months, their flesh turning red and raw where the metal chafed constantly against it.

So now here he was, immobilized, defenceless, caged like a wild animal, while the four of them sat on the other side of a trestle table and discussed him quietly amongst themselves. A single light bulb was directed straight at him, giving off so much heat Luke found himself sweating yet unable to move his hands to wipe away the droplets that trickled down his forehead and onto his cheeks. Surprising, he thought, how such a tiny thing as that could still be so intensely annoying. All part of their game, he told himself. Then at last someone spoke. It was the suit, the man from the Ministry of State Security.

'Christopher Blanford,' he repeated, reading out the name in Luke's passport that he held out in front of him.

'Yes,' Luke replied, 'that's me.'

'What is the nature of your business here in Macau?'

'No business, just pleasure,' Luke said, in as calm a voice as he could muster. 'We were on holiday in Hong Kong so we thought we'd come and have a look at Macau. You know, sightseeing? Tourism?' Always stick to the cover story and stay as close to the truth as possible. But now he was seriously worried. What did they have on him that had made them escalate straight to these drastic measures? Relations between London and Beijing were close to rock bottom but, still, for them to do this to a foreign national they must have a reason.

'Look,' he protested, with a confidence he didn't feel. 'I think you've made a mistake. We've not broken any of your laws. I insist you let me out of this thing and let me go right now. We were leaving Macau anyway.'

What happened next caught him off-guard. Without saying a word, Tracksuit Man walked around the table to where Luke was sitting, bolted into the tiger chair. His face blank and expressionless, he drew back his arm and gave Luke a stinging backhander to the temple. It hurt but Luke was damned if he'd give them the satisfaction of hearing him cry out. After all, he'd suffered a whole lot worse on other missions.

'I ask you again,' the State Security man said coldly. 'What is the nature of your business here?'

'Bloody hell!' exclaimed Luke, once again feigning righteous indignation. 'Is this how you treat every tourist who comes here? Just what is your *problem*?'

But inside his head the questions kept coming. How much did they know? Where is Jenny right now? Had Mr Lau from the port dobbed them in to the authorities? Or Miss Xinyi? Or the oleaginous Mr Rodrigues? Aside from the false name on his passport, State Security had nothing on him. He just had to keep a cool head and this would all be over soon.

The light in his face was so bright he didn't see it at first but then he realized that his interrogator had come around to sit on the table, his legs dangling casually in front of him, so that he was now uncomfortably close, invading Luke's personal space.

'Do you know what this is?' the man said, holding up a small brown bottle with a red screw top. It had a scarlet label with some Chinese writing on it but nothing in English to reveal its contents.

'It is concentrated chilli oil. Good for cooking.' Luke didn't like the direction this was taking one bit but he said nothing. Silently, the man unscrewed the top of the bottle and took a cautious sniff. He made a point of recoiling, screwing his eyes tight shut for a few seconds as he did so. Then, very carefully, almost like a scientist in a lab, he poured a small amount onto the back of Luke's shackled left hand. This time Luke couldn't help himself and he gasped at the pain. It felt as if someone had just touched a red-hot poker to his hand and already he could see the skin turning red raw.

'I ask you one last time,' the man said. 'What were you doing in Macau? Do not tell lies. We know about you.'

'I'm a tourist, for fuck's sake!' Luke shouted at the room. 'We came here for tourism. What part of that do you not understand?'

They must have rehearsed what came next because it all happened with terrifying speed and proficiency. At a nod from the suit the two policemen rushed up to Luke and forced his head back as far as it would go. He was then aware of a hand being placed over his mouth, it might have been Tracksuit Man's, he couldn't tell. The next thing he saw, horrifyingly close now, was that bottle of concentrated chilli oil coming into his field of vision.

The top was off and the State Security man in the suit was poised to pour it straight into his nostrils. And, for the first time, he was smiling.

63

Chelsea, London

WORRY, CONCERN, EVEN FEAR were etched onto the face of Rear Admiral Jonathan Bucknall. Early morning found him at the Royal Marsden, London's premier hospital for the diagnosis and treatment of cancer. But he was not the patient. Admiral Bucknall, a Navy man for nearly all his adult life and happily married for twenty-nine years, was at his wife's side, watching as she slid motionless beneath the MRI scanner. A sudden scare, no need to panic, just taking precautions. And then, after the consultation, they would take their minds off things with an early lunch in Chelsea. But things turned out rather differently.

He took the phone call from Northwood out in the narrow corridor, clamping the phone to his ear while nurses squeezed past his hunched figure. It was from CJO, the Chief of Joint Operations, with the news that he had been assigned Operational Commander for a highly sensitive mission in the South China Sea. He was needed back at Permanent Joint Headquarters immediately, Bucknall was told. There had been a development and this was an urgent instruction straight from the Secretary of State.

Bucknall didn't complain and neither did his wife. As a duty two-star officer on rotation at PJHQ, he reckoned he was lucky still to be in a job after all the recent cuts across the board. But on the hour-long car journey to Northwood he had to make a conscious effort to put his worries about his wife to one side and prepare himself for the job in hand. From the little he had been told on the phone he knew already this was going to be complicated. And quite possibly infested with Whitehall politics. Bucknall was to command an offshore maritime interdiction in the South China Sea. The sheer logistical challenge of organizing an operation of this nature thousands of miles away in a part of the world where Britain had almost no military footprint to speak of was daunting. HMS *Daring* and the rest of her Task Group were off-limits, he was told, not to be touched, already assigned a crucial role in providing a defensive screen along Taiwan's west coast.

This mission was separate, off-the-books, to be run in conjunction with the Directorate of Special Forces at Regent's Park Barracks and with input from SIS. Sensitive enough, in fact, that Number 10 wanted to be involved and that always brought its own sackload of problems, dealing with unelected special advisers and quixotic politicians who wanted all the glory if an op went well and who were nowhere to be seen when it didn't. Then there would be an entire team at the MoD, all reporting to the Vice Chief of the Defence Staff, currently a Royal Marine general with a background in Special Forces, all working on the policy angles, supposedly in tandem with the Royal Navy ops team at Northwood but often, in his experience, pulling in a completely different direction. The days of the Navy's Fleet Command in Portsmouth having control of an operation like this were long gone, but Fleet still needed to be 'the force generators', providing Northwood with whatever assets the Royal Navy could muster at short notice.

And what exactly did they have 'in theatre', that slightly ludicrous term for any part of the world where military operations were taking place? With *Daring* off-limits, the nearest Royal Navy facility was the British Defence Singapore Support Unit, more than fifteen hundred kilometres away in Singapore's Sembawang naval shipyard, at the wrong end of the South China Sea for this op. But the base was currently empty, with its Riven-class patrol vessel somewhere in the Java Sea, an asset that was anyway unsuitable for a hostile maritime intervention of this sort. There was a survey ship, HMS *Enterprise*, but she was in refit at Changi. That left only one option, the ageing Type 23 frigate HMS *Sutherland*, currently on a port call in Manila as part of the UK's new 'forward leaning' defence strategy.

'Has this thing got a name yet?' Bucknall asked, when he finally trotted up the stairs to the Ops Room at PJHQ and met the team he had been assigned.

'Sir?'

'I said, has this thing been given an operational codeword yet? I need to know what I've been put in charge of.'

'It has, Admiral, yes,' replied his chief of staff. 'It's Op Hamartia.'

'Hamartia? That can't be right. Are you sure?'

'I'll double check, sir, but, yes, that's what the computer has given us.'

A look of intense disapproval came over Rear Admiral Jonathan Bucknall. At Cambridge he had read Classics. His friends had called him 'Bookworm Bucknall'. He had forgotten most of what he'd learnt there but not everything.

And 'Hamartia', he remembered quite clearly, was a term introduced by Aristotle to mean 'error of judgement'.

64

Vauxhall Cross, London

ON THE THIRD FLOOR of the MI6 riverside building the China team was gathered round the table for the daily mid-morning review. When the unit was initially put together, at the direction of Felix Schauer, MI6's Director Critical, there had been some suggestion of calling it the 'China Crisis' team. But then one of the older members present had pointed out that there was actually an eighties band of exactly that name. A short and completely irrelevant discussion had followed, while the only person in the room over the age of fifty tried, unsuccessfully, to remember any of that band's songs. A lot had happened since then.

'So the rescue mission is in play,' said Jack Searle, the China desk head, sitting at the end of the table. 'Top marks to the Chief for getting it authorized so quickly and of course we all hope it's successful in freeing Hannah Slade so we can get our hands on the data we hope she was able to collect from Blue Sky.'

'And simply for Hannah's wellbeing,' Angela reminded him.

'Yes, yes, absolutely,' replied Searle. 'That goes without saying. But moving on, we can't afford to be sitting on our hands while we wait for this treasure trove of raw CX intel from inside the heart of China's war machine.' He wagged a finger theatrically. 'Effects team are already asking what else we can produce in short order that throws some light onto Beijing's intentions,' he went on. 'It looks like Washington is blindsided in this area and they're pretty much reliant on what we and some of our well-placed friends in the region can offer them.'

Unlike their American cousins, the CIA at Langley, MI6 did not have a vast team of in-house analysts. In Britain the analysis was done by the Joint Intelligence Committee in Whitehall or, if it was something technical and military, by Defence Intelligence out of RAF Wyton in Cambridgeshire. Smaller, leaner and more focused than the CIA, the Secret Intelligence Service tended to concentrate its efforts on stealing hostile countries' and organizations' secrets and getting agents into dangerous places where they could best access those secrets.

'So,' continued Jack Searle, 'let's run through exactly what we've got in play. Lucia, let's hear from you first.'

'Microchips,' replied the young secondee from Cheltenham. 'They've become an obsession for Beijing.'

'Go on.'

'We've been taking a close look at China's penetration efforts in the area of these semiconductors and, I have to say, they're certainly persistent. They seem to be stepping up their efforts to get people inside the loop at the industrial park at the Taiwan Semiconductor Manufacturing Company, the TSMC. Taipei station report a recent uptick in both phishing attempts and active recruitment. They're throwing everything at it. It's almost as if Beijing cares more about getting its hands on Taiwan's microchips than it does about taking the island.'

'Hmm. So where are we exactly on "Maiden Run"?' Jack again, his eyes shining brightly behind his Hammond & Dummer designer glasses.

'Er . . . did you mean "Maiden Voyage"? Our double agent inside TSMC, yes?' Lucia Freer was visibly uncomfortable at having to correct her boss in front of others. He seemed not to enjoy it either.

'Yes. That's the one,' he retorted, frowning.

'It's a bit sensitive right now,' she answered.

'Isn't it always? Why, what's the problem?'

'Well, thanks to some tech wizardry by Q Branch, he's started sending us some low- to medium-grade material. It was looking promising but now our Taiwanese friends have thrown a bit of a spanner in the works. Seems they want to cut out the middle man, which is us, and run him themselves.'

'Sounds reasonable to me,' Jack said. 'TSMC is their national asset after all. All right, let it play, and if it starts to look awkward we give Taipei what they want. Next item?'

A hand went up. Ginger hair, freckles, his voice a soft Scottish burr.

'Yes, Donald?'

'We've got the psych analysis back from Behavioural Science. If you recall, we asked them to work up a psych profile on each of the top members of the CCP's Politburo?'

'Good. I'll read that with interest if I ever get a moment. Just give me the headlines for now, will you?'

Donald shuffled some papers in front of him, ordering them, then re-ordering them before looking back up at Jack. 'Well, this won't come as a surprise but all the men at the top are becoming increasingly ideological and at the same time ever more isolated from the population. It probably started about the time of the Third Party Congress, the whole disastrous zero-Covid policy and their endless city lockdowns in 2022. But the net result is we've got a bunch of ageing, insular loyalists running the country who view reunification with Taiwan as some sort of messianic goal. It's become central to their belief in the survival of the Party.'

'Right. Any dissent? Any voices against?'

'There is one, yes. Or, rather, there *was* one. His name's Mingze Zhu. An economist by training. He's been warning them of the consequences if they make a move on Taiwan.'

'And?'

'He's out of the Politburo. Last we heard he's been banished to Urumchi in Xinjiang Province.' Donald sighed. 'Look, it really is a tight clique at the top of the CCP, a closed club, if you like. And when it comes to Taiwan there's not so much as a fag paper between each of them. They're speaking with one voice and they all seem to want to "take back" the island, whatever it costs them.'

'Umm, can I just raise one more thing?' Angela had her hand up, waiting to attract Jack's attention. 'You asked me to look more closely into Miss Xinyi Yip, remember? The lady who works for Rodrigues in Macau?'

'I did, that's right. What have you come up with?'

'To be honest, she's a bit of an enigma.'

'Come on, Angela, you know we don't like enigmas in this organization!' His face was smiling but his eyes were not.

'OK. If I had to put my money on it, I'd say she's a floater. She moves between organizations. We know she works for Rodrigues, ergo she has underworld connections. We know she *doesn't* work for the Canadians and she lied about that. Her tip about Lau, the man in Macau port, proved accurate, although we still don't know for certain if Hannah is on that ship.'

Jack Searle folded his hands together and rested them on the table. 'So what's your conclusion?'

'This is why I say she's an enigma. Because my conclusion is . . . Miss Xinyi is both things at once. She is useful, and she is dangerous.'

65

Macau Airport, China

TRAPPED AND SHACKLED in the hideous iron 'tiger chair', head forced back by two police goons and a hand clamped over his mouth, the only thing Luke could see was that little brown bottle of chilli oil hovering above his face. It had become, in this moment, the entire focus of his world. The State Security man was holding it above his nose, ever so lightly between his thumb and forefinger, so lightly that it looked to Luke as if he might drop the thing at any moment. He knew it was too late to say anything that would save him from the agonizing pain he was about to experience but, still, he tried to shout a protest. The hand on his mouth just clamped tighter.

Luke Carlton braced himself for the flaming inferno that was about to erupt inside his body. He squeezed his eyes tight shut and waited for the inevitable. Seconds went by. Nothing happened. He opened his eyes. The man with the chilli oil was gone, the policeman took his hand off his mouth and now he could hear voices coming through the open door to the holding cell. It sounded like an argument and he strained to hear what was being said but it was all in Chinese.

Suddenly the man from the Ministry of State Security was back. He had something in his hand but it wasn't the bottle of chilli oil: it was Luke's passport. He signalled to the policemen, who released their grip on Luke's head. Now someone was unlocking the clamps around his wrists and ankles.

'Mr Blanford.' The man handed him back his passport with something that looked almost like a bow. 'You are free to go. My officers will escort you to your flight. It has not yet departed.'

Luke stayed silent, not wanting to say anything that could somehow incriminate him, but his mind was in turmoil. Some-one, somehow, had said something in that adjacent room that had saved him from an excruciating fate. Luke was no stranger to torture. He had undergone some deeply unpleasant things during his time, like the agony of having a Colombian narco gang drill a hole through his foot. But chilli oil down the nostrils? No, he didn't think he could have coped with that. He would have told them absolutely everything if they'd inflicted that on him.

And so, as the uniformed policemen lifted him out of the tiger chair, he wondered who or what had saved him at the eleventh hour. It was as they set him on his feet and he shook his arms free that he heard a voice he recognized immediately. It was coming from the next-door room. It wasn't Jenny's. It was that of Miss Xinyi.

66

UK Joint Logistics Support Base, Duqm, Oman

EXACTLY 6600 KILOMETRES to the west of Manila, a group of eight tanned, heavily bearded and well-built men climbed into a pair of blacked-out minivans for the short journey to Duqm airfield, close to the shores of the Arabian Sea. Their Heckler & Koch HK-417 rifles, pistols and other equipment were concealed in weapons sacks and stashed beside them on the floor of the vehicles. They were casually dressed, no uniforms, just jeans, mountain boots and polo shirts.

There was little or no conversation. Each man was wrapped up in his own thoughts, most trying not to think of home as they did the mental prep for the mission to come. It wasn't as if maritime interdictions were something they hadn't trained for, *ad nauseam*, for months, working out of the Special Boat Service base at Poole in Dorset or, more often, off some remote, inhospitable, wind-battered stretch of the British coastline. But every mission carried its own risks and many of the older individuals knew of someone who had either returned with life-changing injuries or had not made it back at all.

Few people in Britain, or indeed in much of the Middle East, were even aware that the UK had a semi-permanent military base in Oman, conveniently situated on the Arabian Sea as a jumping-off point for operations in the Gulf and the Indian Ocean. Run by the MoD's Strategic Command, Duqm had opened in 2018 with a thirty-seven-year lease from the Sultanate of Oman. It had a deep-water port big enough to service Britain's two *Queen Elizabeth*-class aircraft carriers as well as its fleet of nuclear submarines. Inland from the port, Duqm had its own training area, shared with the Omanis, where the eight men of the SBS had just spent the last few weeks honing their desert-warfare skills. Things had changed since Afghanistan, a landlocked country where much of the SBS had spent more time operating in the rugged hills and barren valleys alongside Afghan Special Forces than they had at sea. But since the chaotic Western withdrawal from Kabul in the summer of 2021 those skills were at risk of being forgotten, hence the desert training.

The men now onboard the Airbus A400M transport aircraft still had sand in their beards and dust in their hair as, twenty minutes later, the plane took off into the wind, circling low over the Arabian Sea then heading almost due east, bound for a discreet corner of Manila's Ninoy Aquino International Airport. There were no other passengers onboard.

67

Taoyuan International Airport, Taipei

SANDBAGS. AND HESCO BASTION protective walls. Luke hadn't seen these defensive precautions against bomb blasts and incoming missiles since his days of operating out of Kandahar airfield in Afghanistan. Yet here they were, freshly erected at Taiwan's principal civilian airport. 'This is going to take a bit of getting used to,' he said.

'What – the sandbags and soldiers, you mean?' Jenny nodded towards the armed men in uniform flanking the walls on either side of the arrivals hall. She and Luke were barely off the plane and already they felt as if they had pitched up in a country preparing for war.

'That, yes. But also the facemasks. It's like we've just stepped back into the middle of the Covid pandemic.' He gestured towards the large number of passengers and airport staff wearing pale blue surgical masks. There were still some posters up on the walls warning people to keep two metres apart, and in the middle distance, just before Passport Control, two health officials were in full white protective suits and Perspex face shields, brandishing temperature monitors. The soldiers were masked up too, he noticed, all wearing camouflage clothing and carrying T91 assault rifles with a second full magazine of ammunition taped to the first to save time if something kicked off. He also noted that their boots looked rather too shiny and new to have spent much time outside barracks.

'Masks are a thing in this part of the world,' said Jenny. 'Remember, they had the SARS outbreak long before Covid came on the scene. People here just feel safer that way. Plus they tend to do as they're told. Unlike us bolshy Brits.'

They took their place in the queue at Immigration. Taiwan was considered a 'friendly nation' yet Luke and Jenny were coming in undeclared. That was the way Felix Schauer wanted it. Under the radar. No one else in the country needed to know they were there except the station chief in Taipei. Luke regarded Jenny as they shuffled forward, passports in hand. She was somehow managing to look remarkably fresh despite the long day they'd had already. But then again, he thought, she hadn't been threatened with chilli oil being poured into her nostrils.

'Anyway,' she said, glancing up at him with concern, 'how are you holding up, Luke? Do you want to talk about what happened back there in Macau?'

'Not really.' He shrugged. 'I'm more interested in knowing what the hell Miss Xinyi was doing in that police station at the airport. I'm still trying to process that. She vanished the moment I saw her and then I was being rushed onto the flight. I'm just relieved they didn't get to you as well. I suppose . . .' He stopped to bend down and peel off an adhesive baggage label that had stuck to the sole of his boot. '. . . I suppose I should be grateful to her. She fished me out of that mess. But it's made me think.' He lowered his voice as a space opened between them and the passenger in front. 'She's got to be, hasn't she?'

'Got to be what?'

'She's Chinese MSS. State Security. She has to be. Or else she has connections very high up in Beijing. I can't see how else she could pull rank over those thugs back at Macau airport. Come on, Jen, I only caught a glimpse of her but she was acting like she owned the place. It was almost like she was in charge.'

They had reached the passport counter and a masked immigration officer was beckoning them towards his booth.

'Purpose of visit?' he asked, when Luke approached.

It was such a routine question asked at any immigration booth around the world, yet it resounded in Luke's head and reminded him of why they were in Taiwan: *We're here to debrief one of our people as soon as she's rescued off a ship, someone who's carrying top-level intelligence that might just help stop this country getting invaded by China.*

'Tourism,' he replied. 'We're here for tourism. For two weeks.'

The man stamped his passport and waved him on.

It was dark by the time they emerged onto the taxi rank outside the terminal. Jenny approached the first of the yellow cabs that drew up alongside them but Luke stopped her.

'Always take the second or third,' he advised, 'in case it's a set-up and someone's waiting for you to come out. I know we're out of China but you can never be too careful.' She was looking at him questioningly but he steered them towards the next car in the queue. 'It's a rule I've stuck by after bitter experience, trust me.'

On the long, elevated expressway from the airport to their hotel in town they stared out of the window at the darkened, charmless outskirts of Taipei, each lost in their own thoughts. The traffic ahead was starting to back up as they joined a slow-moving queue near the capital's western suburbs. 'Checkpoint,' announced the driver. When they inched slowly forward Luke could see three concrete-filled oil drums that had been placed halfway across the road next to a sandbagged hut. Soldiers in rain capes with weapons slung over their shoulders were shining torches into cars and asking questions. When they pulled up alongside one he took a brief look at their blue-black British passports, peered into the cab at Luke and Jenny, then waved them on. As they passed through the checkpoint Luke noticed a lone Taiwanese soldier sitting on a swivel chair behind a machine-gun on a tripod. It reminded him of something he had once seen in a tunnel beneath the Demilitarized Zone, the

DMZ, that separates Communist North Korea from its democratic neighbour in the south. There too, a lone South Korean soldier had been sitting behind a machine-gun pointing down the tunnel towards the north, just in case the Communists should choose to invade underground. It was a symbolic gesture of defiance by a country that knew its army was far outnumbered by that of its neighbour, and, to Luke, there was an obvious parallel here with Taiwan and China.

The Service's Taipei station chief had booked them into a suitably nondescript and inexpensive hotel: the Blue World Nanjing. It was in a part of the city so bland and featureless the district didn't even have a name. Just a plate-glass skyscraper on the corner of an intersection where the traffic roared past at all hours and where the perpetual Taipei drizzle cloaked everything, including the lines of drooping Taiwanese national flags that stretched down the street, in a damp, depressing mist.

Checked in and up in his room, with Jenny across the corridor, Luke found he was unable to turn off his air-conditioning, set uncomfortably low at 14°C. Neither could he close the curtains, which meant he was treated to the glare of a neon hoarding across the road, which flashed up an advert for shampoo every few seconds. Wide awake now, he checked his phone once more for messages and found a new one from Angela at Vauxhall Cross: *You have meeting confirmed tomorrow. Useful contact. Meet at 0930 at Chiang Kai-shek Memorial, Dazhong Gate.*

It read a bit stilted compared to Angela's usual style but then, Luke thought, she's probably in a rush. He put his phone away, reached into the cupboard for an extra blanket, pulled it over his head and fell asleep within minutes.

68

Villamor Airbase, Manila

VILLAMOR AIRBASE HAD had plenty of high-profile visitors in recent years, from the US Secretary of State to a mass delivery of Chinese Sinovax vaccines to a contingent of US Marines offloading emergency aid in the aftermath of a destructive typhoon. Today's arrival was rather lower profile.

In the darkened hours before dawn the unmarked RAF Airbus A400M taxied slowly past the reinforced-concrete aircraft shelters and the blue-and-white-painted Officers' Club, coming to a halt in a discreet corner of this Philippines Air Force base. It was shared, as so often happens around the world, with the civilian facility of Ninoy Aquino International Airport. Unseen by all but a handful of security men from the President's office, the eight men of the Special Boat Service disembarked the aircraft and walked quickly into the hangar. They were large men, moving with a loose, easy gait despite the weapons sacks in their hands and the kitbags slung over their shoulders.

It had taken some frantic, last-minute diplomacy to get clearance from Manila for this deployment. The Philippines government had often been nervous of doing anything that might upset its giant Chinese neighbour. But recent clashes between the two countries' navies over a disputed reef in the South China Sea, known as the Second Thomas Shoal, had led to a hardening of attitudes in Manila. Within hours of that meeting in the Travellers Club between the Chief and the Foreign Secretary, frantic cables were winging their way back and forth between King Charles Street in Whitehall and the British Embassy on Manila's Upper McKinley Road. With some delicate diplomacy, agreement was reached after a solemn written undertaking was given by London that any action launched by the SBS unit from Philippines soil would be solely against organized criminal networks and not against a sovereign government in the region.

They were not long on the ground. Waiting on the tarmac just outside a hangar, the Royal Navy Merlin Mk 4 helicopter already had its rotors turning, ready to ferry the assault team out to sea. There, the ageing Type 23 frigate HMS *Sutherland* had slipped her moorings in Manila Bay and was now heading towards a point in the South China Sea midway between the coasts of Taiwan and the Philippines. The transfer time at Villamor airbase was tight. Just twenty minutes to get the whole squad and their kit off the plane from Oman, into the base facility for a quick 'comfort break' and to pick up some rations, then filing up the grey-painted back ramp into the gaping maw of the waiting chopper. Minutes later the pilot had the cyclic building to full pitch and they were lifting off northward, then angling left to follow the route of the C-4 highway, lit by streetlamps below, flying over the district of Pasay and out over the dark waves of Manila Bay.

MI6's Manila station chief and her deputy had been busy while the SBS team was inbound from Oman. Working in tandem with Defence Intelligence and Fleet Command, they had delved deeper into the ship suspected of holding Hannah Slade. It turned out there were at least four vessels around the globe going by the name MV *Ulysses Maiden*, mostly medium-sized bulk carriers, registered in Vietnam, Malaysia, Palau and Panama. But it was quickly apparent that the vessel now in transit from Macau to Taipei was up to no good. Every ocean-going ship was supposed to carry a tracker, a VHF broadcast transponder known as Automatic Identification System, or AIS, that revealed to the world exactly where the vessel was on the map. If a ship had its AIS switched *off*, it could mean only one of two things: either the system had broken down, which was rare, or more likely, that it was doing something secret, illegal or dangerous. Or all three.

The last message the Officer Commanding of the SBS detachment received on his phone, just before they all filed onto the Merlin, informed him that *Ulysses Maiden* had indeed switched off her AIS beacon. The suspicions already growing in Whitehall, PJHQ and Manila were now confirmed.

69

Taichung City, Taiwan

BO – THE MAN SOME CALLED Smiley Face – had not always been as he was today. For anyone who worked for him now it was hard to believe it, but he had once been a choirboy. Raised by a God-fearing Catholic family, part of the two per cent of Taiwan's population that follow the Roman Catholic faith, the young Bo had attended the Church of the Immaculate Conception in Taichung City. He said his prayers, went to Mass and did as he was told. Until he was fourteen and met Feng.

Feng's weathered face looked prematurely aged for a boy only just into his teens. It spoke of a hard life on the streets after escaping from an abusive orphanage. But Feng had something that impressed the young Bo: money. Lots of it. He would wait for his friend outside the church after choir practice, then take him for an ice cream at a place round the corner where the staff seemed strangely respectful to one so young, treating him and his guest like VIPs. Often he'd be wearing designer clothes, a brand new watch or showing his friend the latest gadget he'd acquired, without ever giving an entirely clear answer as to where these things had come from.

It was several weeks into their friendship when Feng showed him the packet wrapped in cellophane. The proposition was simple. Take this to the address I'm about to give you and there's a reward in it for you.

'What reward? Show me!' the young Bo had replied.

Feng had given him a knowing smile as if this was exactly what he had expected him to say. He put his hand into his pocket and took out an envelope. It had Bo's name written on it.

'Open it,' he said, and Bo did as he was told.

His fingers closed around three crisp banknotes, which he pulled out. 'Three hundred US dollars? This is for me?' He was incredulous.

The errand was straightforward. What Bo didn't know at the time was that this was just a test, set up by the people who controlled Feng. The packet contained nothing more exciting than a few grams of sugar. It was a simple initiation measure to see if he could follow orders and be discreet. Bo passed.

By the time he turned fifteen he had left the church and the choir far behind. By now he was making regular deliveries of methamphetamine to addresses all over town. Bo's own parents could see the change in him and they did not approve. They thought about sending him away to a strict academy, but a visit from a well-dressed man made it clear, in no uncertain terms, that this would not be advisable. 'Your son Bo,' he informed them, 'has a promising future in "a business enterprise",' and depriving him of that 'would not be good for anyone's health'. Scared and powerless to intervene, the couple watched their only son morph into a person they hardly recognized. He treated the family home like a hotel, coming and going at all hours, bringing girls back at two in the morning and indulging in noisy sex in his room without the slightest concern for his parents next door.

But Bo's carefree existence was about to come to an abrupt halt.

It should have been a simple delivery. His friend Feng was driving, Bo beside him in the passenger seat, and in the back, some new kid they were supposed to be mentoring. It was a late-night drop-off outside a club in the Dajia district of the city, not a part of town they knew well. They pulled up, as arranged, on the opposite side of the street from the club and in the darkened

240

space beyond the streetlamps. Nearly twenty minutes had elapsed and still there was no sign of the customer. It was time to go. Feng reached forward to put the key into the ignition. The figure appeared suddenly at the passenger-side window.

Later, Bo found he could remember every detail of what had happened that night: every moment, every word, every bloodstain. The figure at the window was that of a short, well-built man in his late twenties. He motioned for Bo to wind down his window. Bo shook his head. 'Let's go!' he shouted to Feng, but it was already too late. In the few seconds it had taken for their attention to be distracted someone else had crept unseen to the driver's side, another muscled figure, his face in shadow. He yanked open Feng's door and, with his left hand, he grabbed his ponytail, pulling his head back. In the same instant his right arm shot out, his hand holding a long, cut-throat razor. The next thing Bo saw was a crimson fountain of blood as it spurted in an arc from his friend's throat, splashing over the dashboard and windscreen.

Bo didn't hesitate. Driven by an instinctive, animal sense of survival, he shoved open his door, sending the man on his side sprawling onto the asphalt. Bo was out and running for his life before the man could pick himself up and recover. Bo had no idea where he was heading: all he knew was that he had to get away. He zigzagged through the empty, darkened streets, past the shuttered shops and the empty market stalls, nearly tripping over discarded packaging as he heard the clatter of running feet on wet pavements closing in on him from behind. There were at least two of them, maybe more, he couldn't tell. He never spared a thought for the kid in the back seat. Not his responsibility. He would just have to fend for himself.

Bo spent that night hiding in a large rubbish bin. He covered himself in discarded fast-food packaging as his pursuers went past, then tried to ignore the cockroaches that crawled all over him. Cockroaches didn't carry switchblade razors. At dawn he made his way back to his neighbourhood. He didn't go home. He went straight to the Collection Point, the place where he and

Feng were given their assignments, and their cellophane-wrapped packages. He asked – no, he demanded – to see the *dai lo*, the boss, and he was eventually granted a five-minute audience. He spared him no detail, he described the arc of blood that had jetted out from Feng's slit throat, he gave the best description he could of the man at the passenger-side door. The *dai lo* nodded. He seemed to know exactly who had done this. It was all part of a turf war and these boys had stumbled into it. He reached into his breast pocket, took out a roll of banknotes, peeled off ten and handed them to Bo.

'Give half of these to Feng's family and keep the rest for yourself,' he told him. 'Now, go.' Silently, Bo put five of the notes into his pocket and handed the rest back. This was not what he had come for.

The *dai lo* threw him a menacing glance. 'I told you to go. Why are you still here?' he said.

'I want a job. A proper one.'

The *dai lo* gave him one.

By the age of seventeen, Bo had become 'a cobra', a hitman, for the triad. The fact that he was still technically a child meant his targets often didn't see him coming until it was too late. And he was good at it too. A fast learner, he watched how others carried out their work, then developed his own subtle variations. But what everyone noticed was that whenever the hit went down, whether it was bullet or blade, Bo could be seen smiling.

He had become Smiley Face.

70

Onboard HMS Sutherland, *South China Sea*

THE OPS ROOM onboard *Sutherland* was even more cramped, crowded and noisy than that of her more modern equivalent, *Daring*. What they had in common was an incredible concentration of high-spec electronics and technology that, despite this Royal Navy frigate's near thirty years of age, gave her eyes and ears that reached far beyond the horizon.

Against one bulkhead there was a jumbled and confusing bank of screens and monitors, festooned with cables. On one screen streams of coordinates in red and on another a blue radar map showed the ship's position in relation to nearby vessels. Royal Navy operators in dark blue working dress sat at their consoles, sleeves rolled up, silver-coloured headphones clamped over their ears, eyes straining in concentration.

'So not a sign, then?'

'Nothing, ma'am.'

One of the two figures conversing near the operators was *Sutherland*'s Principal Warfare Officer, while the other was Commander Stewart, the Captain. They were standing at a console known as the general ops plot, staring at a computerized screen showing the positions of all the shipping in that part of the South China Sea out to a twenty-four-mile radius. *Sutherland*, like any modern warship, was carrying a suite of electronic support measures used to analyse any transmissions in the area, both radar and radio comms. As a form of passive surveillance, it allowed the ship to gain a bearing on a contact without giving away its own position.

The ship's intel cell had already received a full classified description of *Ulysses Maiden*, its predicted current position and direction of travel. The intel had been collated and sent by PJHQ at Northwood, a whole 10,600 kilometres away, with input from Defence Intelligence and Vauxhall Cross. Registered in the Pacific island nation of Palau, the suspect vessel was a 16,000-tonne carrier and, having been launched in 1997, she was nearly as old as *Sutherland*. Her tracking data showed that after departing the port of Macau she had headed out to sea on a north-easterly course, on a bearing of 55 degrees, in the direction of Taipei. But it was at just fifteen nautical miles out from the coast of the Chinese mainland that *Ulysses Maiden* had simply 'gone dark' by switching off her AIS tracker. Finding her without that, somewhere in the South China Sea, would be like hunting for the proverbial needle in a haystack.

Shortly before dawn, the Merlin, flying close to the limit of its range, had landed on *Sutherland*'s deck from Manila with its human cargo of Special Boat Service operatives. Buffeted by a headwind it took several seconds for the helicopter to settle on its wheels. The men from Poole were then given a hot meal, a bunk to grab some sleep on and a space to prep their weapons. At 0850 the Captain summoned the Assault Team Commander, Major Barrett, with her Principal Warfare Officer and the Merlin Flight Commander for a briefing in her cabin.

'Come in, come in, take a seat,' Commander Stewart greeted them briskly. 'Hope your team managed to get their heads down for a few hours, Major?'

'We did, thanks, ma'am.'

'Good. So let's just recap where we are. Our priority task right now is to locate, intercept and board *Ulysses Maiden*. We need to do this in international waters or it gets complicated.' She allowed herself a grim smile. 'And I, for one, do not intend to spend the

244

rest of this deployment sitting in the Taipei harbourmaster's office arguing with lawyers. My understanding – and please correct me if I'm wrong, Major – is that a high-value person, an illegally detained British national, is onboard that vessel and that your mission is to rescue them and bring them out alive. Is that correct?'

The SBS Major nodded, his face impassive. It still bore faint white lines along the temples from weeks of wearing wraparound sunglasses in the searing Omani deserts of Dhofar.

'But we have a problem, don't we?' She looked around the table, from one to another as she spoke. 'Because, as it turns out, *Ulysses Maiden* is a wrong 'un. They've gone and switched off their AIS tracker, so we know they don't want to be found, by us or by anyone. So, Tom . . .' She turned to her Principal Warfare Officer seated on her right. 'Take us through the options, will you?'

Lieutenant Commander Tom Carnell, an engineer by training, looked older than his years. Still in his thirties, his hair had started to recede even before he had completed the forty-five-week PWO course at HMS *Collingwood* in Hampshire. His brain positively bulged with technical data, like the integrated use of *Sutherland*'s weapons systems and sensors, her anti-submarine warfare capabilities and all her communications and electronic warfare systems. But this was the first time he had been tasked to hunt down a rogue vessel plying the South China Sea.

'Well, we're running blind here,' he began. '*Ulysses Maiden* went dark almost the moment she left Chinese territorial waters. So we have to start with the data we have, working from her last known position and course. Normally –' He was looking directly at the Assault Team Commander as he spoke. '– we would work on the basis of the furthest-on circles. That allows us to predict with some accuracy where a vessel is likely to be, based on an assumed speed – ten to twelve knots in this case – after a certain period of time. But *Ulysses Maiden*'s last-known position was several hundred nautical miles north-west of here so that spreads the arc of her possible current location too far and wide to predict with certainty.'

Commander Stewart watched the SBS Major's face for a reaction as this scenario was set out for his benefit. There was barely a flicker. 'Right,' she said crisply, glancing at her watch. 'Let's move on to courses of action.'

'Yes, ma'am,' replied Carnell. 'From where we are now, positioned north of Luzon, we should soon have a clear radar surface picture of every vessel heading towards the coast of Taiwan, from the smallest fishing boat to a Panamax tanker. Anything the size of *Ulysses Maiden* that's got its AIS switched off will automatically become an immediate vessel of interest.' He was now facing the ship's helicopter flight commander as he spoke. 'But I don't propose we sit passively waiting for her to pop up on our radar. We need to take proactive action.'

He looked to the Captain, who nodded for him to continue. 'So, I propose we deploy the Merlin on a schedule of spaced four-hour sorties on a hundred-mile radius, using her suite of electronic support measures to identify the target. I suspect we might have a better chance at night using infrared. Once the target is located it is then obviously the Captain's call to deploy Major Barrett to execute the mission. Any questions?'

71

South China Sea

HANNAH SLADE WAS ASLEEP when the door to her cabin burst open. Three masked men ran in. They came straight to her bunk and, without a word, lifted her off it and carried her out through the bulkhead door. She let out a scream of protest but quickly felt a hand placed over her mouth. Her nostrils registered an overpowering smell of diesel oil.

Was she being rescued? Was this the moment she had longed for ever since she had been overpowered by those two men in the Kowloon café? 'The Service never leaves an agent behind.' That was what they had kept telling her in all those clandestine park-bench meetings in Kensington Gardens. But she wasn't strictly an 'agent', was she? She was a collector. Maybe they secretly had different rules for people like her. All these thoughts had been playing on her mind as she lay there, trapped in that tiny prison of a cabin, while an unseen engine took her across the sea to an unknown destination.

She was being rushed down a corridor until they stopped by a bulkhead door and now someone was pulling a black hood over her head. This did not feel like a rescue. Hannah fought to control her rising panic. Then she remembered the gum. Her tongue curled upwards inside her mouth, flicking over the wad containing the chip she had repositioned earlier, behind her molars. It had been a close-run thing when it had fallen out: she had nearly swallowed it by accident, and she didn't want to think what that would entail. So now it was back in place, but for how much longer? She clamped her teeth together as she felt the men shift their position and start moving again. She heard the scrape and rasp of a metal bulkhead door being pulled open and now she was being carried down steps. One of the men holding her briefly lost his footing and they nearly dropped her. She emitted a silent scream inside her hood. Another stop and what sounded like another bulkhead door. A change in air pressure and a new sound: waves. It was daylight and even with the hood loosely covering her face she was aware of the warm, damp ocean air. Oh God, she thought, they're about to throw me overboard! She screamed once more and a voice shouted: 'Quiet! Be still! You are safe.'

Safe? That was the last thing Hannah felt. She could feel hands grabbing her as she was lifted up again and deposited roughly on something soft and rubbery. There was the sound of an outboard engine revving up, then a sudden lurch, which tipped her sideways. She was on a Zodiac, an inflatable speedboat. That much she knew. But she had absolutely no idea where they were taking her. Dr Hannah Slade, respected climate scientist from Imperial College London, and part-time covert collector for the Secret Intelligence Service, felt utterly helpless.

72

Taipei, Taiwan

NINE O'CLOCK IN the morning and the Taiwanese capital was shrouded, as it so often is, in a blanket of cloud and drizzle. The taxi deposited Luke and Jenny at a busy intersection where lines of motorcycles and their riders were waiting patiently for the lights to change. People were pulling on waterproofs as the drizzle turned to rain, falling in sheets from a sullen grey sky.

'This country is so well-behaved,' Luke said, 'I haven't seen one person jay-walking yet.'

'It's an obedient population,' Jenny replied, 'but it's still a democracy. They really don't want to be ruled by China and end up living under an autocracy in Beijing. Come on, let's cross.'

Luke had slept fitfully the night before. Angela's last message from VX had left him puzzled. *You have meeting confirmed tomorrow. Useful contact. Meet at 0930 at Chiang Kai-shek Memorial, Dazhong Gate.*

Angela was very thorough and she normally provided more detail than that, or at least a follow-up call. But when he'd tried to call her it had gone straight to voicemail and he didn't feel like leaving a message. When he'd shared his concerns with Jenny over breakfast she had dismissed them with a shrug.

'They're flat out on the China team, remember?' she told him. 'I don't suppose any of them are getting much sleep.'

Now they were walking into the Chiang Kai-shek Memorial Plaza as per Angela's instruction, and it was as if they had left the city behind them. All the ugly brown and grey buildings, the satellite dishes and the rush of traffic faded away amid the hushed serenity of the vast park. Luke pulled the peak of his baseball cap down to shield his face from the rain. They had stopped beside a guide plan on a plinth that showed the park's layout. A central open space was named 'Democracy Square' and two archways at the side marked 'The Gate of Great Piety' and 'The Gate of Great Loyalty'.

'Loyalty to whom, I wonder? Certainly not to Beijing,' remarked Luke, as they crossed the central plaza and headed as instructed towards the Gate of Great Loyalty.

'It's just an expression, Luke. It comes from the saying "Both loyalty and filial piety are attained."'

'Well, this is a monument to a man who ruled Taiwan with practically an iron fist. Chiang Kai-shek. Hardly the world's greatest democrat. In fact, they didn't have democracy here until 1996, did they?'

Jenny smiled in agreement. 'Point taken but you know what, Luke? It's their country. Let them tell it how they want to. Now, which way is this Dazhong Gate?'

He pointed towards a broad white-columned ceremonial archway. Rows of Taiwanese flags were planted every few metres amid the Chinese junipers in the surrounding gardens. The flags hung limp and forlorn in the rain and the place was all but deserted. Just a couple in bright yellow mackintoshes, and they were leaving. Luke checked his watch: 0925. 'We're right on time but I don't see anyone waiting, do you?' he said.

'Nope.'

'OK, let's split up,' he suggested. 'You stay close to the gate. I'll check around these gardens.' Luke set off at a brisk pace, quartering the area to be searched methodically in his head. He could see squirrels with dark grey fur and a rat-like appearance

250

foraging around a clump of pine trees while a lone pigeon considered its reflection in a puddle with its head to one side. He stopped to scan the empty benches as an old man in a facemask jogged slowly past ignoring him, his outsize shorts flapping against his bare knees. But of the contact there was no sign. He looked back towards Jenny, who was standing alone beneath the Gate of Great Loyalty.

'It's beautiful, isn't it?' The voice came from behind him and Luke whirled round, surprised and annoyed to be caught off-guard. It was the elderly jogger with the facemask. He peeled off the mask to reveal a face lined by the years. Tiny vertical grooves on his upper lip told of a lifetime of smoking and there was a deep scar next to one ear that did not look like the work of a careful surgeon.

'I believe you are looking for someone,' said the man. 'Perhaps I can help . . . Mr Blanford.'

Luke smiled and held out his hand and the man gave him a crushing handshake in return. So this was the contact Angela wanted them to meet. Nice move – a jogger. He hadn't seen that coming.

He signalled to Jenny, who hurried over. '*Zaoshang Hao*,' she greeted him in Mandarin. 'Good morning.'

The man pointed towards a bench in the shelter of an arch. 'Better out of the rain,' he said.

'So,' he began, once they were seated in a deserted colonnade at the far corner of the park. 'I understand you would like to meet my employers.'

My employers? Luke threw Jenny a glance. Angela hadn't mentioned anything about this. Her message had given the impression the man they were meeting was on the home team.

'Your employers?' Luke replied.

'Yes. I'm sorry if my English . . .'

'No, no, your English is fine,' Luke reassured him. 'It's just . . . could you tell us a little about your employers?'

He did not want to enquire immediately about Hannah – it went against everything they taught on the agent-running course

251

back at the Fort. But Luke had a rising sense there had been a major misunderstanding here.

'You will meet them, my employers. Today,' the man said, ignoring Luke's question. As he spoke, Luke noticed for the first time he had a blackened front tooth but he tried instead to focus on the eyes. 'Arrangements have been made,' he continued, folding his hands on his lap with an air of finality.

'OK, just hang on here,' Jenny interrupted. 'We haven't agreed to that yet. I think we need to establish some ground rules here. We'd like to choose the venue, if you don't mind.'

The man smiled. He seemed to Luke to be very sure of himself. 'You want information about your Miss Slade, yes? Then we will choose the venue.' He rose to his feet and began to replace the mask around his mouth. 'Please be at your hotel at three p.m. this afternoon. Don't bring anyone else.'

'Don't you need the address?' Luke said.

'We have the address,' he replied, his words slightly muffled now by his facemask. 'You are at the Blue World Nanjing.' He gave them a very slight bow, then broke into a stiff jog and was gone.

73

Chiashan Airbase, Hualien, Taiwan

HIDDEN FROM THE AIR, hidden from satellites, Taiwan's Chi-ashan airbase lay deep in granite-reinforced bunkers on the eastern side of the island. Officially, it had not even existed until a decision to go public was taken in the summer of 2022, around the time of a tense phone call between the US and Chinese presidents over the status of Taiwan. Even before the latest crisis, with the rhetoric from Beijing growing ever more strident on the need to 'return the renegade province to the motherland, by force if necessary', Taiwan had long been boosting its defences.

Taking a leaf from Iran's nuclear playbook, the self-governing island had decided it needed to squirrel away some of its most precious assets in a subterranean cave complex so well protected that not even a powerful bunker-busting bomb could reach them. And those assets included a wartime command and control centre and at least a hundred of the island's most advanced fighter jets: the F-16 Viper, capable of detecting and tracking targets in all weathers using its active scanned array radar.

Taiwan's Ministry of National Defence had taken an extremely close interest in the war in Ukraine, as had China. The parallels were clear to see: huge, nuclear-armed country invades much smaller neighbour in the expectation of a swift victory by overwhelming force of arms. Smaller country puts up surprisingly strong resistance, reinforced by recent years of help from the West. Taiwan did not intend to be caught napping by a surprise attack from the mainland.

Today was drill day and all across the base the sirens were blaring, from the sodium-lit tunnels to the massive earth revetments outside, designed to interrupt the path of an incoming missile. Pilots were scrambling for their planes, ground crews rushing to make final adjustments to the weapon loads, from Sidewinder air-to-air missiles to Harpoon anti-ship missiles to take on the enormous amphibious fleet China could be expected to send in the event of an actual invasion.

Standing alert and tense in his underground command centre, Air Force General Chun-chieh Yang and his staff watched the proceedings with mounting impatience. They had one eye on the video feeds coming in from all points on the base, some even from inside the F-16 cockpits, and one eye on the clock. The exercise completed, he addressed every member of the base using the PA system.

'You performed well today,' he told them, 'but not well enough. We are still nearly four minutes over time. And what does that mean? Let me tell you. It means four minutes more for the invaders to reach closer to our shores. Four more minutes for them to attack your families' homes, our farms, our cities. Those four minutes could mean all the difference if it comes to war. We don't want this war, of course not, none of us do. But, like our brothers and sisters in Ukraine, if it comes to war we will fight back with everything we have. Now go and clean up, take some rest, and think about how you can improve your performance. Because the fate of the republic, and our whole democracy, depends on you.'

74

Taipei Botanical Garden, Taiwan

MID-MORNING, AND THE RAIN had cleared as Luke and Jenny sat on a stone bench beside the lotus pond with the man from the British mission in Taipei. Great Mormon Swallowtail butterflies, each the size of a child's hand and coloured black, white and crimson, floated and glided amid the lush plants that grew all around. From the tree canopy above, a chorus of trills and squawks from tropical birds.

Britain doesn't have an embassy in Taiwan. The island may be self-governing but it is not recognized as an independent country. Instead, His Majesty's Government website lists its presence in Taiwan as 'The British Office in Taipei', which 'maintains and develops relations between the UK and Taiwan'. Even that was enough to annoy the men with lacquered hair and dark suits in Beijing, who raised furious complaints every time a Western government minister had the temerity to pay a visit to this rogue 'breakaway province'.

The official cover for Graham Leach, the man from the British Office, was 'First Secretary Economic'. He was also the MI6 station chief in Taipei. Since Taiwan was considered a friendly nation he was 'declared': the authorities had been told exactly who he was. A graduate in Mandarin and Oriental studies from SOAS,

London University, followed by a short service commission in the Intelligence Corps, this was Leach's first overseas posting. A cautious man by nature, he was acutely aware of the need to avoid hostile surveillance. When he suggested the botanical garden for their meeting he judged that to be the safest place to avoid the infiltrators and paid informants from Beijing who were known to be operating around the island and in the capital.

'So let me get this straight,' he began, and stopped almost immediately as a woman approached, wheeling a pram. 'As I understand it,' he resumed, once she was out of earshot, 'your contact has offered you a meeting this afternoon with the organization that seized Hannah Slade? And this has come via Angela?'

'That's correct,' Jenny said. Luke remembered that this wasn't the first time she and Leach had met. Jenny had told him she had sat on one of the recruitment boards at a country house in Buckinghamshire when Leach was joining the Service. She'd had misgivings about his rather stiff personality but his knowledge and understanding of China and its culture had impressed her.

'I'm not sure we need this, do we?' Leach wondered. 'I mean, if this maritime operation goes as planned, we should have Hannah safely back here and ready for the debrief within the next twenty-four hours. There'll be some arrests onboard, I believe. So I don't think it's sensible to risk sending you off to meet these people. The triads here are not as violent as they are on the mainland but, believe me, you still don't want to mess with them.'

Luke shifted himself along the bench into a patch of shade. The sun had finally broken through the cloud and shafts of light were lancing down through the glistening foliage where the butterflies still fluttered and flitted.

'That's rather a big "if", Graham,' Luke reminded him. 'This maritime interdiction is a bit of a fishing expedition. We don't even know for certain that Hannah is on that ship even if the Navy manage to find it in the middle of that ocean out there.' He gestured in a vaguely westerly direction. 'Let's look at it this way. The Service – or let's be specific here – the Chief has decided to send us all the way out here as it's a Tier One priority. If we can get Hannah off that ship and back here with whatever intel she's carrying, then great. Fantastic. That's the result we're all rooting for, right?' He could see Jenny was giving him an uncertain look, as if to say, 'Where are you going with this, Luke?' He pressed on. 'But I'm sure you'll remember the phrase "concurrent activity" from your days in uniform. I think it makes sense, unless you have strong objections, that we use this time here in Taiwan to find out all we can about the people who've taken Hannah, don't you? I mean, for a start, if this abduction is a Chinese state op, if it's MSS, then they have most definitely crossed a line.' Even as he said this, Luke was thinking of his close encounter with the chilli oil the day before, and the last-minute intervention of Miss Xinyi. 'More than that, Graham, it would mean Beijing has torn up the rule book. It would mean none of our officers is safe. Including you.'

He saw Leach wince visibly at this but the man recovered quickly. 'I doubt that,' Leach retorted. 'It would hardly make sense for Beijing to send Hannah Slade all the way here if they had her in their clutches in Macau. Can you tell me more about this "contact" Angela set you up with?' he asked. 'I'm just rather surprised she didn't let me know about this.'

'Let's call him the Jogger,' Jenny said. 'He gave very little away but I don't think he's too far up the food chain. Whoever he works for is not going to risk anyone valuable for a first contact. But I'm with Luke on this one. I think this is a stone we can't leave unturned, not when we've got a lead and a firm rendezvous.'

Leach looked down at his shoes. There was a long pause before he answered. 'All right,' he said. 'But we can't have you two walking into the lion's den unprotected. I really don't want to be calling Vauxhall to tell them we've now got two kidnapped officers held God-knows-where in this country of twenty-four million people.' He stood up abruptly. 'This doesn't leave us a lot of time, but I'm going to sort out what back-up I can. You won't see them but they'll be there, watching you. And don't worry, they're very proficient at this.'

75

US Seventh Fleet HQ, Yokosuka, Japan

IN TIMES GONE BY, the wardroom might have been thick with cigarette smoke, and probably that of a fair few cigars. Certainly more than one of the senior US naval officers gathered in the briefing room that day could have done with something, anything, to ease the tension, but this was the twenty-first century and, back in Washington, the Secretary of the Navy was known to have strict views when it came to smoking.

Midday, Tokyo time, and the men and women at the top of the chain of command of America's massive Seventh Fleet had assembled onboard the command ship, the USS *Blue Ridge*. It was moored inside the port, a short distance from where the US Navy's only permanent forward deployed aircraft carrier, the USS *Ronald Reagan*, was berthed when it came into port for maintenance. 'Forward deployed' meant that instead of sitting comfortably back Stateside or even at Pacific Fleet headquarters in Hawaii, Carrier Strike Group 5, as it was designated, was placed deliberately close to the action, should any develop. And now, given what was building in the Taiwan Strait, that looked like a dangerously real possibility. For years, Navy doctrine had maintained that there were only two places where that action might kick off: the Korean peninsula and the South China Sea.

With North Korea and China possessing nuclear weapons it was a doomsday scenario that nobody wanted to contemplate. But today they had to.

Addressing the room was the three-star Fleet Commander, Vice Admiral Dean B. Kovitz III. His deeply tanned and lined face contrasted with the crisp white of his short-sleeved shirt, topped by his admiral's gold epaulettes and emblazoned with rows of medals. Kovitz had been a lowly Navy ensign on his first operational tour during the Desert Storm campaign of 1991 but he had caught the eye of his superiors even then by leading the rescue of a downed Navy pilot whose F14 Tomcat had careered off the deck of a carrier.

Next to him was the *Blue Ridge*'s Commanding Officer and his Chief of Operations. Outside, beyond the gunmetal grey deck of the 19,000-tonne amphibious command ship, clouds gathered over the entrance to Tokyo Bay and from across the water came the long, mournful blast of a ship's horn as it entered one of the world's most economically prized waterways. It seemed a fitting backdrop for the gravity of the situation.

'I have today received orders,' announced the Vice Admiral, 'that the *Ronald Reagan* and its Carrier Strike Group are to deploy to a patrol vector just north of the Taiwan Strait. The Navy has also put this command on notice that as the unfolding situation with China develops – or deteriorates – we should expect to move to a deployment level in excess of ninety per cent of our assets.'

He took several paces to his left and pressed the clicker in his hand. A map came up on the wall screen showing Japan, Taiwan, the coast of China and the East China Sea that connected them all.

'I'm going to be straight with you,' he continued. 'This puts many of our surface ships within range of the PLA's coastal missile batteries, including their latest variants of hypersonic glide vehicles.' As he said these words a sound like a massed sigh, or perhaps a faint gust of wind, passed through the room. China's HGV missiles had become something you did not mention unless you had to in polite naval circles. Everyone in the room had read

259

the reports in the Navy journals about China's 'carrier killer' arsenal that could, it was boasted by Beijing, send the pride of the Seventh Fleet to the bottom of the ocean, along with all 5600 of her ship's company.

'For that reason we will be conducting a constant programme of evasive manoeuvres, making the passage of our vessels as unpredictable as possible. Appropriate active defence measures will also be taken. I should add that the Chief of Naval Operations and his staff are keeping this posture under continual review until further notice.'

The Vice Admiral, a former ballistic-missile submarine commander, was a shrewd judge of people and he was quick to read the atmosphere in the room. 'OK, so I'm seeing some anxious faces here today and, frankly, I'd think less of you if you were not concerned. As of right now, neither the Department of the Navy nor our combined intelligence community has reached a conclusion as to whether China's aggressive moves towards Taiwan are a bluff or whether this is the precursor to a full-scale invasion. But, ladies and gentlemen, we must be prepared for all eventualities.' Nods all round in the wardroom. 'What we do know is that the President has committed us to help defend Taiwan and this is where we should be proud to play our part. This is what you all trained for. It's what you joined the Navy for. As from today we are moving to a combat posture and this, ladies and gentlemen, is not a drill.'

76

Taiwan Strait

HANNAH SLADE DIDN'T know it but at noon that day she was less than fifty nautical miles from HMS *Sutherland* as it steamed northwards towards the coast of Taiwan. The Type 23 frigate's Merlin helicopter was deployed and airborne, scanning the ocean for a medium-sized 16,000-tonne commercial ship with its AIS beacon switched off.

But Hannah was not on that vessel.

Somewhere to the west of the southern tip of Taiwan, just outside the maritime boundary and at a latitude close to 22 degrees north, her captors had transferred her to a small and barely seaworthy fishing boat. Still hooded and with her wrists tied behind her, she was sitting on the heaving deck on a coil of thick ship's rope, beneath a metal cowling. At one point she could just make out the faint sound of a helicopter in the distance. The sound grew louder but she refused to get her hopes up. Before long it had faded away. The *Sutherland*'s Merlin had gone off to search elsewhere.

Two hours later the boat carrying Hannah joined dozens of similar vessels as they crowded into the fishing port of Keziliao, just north of the city of Kaohsiung. It attracted little interest from anyone as it moored beside the bustling quayside. No one paid any attention to the crew as they unloaded their small catch, contained in white crates, or the large roll of green tarpaulin that was swiftly hoisted onto the back of a small truck. With a crunch of gears, the vehicle turned and made its slow and inconspicuous way out of the port area. Soon it was on the road and heading for the Central Mountain Range.

77

Piccadilly, London W1

SIMON EUSTACE WAS a troubled man. This was the last thing he
needed. Whisked away to Whitehall in his ministerial car after
an early breakfast at the Cavalry and Guards Club, Britain's Secretary of State for Defence sat in the back of his 5-litre V8 Range
Rover Sentinel, glaring at his phone.

'That bloody man!' he exclaimed. His driver said nothing: he
knew better than to presume that any of his passenger's invec-
tives were meant for his ears. 'Why can't he mind his own
damned business?' Eustace muttered. 'As if we haven't got
enough on our hands already in the South China Sea.'

His ever-efficient SPAD had sent him the article from one of the
red-top tabloids he knew full well his boss would never be seen
reading otherwise. 'MP Enrages China' ran the headline. It seemed
that the Honourable Member of Parliament for south-east Norfolk, a noisy backbencher and a renowned hawk on China, had
infuriated the Chinese Embassy by what he had said the night
before in a speech to Britain's captains of industry, an event
attended by none other than the Chinese commercial attaché.

Britain, the MP had argued, should not be sitting on the fence
when it came to Taiwan. Quite the opposite, it should be rushing
to that island's defence in close coordination with our US and

Australian allies, forging a bond of like-minded liberal democracies. Did our principles in foreign policy not count for anything these days? he had asked. Was Britain so weakened by the years of Covid, Brexit and soaring government debt that it no longer had a voice in the world?

'For crying out loud, what does he *think* we're doing?' demanded Eustace to himself.

He read on. The response from the Chinese Embassy on London's Portland Place had been fast and furious: 'These wrongful words were a gross violation of the one-China principle agreed upon by all parties and which form the basis of UK–Chinese diplomatic relations,' thundered the posting on the Embassy's website. 'We strongly condemn this interference in China's internal affairs, which clearly undermines the peace and stability of the Taiwan Strait.

'Is this British politician so ignorant of geopolitics,' it went on, 'that he does not understand that the breakaway province of Taiwan is an inalienable part of China's territory? Politicians like him should study their history and understand that this is a matter for the Chinese people alone. Troublemakers,' it concluded, 'who dare to provoke the Chinese people are doomed to failure and will come to a no-good end. We will not take such provocations lying down.'

78

Taipei, Taiwan

THE SILVER-GREY MINIBUS that pulled up outside was emblazoned with a logo of white Mandarin characters above the words
'Big Emerald Tours'. Watching through the window of the hotel's
ground-floor coffee shop, Luke, who had once tried to teach himself some elementary Chinese, recognized the Chinese character
for 'big': a symbol of a stick man with outstretched arms. He also
noted the number plate, which, in accordance with Chinese culture, did not contain the number four as it is considered to be
unlucky. But, more importantly, he recognized the man behind
the wheel. It was their contact from that morning: the Jogger.

'Three p.m. He's bang on time,' Luke said to Jenny, as he put
down his half-drunk cup of coffee. Discreetly, when he reckoned
no one was looking, he took a photo of that number plate with
his phone and pinged it over to Graham Leach. Just a precaution.
Then they picked up their holdalls and walked out to the waiting
vehicle, Luke making a conscious effort not to scan the surrounding streets for their back-up team. 'Bring no one else,' the Jogger
had instructed them, and Luke certainly had no wish to spike
this endeavour before it had even begun.

Leach had worked fast since their meeting in the botanical gardens. After liaising with Security Section back at Vauxhall Cross

he had arranged for a team of two vetted and cleared former Special Forces NCOs, who had done the evasive-driving course, to shadow Luke and Jenny at a safe distance in an unremarkable car. One would be 'carrying', keeping a loaded sidearm in the glove compartment for insurance. Leach had also remotely installed Tracker27 on Jenny and Luke's phones, a GPS locating device powerful enough to beam out a signal from anywhere across the whole of Taiwan and complete with a panic button in case the proverbial hit the fan. But that, he reminded them, was a last resort as it would almost certainly mean having to call for help from the Taiwan police and that meant there would be a lot of explaining to do. This wouldn't be the first time MI6 had run into trouble conducting an undeclared op on friendly territory without first informing the authorities. And Taiwan was most definitely considered a UK ally in this part of the world, along with Japan and South Korea. But a decision had been taken in London that there was too much at stake. The risk of infiltration by either the criminal underworld or the agents of Beijing was simply too great. They'd kept the circle of trust as tight as possible, which meant that not even the FCDO man in charge of the British Office in Taipei had been informed as to what was about to go down.

The Jogger leapt down from the minibus, greeted Luke and Jenny with a toothy smile and ushered them into the vehicle as if they were day trippers, off for a picnic on the shores of the South China Sea. He told them his name was 'Win', which Luke thought rather ironic for someone who didn't look like one of life's winners, but this afternoon he was in a chatty, expansive mood. His English was better than Luke remembered.

'You see the Chelsea game this week?' he asked, as they moved out into the afternoon traffic, Luke and Jenny sitting in the row behind him. 'My team won. Two–nil. Look!' He twisted in his seat to show them what he was wearing. 'I even have a Chelsea shirt.' Watching a football match on television in the middle of such a perilous mission was about the last thing on Luke's wish list. But maybe there was an opportunity worth exploiting here.

'Congratulations,' he said amicably. 'By the way, where did you learn your English?'

'In London,' came the reply.

'Really? Whereabouts?' This was getting interesting. If he could get more details there might be something they could pass on to MI5 to see if the Security Service could track down this man's real identity and who he worked for.

'All over,' Win answered noncommittally, and that was it. He fell silent.

Win's minibus had those annoying black netting blinds on the windows that hid much of the view. What little Luke and Jenny could see hinted at rows of car-mechanic workshops, tyre-repair outfits and mobile-phone shops. Win pulled up suddenly outside a property sandwiched between two garages. It appeared to be a shop of some kind. He turned off the engine and held up a finger.

'One minute. Back in a moment,' he grunted. Then he was out of the door and walking over to the plate-glass-fronted shop.

'What do you think's going on here?' Luke said, peering through the netting. A girl was standing in the doorway dressed in a bikini that left little to the imagination. 'Is our jogging friend popping in there for a quick one?'

Jenny had her hand hooked around the edge of the window netting, moving it to one side for a better look. She shook her head. 'I know that's what it looks like but, no, this is a betel-nut shop. They have them all over Taiwan. That girl in the doorway is just a marketing gimmick to pull in the punters. Nothing happens in there. Or so I'm told.'

Seconds later, Win came back, clutching a bag of what Luke assumed must be betel nuts, along with two cans of iced coffee, which he offered to his passengers. They moved off, back into the Taipei traffic.

Win's manoeuvre, when it came, caught them off-guard. Without warning, he suddenly accelerated, then veered off the main road, turned sharply round a corner and sped down a side-street. Luke and Jenny found themselves hurled against the side of the minibus.

'Christ alive!' Luke shouted, struggling to regain his balance. 'What the hell are you doing?'

He heard Jenny gasp as he looked round for the handle on the sliding passenger door, but they were moving too fast. The next thing he knew the daylight had vanished as they raced down a ramp into an underground car park. Luke tried to rise from his seat to grab hold of the steering wheel, but Win's deliberately chaotic driving kept him off-balance, making it impossible. The tyres screeched as he threw the vehicle to left and right, hurtling past rows of parked cars, down another storey, then braked to a sudden stop and leapt out. The next moment, Win was yanking open the side door and all the bonhomie of earlier was gone as he ordered Luke and Jenny out.

Through the open minibus door Luke could see three muscular young men dressed in bomber jackets and dark glasses. They were standing, hands on hips, beside a large cardboard box. They looked as if they had been waiting for this moment. A flash caught Luke's eye. The car park's yellow sodium lights glinted off a steel blade: the largest of the three men held a vicious-looking meat cleaver, the sort of razor-sharp implement that waiters in the finer Chinese restaurants might use to tackle a Peking duck. As Luke and Jenny stepped down from the vehicle the man with the blade came forward and waved it in their faces. He was close enough for Luke to smell his breath.

'Take off your clothes,' he ordered. 'All of them.'

79

Vauxhall Cross, London

0830 IN LONDON and Angela Scott was back at her desk with a steaming cup of Earl Grey tea. No sugar, no milk: that was just the way she liked it. She had been at work since seven that morning, as she often was. Angela was exhausted – they all were on the China team. It had been four days since Hannah Slade, the collector, had been snatched in Hong Kong but the pressure from Cabinet Office for secret intelligence on China's intentions was mounting by the day. Whitehall wanted results and the Service was struggling to deliver.

The fact that Angela was often to be seen beavering away inside Vauxhall Cross late into the night would perhaps account for her perpetual pallor and the faint grey bags beneath her eyes. Unlike most of her fellow case officers, she had been single for as long as anyone could remember, and she seemed to have no social life that anyone was aware of. None of that mattered at work, of course. She was regarded by everyone there as a first-class case officer with an impeccable record. Which was why what followed was all the more shocking.

Her cup of tea was still too hot to drink when three people, all men, walked rapidly and purposefully up to her desk. They were all wearing white forensic gloves and carrying see-through evidence bags with seals. She recognized two as being from Security Section, an in-house division of MI6, often staffed by ex-policemen and soldiers – people whose job it was to keep officers and their agents safe and alive. The other identified himself to Angela as having been sent by the National Cyber Security Centre. They surrounded her and her workstation. The shortest of the three seemed to be the one in charge.

'Do not touch anything!' he barked. 'Angela Scott . . . I'm going to ask you to please stand up, move away from your desk and wait over there.' He pointed to the middle of the room. Angela sat there, open-mouthed.

'I'm sorry, is this an exercise?' she protested, her jaw thrust out defiantly. 'Because if it is, then it's highly inappropriate. We're in the middle of a live operation here. Who authorized you to come barging in like this?'

'I'm aware of that, ma'am, but, no, this is not an exercise. Would you please vacate your workstation.'

Slowly, Angela pushed back her chair, stood up and walked to the middle of the room as instructed. Her colleagues looked on, stunned.

'Yes, just there where you are now and please don't move,' the short man continued. 'Now, without touching anything, can you indicate to us exactly where your mobile phones, iPads, tablets or any other communication devices are located? And if any of them are sealed away in a locker, then I must ask you to give us the key.' Angela felt her composure return enough to ask what the hell was going on.

'Ma'am, all I am authorized to tell you is that your mobile phone has been compromised.'

'Compromised? By whom?'

'By hostile intelligence.'

'What?' she gasped, her hand instinctively going to her throat as if she could somehow choke off this source of bad news and make it go away. 'That's not possible, surely.'

'Not only possible, Ms Scott, but it's happened. There's been a data breach and it's come from your phone.'

As he spoke, his two colleagues began opening drawers and searching shelves as if she were a criminal suspect. It was then that a terrible thought struck her. 'Wait – I hope no one is suggesting it's deliberate on my part? I had no idea . . .'

The security officer folded his arms and stood looking at her. He might have been slightly shorter than she was but Angela found herself distinctly intimidated by him. She could feel her cheeks reddening with embarrassment.

'That's not for me to say, ma'am,' he replied at last. 'There'll be a full investigation, obviously, and we'll need to go through your complete digital history.'

'Am I being charged?' Unthinkable as it was, she had to ask the question.

'Again, I'm not at liberty to say. The Chief would prefer to keep this in-house for now, but I can't rule out Scotland Yard's SO15 being brought in to investigate.'

The Chief? How long had *she* known about this? Angela's shoulders slumped. Suddenly, like a sad ending to a film she had already watched, she could see her entire career disintegrating before her eyes. Everything she'd worked for, all those joyless evenings spent late in the office, the pre-dawn starts, the bank holidays and the weekends sacrificed, not to mention the nail-biting stress and angst of sending agents and case officers into hostile territory . . . and all for what? An ignominious exit from the job she loved, dismissed without honours. There would be no criminal prosecution, she was pretty sure about that. The Service had a visceral aversion to airing its dirty laundry in public.

In her own mind Angela knew she had done nothing with malicious intent and there was not one scintilla of evidence to indicate she had been cooperating with a foreign power. But the bar for digital security was set low right across government and as she stood there, helplessly watching these uninvited men rifle through her workstation, she recalled it wasn't so long ago that a home secretary had had to resign after sending an official document from her personal email account, breaching ministerial rules.

So Angela Scott, lifelong employee of Britain's Secret Intelligence Service, respected case officer and former station chief, knew exactly how this would go down from here. Even if she were exonerated – and she still wasn't clear what had happened, how or when – the pall of suspicion would never completely lift from her name. Even if she managed somehow to cling on to her job her security clearance would likely be downgraded. She would be lucky to be given some mind-numbing admin role with no access to sensitive intel.

And as she was escorted from the building that day, a slight tremble in her hand as she passed through the ground-floor foyer, flanked by security men, a voice in her head kept repeating the awful truth: 'It's finished, Angela. Your days in this organization are over.'

80

UK Defence Intelligence

To all UK Media Outlets:

INTELLIGENCE UPDATE

- China's People's Liberation Army (PLA) Navy has moved 11 warships into the Taiwan Strait. Satellite evidence reveals that commercial ships are being concentrated in ports close to the city of Xiamen. PLA Marines and Infantry units are being moved to bases along the coast opposite Taiwan.

- Taiwan's defence ministry said today it had detected 19 Chinese military aircraft flying inside its Air Defence Identification Zone (ADIZ). These include nuclear-capable strategic bombers, ground attack aircraft and electronic warfare aircraft.

- Taiwan's Ministry of National Defence further detected a surveillance balloon that had crossed the Taiwan Strait median line.

- The UK, in cooperation with its allies and partners in the region, condemns China's military build-up and warns against any attempt to threaten or invade the self-governing island of Taiwan by force.

81

NO ONE WHO worked at Vauxhall Cross had ever seen Felix Schauer without his trademark bow-tie. No one had ever seen him late, flustered or in any way losing his cool. Today MI6's Director Critical was all of those things.

'Into the conference room now. All of you,' he announced, rushing into the third-floor open-plan office used by the China team. 'Please,' he added, as an afterthought.

'I have just been informed by Security Section,' he began, barely waiting for the last person to take their seat, 'that the data breach on Angela's phone is even worse than we thought.' He shook his head and closed his eyes for a moment. To those around the table it was almost as if he were in physical pain. 'Yes, it's bad, very bad,' he continued, as if answering a question that no one had asked. 'Someone, and we don't yet know who, has been sending text messages from Angela's phone to Luke Carlton in Taiwan. Unbelievable, I know, but her phone was taken over by a malign operator. Zombified, I think they're calling it. We're still trying to find out exactly when this happened.'

He looked around the row of shocked faces.

'I want you all to stay calm,' he continued. No one had moved a muscle so far. 'But now we have to take some drastic action.

You!' He pointed at the fair-haired, freckled Scotsman in the room.

'Director?' Donald answered.

'I need you to contact Luke and Jenny once I've finished here . . . No, go and do it now. Tell them to ignore any instructions they received from what they will have presumed was Angela's device. Those orders will almost certainly lead them on a false trail . . .' He paused briefly, shaking his head from side to side in disbelief. 'Oh *mein Gott*. This is a disaster.'

Felix Schauer stayed talking for a few more minutes, going through some of the operational changes this would mean for the team. It was then that Donald returned, his face paler than ever. 'I've tried both their phones,' he said. 'They're switched off. So I contacted our station chief in Taipei instead.'

'Yes, good. Graham Leach. And?'

'They went to meet the opposition. It was at an unspecified location. He said the instruction came directly to them from Angela's phone.'

'Oh Christ,' exclaimed Schauer.

'One more thing,' Donald said. 'Leach arranged for them to be shadowed to the meeting but now the comms are down. It seems we've lost contact with Luke and Jenny.'

82

Army Command College, Nanjing, China

JIAN ZHANG STOOD stiffly to attention, head held high, chin out, eyes straight ahead, not a muscle moving. No longer a private first class, he was now a *xia shi* – a junior sergeant – having been promoted for his exemplary performance on manoeuvres so soon after his recovery from wounds incurred on the Lieyu Island operation. His training and his absolute loyalty to the Party demanded he stand to attention whenever there was a visit from a senior officer or, like today, a member of the Politburo. But Junior Sergeant Jian Zhang was silently bursting with pride. Not all the members of his unit had been selected for this briefing, but he had been told that he was one of the chosen few. He was about to be initiated into secrets that he could share with no one. To do so would be treachery, the penalty death. That, too, had been made very clear to him by his commanding officer.

There were thirty of them, each at attention beside a bare desk in the lecture room, and when the order came to take their seats they sat down as one: no scraping of chairs, no coughing or clearing of throats, just a silent air of expectation. The blinds were drawn, and the lights were turned out. And then the first image appeared on the screen in front of them. It showed a modern hi-tech industrial park, a place of clean lines and green lawns. It could have been any tech park from Palo Alto to Bangalore. But it was a lot closer to home than that.

'You have all been selected,' began the man from Beijing. His face in shadow, he stood to one side of the screen, flanked by a senior officer of the PLA, 'for your special qualities. These have been recognized and acknowledged by the Central Committee of the CCP. You will now be informed of the special mission that has been assigned to you when the time comes.' Had this been a Western audience, one composed of US or British servicemen and -women, for example, there might have been some subtle murmuring at this point, maybe the odd elbow jab in the ribs. But not in Lecture Room 32 in Army Command College that day. Only an obedient silence as they awaited their orders.

'The photograph you see,' continued the Politburo man, 'is of the Hsinchu Science Park. It is situated close to the city of Hsinchu in the north-west of the misguided and corrupt province of Taiwan. This place is of special interest to us for a reason. It is home to the TSMC. That stands for the Taiwan Semiconductor Manufacturing Company. It produces 90 per cent of the world's highest-quality semiconductors. These are the essential components for everything the world wants – mobile phones, computers, cars, planes – everything.' He paused to take a sip of water while the room waited.

'It had been hoped by all peace-loving nations,' resumed the visitor from Beijing, 'that the renegade province of Taiwan would come to its senses and quickly reunite with the motherland following their sham elections last January. By now such production facilities in Hsinchu should be serving the People's Republic. Instead, they are serving the greedy capitalist pockets of their imperialist masters in Washington. This must be corrected.' He paused again. A cadre of recruits jogged past outside the building with an accompanying chorus of martial chants. Now another image filled the screen, a photograph of a military airbase, with hardened shelters that had camouflage-patterned walls and grass-covered roofs. The silhouette of a city quivered in the heat beyond.

'Hsinchu airbase,' said the lecturer, 'is the first line of defence for the TSMC. A decision has been taken by the Central Committee that this is a cancer that must be cut out, an obstacle that must be neutralized, in order, when the time comes, for the People's Liberation Army to achieve its rightful goals. You –' He jabbed a finger towards his audience. '– you will be playing your part in this, in serving your great nation. In fact, you will be staking a place in history itself. Yes! Because following the appropriate rehearsals and training, your task will be to capture and take control of Hsinchu airbase. When they come to write the history of how the province of Taiwan was joyfully returned to the motherland it will not be forgotten that it was you, yes, all of you in this room, who struck the first blow, in enabling us to become the greatest economic power on Earth.' And now it was his turn to stand to attention, facing the front, as he shouted the slogan circulated by the Central Office of the CCP to mark the anniversary of the Chinese Communist Party.

'No person and no force can stop the march of the Chinese people towards better lives!'

And, as one, the lecture hall rose to its feet, Zhang included, bellowing the words as they erupted in applause.

83

Wimbledon Common, London

THE SERVICE CAR had deposited Angela Scott at the end of her street, and she was back in her Wimbledon flat by late morning. It had already been searched. The Service had made no secret about that, they just weren't telling her what, if anything, they had found. Suspended on full pay, pending the investigation, she was under strict instructions to speak to no one about her employment situation. If anyone asked what she was doing at home at that time on a weekday she was to say she was suffering from a mild cold. And what exactly, she wondered, as she looked around her silent kitchen, *was* she going to do now? Being at home during working hours was utterly alien to her, apart from those brief, unhappy months of lockdown during the pandemic. No, she shook her head, this wouldn't do. She needed to get out and clear her head.

Locking the front door behind her, she walked purposefully up Wimbledon Hill Road, past her favourite Japanese restaurant, along the quaint, curved high street of Wimbledon Village, where she couldn't afford to live, and out onto the open space of the common. She needed to make sense of what had just happened. A serious lapse of digital security. A breach in the Service's firewalls that had been traced back to her phone. OK, that was bad, she'd be the first to admit it. But what had she actually done wrong? No one had explained that to her. They had sent her home, like a disruptive schoolchild, banished from the community she had served for more than two decades. There were no charges – yet – but those grim-faced men from Security Section had made it abundantly clear: she was under suspicion of committing 'digital negligence', of allowing a hostile state to insert a 'worm' into the system.

She stopped by the pond and sat down on an empty bench. A light breeze was sending ripples across the dark surface of the water and ruffling the feathers of the two swans that paddled up to take a look at her. For a moment, she envied their innocence.

'*You*'re not being investigated by Security Section, are you?' she found herself saying to them, mouthing the words inside her head. '*You*'re not under suspicion of committing a gross error of negligence that's about to cost you your whole career. No, *you*'re doing just fine. Well, aren't you the lucky ones?' Seeing she had nothing to offer them, the swans soon lost interest in the woman on the bench and went on their serene way.

The few people out and about on Wimbledon Common this lunchtime all seemed to have dogs, calling after them in commanding, strident voices, and she almost wished she had one of her own to take her mind off other things. But, no, Angela was a cat person, always had been, always would be. Her own animal, Faustus, was twelve years old now and spent most of his time asleep on his favourite cushion or watching her, eyes half closed and barely moving.

She leant forward on the bench, put her head between her hands and closed her eyes. How, in God's name, could this have happened? She had lost count of the number of in-house digital safety courses she had attended – the Service was understandably obsessive when it came to this – so how could she have been so careless? Then she sat up, eyes wide and alert. Where would this leave Luke and Jenny? Still out in the field, trying desperately to track down the collector, Hannah Slade. With her phone taken from her, she had no means of contacting them. Now, she supposed, Luke's incoming calls would go straight to the duty officer at Central Collection Point where they'd be logged, transcribed and passed to someone else when it should be her, Angela, who was shepherding them through this mission.

Angela still had no idea, as she stood up and began to walk wearily back to her flat, that her phone had sent Luke and Jenny right into the path of danger.

84

Somewhere in Taiwan

CRAMPED, PAINFULLY UNCOMFORTABLE and most of all angry, Luke tried to shift his position as he felt himself jolted around in the dark with each movement of the vehicle. His hands tied, a gag around his mouth, he had been squashed into the boot of a car. He hoped Jenny was OK. And what had happened to Leach's back-up plan? He suspected he knew the answer. However good Leach thought his team were, these guys were one step ahead. They must have guessed there would be a tail and aimed off accordingly. Hence the swift vehicle change in the underground car park. In those brief but vital few seconds, while Win was getting out and hauling open the side door of the minibus, Luke had at least managed to activate the emergency Tracker27 button on his mobile and sound the alarm. To hell with the political consequences if some Foreign Office suit had to make a grovelling apology to the Taiwan authorities in the days ahead: his life and Jenny's were worth more than that. But that had been when they were already underground, at least two floors down, and he couldn't be sure that the signal had got through.

The vehicle wasn't the only thing that had been changed. The meat-cleaver trio were taking no chances. They had made him and Jenny take off everything, dump their clothes in the cardboard box and put on what looked like prison-issue grey tracksuits. Jenny, at least, had been allowed to change behind the van before he saw her bundled into a separate vehicle. There had been a moment when Luke had thought seriously about taking them on. But the odds were terrible: four of them, plus that wicked meat cleaver. Not good. They did not look like the kind of people who would have any qualms about using it. Perhaps if it had been just him, he might have had a go, but the thought of what they might do to Jenny restrained him. Both of them were now minus their phones with the precious GPS trackers. No surprises there. Their captors would have ditched those immediately. At this very moment, he thought, Leach is probably sending his driver off to look for them in some municipal rubbish dump on the edge of Taipei.

Eyes shut, hands cramped, Luke listened for tell-tale changes in the sound of the engine. When they stopped, he assumed at traffic lights, it told him they must still be in an urban area. Then later he could hear the call of birds, meaning they were now in the countryside. And then an audible shift in the pitch of the engine. They were climbing a gradient, making their way up a twisting vertiginous road. Again, his thoughts turned to Jenny. How was she coping with this? Jenny was tough but there would still be the inevitable gnawing fear of what lay in store for them at journey's end. And where was that? Taiwan was a mountainous island and it offered their abductors any number of possible hideouts.

A sudden lurch and the car stopped. Low voices and the crunch of feet on stony ground. A metallic rasp and someone was unlocking the boot. Luke braced himself. The first thing he took in, apart from the welcome rush of fresh air, was that it was twilight, which meant they must have been travelling for at least four hours. That, and the temperature. It was significantly cooler here than down in the city. So they must be somewhere in the Central Mountain Range. Muscular arms reached in and he was pulled out of the boot. Even in the half-light he recognized the three men in bomber jackets from the underground car park.

Behind them, smiling, was Win, 'the Jogger'. They hauled Luke to his feet and roughly untied the gag but his wrists remained bound behind his back. He spat on the ground, trying to rid himself of the bitter, metallic taste of motor oil and dust. He looked around. There was no sign of Jenny. He turned to Win, didn't raise his voice, didn't shout – no point up here in these mountains. He just needed to know straight away. 'Where is she, Win? What have you done with her?'

'Your partner? She is here. She is with us. She will join you presently.' And with that he flung his arms wide. 'Welcome to the mountains!'

Welcome to the mountains? Luke snorted in disbelief. Like this was some sort of organized package tour? 'What the fuck, Win?' he demanded, clenching and unclenching his hands behind him in an attempt to get the blood flowing. 'Was all this necessary?' He tipped his head towards the vehicle they had just brought him in.

Win spread his hands again in a gesture of apology. 'You must forgive us, but, yes, these were very necessary precautions,' he replied. 'The man you are both going to meet, he really doesn't like uninvited guests.'

'OK, I get that, but do you really need to keep my hands tied like this? I mean, come on, what am I going to do with them up here in these mountains?'

Win appeared to think about this for a few seconds and then spoke to the men in bomber jackets. Without a word, one stepped behind Luke and untied his wrists. As he rubbed them, he heard another vehicle approaching. It was an ordinary saloon, and as it pulled up next to them Luke once more made a mental note of the number plate, just one of the many details, however trivial, he was storing up in his memory banks.

The driver got out, walked round to the boot and unlocked it. The bomber-jacket crew went over and lifted out a bound and gagged figure. It was Jenny Li. This time Luke ignored the presence of the meat cleaver and went straight over, shoving them gently but firmly aside to reach her. He heard Win mutter something in Mandarin and the gang backed off.

'Jen!' He held her upright – she was swaying slightly. Even in the fading light he could see she was pale and probably in shock. 'Are you all right?' She nodded, as Luke fumbled with her gag.

'Please . . .' Win said, when he had finished. He indicated a path that led up a slope above the clearing where they were parked. 'This way.'

In silence they trudged uphill in single file, Win in front, then Luke and Jenny, the bomber-jacket crew behind. Luke's eyes had already adjusted to the near darkness but Jenny was having difficulties, walking unsteadily and stumbling. Her hands now free, she twice grabbed his arm to stop herself falling. As he walked, Luke scanned the vegetation beside the path, hunting for possible exit routes and hiding places they might come to need. But he had no illusions. If they had to make a break for it, the odds would be against them. Given the obsessive precautions these people had taken to get them there, he suspected there would be no one else around for miles and this gang would know the terrain by heart. And where would that leave Hannah Slade, the person they'd come all this way to try to find?

Through the gloom a small log cabin appeared, pine trees whispering and sighing in the chill evening breeze. 'This,' explained Win, like some hotel concierge, 'will be your accommodation during your stay with us.' He pushed open the door and stepped aside for Luke and Jenny to enter. A single room, with two single beds and a basic bathroom. A tin of biscuits, a few packets of crisps and canned soft drinks on a table to one side, spare blankets piled in the corner. On the windows: bars.

'When they are ready,' Win announced, 'they will call for you and I will escort you there myself.' Luke found his courtesy confusing. They had been abducted. Kidnapped. Held against their will by cleaver-wielding thugs. And yet this man was addressing them as if they were honoured guests.

'"There"? Where's "there"?' Jenny said, her voice little more than a whisper. Win ignored the question. Instead, he fished out an old-fashioned key and held it up with a smile.

'You must excuse me,' he said, with exaggerated politeness, 'but I have strict instructions. I hope you understand.' And with that he turned and walked out of the cabin, closing the door behind him. There was a loud click, and Luke knew they had just been locked in for the night.

85

Wimbledon, London

ANGELA SCOTT COULD not remember a time when she had felt so redundant, so utterly devoid of purpose. The Service hadn't exactly fired her, at least not yet, but she knew she was under a great black cloud of suspicion for this serious lapse in digital security and she was canny enough to know she needed to plan for the worst. What she needed now, she decided, was a fight-back plan. She was damned if she was going to roll over and accept her fate, not when she had done nothing wrong. Hostile surveillance was a fact of life in her business. You were told to take precautions and she had taken them. So how could this have happened? She still didn't know. She remembered an infamous incident some time ago when someone had ordered pizzas to be delivered to the office and a virus had been embedded in the pdf code for the pizzas, thereby compromising their phone. But that wasn't her. She was wise to that one and would never dream of doing such a thing.

With a shock Angela realized she didn't have a mobile phone any more – her devices were now being taken apart forensically by the Security people. When was the last time she had been without one? 1995? 1996? No, this wouldn't do. She walked down the hill towards Wimbledon station, went straight into

287

Phones4u and asked for the cheapest deal on offer. As she walked home to her flat thirty minutes later, armed with a new phone and a new number, she wondered how the Service would contact her now. They didn't know this new number and she decided she wasn't going to share it with them straight away. The decision sent a strange frisson of excitement down her spine. Safe, dependable Angela, who in more than twenty years had never done anything remotely underhand behind the Service's back, was crossing a line here.

She turned down her street just off Alexandra Road, walked up the three steps to her front door, put the key in the lock and let herself in. That was odd. The vase of red gladioli on the table in the hallway just inside the door was in a different place from where she'd left it this morning. Instantly alarm bells went off in her head. Her cleaner often moved the flowers but she wasn't due in until next week. And now she could see that the mail that had been posted through the letterbox was on a different part of the floor from where it usually landed. Angela noticed these things and knew straight away what they meant: someone had been inside her flat. With a sudden pang of fear, she realized that, quite possibly, they were still in there.

86

Vauxhall Cross, London

'CALL FOR YOU, CHIEF.'

The Chief of MI6's young, enthusiastic PA put his head around the door, as she had encouraged him to do. 'I run an open-door policy here, I hope you'll make use of that,' she had told him, on the day he was assigned to her private office.

'Who is it, Sean?'

'It's the Secretary of State for Defence, Chief.' He lowered his voice. 'He doesn't sound very happy.'

Alex Matheson had had thirty years of dealing with Whitehall mandarins of all moods and temperaments so she smiled wryly. She had had her fair share of bolshy ex-Guards officers in her time. 'Put him through, will you?' She took the call at her desk, looking out through the window at the perennial cranes and then beyond, across the river, at the clouds scudding over Pimlico.

'Simon . . . always a pleasure,' she soothed.

'Not today it isn't,' thundered the reply from the other end. Alex Matheson got up and quietly closed the door to her office. She had a feeling she knew what this was about.

'I'm going to do you the courtesy of getting this off my chest here and now, over this means, rather than raising it at the next COBRA, which will be embarrassing for all of us.'

'I'm listening, Simon.'

'I wanted you to be the first to know,' continued Simon Eustace, the Defence Secretary, 'that we have just wasted an inordinate amount of time and resources carrying out a maritime interdiction in the Taiwan Strait . . . on a *completely innocent cargo ship!*'

She had to hold the receiver away from her ear at this point, he was shouting at her so loudly down the line. But Alex Matheson's heart still sank at hearing these words. It was the news she had dreaded. They had failed to locate Hannah Slade onboard *Ulysses Maiden*.

'I understand this came from a meeting in person between you and the Foreign Secretary at the Travellers?' he continued, only marginally quieter.

'Yes, that's correct. My Service reports directly to him, as you know,' she replied evenly.

'Well, the next time you feel inclined to request an operation involving a Royal Navy frigate, a helicopter and eight of my Special Forces operators deploying to the other side of the world you might want to include me in that initial conversation. Because it was a complete fucking waste of everyone's time!' His voice was back up to full pitch again. 'Do you realize just how much I've already got on my plate in that part of the world without having to hive off precious resources to go looking for one of your cloak-and-dagger types – who isn't even onboard the bloody ship in question? Hmm? Not to mention that the two-star we put in charge of this op has now missed being present at a serious medical diagnosis for his wife.'

The Chief took his rudeness in her stride: there was no point responding in kind. She had bigger things to worry about now.

'Look, I'm very sorry for all the trouble you've gone to, Simon, and please pass my apologies to your general. I do appreciate your help. But, as I'm sure you know, this had the PM's full backing. So, yes, of course I promise to include you in any initial conversations another time. But if you want to take this further then I really think you'll have to take it up with Number Ten.'

'Oh, I will, Alex. I will.' The Defence Secretary hung up.

Alex Matheson let out a weary sigh and asked her PA to send in Felix Schauer.

'Take a seat, Felix,' she said, when he appeared in her doorway shortly afterwards. 'We've got rather a lot to discuss and I'm going to get straight to the point.' Her tone was brisk. This was going to be what was known in the business as 'an interview without coffee'.

'From where I'm sitting,' the MI6 Chief continued, 'this whole op is starting to descend into a complete bag of shit. We've lost track of Hannah Slade, we've lost track of Luke and Jenny, Angela's phone has been compromised by Beijing and we don't seem to be any closer to getting our hands on the intel we sent Hannah to retrieve. Meanwhile I've got Cabinet Office panting down the phone every two hours asking what we can give them on China. Not to mention a very angry Defence Secretary, who's just crossed me off his Christmas card list.' She gave him a hard stare. 'Felix . . . there's no getting round this, it's all on your watch. So I'm keen to hear what you plan to do about it.'

87

Wimbledon, London

IF ANGELA SCOTT had been thinking straight that afternoon she would have done the sensible thing: bolted out of her flat in a flash and called the police, the Service, or a neighbour, or just about anyone in fact. What, under normal circumstances, she would never have considered doing was something so rash as venturing inside her flat, alone and unprotected, knowing that an intruder might still be in there, biding their time, waiting for her. The Service had a protocol for this kind of situation, one more intended for officers posted overseas in hostile countries but, still, a global system designed to keep its personnel out of harm's way. But Angela's world had been turned upside down the moment those men from Security Section had come marching into her office that morning. Now, despite all her years of training and experience, something was urging her to confront whoever had dared to invade the sanctity of her home.

'Hello? Who's there?' Her words echoed back to her down the silent hallway, her voice sounding higher-pitched and more uncertain than she would have liked. No answer. She picked up an umbrella from its place beneath the clock, not exactly a lethal weapon but it gave her some comfort to hold it out in front of her. She turned the corner into the living room and stopped.

There were three of them sitting on her sofa. *Her* sofa. That already felt like a violation. All men, all appeared to be Chinese.

'Is it raining?' one asked, nodding at the umbrella, a faint smile playing around the corners of his mouth.

'What?' Angela had so many things going through her mind right now that the question threw her off-balance.

'Your umbrella. Is it raining outside?' he repeated. The two men sitting on either side of him stared at her impassively.

'I'm sorry,' she said, without any trace of apology, her anger having quickly overtaken her surprise, 'but who the hell are you and what are you doing in my flat? I've called the police, you know. They'll be here at any moment.'

'No, you haven't,' the man replied, his voice flat. He seemed very sure of himself. It was then that she noticed the laptop open on the low table in front of them. Her table, not theirs; they had no right to be placing anything there. He gestured for her to sit down. In her *own* damned living room. Angela felt as if she were attending an interview for a bank loan, not facing down three unknown intruders. And yet here she was, taking a seat, waiting to hear what the three strangers had to say. Admittedly they didn't look very threatening. There was no duct tape or plasticuffs that she could see, only the laptop, which remained facing away from her.

'I hope you will forgive this unorthodox approach,' the man continued. His English was perfect, she noted. He had clearly spent some time living in Britain and she wondered if he might even be a UK citizen. But whoever these people were, a voice in her head was shouting: Chinese Ministry of State Security.

'Well, not really, no,' she cut in. 'You still haven't told me who you are and why you've broken into my home like this.'

'Of course. We had no wish to alarm you but my associates and I ...' He gestured to his two silent accomplices. '... we needed to speak to you in private and, I think it's fair to say, we have your attention, yes?'

Angela folded her arms and said nothing. She was starting to regret not calling this in the moment she'd walked into the hallway. But it was a little late for that now.

293

'So,' said the man on the sofa, his tone almost convivial, 'we represent a company based in Hong Kong: Wing Oh Terminals. Perhaps you have heard of them? No? Well, you can google them after we leave.'

Good. That last phrase was a relief to hear.

'But, please,' he held up a hand, 'first, hear me out. Look . . .' He was leaning forward now, speaking in a low, confiding tone as if about to impart some great secret. '. . . we understand you are having some difficulties at work and we'd like to help. My principals at Wing Oh would like to make you an offer. There is great demand for someone of your skills and—'

'My skills? Sorry, but what are you talking about? I work at the Foreign Office. I'm a diplomat. What possible use could a Hong Kong company – what was it, Wing Ho Enterprises? – have for that? If this is a recruiting pitch, it's a pretty transparent one!'

The expression on his face didn't change as she said this but he exchanged a knowing glance with the man on his left, who nodded. Angela had the distinct impression they had already talked through in advance exactly how they thought she would react and she was about to hear a Plan B. She wasn't wrong.

'So. As you wish,' he said, but the smile had disappeared. 'We can play it that way, if you prefer.' He now turned the laptop so that, if she leant forward, she could read what was on the screen. 'On here, on this laptop – oh, and don't worry, we have it backed up – is every message you have sent and received from your phone, going back quite some time, I think.' Angela looked down at the screen and found it hard to disguise her horror. It was true. They had hacked into her phone and got everything.

'Awkward, isn't it?' he said, sounding almost sympathetic.

Angela shrugged, feigning nonchalance. 'Not really. My employers know my phone was hacked. There are no surprises there. So, is this your best shot?'

The man sighed as if all his attempts to be reasonable were being met with stubborn pig-headedness on her part.

'Angela, if I may call you that,' he resumed, 'for now, none of what is on this laptop is in the public domain. But it could be.

294

Very quickly. And meanwhile I think we must accept that your career as an intelligence officer at SIS is now over. They'll be investigating you as we speak. You'll be facing a commission of inquiry. You'll have to face a lot of questions and it won't be pleasant. And even if you are "forgiven", shall we say, you will never get your strap-level security clearance back. You are finished working for your government.'

He turned the laptop away from her and closed it with a snap.

'But it doesn't have to be all doom and gloom. There is a light at the end of this tunnel. We can offer you a very generous package. You will be living in a nice apartment in Hong Kong. In the mid-levels on the Peak. One with a proper view.' He cast a meaningful glance at the living-room window of Angela's flat. It looked out onto the grime-blackened wall of a local school. His eyes returned to Angela as he reached into his breast pocket and fished out a business card. With a flourish, he laid it on the table between them. 'You don't have to decide now. Take your time and call this number when you're ready. It might be the smartest decision you ever make.'

With that he got up, gave a slight bow and left, clutching the laptop, followed by his two silent accomplices.

88

Dasyueshan Mountain Forest, Taiwan

THEY CAME FOR Luke and Jenny just after 9 p.m.

A loud rap on the door of their log cabin, the sound of a key in the lock and a male voice that sounded distinctly American. Jenny looked up expectantly but Luke shook his head. 'Don't get your hopes up,' he told her, as he walked to the door. 'I doubt this is the cavalry coming to our rescue.'

When the door opened Luke was proved right. It was a big, fair-haired, broad-shouldered man sporting a tight-fitting khaki T-shirt despite the falling temperature. He wore brown mountain boots beneath baggy cargo trousers that supported a black holster and sidearm on his right thigh. Luke put him at around forty. In his meaty hands he cradled a Heckler & Koch MP7 submachine-pistol, a weapon he handled with the sort of casual ease acquired by someone who's spent an awful lot of their life in the company of powerful automatic firearms. Standing in the open doorway, Luke could just discern the outline of two more men behind him. They looked like locals.

'Ma'am, sir,' said the American, politely but firmly. 'They're ready for you. I'm here to escort you to your meeting.' He kept the barrel of his MP7 facing downwards but it was still clear that this was an order, not an invitation. And yet Luke hesitated.

There was something familiar about this big American, but he couldn't quite place it.

'Where's Win?' Jenny asked, as they filed out of the cabin. 'I thought he was escorting us?'

'I know no one of that name, ma'am,' came the curt reply. He pointed at the outline of a 4x4 parked beneath the pine trees. 'Will you step into the vehicle, please?'

Where had that come from? Luke wondered. It was a black Mercedes-Benz G-Class, more jeep than car. Somehow the gang had driven it up a track to the hut without him hearing it. For a few brief moments Luke had a chance to relish the cool night air tinged with the scent of pines, before the American prodded him and Jenny into the back of the 4x4. Well, at least we haven't been bundled into the boot this time. That's progress, Luke thought, as they drove off through the trees. But it seemed the gang were taking no chances. The big American sat in the front passenger seat, the MP7 automatic weapon wedged between his knees, while half turning to keep watch over his two passengers in the back. Luke could see he had unclipped the pistol from its thigh holster and this now lay on the dashboard, within easy reach of those rather large hands. The driver was a local. Glancing behind him, in the fading light Luke could just make out the other two men following in a second vehicle. This was not a scenario that seemed to offer up any easy means of escape.

Three kilometres, Luke estimated, or maybe four, but no more than that. That was how far he reckoned they'd driven from the log cabin when they pulled up in a clearing in the forest. The first thing he saw was what looked like the entrance to a temple of some sort, lit by yellow lanterns that hung from each corner of the roof, and in the pale golden light, a courtyard, and a large ceremonial bell beneath a stone archway emblazoned with Chinese characters. Several cars, all top-of-the-range SUVs, were parked on a flat, grassy space in front of the structure. And there, incongruously, to one side, a forklift truck beside bulky, tarpaulin-covered pallets. What's that about? Luke wondered. Are they stocking up supplies for something?

People milled about, some armed, some not. And now there was a new smell, mingling with the sweet scent of pine resin that came off the trees: incense.

'What is this place?' he asked, as the American pulled open one of the Merc's rear passenger doors. 'Is this a temple?' The American ignored his questions and steered them forward.

'Keep walking right ahead,' was all he could get out of the man. And yet he had met him before, Luke was sure of it now. He just couldn't place him.

With the American just a few paces behind them, the MP7 in his hands, Luke and Jenny walked as directed, heading straight for the stone archway. A few heads turned to stare, people stopping whatever they were doing to look at the two newcomers. Luke shivered. He had a sudden, uncomfortable feeling they were being led towards some sort of ritual sacrifice.

In silence he and Jenny walked through the archway. Glazed Buddhas to their left, a pair of stone lions on either side, dragon motifs everywhere, and a large bronze urn supporting a cluster of incense sticks. White smoke coiled up into the night sky. An elderly man, Chinese, wearing a red ankle-length robe, bowed deferentially and gestured for them to continue into the temple. Luke glanced at Jenny. She looked every bit as worried as he felt. He looked up – a row of red lanterns had been lit above a string of strips of red paper.

'Offerings to the gods,' Jenny whispered. 'I think this is a Taoist temple. Or at least that's what it's pretending to be.'

'OK, hold up right there, you two,' said the American. He turned to speak to one of the local guards.

Luke suddenly grabbed Jenny's arm. 'I don't believe it,' he hissed. 'I *knew* there was something about him – I'm certain I know this guy!'

'Stop it, Luke. That isn't funny.'

'No, Jen, I'm serious,' he said, keeping his voice low. 'We trained together in the US. I met him on a course at Fort Bragg. I remember his name . . . Tad something. Yes, Tad Kreutzer, that was it.'

The American had just finished talking to one of the local men when Luke coughed loudly and called a muffled 'Kreutzer'. The man whirled round, visibly surprised, a flicker of recognition in his eyes, but no handshake of welcome. Instead, a scowl, as he marched over to them.

'Luke Carlton, right?' He almost spat the words into his face. 'I do remember you. You were the Brit that flunked the special-weapons course at Bragg.'

Luke was about to point out that quite the opposite was true but Kreutzer had more to say. He glanced around him, then shook his head as he looked from Luke to Jenny. 'Oh, man,' he said. 'I don't know what the fuck you people are up to but, boy, have they got plans for you. Big mistake coming here.'

89

Hsinchu City, Taiwan

THE NEW ARRANGEMENT was doomed from the outset. Later, when the two officers from Taiwan's National Security Bureau would write up their reports, they admitted that, with hindsight, Chen Chin-lung had not, after all, been a suitable candidate as a double agent.

Incapable of concealing his nervousness, he had immediately aroused the suspicions of Lihua, his Chinese handler, within minutes of his arriving for their first meeting following his arrest. His hands trembled, his voice was different from last time and he kept avoiding eye contact. All these things she noticed because Lihua, which, of course, was not her real name, was a highly trained operative with China's Ministry of State Security. She already had four years of agent-running under her belt before she had even approached Chen for recruitment.

'Is everything all right?' she had asked him gently. 'Has something happened?' She was giving him a last chance to confess that he had been turned, but Chen had brushed it off, just as the two women from the NSB had taught him to. Troubles at home, he had explained, nothing more than that. Unfortunately for Chen, Lihua could see through him like a glass door. She knew at once what had happened. But she was canny enough to say nothing, not until she had sent off his latest packet of material to Beijing for analysis.

And the response that came back from MSS headquarters, at 100 Xiyuan in Beijing's Haidian District, confirmed her suspicions. The intelligence Chen had supplied was corrupted. As far as Beijing was concerned, he was now a burnt asset, and expendable. Lihua knew exactly what she needed to do.

So she brought forward their next meeting, greeting Chen with the warmest of smiles from her quiet corner in the café. She even touched his arm as they spoke, putting him at ease, softening him up for what was to follow. Lihua had arranged for a particularly attractive waitress to be working the tables that afternoon. She needed him to be distracted. And while the man's gaze was otherwise engaged, she acted. Chen Chin-lung never saw the thin stream of colourless liquid Lihua squirted into his cup or the tiny syringe being popped back into her purse. It was not until eighteen minutes later, having finished his drink, that he began to experience a tightness in the chest. He complained of a feeling of an unbearably heavy object pressing down on him. She observed him dispassionately as he clutched first his arms, then his throat. He appeared dizzy and short of breath. Chen Chin-lung gripped her wrist, his eyes wide with terror, his lips silently pleading for help. And Lihua was gentle and attentive in those final moments. With her free hand she stroked his hair, and mopped his sweating brow with a napkin from the table. It was only when he finally slumped forward, his eyes open but lifeless, that she called across the café for help. 'An ambulance!' she cried. 'I think this man's having a heart attack!'

Lihua – Pear Blossom – hurried outside for help. And did not return.

90

National Security Council, Whitehall, London

'UNBELIEVABLE. JUST UN-BLOODY-BELIEVABLE.'

The PM was glaring around the room as if all those present at this National Security Council meeting were somehow responsible for the bad news coming out of China. 'First, they fire a missile across the bows of our warship, then they land a load of troops on a Taiwanese island and murder the garrison there. Now this. Seventy-five million!' He was banging his fist on the table now. 'Seventy-five million malicious attempts, every *minute*, yes, every minute, by hackers to bring down the website of Taiwan's Foreign Ministry.' He looked down at the GCHQ briefing document in front of him. 'It's a wonder they haven't had a go at ours.'

'They have, PM. Several times,' interjected the Foreign Secretary, 'but we can usually thwart them. It's a game of cat-and-mouse. They keep having a go, we keep trying to stop them.'

'Right. Exactly.' The PM was now seemingly warming to his subject. 'And the point is . . .' He searched through the text on the briefing paper. '. . . the point is, that almost every single one of those malicious attempts, I'm told, originates in either China or Russia. What a surprise.'

He turned to face Hugh Rawlinson, sitting just to his right.

'Foreign Secretary, could you read out the text of the statement you're about to put out so everyone here is in the picture.'

'Yes, of course, PM.' He hunted around until he found his glasses, then began to scroll down the text on the tablet in front of him. 'Yes. Here we are, bear with me.' A short pause. 'So, this is what we plan to publish shortly. It will be on the FCDO website and sent out to the media: *"The UK and its G7 partners condemn in the strongest possible terms China's unacceptable military escalation in the vicinity of Taiwan. We have instructed our officials to summon the Chinese Ambassador to explain her country's actions. The United Kingdom and her allies impress upon China the urgent need to de-escalate tension in the region and to resolve any differences by peaceful means."'*

'Um ... could I just say something?' Zara Simmons, the National Security Adviser, a lady with few friends in Cabinet, was armed with a formidable temper and an uncanny ability to win arguments. Ergo, not to be messed with. 'Look,' she said, with an attempt at a smile, 'I think we all know, don't we, that the CCP in Beijing won't give a stuff about whatever statement we put out? We summon their ambassador here, they just summon ours over there. It's how it works, isn't it?'

'Where are you going with this, Zara?' said the PM. He looked tired.

'Well,' she began, using a cosy book-at-bedtime sort of voice, 'I would humbly suggest that the only way they're going to take any notice of us is when force meets force. We have to show resilience. We have to show strength! I would venture that we need to up our military presence in the region, dramatically and without delay.' It was no secret to anyone in the room that Zara Simmons, ever hawkish, had ambitions for the top job.

'Well, within reason,' observed Simon Eustace, the Defence Secretary.

'Excuse me?'

'I said, within reason,' he replied tersely. 'It's all very well sending *Daring* or the *Queen Elizabeth* strike group steaming through the South China Sea in peacetime on a freedom-of-navigation gig. It's quite another matter if China is firing off ballistic and cruise missiles. And just a little reality check here: China's Navy is the largest in the world. It's been growing by the same size as the French Navy every single year. So, I'm sorry, Zara, but I'm not prepared to take the risk of our warship being sent to the bottom of the Taiwan Strait by one of their hypersonic missiles. It's just not happening.'

'Which begs the question,' she countered, her sculpted eyebrows arching in disapproval, 'what is the point of having a navy at all?'

'All right, just hold your horses!' interrupted Admiral Seaton, the First Sea Lord, a youthful fifty-four-year-old with a string of operational tours under his belt. 'I think, PM, if I may interject here, this conversation is getting a bit out of hand. The Royal Navy is there to guarantee freedom of navigation on the high seas, wherever we are in the world, whether it's the Red Sea or the Taiwan Strait. We've been doing it since the time of Henry the Eighth and we're not about to shirk our duties now!'

'Right, that's enough of this,' concluded the PM. 'Simon, I am tasking you and Defence Intelligence to come up with a rapid assessment of where best we deploy our assets in theatre and in coordination with our US, Australia and Asia Pacific allies. I want to know the risks, the rewards and the likely response from Beijing. Oh, and, Hugh,' he turned to the Foreign Secretary, 'let's hold off on that statement. Zara is right. It's pointless.'

91

Dasyueshan Mountain Forest, Taiwan

LUKE WASN'T SURE what he expected the man at the top of this underworld organization to look like. In fact, he couldn't be sure it would be a man. It was just that there were very few women in high positions in the triads. Were they about to meet the archetypal Mr Big, reclining on an overstuffed couch, surrounded by bejewelled women and a slew of mobile phones, like some Colombian drug baron? Or would he be an ageing street thug, scarred and brutish, his face blued with clan tattoos? Or perhaps a tech obsessive in milk-bottle glasses, barely able to tear himself away from his bank of screens?

And this was a triad set-up they had walked into, no question. Who else would risk kidnapping two foreigners like this? Sure, the triads did things to each other on their own turf but abducting two Western visitors? From a country likely to make a big fuss? That was in a different league. So there must, he reasoned, be a good reason for it. They wanted a trade, he was certain. But for what?

Candles and incense flickered and bent in the breeze from outside as Luke and Jenny made their way deeper into the inner sanctum of the temple, prodded on at gunpoint by the taciturn Kreutzer. His words of warning were still ringing in Luke's ears.

'Have they got plans for you.' What plans? What had he meant by that?

Through an open doorway and into a low-ceilinged room, a single light shining in the corner. Luke took in their surroundings: a large wooden desk, a sofa, some chairs and cushions. Almost nothing in the way of decoration. From somewhere outside came the distinctive hum of a generator. Two men waited for them. One standing, one sitting. The man on his feet was, Luke assumed, another American or European. Clearly a bodyguard as he wielded an automatic weapon. But it was the man sitting behind the desk who drew Luke's attention. Was this the man they had been brought to meet?

A long silence. Nobody moved, nobody spoke. The man sat, half hidden, behind his desk, busy reading something and ignoring his visitors. Luke watched him closely. He was a stocky middle-aged man with shiny lacquered hair and glasses. Luke turned to Jenny, who gave a slight shrug. Kreutzer, he noticed, was standing almost to attention. How much, Luke wondered, was he being paid as a gun-for-hire for this gangster?

Kreutzer cleared his throat and the man looked up. His face broke into a sly smile as he put down his papers, took off his glasses, got up and came round the desk to greet them. He was short, Luke could see that now, which probably explained the cowboy boots with their stacked Cuban heels. Luke watched him approach. Tight-fitting jeans and a chequered shirt beneath an aviator's jacket with a sheepskin collar. A sort of faux-*Top Gun* look. His face was deeply tanned and lined, a slightly bulbous nose. His eyes, dark and glinting, appeared to be set back deep in his skull, and flickered constantly from side to side. The man put Luke in mind of the venomous pit viper he had once encountered while on secondment to Colombia's Special Forces.

'Lady . . . gentleman . . .' the man began. 'How very good of you to visit us! Please.' He gestured towards a couple of incongruous white plastic chairs, the sort you might find in a school assembly hall. 'Take a seat.'

'Thanks, we'd prefer to stand.' Luke was damned if he was

306

going to give this man the upper hand but then he felt something blunt and solid digging into his kidneys from behind. He turned his head and looked down to see the muzzle of Kreutzer's Heckler & Koch pressing into his side. He sat, as instructed.

'Let me introduce myself,' the man said, pulling up a chair and sitting down to face them. 'My name is Bo and you are my guests here.'

Bo? That set off alarm bells. Wasn't it the name of one of the handful of triad heads whom the China team back in London believed could have taken Hannah Slade? So they were in the right place, but in the wrong situation. Luke tried to catch Jenny's eye. He had read the brief on Bo. The man was practically a psychopath. He had people killed, in horrible ways, at the click of his fingers.

'Take some tea with me,' Bo continued affably. 'You like oolong tea? We grow it up here in the mountains, you know.' His English was good, but had a marked transatlantic accent. 'Yes,' he continued, eyes darting from Luke to Jenny. 'Oolong tea is much in demand . . . Rather like your Hannah Slade.'

92

Vauxhall Cross, London

'I'VE CALLED YOU all in here,' announced Jack Searle, head of the China team, 'because the Chief wants an update on exactly what intelligence we think is on the flash drive that Hannah *may* still have in her possession. I'm talking about the raw CX she went to collect from Blue Sky in that Hong Kong café before she got lifted.'

There were nine people around the table that afternoon and not a single Chinese among them. Jenny Li was a notable exception in the Service. Other than her it was proving too difficult to get candidates with Chinese backgrounds through the rigorous Developed Vetting process. Donald, the lone Scotsman on the team, raised his hand.

'Yes, Donald?'

'A question,' he began. 'I hate to mention the elephant in the room but we've now got three missing people on this operation and surely our priority needs to be tracking down Jenny and Luke. Plus, is there not a risk that this entire operation is compromised after Angela's phone was hacked?'

There was an audible intake of breath at the mention of Angela Scott. The chair she normally sat in was now occupied by someone else. Her absence was an awkward reminder that one of the most loyal, stalwart intelligence officers in the Service was also responsible for the worst breach of digital security anyone could remember.

'I hear you,' Searle retorted, 'I really do. But Security Section is taking care of all that and they're working closely with Taipei station. We're sending two officers out there to help with the search. Now, Lucia. Your thoughts, please.'

Still only in her twenties, the girl on secondment from GCHQ sometimes found it hard to believe how much responsibility she was being given so early on in her career. The next-youngest person in the room was twelve years her senior. Lucia was also sufficiently new to the job to be unfazed by the low pay and long hours.

'I've been going through the whole file on Op Boxer with Donald,' she said, 'and there's no question that Li Qiang Zhou was incredibly well-placed. So—'

'Please use his designated codename, Lucia, if you don't mind,' interrupted Searle. 'Thank you.'

Blushing, Lucia pressed on. 'Sorry. Blue Sky was incredibly well-placed inside the Central Military Commission. He had top-level clearance, which gave him access to practically everything. So what we've done is to produce a shortlist – well, a sort of shopping list, if you like – of all the areas of interest to us that he *could*, in theory, have placed on that drive.' She looked across at Donald. 'D'you want to . . .?'

'Yes, I can pick it up from here.' Donald nodded. 'Let's start with procurement.'

'No, let's not,' interrupted Jack Searle once more. 'We're in the middle of a full-blown crisis in the South China Sea. The Chief wants something she can take to the Joint Intelligence Committee. She's not going to want to hear about long-term future items, like procurement. Can we cut to the good stuff?'

Now it was Donald's turn to blush. 'Of course, Jack,' he said. 'So Blue Sky would have known exactly what the Central Committee's plans for Taiwan are. He would have known if they were serious about going for a full-on invasion or just bluffing in order

309

to put the squeeze on Taipei. He'd have known about timings, troop movements, requisitions of commercial shipping to get troops across the Strait. But most of all,' and here he exchanged a knowing glance with Lucia, 'he would have had access to the launch codes for their entire arsenal of hypersonic missiles.'

93

UK Defence Intelligence

UPDATE ON CHINA / SOUTH CHINA SEA

To all UK Media Outlets:

INTELLIGENCE UPDATE

- In the last 24 hours a Chinese Coastguard vessel operating more than 650 nautical miles off the coast of the People's Republic of China in an area of the South China Sea known as the Second Thomas Shoal has deliberately rammed a supply vessel belonging to the Philippines Navy.

- Two Filipino sailors were killed in the incident and six more have been hospitalized with injuries. The Chinese Ambassador has been summoned to the Foreign Ministry.

- China's Foreign Ministry maintains that moves by Chinese Coastguard were 'professional' at all times and it has lodged firm representations with Manila.

- HMS *Daring*, a Royal Navy Type 45 destroyer, along with accompanying vessels from the US and Australia, is currently deployed in a defensive posture in support of Taiwan and to help provide security in the South China Sea. No UK assets were involved in the incident.

311

94

Dasyueshan Mountain Forest, Taiwan

HANNAH SLADE . . . Bo's stating her name came like a thunderclap. She is 'much in demand', he just said. So there it was, their suspicions confirmed: Bo was holding the collector. But where? And why?

Luke lurched forward in his chair but Jenny got there first.

'Where is she?' she demanded. 'Are you holding her?'

Bo's eyes narrowed, and Luke saw the pit viper sizing up its prey. The triad leader wagged an admonishing finger at Jenny. He had remained seated while Luke and Jenny were half out of their chairs. He calmly exuded an air of suppressed malice and power.

'Not so fast, young lady,' came the reply. 'We will come to Miss Slade in a minute. Unless, of course, you have somewhere you need to be right now?' He cackled with laughter at his own joke, nodding and winking at the bodyguard who remained standing silently in the corner. Once he'd composed himself, he called out in Chinese. A hidden door behind Bo's desk that Luke hadn't seen until now opened, and a couple of local men came shuffling into the room, carrying two boxes.

'We thought,' Bo turned back to Luke and Jenny, 'you might like to have your own clothes back. They are in the first of these two boxes. We've brought them all the way here from Taipei for you. See, we are not the barbarians you might think we are!' Again, that strange, demonic cackle. 'But this is not the only gift we have brought you from the city . . .'

The man's smile remained, but Luke could see the hardness in his eyes.

'Do you not remember what my man Win told you about the importance of coming alone?' Bo said. 'No? Strange, as I believe he made our instructions very clear to you.'

Luke did remember. It was 'Don't bring anyone else' but Leach, the station chief in Taipei, had organized the discreet tail that was supposed to keep them safe. And now Luke had a sick feeling in the pit of his stomach. Everything about this gangster caused alarm bells to go off in his head.

'That wasn't very smart of your people,' Bo continued, as if reading Luke's mind. 'Taipei is our city. We spotted them straight away. Of course we did. They are not – were not – very good at their job. My son could have done better. Still, I am pleased to say they are still here with us.'

Luke and Jenny exchanged glances. Bo waved, and the two men scuttled over and placed the second box in front of them. It looked like the sort of thing motorcycle couriers used to transport urgent blood supplies.

'Please,' Bo gestured with his hand, 'open it.'

'We're not playing your games,' Luke said, folding his arms. 'If you're holding Hannah Slade, we'd like to negotiate her release and be on our way.'

Bo didn't reply. Instead he made a scolding sound, looked up at Kreutzer, who was standing behind them, and nodded. Luke felt the cold metal of the MP7's muzzle digging into the back of his neck. He shivered in spite of himself.

'Open it,' Bo repeated.

Slowly, reluctantly, Luke leant forward and released the catch on the top of the case.

The moment the lid sprang open the smell hit them. Luke recognized it from his time serving in Afghanistan. It was the smell

313

of an informant caught by the Taliban and left to rot in the sun after suffering an excruciating death. It was the smell of three Pashtun farmers they'd come across who had been strafed in error by a NATO warplane. It was the smell of decaying human flesh.

'Jenny, for God's sake, don't look!' Luke shouted, holding her back as he forced himself to glance inside. But his words and actions came too late. He heard her gasp in horror, and choke back a sob as she clasped her hand to her mouth. Throwing herself to the side of the room, she was violently and noisily sick; nobody stopped her.

Luke never did have the chance to meet the two protection officers Leach had arranged to shadow them and now he never would. Because staring up at him from the Styrofoam case were two severed human heads.

95

Wimbledon, London

FOR A FULL FIVE MINUTES after the men had left her flat Angela Scott sat, stunned and motionless. Although none of her three uninvited Chinese visitors had laid a finger on her, she still felt defiled. Doubly defiled, in fact, because not only had they broken into her home with apparent ease, they had also broken into her digital history and that, right now, was by far her biggest worry. When had this happened? How far back did it go? That was something the investigators would be probing into at this very minute at Vauxhall Cross. She squeezed her eyes shut as she remembered a text conversation that she probably should not have had on that phone – her three tormentors would doubtless have spotted it. It was what the Russians would call *kompromat* – compromising material used to blackmail a victim.

She stood up abruptly, went to the fridge, took out a carton and poured some milk for Faustus into a shallow saucer. Then she grabbed her keys and walked out of her flat. It seemed almost pointless locking the door behind her now but she did so anyway. She knew where she had to go and who she had to talk to, and it wasn't Vauxhall Cross. She didn't feel she could face talking to anyone there, not right now, not when they would be judging her. No, she needed some neutral, impartial advice before she made her next move.

Angela walked briskly to Wimbledon station and hailed the first cab in the waiting rank. 'Selkirk Road, please,' she instructed the cabbie. 'It's just opposite Tooting Market. Hang on, I'll find you the postcode.'

"S all right, love,' he replied, already pulling out into the traffic. 'I know where that is.'

The journey didn't take long in the mid-afternoon traffic, just a seven-minute ride – across the River Wandle, past St George's Hospital – and then they were pulling up in the quiet, mostly residential street with its solicitors' office, minimarket and rows of modest terraced houses. She paid by cash, walked up to the house with the black cat in the window and pressed the bell. As she waited outside on the doorstep, Angela looked back down the street, checking to see if anyone had followed her. They hadn't, but after what had just happened inside her flat she couldn't be too careful. Then, from the other side of the front door, she could hear the familiar slow, heavy footsteps followed by a gruff 'Who is it?' Without waiting for an answer, the voice's owner swung open the door.

Professor Charles Beck had been Angela's tutor at Oxford when she was studying for her Politics, Philosophy and Economics degree. He had coached her to a first but Charles Beck had been so much more than simply a brilliant teacher to Angela. Over the years she had come to value his consistently wise counsel, advice that went well beyond the field of academia. She trusted his opinions – and Angela didn't trust many people – such that when he eventually retired and moved to London to live close to his sister, she would often drop in on him. Her visits were often unannounced as he had a habit of ignoring the phone.

And here he stood now in the doorway, older, greyer than she remembered him from last time, but still sporting his trademark baggy green cardigan with those knobbly brown leather buttons, like polished conkers, and the pervasive smell of pipe tobacco that filled the hallway.

'You'll have to excuse the clutter,' he said, as they squeezed past several piles of magazines tied up with string. She remembered them being in exactly the same place the last time she'd popped round, and smiled.

Once he'd made them a pot of tea, they sat in his living room, his cat curling its tail around Angela's ankles and purring as she stroked its back.

'Now, then,' he said, leaning back in his armchair and pulling out a pouch of tobacco, some of which he started to tamp down in his pipe, 'how can I be of assistance?'

She told him everything, even recounting the scene with the grim-faced men from Security Section back in her office, painful as that was. Professor Beck was one of only three people to whom Angela had revealed where she worked. Another was her late mother, and the last had been an early romance that had once looked like being serious but had quickly gone south after her posting to Damascus.

'You know what I ought to be telling you, don't you?' There was a twinkle in his kind eyes that shone out from a face etched with spider veins and the signs of advancing age.

'Which is?'

'Walk out of here right this minute. Go straight back to Vauxhall Cross and tell them everything that's just happened. Anything other than that will put you in breach of the law. You do see that, don't you?'

'I do . . . It's just that . . .'

'Just that what?' He paused. 'For God's sake, Angela, you're not seriously thinking of going to Hong Kong? To sell your soul to Chinese intelligence and betray everything you've worked for?' He had put down his pipe now, unlit, and gripped his arthritic knees as he addressed her. 'Because I know you well enough to tell that you couldn't live with yourself if you did that. That is simply not you, Angela Scott.'

For a long moment they looked at each other, his eyebrow raised, before he broke the silence. 'Oh, hang on, I get it. There's more that you haven't told me, isn't there?'

Angela nodded.

'Well, you didn't come all this way just for me to give you half-arsed advice. Here . . .' He reached over with the teapot. 'Let me pour you a refill.'

'It's the *kompromat*,' she said at last. 'It's the text exchanges they will have found on my phone.'

'And?'

'Well, they are – how can I put this? – rather more intimate than I'd have liked.'

'I see.' There was silence as the retired professor resumed the careful business of stacking his pipe with tobacco. 'So, you've got a new chap. You haven't told me about this.'

'It's not a chap.'

He paused for a moment before going back to his pipe with a wry smile. 'Well, I'm happy for you,' he commented, 'but why is that a problem? This isn't the 1970s, thank God.'

Angela squeezed her eyes shut for a few seconds and passed a hand over her face. All her life, throughout her career, she had played by the rules. It seemed so grossly unfair that she now seemed to have fallen into this metaphorical bear trap.

'It's because of who she is,' she finally replied, her eyes popping open as she looked straight at him.

'And who might she be?' he gently prompted.

'I'd rather not give you the name, although I suppose it's going to come out anyway if I don't take up the Hong Kong offer. We've only been seeing each other for a few months.'

'Well?'

Angela paused. Another silence. 'All right. If you must know, it's Sandra James, the Prime Minister's spokesperson. She practically runs Number Ten. Beijing's going to have a field day with this.'

96

Dasyueshan Mountain Forest, Taiwan

KREUTZER AND ANOTHER MAN drove them back from the temple to their cabin. Jenny Li was next to Luke, bolt upright, her face pale. He reached out and tried to offer her some comfort but she shook him off and now she sat in the back of the 4x4, staring dead ahead.

Luke tried to push the memory of those two severed heads to the back of his mind. He couldn't. His brain was in overdrive, striving to work up an escape plan. But he was angry too. What the hell was Angela doing, sending them off into such an incredibly dangerous situation? Luke wasn't afraid of risk. He would never have made it through twelve years in the Royal Marines if he had been. But he liked to know the odds and what resources he had on his side. Meeting up with the triad suspected of holding Hannah Slade had turned out to be a gamble that had now gone horribly wrong. He had one thought now and one thought alone: they had to get out of here alive.

Outside the log cabin, just visible through the forest canopy, a crescent moon had risen. Kreutzer jumped out, unlocked the rear doors and escorted them to the cabin. Luke noted his finger rested lightly on the trigger guard of his machine-pistol. The American opened the door, calling to the other man to wait, and then he did something unexpected. He followed Luke and Jenny inside, went over to the washbasin and ran the tap. The water came out in fitful splutters but it was enough to hide anything about to be said.

'Take a seat,' Kreutzer commanded, with a wave of the Heckler & Koch. Luke took a good look at the man now. He was markedly older and greyer than he remembered him from that special-weapons course in the States. But he was still in shape, Luke gave him that. They lowered themselves onto the nearest of the two single beds while Kreutzer remained standing. Luke threw a glance at Jenny. He could see she was in a state of shock. Jenny Li knew more about the grisly effects of chemical and biological weapons than anyone else in the Service, and she'd more than proved herself in the field on numerous operations. But the sight of those putrefying heads, well, that was more than anyone should have to see. He wondered what possible reassurance he could offer her now, given their situation.

'OK, I'm going to level with you two,' Kreutzer said. 'You're both in deep shit.'

'You don't say,' Luke retorted, but Kreutzer held up a hand.

'Save it,' he said. 'I know you want to give me a heap of grief about working for this guy but right now that's not going to help you. Listen.' He paused in mid-sentence and seemed to be weighing up just how much to tell them. 'Your friend Hannah, she's got a price on her head. A lot of people want her.'

'Who does exactly?' Luke interrupted. 'And where is she?'

Again Kreutzer held up his hand, tilting his head to one side. Running water gurgled in the background. 'I'm not done yet, Carlton,' he said. 'So, our Mr Bo up there in the temple, well, he just loves a deal and he's going to sell her to the highest bidder. Now, as for you two—' He stopped suddenly. There was a loud knocking at the door and Kreutzer moved to answer it.

'Wait!' said Jenny, leaping up from the bed. 'Tell us. What were you about to say?'

But Kreutzer was already at the door and unlocking it. He turned round, shook his head, and said quietly, 'You'll find out soon enough.'

320

97

East China Sea

MIDNIGHT ON THE OCEAN, around a hundred nautical miles south-west of the city of Yokohama. Under a clear starlit sky the bow of the massive USS *Ronald Reagan* split the waves in two as it forged onwards towards the Taiwan Strait. At more than a hundred thousand tonnes this nuclear-powered aircraft carrier was one of the largest ships in the US Navy, part of one of America's eleven Carrier Strike Groups. Embarked on her deck were seven squadrons of F/A-18 Super Hornet fighter bombers, as well as its normal complement of helicopters and Grumman Hawkeye tactical airborne early-warning aircraft. Flanking her on either side was a protective armada of ten surface ships, comprising guided missile cruisers and destroyers. And unseen, beneath the surface, a nuclear-powered submarine equipped with Tomahawk cruise missiles capable of hitting targets more than fifteen hundred kilometres away.

Onboard the Carrier Strike Group 5's flagship, the USS *Blue Ridge*, Vice Admiral Dean B. Kovitz III, the Commander, was still up on the bridge. He was preparing to retire to his cabin for the night when a junior officer came in, apologized for the interruption and handed him a signal.

'It's from Norfolk, Virginia, sir,' he explained.

321

'Thank you. I can see that,' the Admiral replied drily, as he read the message contents. He frowned. 'Go and wake the Executive Officer,' he ordered. 'Tell him I need him up here. Now.'

He looked again at the signal. From US Fleet Forces Command, it was both succinct and ominous. *Major increase in PLA Navy surface fleet activity detected out of Ningbo*, it read. *China Eastern District missile batteries moved to Alert State 1.*

98

Vauxhall Cross, London

ANGELA SCOTT FELT she was swimming against the tide. It was just past 5.30 p.m. and everyone was streaming out of central London while she was going in the opposite direction, heading up to Vauxhall by train. But it wasn't the reverse commuting that was making her feel like an anomaly, an outsider among all these homebound professionals. Right now, she didn't even know if she still had a job. But she was following orders, just as she had always done, and the order had been hand-delivered to her door. It was waiting for her on the mat when she let herself back into her flat, following her visit to her old tutor.

Be at VX Reception at 1815, it read. *Discuss this with no one. Security will meet you there.* And that was it. No 'hope you're holding up', no 'realize this must be a difficult time for you'. Just a sign-off from Felix Schauer, MI6's Director Critical. Well, at least she would know where she was with Felix. If she was about to be fired he'd give it to her straight, no dressing things up in management gobbledygook. And Angela had been doing a lot of thinking. She had a plan. She was not going to take all this lying down. She was damn well going to fight her corner, even take them to a tribunal if need be. But whatever happened, Angela Scott was not going to let some unintentional digital error torpedo the career for which she had worked all her adult life. No, she was going to fight this one all the way. But first she would have to tell them what had just happened.

They were waiting for her just inside the lobby of that great sandstone and green building at the southern end of Vauxhall Bridge. Angela Scott said nothing as the men from Security Section escorted her to one of the windowless, featureless rooms on the ground floor. Nothing on the table in there save a glass of water and a notepad. So, that was a clue right away. She gave a rueful smile. This was to be an interview without coffee. Without uttering a word, the security men left the room, closing the door behind them.

Angela sat in silence as the clock ticked quietly on the wall behind her. On the floors above, she thought, the men and women of the Secret Intelligence Service were going about their normal business, closing down their workstations for the night, fetching their coats, retrieving items from their personal lockers in the corridor, making plans for the evening. But not her. Instead, she felt like the twenty-two-year-old Angela Scott, still in her last year at university, waiting nervously for that first tentative interview in Carlton Gardens, the encounter with the recruiting officer that would eventually open the doors to all her years as a case officer and station chief.

The door opened. She was expecting it to be Felix Schauer who walked through it, but it wasn't. It was Alex Matheson. Angela saw the MI6 Chief turn to the Security men outside the door and heard, 'Thank you, you can leave us now.'

The door closed and Alex held out her hand. She held Angela's for a few seconds longer than was necessary. Was this to soften her up for the blow to come? Put her off her guard? Angela said nothing, just nodded in greeting.

'How are you bearing up, Angela?' Alex enquired, taking a seat opposite her and pushing away the notepad. 'You've been through it rather, haven't you?' Her face bore an expression of genuine concern. Angela shrugged. She was giving nothing away until she knew where she stood.

324

'So look, Angela, I'm going to give you the bad news first. Brace yourself.'

They're firing me, I knew it. She opened her mouth to say something but the Chief hadn't finished.

'And no, we're not letting you go, in case that's what you thought I was about to say. No. But something very serious has occurred. Something that does involve you directly.'

'The hack,' Angela said. 'I do know about the Chinese hack. Security Section told me this morning. There's something I need to tell you.'

The Chief held up a hand. 'You don't know the extent of it, I'm afraid.'

'Oh?' Angela swallowed hard. Could this possibly get any worse?

'The operation you were working on with Luke Carlton and Jenny Li . . .'

'Op Boxer.'

'Yes. Well . . .' Alex Matheson sighed and looked down at her lap. She almost seemed to be in pain as she spoke. 'The fact is, Angela, that a message they received from your phone has sent them off to meet an extremely violent triad boss in Taiwan and—'

'Wait – from *my* phone? But I never sent them any such message . . .' Angela felt suddenly very cold.

'No, we know you didn't. That didn't take us long to establish. Someone else did, someone who had control of your phone. But the net result, Angela, is that Luke and Jenny have now gone missing, presumed kidnapped.'

Angela felt the colour drain from her face. 'What?' she gasped. 'How can you be so sure?'

The MI6 Chief sat back in her chair and looked directly at Angela. 'They've lost contact with Taipei station. Luke had a tracker on him but of course whoever's got them soon disposed of that. So now we've got one collector and two case officers missing somewhere on an island that is very possibly about to be invaded by mainland China. All of which means . . .'

The Chief let the words hang in the air for a second or two.

'All of which means that you, Angela, are the last person I can afford to let go right now. Yes, you will have to attend the advanced cyber security course at Cheltenham, I'm afraid. Think of it as your penance, if you will. But in the meantime, I need you back on the China team ASAP.'

Angela felt a warm surge of relief ripple through her but she had something to get off her chest. 'Um . . . Chief. There's something you need to know.'

'Go on.'

'When I got home today I found three Chinese nationals – at least I assume they were Chinese nationals – waiting for me.'

The Chief eyed her across the table; she didn't react.

'They'd broken in somehow,' Angela continued. 'But that's not all. They had a laptop that contained all my WhatsApp messages. Nothing classified but some very personal stuff on there. They made me an offer to come and work in Hong Kong. Well, it was really more a case of blackmail, to be honest. I think we should hand this to Thames House, don't you? They're clearly MSS operating on UK soil.'

The Chief paused before breaking into a broad smile. Angela felt perplexed and confused – this was not the reaction she'd expected. 'That,' said Alex Matheson, as she rose from the table, 'will not be necessary. I'm afraid I arranged that little charade. I was the one who sent them. Those men were from T Branch. They work for us. You won't have come across them before and you won't be seeing them again. Just think of it as a test, Angela. And you passed. Welcome back!'

99

Dasyueshan Mountain Forest, Taiwan

DAWN IN THE Central Mountains, the lush green spine that runs the length of Taiwan, from north to south, and Luke Carlton was already up. It wasn't the chorus of birdsong that woke him, or the faint grey light that crept in through the windows of the cabin. No, it was his mind, racing with myriad questions. And how exactly they were going to get out of this place alive was only one of them.

He looked over to the bed next to his. Jenny Li seemed to be asleep. Quietly, so as not to wake her, Luke got down on the floor in the small space beside his bed. Forty press-ups on his knuckles, enough to get his juices flowing for the day ahead. 'Start switching on, Carlton,' he could hear an imaginary voice telling him. He remembered the PTIs, the physical training instructors, down at the Commando Training Centre in Devon, yelling abuse and encouragement in the same breath. Pushing himself physically, Luke found, helped focus his mind.

So it was Bo's organization that had seized Hannah Slade and she clearly had a price on her head. But where were they holding her? Surely not on that cargo ship, *Ulysses Maiden*. If everyone was doing their job in the UK she must have been raided at sea by now. And yet Bo was speaking about Hannah with the irritating complacency of a man who thinks he holds all the cards.

Then a shadow moved across the window. Footsteps outside the door and the sound of a key turning in the lock. A voice, a command: 'Two minutes, people. Grab your things. Mr Bo wants to see you.' It was Kreutzer.

Luke could hear an engine revving. Jenny, who had seemed moments earlier to be fast asleep, was up and out of the door before him. In the chill mountain air, a thick mist had descended on the forest and drifted eerily between the pines. Good cover for a getaway, he noted. Kreutzer was waiting by the Mercedes 4x4. He appeared to be making no concessions to the cold and wore a white T-shirt.

It was as Kreutzer held open the rear door of the 4x4 for them to get in that Luke noticed the hunting knife strapped to the American's calf. He recognized it as a Yarborough, a knife that held a special place in the heritage of US Special Operations. Awarded to the elite few who passed the gruelling selection process for the Green Berets, each had a unique serial number engraved on the blade. So Kreutzer had passed 'Selection'. Luke momentarily wondered what could have driven the American to turn his back on all that to work for a psychopathic triad boss in Taiwan. But he was more interested in something else. The knife and its sheath had a quick-release catch.

Luke felt every lurch of the vehicle as they drove, faster than usual, along the track up to the temple. Jenny, still silent, swayed and bumped against him. Ghostly shapes loomed out of the mist, gnarled branches reaching out as if to grab the passing vehicle before receding behind it. The moment they arrived at the temple, he sensed a difference from the night before. The atmosphere had changed. If anything, it felt even more sinister. No more people casually milling around. Now there was a reception committee waiting for them. Rows of people, all local, were lined up on either side of the entrance, bowing and smiling, forming a funnel through which he and Jenny were now expected to walk. And they were all wearing white – what was that about?

'This doesn't look good,' he murmured to Jenny. 'Isn't white supposed to be the colour of death over here?'

She mumbled something back but so quietly he didn't catch it. From inside the temple, the sound of a bell tolling and everywhere the intoxicating smell of incense. Then from far away down in the valley he heard the rhythmic thud of rotor blades. Luke looked up sharply. A search helicopter? A rescue attempt? But the sound faded almost as soon as it had begun. No one paid it any attention.

Side by side, Luke and Jenny entered the temple, past the stone lions with their gaping jaws, Kreutzer right behind them. If this was it, if this was the endgame, then Luke vowed he would go down fighting, and do his damnedest to let Jenny get away alive. Then came the clapping, a slow, rhythmic sound – the sort of mocking sound an audience makes when it doesn't think much of a stand-up comic. They rounded a corner and there was Bo, dressed in a white silk robe tied at the waist with a crimson sash. Around his forehead, a white headband, inscribed with Chinese characters. Luke knew he should probably keep his mouth shut, but he had to say something.

'You've been watching too many Bond films.' He gestured at the whole theatrical scene around them. 'Don't get me wrong, I love what you've done with the place, but can we just get on with the negotiation?'

'Luke!' Jenny hissed. 'Show some respect!' But he shrugged. He wanted this jumped-up crime boss to know he wasn't afraid.

Luke caught the momentary flash of anger in Bo's eyes but when he spoke the triad boss's tone was calm, almost genial. 'You will have guessed by now,' he told them, 'that I am not a religious man. This place . . .' Bo gestured dismissively towards the temple walls and the coils of incense spiralling up to the ceiling. '. . . it serves my purposes. But for others, it is a spiritual place. And we must all play our part.' He patted his white robe and sash, then pointed. 'Even you.'

Bo held Luke's gaze as he raised his right hand. Was this a prearranged signal for something? Oh God, Luke thought, please not more severed heads. He moved a step closer to Jenny in readiness.

More men shuffled into the inner sanctum of the temple, this time carrying a large wooden crate on poles. Setting it down in the centre of the room, a crowbar was produced and the lid prised off with a creak and a sudden snap. Luke had a terrible feeling they were about to see the headless body of Graham Leach, the SIS station chief in Taipei. He heard Jenny's sharp intake of breath but he forced himself to watch as Bo's people reached into the crate . . . and gently lifted out a living human figure.

It was Hannah Slade.

100

UK Defence Intelligence, RAF Wyton

DEEP IN THE BOWELS of the Pathfinder building, in the heart of the flat Cambridgeshire countryside, Emma Saye had almost forgotten about the two visitors from MI6 she had recently briefed on the intricacies of China's latest weapon systems. As one of UK Defence Intelligence's in-house specialists, her workload had speeded up dramatically since then. It was evening and well past Whitehall working hours but she was giving a detailed briefing to the Chief of Defence Intelligence, or 'CDI' as he was known.

'Combat drones,' she announced. 'We all know they're a game-changer – we saw that in Nagorno-Karabakh, and God knows we've seen it in Ukraine. While our friends in Beijing may have been a little late to the party in this sphere, they've been busy catching up. And one of the items of kit they've deployed in the Taiwan Strait is the Tengden TB-001. You may have heard it referred to as "the Two-tailed Scorpion".' She looked up and, yes, she had the CDI's full attention. 'That's what the Chinese like to call it anyway. It can carry a variety of payloads, mostly Blue Arrow air-to-ground missiles, and it can loiter for up to thirty-five hours over a target. But . . .' She held up a warning finger. '. . . what sets this beast apart from the rest of the pack is that it can operate at altitude. It can launch one of its AR4s – that's another air-to-ground jobbie – from seven thousand metres up.'

The CDI wasn't taking notes that evening – someone else was doing that for him – but he was listening attentively. 'How does that compare with what the Americans and the Taiwanese have got?' he asked, one silver eyebrow raised.

'Annoyingly well is the answer, General. Take the standard NATO US Hellfire Longbow missile, for example. It has a range of eight thousand metres. Its Chinese competitor can deliver an eighty-kilo warhead to a target twenty kilometres away. They've been in production since 2017 and they're only going to go further and faster. They're working on new variants all the time. So, yes, when it comes to drones, Taiwan is outclassed and, to be honest, there's not a lot we can give them to level the playing field.'

The CDI shifted in his chair, as if he'd just discovered he'd been sitting on something that wasn't supposed to be there. 'All right.' He sounded tired. 'What else? And for God's sake, please give me some good news, Emma. Remember, I've got to brief a bunch of chippy journalists in Cabinet Office in the morning. If they get a whiff our allies are outmatched in the South China Sea it'll be headline news the next day.'

'Sooner, in fact,' she corrected him. 'We live in a digital world, I'm afraid, General.' She threw him an apologetic smile and, for a moment his aide stopped writing to look from one to the other. 'Right,' she continued. 'I'm not sure I can send you away with too much to write home about there. We do know the Chinese are having trouble with the guidance systems on one of their Dongfeng missiles but, again, they're working on it and those coastal batteries are spooking the US Seventh Fleet. Ten years ago they'd be all over the Taiwan Strait. Not now, not with those hypersonic missiles. If this situation turns fully kinetic then a lot of the action is going to be with long-distance stand-off weapons. But it won't just be here on Earth.'

The CDI's chin rested in his hands as he considered all this. 'You mean it will be fought in space?'

'Very much so. We're talking satellite jamming, even lasers

aggressively trying to neutralize our own satellites. Beijing's intention will be to "blind" us from Day One.'

The Chief of Defence Intelligence sat forward in his chair, eyes fixed on the young specialist who was briefing him. 'So, if we lump everyone together for a moment,' he said, 'that's us, the Americans, the Japanese, the Australians, South Korea and, of course, Taiwan, where would you say we stood, on balance?'

'Just in terms of weapons?'

'Yes.'

'Conventional only?'

'Christ, yes.' The CDI winced at the thought of anything else. 'Let's leave nukes out of the equation.'

'Right, well, discounting nukes,' Emma chose her next words carefully, 'I'd say we might still be ahead on quality, except when it comes to hypersonic glide vehicles. China definitely has the edge there. Their command and control is still very rigid, very Soviet era, just like the Russians in Ukraine. No room for initiative by junior ranks at all. But do you know what, General? I'm not sure that matters when it comes to Taiwan. This is a numbers game, and if Beijing really wants to do this thing and invade, the sad fact for us is that they have enough men and weapons to throw at it to eventually get the job done. They will have looked at what Putin achieved in Ukraine by mass alone and may just decide that's the route they want to go down.'

The CDI rose wearily to his feet. 'Well, thank you *so* much for that, Emma,' he said. 'You've cheered me up no end. I do look forward to explaining this to all those defence and security correspondents in Whitehall.'

101

Nanjing Army Command College, China

JUNIOR SERGEANT JIAN ZHANG'S commanders were wasting no time. Less than twelve hours had elapsed since the address to his unit by the Party official from Beijing and already each man had been assigned specific tasks for the planned capture of Taiwan's TSMC microchip facility in Hsinchu. Multi-skilled by training, it was a lottery as to who got what. Some were assigned to the Electronic Warfare and Communications Unit, their job to cut off Taiwan's premier semiconductor facility from the outside world. Others were part of a diversion force, their aim to distract Taiwan's ground forces to make it harder for them to regain the initiative once Zhang and his team arrived on the scene. A separate paramilitary police unit was assigned to enforce control of the population, supported by scores of trained investigators from the Ministry of State Security who would soon be scouring the records of every employee, searching for those least sympathetic to Beijing.

Zhang was fiercely proud of the role he had been given. He had been specially selected to be part of the high-value target team. Their job, it was explained to them, would be to locate and hunt down every senior scientist and technician at TSMC, whether they were on shift at the time or at their homes in Hsinchu. From now on, he and the rest of the team would be required to familiarize themselves with every name, face and address on the lists provided by the Ministry.

The People's Liberation Army would not just be capturing the physical entity of the company. When the day came, it would be seizing the beating intellectual heart of Taiwan's entire economy.

102

Dasyueshan Mountain Forest, Taiwan

HER HAIR WAS matted and dishevelled. Her grey tracksuit was filthy, rumpled and stained, while her face looked years older than the photograph Luke and Jenny had been given by the China team back at Vauxhall Cross. But the woman standing unsteadily in front of them was unmistakably Hannah Slade.

The collector was alive.

Five days. That was all it had been since she was snatched from the café in Kowloon yet Luke could only imagine what she must have gone through. She looked dazed and bewildered, her eyes darting nervously from left to right. Before Luke could say anything, Jenny rushed forward and hugged the scientist. He could see Hannah was struggling to adjust to the light, turning her head from one side to the other as she mumbled something to Jenny. He wondered how long these bastards had kept her inside that crate.

And did she still have it? Had Hannah Slade somehow, despite everything, managed to keep hold of the prized intelligence she had been sent to collect from Hong Kong? Luke had his doubts, but the question still burned. He had to know. Yet he couldn't ask her. Not here, not now, not with Bo and his bodyguards watching their every move.

Luke glanced across at Bo. The sickly grin remained plastered across his face, his lacquered hair still slicked back. And dyed jet black, Luke thought, just like a member of the Beijing Politburo. The triad leader stood to one side, arms folded, watching Jenny comfort his star captive. This was his party and he was the affable host. He gave them a minute and then Luke saw his expression change, the smile fade. He looked up and clapped his hands for attention.

'To business,' Bo announced, like someone welcoming friends to a game of poker, which in some ways was exactly what this had become, although for lethal stakes. Luke could not erase the fact that less than twelve hours ago this man had presented them with two severed heads in a box.

Bo pointed to three chairs. 'Sit,' he said. He remained standing. Beneath the hem of his white ceremonial robe, Luke noticed, he still wore the boots with the stacked Cuban heels. Bo turned to the other American bodyguard and waved a hand in dismissal. That left just Kreutzer, leaning with his back against the wall, still covering them with his Heckler & Koch. But Luke's senses were wired. The odds had just changed.

'You are a popular lady.' Bo was addressing Hannah as he said this. His eyebrows arched in feigned surprise. 'It seems everyone wants a piece of you!' Luke looked across at Jenny, who was holding Hannah's hand as they faced the triad leader.

'Our friends across the Strait in Beijing,' Bo continued, counting off on his fingers, 'those crazy dudes with the nukes in Pyongyang, certain people here in Taiwan and, of course, we mustn't forget your two friends here . . .' He pointed at Luke and Jenny. 'They all want you *sooo* badly. So, what do we do? Hmm?' He rubbed his hands together. Luke could see he was loving every minute of this, drawing it out to feed his ego. 'You must have something they all want and that means, my dear Miss Slade, that you command a high price.'

'My employers are willing to pay.' It was Jenny who spoke, her voice surprisingly calm and assured, given what she had seen in this room.

'Oh, I have no doubt about that, lady. That's why I've had your friend brought here to me,' Bo replied, the hint of a transatlantic accent creeping into his voice again. 'But then maybe I don't want to let her go. Had you thought about that?' Bo looked from Jenny to Hannah and then to Luke.

In the silence that followed, Luke ran through their predicament in his head. How much did Bo know about him and Jenny? Was there a price on their heads too? All right, so this was about money and power, all part of Bo's shoring up his position in the criminal underworld. But something else was at play. This was a game to Bo – the man was toying with them. And if Hannah was the prize then he and Jenny were expendable. It was time to remind Bo of some hard truths.

'Look, you've got to face facts here,' Luke told him. 'And the truth is, Mr Bo, that time is not on your side, is it? Because by my reckoning we've been missing now for, what . . . getting on for sixteen hours or thereabouts. This is not a big country and they'll find us here before long. This is the twenty-first century, with all the tech that goes with it. You know that, I know that. So let's just agree a deal and we'll be on our way. All right?'

A slow, sarcastic handclap from Bo. 'Bravo, my friend,' he said. 'That was quite the little speech.' He smiled across the room at Kreutzer. The American was still leaning against the back wall. Luke could see he had a wide arc of fire that allowed him to cover all three of his boss's prisoners without having to shift his position. 'Didn't you like his speech?' Bo asked him. 'I did.' Kreutzer grunted something in reply that Luke didn't catch.

'No,' Bo continued, turning back to Luke with an air of finality. 'You people have no idea what you've got yourselves into, have you? We're about to have a war here on this island and I can tell you that a high-ranking British intelligence officer is a prized . . .' He rubbed his thumb against the tips of his fingers. '. . . commodity.'

'But she is not an intelligence officer,' Jenny interjected. Service policy was always meant to be NCND, neither confirm nor

338

deny, if someone worked for MI6. But Jenny had decided that in this instance it was worth breaking protocol.

'Of course she is! That's why you are here. And, yes, she is also a commodity!' Bo's voice went up an octave. 'To be bought and sold. I own her and I alone will decide what we do with her. And you, Mr Carlton, you talk about time not being on our side, but you are wrong.' He wagged a forefinger to and fro in Luke's direction. 'Let me tell you, at this very moment two delegations are waiting in Taichung for my decision. You could call them "commodity buyers", if that pleases you. One is from mainland China, the other from the Democratic People's Republic of Korea. They would very much like to take delivery of your Hannah Slade today. And if they do . . .' Bo sighed and shrugged. '. . . well, it might be weeks before your people even know she has left the island.'

Hannah had yet to speak, but Luke saw her flinch as she took in Bo's words. It was Jenny who spoke, breaking into Mandarin. Unable to follow what she was saying, Luke watched Bo's face for a reaction. The triad boss looked surprised, then answered her in the same language. Jenny frowned and nodded. This was like watching a foreign-language film without the subtitles. Bo spread his hands and beamed.

'Your lady here is very brave,' he announced, 'and most honourable. Because she has just made a most interesting proposal. She would like to offer herself in exchange for your Hannah Slade.'

103

Zhanjiang Naval Base, China

AT 0830, ON A CLOUDLESS blue morning in the South China Sea, the latest, most modern of China's three aircraft carriers slipped her moorings and steamed out of Zhanjiang naval base on the southern coast of the People's Republic, bound for the Taiwan Strait.

The 80,000-tonne *Fujian* had only recently completed her sea trials but now she carried a full complement of forty-two fourth-generation Shenyang J-15 'Flying Shark' fighter aircraft, ready to be launched by electromagnetic catapult, a system employed by only the most advanced US and Chinese carriers. Larger than any ship in the Royal Navy or the French Navy, *Fujian* had a capacity crew of 2020 sailors and nearly a thousand air crew. Most of the ship's company had been told they were departing on an exercise, ready to carry out important naval manoeuvres in the defence of the motherland. Only the most senior officers onboard had been fully briefed on her classified mission.

Aircraft carriers do not sail alone or they would be sitting ducks for incoming enemy missiles and attack submarines. When *Fujian* left port that morning she was escorted and protected by a fleet of guided missile destroyers, frigates and – ominously for the Western intelligence analysts who were already studying the satellite images – no fewer than six amphibious landing ships.

Invisible from space once they deployed to the open ocean, *Fujian* was also being shadowed beneath the surface by a pair of Yuan-class stealth submarines, with their dramatically reduced active sonar signature.

As the US Navy's Seventh Fleet Carrier Strike Group 5 steamed in the opposite direction, heading south-west across the East China Sea, the People's Liberation Army Navy was now moving to a more active phase. It was preparing to meet the US Carrier Strike Group head-on.

104

Dasyueshan Mountain Forest, Taiwan

LUKE WASN'T SURE if he'd heard correctly. He stared at Bo and then at Jenny. 'What? Jenny, is that right? You've offered to trade places with her?' He indicated Hannah.

His colleague – her face tight-lipped, her jaw set – replied with a nod.

Luke had an inkling he knew what was behind this. Was it because Hannah still had the flash drive? And Jenny was prepared to make this sacrifice to get it safely away to where it was needed? An incredible act of self-sacrifice to help avert a devastating war. He could think of no other explanation. But he still couldn't let her do this. There had to be another way. His thoughts were already heading into dark places, weighing up tough choices, making the most cynical of calculations. He and Jenny were highly trained and valued intelligence officers; Hannah Slade was not. She was a collector. Someone off-the-books. A deniable asset. That didn't mean she was expendable, but if there was a way to transfer whatever data she was carrying to Luke and Jenny, he knew exactly what course he would be expected to take.

'Um. No. Sorry,' he said firmly. 'That's not happening.' This was not a discussion he wanted to have in front of their captors

342

but Luke knew he needed to quash this idea immediately. 'Jen, just think about it. Just . . . no.'

'I *have* thought about it, Luke,' Jenny Li replied, 'and this is my decision. It's the right thing to do.'

And yet something else was playing out in the back of Luke's mind. It was something deeply sinister that Kreutzer had said to them last night, just before he left them in their cabin. Something about Bo's plans for them. 'As for you two,' he'd said, 'you'll find out soon enough.' That didn't sound like a scenario that saw any of them leaving this place in one piece. It was time to find out.

'OK, Mr Bo, let's negotiate,' Luke said, addressing the gangster. 'What *exactly* do you want from us?' But Bo, he realized, wasn't listening. The man's expression had darkened. No more the genial host.

'Enough of this!' Bo announced, waving over Kreutzer. 'It's time. Take them to the cage.'

The cage? If ever there was a trigger word for Luke, it was this. He knew, through training and painful personal experience, that the best time to escape was in the early moments of capture. After that, your options dwindled dramatically, especially if you were restrained with wrist-ties or leg-irons. They had already missed one opportunity back in that underground car park in Taipei. He wasn't going to pass up another. It was time for direct action.

As Kreutzer came up to him, Luke raised his right hand and wagged a finger in the American's face. 'No wrist-ties,' he told him.

It took only a second to distract Kreutzer's attention but it was enough. With his left hand, Luke reached down, quick as a flash, and grabbed the handle of the knife, lifting it clear from the sheath strapped to Kreutzer's calf. In a lightning-fast move, he thrust it halfway to the hilt, right into Kreutzer's stomach, causing him to cry out and drop his weapon with a clatter to the floor as he clutched his hands to his abdomen. It was a calculated, calibrated attack. Luke could have stabbed Kreutzer in his femoral artery, making him bleed out in under three minutes. He could have gone straight for the jugular and done it even quicker. But he didn't. Instead, he had given Kreutzer a wound he could probably survive. And now he had his Heckler & Koch.

Luke dropped the knife and snatched up the machine-pistol, instinctively checking that the safety was already off, then dashed over to where Bo stood, open-mouthed in shock. The triad man wasn't smiling now. For the first time Luke saw something different in his eyes: fear.

Luke jabbed the muzzle of the weapon hard into Bo's ribs, probably harder than he needed to but everything was happening in double-quick time and he could feel the adrenaline surging through his veins. 'Put your hands up behind your head,' he ordered.

A low groan came from where Kreutzer lay prone on the floor, a dark pool spreading next to him. Bo was still speechless but Luke knew that wouldn't last, that any second now he would raise the alarm and there were a great many more men with guns on the other side of that door. They were not even close to getting out of this, but Luke had a plan forming fast in his head.

105

Vauxhall Cross, London

IF FELIX SCHAUER had had the slightest idea of what Luke, Jenny and Hannah were going through he might have lost his cool altogether. As it was, he had a strong feeling that things were spinning out of his control. As MI6's Director Critical it was his job to stay on top of a crisis situation. For a man with an obsession for details and order, nothing was going to plan. Hannah Slade and the raw CX intelligence she was supposed to collect were both still missing, presumed somewhere in Asia but no one on the team could be sure. Two of his best case officers, Luke Carlton and Jenny Li, had also gone completely off-grid. Graham Leach, the Taipei station chief, seemed not to have the faintest idea where they were. The two sleuths from Security Section he'd dispatched to Taiwan to help find them had gone down with food poisoning almost the moment they'd stepped off the plane. They were now holed up in a Taipei hotel at the British taxpayers' expense and contributing absolutely nothing to anything. And as for Angela Scott . . . Well, Felix Schauer had never much cared for her, although he had wisely kept his views to himself. But after her digital disaster he had expected to have seen the last of her at Vauxhall Cross. Which was why he had found it hard to conceal his dismay on bumping into her this morning, helping herself to a cappuccino at the machine on the second floor as if nothing had happened. Schauer had beaten a hasty retreat to his office and now, faced with a mounting number of unanswered questions and loose ends, he did what came naturally. He called a meeting.

Quoting the words of the late US Defence Secretary Donald Rumsfeld, he reminded everyone from the China team that there were 'known knowns, things we know that we know'. And then there were 'known unknowns'. In other words, things we knew that we didn't know. But then, even more confusingly, there were the 'unknown unknowns' – the things we didn't know that we didn't know. It had all sounded like a load of Pentagon gobble-dygook when Rumsfeld had first aired this theory in the year before America had gone blundering into Iraq in search of Saddam Hussein's non-existent weapons of mass destruction in 2003, aided and abetted by flawed intelligence from MI6. But over the years historians and intelligence analysts had come to recognize that while the invasion had been a disaster there was a certain twisted logic to Rumsfeld's words. If you could at least identify the facts you needed to know, that was halfway to containing and solving a problem. Felix Schauer was now using this to illustrate his China team's predicament.

'So let us remind ourselves of the facts,' he began. 'Hannah Slade was abducted in Hong Kong. That's a known known. How did we respond? We sent Jenny Li and Luke Carlton to the region to try to secure her release. Again, a known known. But what we *don't* know is whether Hannah had time to get the flash drive from Blue Sky before she was taken. Was she able to conceal it as she had been trained to, or has this whole exercise been a futile waste of time?' He faced a table full of anxious faces. This was the exact opposite of a pep talk.

Schauer got up to do his usual pacing around the small space between the table and the door, talking as he walked. 'Our people in Hong Kong have tracked down the café in Kowloon where she was taken,' he said, 'and they have gone over every millimetre of that place in case she somehow managed to hide it in there. No joy. We've run an extensive background check on the woman who runs the café. Again, nothing. At least, nothing that would connect her to Beijing.'

He stopped pacing and leant forward, both hands resting on the table.

'So, now we come to the tricky part,' he said. 'Who has taken Hannah and why? Is it the same people who murdered our agent Blue Sky in Hong Kong? I think not. Why? Because her body would have turned up by now. More importantly, who is holding her now? Is it a mainland Chinese triad? The Russians? The North Koreans? Or is it people we haven't even considered yet?' He stood up straight and spread his hands to illustrate the point.

Often a man of few words, Schauer was now working himself up into full-on football-coach mode, urging on his team to get results. 'So, I want all of you in this room to be working every angle. Go over every intercept that might be relevant with our colleagues from Cheltenham, talk to the Americans, see what they know, check the data for every port in Taiwan, every vessel that's come in from Macau, get the manifests, work the numbers, look for anomalies. So, yes, it turned out Hannah wasn't on *Ulysses Maiden* when the Navy team raided her. But one of the crew is talking and there is every indication she was taken off it somewhere out at sea.'

Schauer clapped his hands. 'So, come on, people, I shouldn't have to tell you how to do your jobs. Somewhere out there is a missing collector with intelligence that could stop a war in the South China Sea. A war that could start any day now, so you don't have a minute to spare!'

347

106

Xi'an Satellite Control Centre, Xi'an, China

THEY WORKED LONG SHIFTS at the Xi'an Satellite Control Centre, the teams who monitored the incoming data beaming down from China's galaxy of satellites, the eyes and ears of the People's Republic looking down on Earth from up in space. Reporting to the PLA's Strategic Support Force, their secretive workplace was also known to those in the military as simply 'Base 26'.

Thanks to the wonders of artificial intelligence and quantum computers, those who worked there were able to download, analyse and disseminate nearly all the raw data coming in from outer space at speeds that would have been unthinkable just five years earlier.

And what was coming in that morning was triggering a flurry of urgent radio messages to the Central Military Commission in Beijing and to the PLA Navy's Eastern Theatre Command at Ningbo, 1280 kilometres to the east of Xi'an and just down the coast from Shanghai. Chinese military satellites had picked up the movement southwards from the East China Sea of two US Navy warships, heading for the Taiwan Strait. Digital magnification and detailed analysis revealed them to be two Ticonderoga-class guided missile cruisers: the USS *Chancellorsville* and the USS *Antietam*, both part of the US Navy's Seventh Fleet based out of Yokosuka in Japan.

On the ground at Base 26, beneath the bristling array of radio masts and antennae, the analysts noted that this would not be the first time that the meddling and neo-imperialist United States had sent these two warships through the Taiwan Strait on one of their FONOPs – freedom of navigation operations. Beijing had complained before about what it called 'this unnecessary and provocative act that threatened the peace and security of the western Pacific region', but this time appeared to be different. Rather than transiting through the Strait and on into the South China Sea, the two US warships appeared to be stationing themselves at the northern entrance to the Taiwan Strait, bolstering the already unwelcome presence of those three AUKUS warships from the US, the UK and Australia.

The People's Liberation Army Navy had extensive files on every single aspect of the US Navy's Seventh Fleet. It knew, for example, the names and home addresses of each vessel's commanding officer. Its analysts had done extensive research on the combat capabilities, strengths and weaknesses of every single warship in their opponent's fleet. It knew that these two guided missile cruisers were first deployed over three decades ago, yet they were armed with sophisticated weaponry including Tomahawk land attack cruise missiles and medium-range surface-to-air missiles capable of taking out any aircraft flying across the Strait.

Within hours of this development reaching the Central Military Committee an executive order was issued. Land-based missile units of the PLA's Eastern Theatre Command should draw up contingency plans for the targeting of both US warships with a series of hypersonic missiles in the event that the geopolitical situation deteriorated further. Such an intrusion by a hostile and malevolent power so close to the coast of the motherland could not be tolerated, it was concluded, and therefore the use of force must not be ruled out.

107

Dasyueshan Mountain Forest, Taiwan

REMORSE, LUKE FOUND, tended to be something that happened to other people. Remorse meant you had made a mistake, that faced with that choice again you would have chosen a different course of action. Glancing down at the contorted, groaning Tad Kreutzer, Luke had no regrets. He had assessed the American to be an integral part of the threat they faced; Kreutzer had stood between them and their path to freedom. But it was the mention of 'the cage' that had driven Luke to do what he'd done. He had seen too many hideous terror videos from his time in Special Forces to take a chance on something like that.

He wiped his hand, still slick with Kreutzer's blood, on the side of his trousers, then pressed the muzzle of the Heckler & Koch once more into Bo's ribcage. 'Not a word from you,' he told him.

Seeing what Luke had just done to his bodyguard had a some-what chilling effect on Bo. He complied, but his eyes were still darting around the room. That animal cunning again, Luke thought, looking for an opportunity to turn the tables and seize his moment. Lose control of the situation now, and his revenge is going to be off-the-scale. And any minute now someone is going to come through that door to investigate and I'm going to have to shoot them. So I need every second I've got.

Jenny was already kneeling beside the bleeding Kreutzer, pressing a rolled-up scarf she'd found against his wound as he gripped his legs in pain. Hannah stood back from the whole scene, her face a mask of horror.

'OK.' Luke turned to them, the MP7 now firmly in his hands. 'This is what's going to happen. Jenny, Hannah, we're going to walk out of here, all four of us, and use one of those vehicles out there to get ourselves off this mountain.'

'All *four* of us?' Jenny questioned, looking up from attending to Kreutzer.

'That's right. Not him. Our man Bo is coming too. He's our insurance.'

'You mean he's our hostage,' she corrected.

'Exactly. So, Hannah, I need you to look around this room and find something to tie him up with. Can you do this?'

Hannah Slade nodded silently and gave him a wan smile. She started to search along the shelf that ran next to Bo's desk. 'Will this do?' She held up a length of cord, frayed at one end.

'Perfect,' Luke said. 'Now I need you to tie his wrists together behind his back – like this.' Gripping the machine-pistol with one hand, Luke yanked Bo's hands down with the other, placing them where he wanted them. 'Make it tight but not so tight it cuts off the blood flow.'

Bo suddenly broke his silence, opening his mouth for the first time since he had watched his bodyguard topple to the floor. 'Listen,' he rasped. 'I have eight armed men on the other side of that door. You have no chance, no chance at all. You know, I was even going to let one of you go. Maybe I still will. So, give up now and I promise you a quick and painless death. Otherwise . . .'

'Shut it,' Luke told him, ramming the barrel of the weapon hard against one of Bo's kidneys, hard enough to make him wince. The triad boss's wrists were now securely tied behind his back but Luke had one more detail to attend to before he was ready.

'Jen – can you grab the knife?' He jerked his head towards the floor where he had dropped the blood-stained Yarborough knife, close to where she knelt.

Jenny placed both of Kreutzer's hands on the scarf she had been pressing against his wound. His eyes were squeezed tight shut but he was still conscious. Gingerly, she retrieved the knife and stood up, holding it as if it were a filthy object to be urgently disposed of. Luke could hardly blame her. MI6 case officers tended to spend more time in front of a computer screen than picking up bloodied hunting knives. But if they were going to get out of here alive, he needed her to be ready to use it. He knew the odds were stacked against them – this was a game of chess where your opponent has taken your queen and you're down to your last few pieces. They needed every weapon they could lay their hands on.

'When we walk out of here, Jenny,' he said, 'I want you to keep close behind him like this.' He lifted her left hand and put it on Bo's shoulder. 'Now I need you to grip the knife . . . Yup, that's it. Hold it tight and keep the tip of the blade resting right up against the small of his back . . . like this.' Bo flinched as the blade tip pierced his robe. 'If he tries to escape, just drive it in. Hard. You OK with this?' Jenny swallowed and nodded.

'Is this going to work?' Hannah Slade interjected, her voice hoarse. She looked petrified.

'Definitely,' Luke replied, with a confidence he didn't feel. 'Come on,' he said, and moved towards the door that opened out to the rest of the temple complex. He had no idea what to expect but knew full well it might be the last door he ever walked through.

108

Wimbledon, London

ANGELA SCOTT COULDN'T SLEEP. There was a glass of water on her bedside table, an opened packet of sleeping tablets next to it and a half-read novel lying upside down on her duvet. She had dozed fitfully for a couple of hours but it was still the middle of the night and she was wide awake. She had a lot to worry about.

She knew her rehabilitation into the arms of the Secret Intelligence Service was only half complete. The in-house Service investigation into how Chinese hackers had got inside her phone had yet to run its course. Officially, she was back in Vauxhall Cross, and back on the China team, but people were looking at her differently, she could tell. Walking down the corridor on her floor of the building she had turned a corner and recognized a colleague coming towards her. She was about to greet them with a smile, only for them to turn quickly on their heels and disappear off in the opposite direction.

But Angela had other worries too. The Service – her Service – had sent three strangers to break into her home. She couldn't get over that. All right, so it had been a test and she'd passed, but it still felt like a violation, a betrayal. How could the Service treat her like this after all she had given it over the years? She couldn't help but feel that the scheming Felix Schauer must have had something to do with it.

Throwing back the duvet, she swung her legs out of bed and went to make a cup of tea. Faustus stirred in his basket and blinked at her, no doubt curious as to why she was up at that time of night. No, she concluded, as she sipped her drink, these were all trivial worries and she couldn't afford self-pity, certainly not now, not when Luke and Jenny were missing somewhere in East Asia and the Service was further than ever from retrieving the collector's intel. The notion that it was *her* phone that had somehow, unbeknown to her, sent Luke and Jenny off into the path of danger appalled her. If anything now happened to them as a result of that, she decided, she would do the honourable thing. Angela Scott would resign and turn her back on the world of secret intelligence for ever.

109

Dasyueshan Mountain Forest, Taiwan

OK. DEEP BREATH. FOCUS. Left hand on the door handle, machine-pistol gripped in the right. Thirty-round magazine full and checked, but no spare magazine. No Glock sidearm Velcroed to the thigh either, just Kreutzer's gore-smeared but razor-sharp Yarborough knife wielded by Jenny, ready to face whatever was on the other side of that door.

Luke turned to Bo, who seemed a much diminished figure now, his hands tied behind his back, a knife against his skin, his chief bodyguard lying disarmed and immobilized. 'When I open this door,' Luke told Bo, 'you're going to be the first one through it.'

The gangster's eyes narrowed but he said nothing.

'So I would advise you,' Luke continued, 'to shout a warning to your guys and tell them not to shoot. You got that? It's your call.'

Bo sniffed, tilted his head and grimaced. He obviously wasn't enjoying being told this.

'Right,' Luke said, his voice hushed. 'Here we go . . .'

A shove against the door, a roll to the side, then Bo was through, propelled by Jenny, screaming out for his bodyguards not to open fire. Next through, Hannah, followed by Luke, finger on the trigger of the Heckler & Koch, its safety off and muzzle sweeping the room. First thing in vision: a massive cage, door swinging open – their intended fate. Then he saw the Americans, two of them, legs braced, backs against the wall, eyes wide in surprise but guns raised.

'Tell them to lower their weapons,' Luke shouted. How much longer was the triad leader going to comply? Not long, he reckoned. The slightest hesitation and Bo and his people would rush him. That would be that. It would all be over.

Bo obeyed.

Keep moving, got to keep this group moving. Don't stop for a second or they'll have you. Keep your gun trained on the Americans. Out of the temple, past the stone lions, a stumble by Hannah, then a recovery, and they were into the forecourt. Early-morning mist had given way to blazing sunshine and a blanket of heat. More people, all Chinese, motionless and watching open-mouthed. Bo was playing up, walking deliberately slowly, dragging the pace.

'Speed up,' Luke told him, and cuffed him hard on the back of his head.

A row of jeeps, all black, all 4x4s. One with its engine running. That was his target. Still a hundred metres to go and any second now the bullets could rip into them. A trained sniper could take out Luke and Jenny with a quick double-tap. But not today, not that morning, not with Bo as their hostage and the jeeps just twenty paces away.

It was another Mercedes-Benz G-Class, gleaming new, a muscled thug beside it, half-smoked cigarette falling from his parted lips.

'Fuck off somewhere else,' Luke told him, waving the machine-pistol at the man, who slunk away.

'Hannah – can you drive?' She nodded. Good. He'd worked out that was the only way this would work. 'In the back. Yes, you,' he told Bo. 'Jen – go next to him. Keep that knife on-point.'

A hesitation, Bo standing his ground, looking around for help from his people. Time to step it up. Luke aimed the Heckler & Koch at a spot between the man's feet and loosed off a single round. The sound reverberated through the forest. Bo yelped and scrambled into the vehicle, like a frightened child. One more round, into the air, to keep Bo's people at bay. He could see them, gathering at the edge of the temple, watching, waiting for their moment to give chase.

Keys already in the ignition, everyone in, dirt track in front. No time for choices, they'd have to take this route through the forest.

'Go!' Luke shouted at Hannah. 'Drive! As fast as you can! Go straight ahead!'

A lurch forward, wheels spinning on stones, then sudden traction and a jolting, jarring acceleration down the track, pine trees crowding in on either side. Hannah's face, pale and taut yet grimly determined, as she hunched over the wheel.

A sharp crack, like a piece of wood being snapped in two.

'Luke!' Jenny yelled from the back. 'They're shooting at us!'

'Just warning shots!' he shouted back. 'They're not going to risk killing Bo.' Window down, level the Heckler & Koch and loose off another shot at the road behind.

Round a bend in the road, picking up speed now, putting some distance in. No sign of pursuit yet. Tall stands of bamboo waving in the morning sun. Then ahead a fork in the road. Both tracks identical, left and right.

'Go left!' Luke shouted.

The Merc surged. Down a slope, going ever faster. We're going to do this, we're going to get away. But then a sudden jam on the brakes, hands out in front, forcing him to drop the machine-pistol in his lap. And they skidded to a stop.

'Jesus, Hannah?' Her eyes were wide, knuckles white as she gripped the steering wheel. 'Oh shit,' Luke muttered.

Ahead, lying across the track and completely blocking their escape route, was a large fallen tree.

110

High Wycombe, Buckinghamshire

THE CALL FROM PINDAR came through on the secure line just after 4 a.m. It rang only once before someone reached out and grabbed the handset. Pindar was the Government's secure Defence Crisis Management Centre, buried deep beneath the Ministry of Defence in Whitehall. In fact, so far underground that it could supposedly withstand a nuclear attack.

'Crosland.' Always a light sleeper, Air Chief Marshal Chip Crosland was immediately awake and firing on all cylinders. As Britain's Chief of Defence Staff and a former head of the RAF, he knew no one would be calling him at this hour unless it was a matter of extreme national security. The last time anyone had done so was when the Russians had kicked off their full-scale invasion of Ukraine.

'Sir, there's been a development. I've been asked to wake you.'

'Go on. Who am I speaking to?'

'Major Bradshaw, sir. I'm the duty SO2 here at Pindar. It's Russia—'

'Oh Christ. Not the Baltics?' The Air Chief Marshal clapped his free hand to his forehead. This was the nightmare scenario he'd long anticipated. 'Is it Estonia?'

'No, CDS. It's Taiwan. Moscow is mobilizing its Pacific Fleet.

We think it's in support of China's claim to the island. Chief of Defence Intelligence thought you should know.'

Too bloody right he should know. A long pause. This tipped everything upside down. Standing up to the PLA Navy was one thing but Russia and China combined? 'All right,' he said calmly. 'Who else knows?'

'They're waking the Secretary of State now, sir. Then we'll cascade it to Strategic Command at Northwood and Commander in Chief Fleet.'

'Right. Give me the details.' Crosland reached across the still sleeping form of his wife to grab a notepad and pen. 'OK. Tell me.'

'There's a full briefing on its way over to you now, sir. But the top line is that Fokino's moved up to maximum readiness and—'

'Fokino? Hold on, where's that?'

'Formerly Vladivostok. It got renamed.'

'Yes, of course. What else?'

'Likewise their fleet based in Petropavlovsk-Kamchatsky. Same with their submarine base at Vilyuchinsk. We've picked up two of their latest ballistic missile SSBNs leaving port.'

The Chief of Defence Staff frantically scribbled all this down. He didn't have time to wait for the full briefing. The Secretary of State was going to want a preliminary assessment right away. Crosland thanked the duty officer and hung up. Then, moving carefully so as not to wake his wife, he grabbed his dressing-gown and went through to the kitchen. There he paused, took a deep breath and dialled the private number of the Defence Secretary. Everything had changed now.

This was going to be a long night.

111

Dasyueshan Mountain Forest, Taiwan

A BLOODY GREAT tree trunk. Right in their path. Too big to drive over, too heavy to move. And too many trees to allow them to drive round it. Luke was thinking fast. Only two choices: go back up the hill, and risk driving right into their pursuers, or abandon the vehicle.

'We should get out. Now!' Jenny called from the back seat.

'Agreed.' Luke swivelled round. Bo stared back at him, a smug grin all over his face, his ridiculous white priest's gown bulging at the midriff. Luke's plan was unravelling fast and Bo knew it.

'Quick! Quick!' Bo mocked, head bobbing, eyebrows raised in a parody of fear. 'They'll be here any moment. Hurry, hurry, or they'll catch you!'

'Jen, we'll leave him here. Hannah, let's go!' Grasping the Heckler & Koch, Luke pushed open the Merc's door and leapt down, listening out for the sound of pursing vehicles. And there they were, up the hill they'd just come from, maybe two hundred metres away at most. Movement in the back of their 4x4. Bo was rocking from side to side, struggling to free his bound wrists. No longer afraid, he was starting to shout too.

'Hannah – kill the engine and grab the keys from the ignition,'

Luke called. 'Lock him inside – doors, windows, the lot – and chuck the keys into the forest. Might buy us a bit of time.' He turned to Jenny, the blood-smeared hunting knife still in her hand. 'Jen, we need to split up. You take Hannah, get past that log and get as far down the track as you can. I'll catch you up.'

'But what about—?'

Luke patted the machine-pistol. 'I have this. Now, go! Run!' He saw Hannah fling the Mercedes keys deep into the undergrowth, and Bo's grimacing face peering out from the vehicle's rear window, then she and Jenny took off.

Luke paused. Think, Carlton, think! Got to delay the pursuers. Buy the others time. Give them the best chance to get away. He hefted the weapon: three rounds fired already. That left twenty-seven in the magazine. He knew he was heavily outgunned, no question, but he'd make every damn bullet count.

Luke scrambled up the steep slope at the side of the track, grasping at roots, branches, hauling himself up until he was deep in the undergrowth. The growl of vehicles coming down the track now, drawing closer. Need to find a good firing position. A solid fallen tree trunk with a field of fire and an exit route. No time to be choosy. He squatted down behind the first he saw and hurriedly unfolded the stock of the MP7. Controlling his breathing, he steadied the weapon against the dank, moss-covered trunk and pulled it into his shoulder. Squinting through the optical sight, he aimed the red dot at the windscreen of the first vehicle that was now powering down the track. He squeezed the trigger. A sharp crack, minimal recoil and a grunt of satisfaction as he watched the jeep career off the trail and tumble over the side into the forest below. Twenty-six rounds left. Grabbing the weapon, he turned and charged through the undergrowth, branches whipping at him as he ran. Hurling himself down the slope, he rejoined the track a hundred metres or so further on. There, a large boulder, right beside the road: perfect cover. Ducking behind it, Luke took up a firing position, readying himself to take out the next vehicle. Nothing yet. For now, his plan seemed to be working.

'Luke!' He whirled round. It was Jenny, standing alone at the edge of the forest. No sign of Hannah or the hunting knife.

'Are you OK? Where's Hannah?'

'She's back there. Listen . . .'

He noticed a tremor in her voice. 'What is it, Jen? We've got to keep moving.' A glance back up the track, still nothing. But they'd be coming, and they'd be on foot as well, fanning out through the forest, intent on cutting them off.

'It's Hannah,' Jenny continued. 'She's got the flash drive.'

'Wait. What? That's fucking fantastic!' Luke felt like hugging her but Jenny wasn't smiling.

'There's something else,' she said grimly. 'I think she's broken her ankle. She's in a lot of pain. She can't move.'

112

National Defence HQ, Taipei, Taiwan

VERY FEW PEOPLE knew about the announcement in advance. The White House was tipped off, so was Langley, Virginia, and so were a select few leaders of Allied nations in the region. But for the vast majority of Taiwan's twenty-four-million-strong population, the news came as a shock.

At exactly midday, Taipei time, the order was beamed out from the grey, white and glass Ministry of National Defence on the north bank of the Keelung River to every news agency. As from today, every able-bodied male between the ages of eighteen and fifty-five must report for duty at their local mobilization office. Addresses for these would be published by the end of the day. It was stressed that this was a national duty in the face of unprecedented and unjustified military pressure from the People's Republic of China. Exceptions would be viewed harshly. Everyone must do their duty to preserve and safeguard the freedom-loving and democratic ideals of Taiwan, the Republic of China. Submission to the will of Beijing was not an option. National and patriotic resistance was the only way to guarantee peace and prosperity.

Citizens should stand by for further announcements on a series of imminent civil-defence drills, which will involve the entire nation.

113

Dasyueshan Mountain Forest, Taiwan

HANNAH WAS IN AGONY. Luke saw that at once.

'I've strapped up her foot as best I can,' Jenny said. Even through the makeshift handkerchief bandage on Hannah's exposed ankle, he could see the bruising, the flesh turning a livid purple. The older woman rocked to and fro, clutching her leg, digging her fingertips into her thigh again and again to distract herself from the pain. She was biting her lip, trying not to cry out. As Jenny knelt beside her, Luke cursed silently as he ran through their options.

Got to get off this track. We're too exposed here. It's two minutes, tops, before Bo's thugs reach this point, less if they can shift that tree trunk. We've two choices: head up the slope or down. Never take the obvious path. They'll be expecting you to go down the hill. That means . . .

He looked at Hannah Slade. 'OK, Hannah, we're running out of time. I'm sorry, but we've got to move so—'

'No, you can't! You're not leaving me, are you?' Her voice shook. Pale, exhausted, racked with pain, she stared up at him. 'Please! You can't leave me with those psychopaths!'

'God, no. But I do have to carry you. And we have to go right now. Jen? Can you take this?' He flipped the safety on the Heckler

& Koch and handed it to his colleague. A beat as Jen held his gaze. Was that rebuke in her eyes? For Kreutzer? They would have to settle this later. If they got to live that long. Then he squatted in front of Hannah, his back to her. 'Put your arms around my neck, link your hands tight and hold on.' He reached behind him, taking the weight off her legs and stood, muscles screaming. Hannah groaned but didn't cry out. A couple of seconds to adjust his balance and they were off down the track at speed, Luke half running, Hannah on his back, as Jenny kept pace beside them.

A short, frantic scramble up a bank, through the bushes and into the pine forest. Got to put the distance in. It was like a voice in his head, over and over, like a mantra. A hundred metres, two hundred, three. Then he stopped and set Hannah down, as gently as he could. 'You doing OK?' he asked her. He sensed Jenny turn to look at him.

Hannah glanced up at him, nodded, clenching her jaw. He could see she was fighting through the pain. Then he had to ask the question, had to hear it for himself, even though Jenny had told him. 'So, Hannah, the file, the flash drive . . . You've got it?'

And for the first time since the moment Bo's people had lifted her out of that box up at the temple, Hannah's face broke into a broad smile, in spite of her ankle. It was a smile of triumph. 'I certainly have,' she said, and pointed towards her mouth. 'It's still in there.'

Luke took a deep breath and grinned at her. 'God, fantastic job. I can't think what you've had to go through to keep it safe.' He reached down and gave her hand a squeeze. 'Look, um . . .' What he was going to say next was difficult. He wished he'd spoken to Jenny, asked her to do it because she'd have handled it better, but she was preoccupied, scanning the track for their pursuers and this couldn't wait.

'Look, Hannah, I have to ask this,' he went on, 'but would you mind if I took the flash drive now? It's better if I get caught with it than you.' That wasn't his reason for asking and she probably knew it.

'Why? I've kept it safe all this time.'

'Yeah, I know. And you deserve a bloody medal for that, seriously. But it's Chief's orders. The Service was very specific about this, that we should take possession of it as soon as we found you.' It was a lie, of course. Hannah regarded him coolly for several seconds.

'All right,' she said at last, with a sigh. 'But you'd better take good care of it.' And she inserted her thumb and forefinger into her mouth. Moments later she held out the grey wad of chewing gum, long solidified around the miniature flash drive.

Luke paused as he took it, wondering how something so small could be so valuable before tucking it deep into the breast pocket of his shirt and buttoning it up. 'We will. I promise.'

'Luke!' Jenny hissed. Voices were coming from the trail, not far below them. They sank to the ground, pressing their bodies to the cool, damp earth of the forest floor, as the sounds drew closer. There was birdsong too, in the treetops high above them. Luke listened – he was on the alert for something else: dogs. If they bring tracker dogs we're stuffed. Keeping his movement to the minimum, he reached over to Jenny and took the MP7, silently flipping off the safety. Twenty-six rounds left. Not enough if Bo's people found them. He didn't want to think what would happen to them if they did.

He raised his head a few centimetres above the ground, enough to catch a glimpse of their pursuers. Squat, broad-chested men: some carried guns, others long bamboo staves. One had a net. Suddenly they stopped. One pointed up the hill towards where the three of them lay. Oh God. Don't come up here. Please don't come up here. A crackle of walkie-talkies and then he heard them. Dogs.

114

Whitehall, London

THE ARMOURED AND supercharged five-litre Range Rover Sentinel carrying the Chief of Defence Staff made the journey from High Wycombe to Whitehall in under fifty minutes. As his driver barrelled down the darkened and largely empty M40 motorway, Air Chief Marshal Crosland used the time to get up to speed on Russia's Pacific Fleet. You could ask Crosland anything about the range and payload of a Russian Tu-22 Tupolev bomber, the number of F35s you could fit onto the deck of an aircraft carrier, or the explosive power of a Russian Kinzhal hypersonic missile, but when it came to what the Russian Navy was deploying out of Vladivostok he still had a lot of catching up to do. By the time they drove through the police checkpoint where Horse Guards Road meets the back of Downing Street he had fired off no fewer than eighteen questions to his Chief of Staff. CDS had no wish to look foolish on a day like today.

Crosland had already been in Downing Street for more than two hours before all the senior figures of Britain's national defence and security establishment began arriving for the early-morning emergency COBRA session. First, he had a meeting upstairs with the National Security Adviser and the Defence

Secretary, then fifteen minutes with the PM before they all moved below ground for the COBRA.

'As of this morning,' declared the PM, 'we are in a different paradigm. The risk level on this whole Taiwan situation blowing up in our faces has just gone through the roof. CDS, can I ask you to give everyone here a read-out of the CRIP?'

On both sides of the road that divided Cabinet Office from the MoD Main Building in Whitehall, teams had been working through the early hours to produce a document known as the Commonly Recognized Information Picture, or CRIP, a tool usually reserved for the aftermath of a terrorist attack.

'Certainly, PM.' Air Chief Marshal Crosland removed his glasses and straightened in his chair. 'At latest count, Defence Intelligence report a total of thirty-seven Chinese and Russian surface vessels deployed from port and heading for the area of the Taiwan Strait. We can expect more to deploy in the coming hours. Plus an unknown number of SSNs and SSBNs.'

'Sorry, SSNs? SSBNs?' The Home Secretary, grappling with the military's love of acronyms and jargon.

'Submarines, Home Secretary. Stands for sub-surface nuclear-powered and sub-surface ballistic nuclear. We can't always know where they are but we have to assume both fleets will be deploying them.'

'Strewth.'

'Exactly. On our side of the equation, we've got the US Navy's Seventh Fleet Carrier Strike Group moving into position close to the 26th north parallel. We've got *Daring* in a defensive posture west of Taiwan alongside her sister ships from that AUKUS patrol.'

'The one the Chinese fired a missile at, across her bows, five days ago,' the National Security Adviser chipped in.

'Indeed, Zara, yes, that one,' Crosland continued. 'Now, we've had strong messages of support from Japan, South Korea and the Philippines but for now they're staying out of this. Keeping their heads down. So, the question we have to address in this room is how do we respond?'

'Weakness.'

'Excuse me?' All eyes turned to the National Security Adviser.

'Weakness and hesitation,' Zara Simmons said. 'That's what Moscow and Beijing will be looking for. The Kremlin knows full well they managed to spook us into not sending enough kit to Ukraine in 2023 until it was so late their summer counter-offensive flopped. They're looking to bully us into making exactly the same mistake now and abandoning Taiwan to its fate.'

'Hold on a minute there, Zara.' Hugh Rawlinson, the Foreign Secretary. 'The stakes are rather different now, wouldn't you say?'

'All the more reason for us to show strength,' she retorted. 'I would propose we send the *Queen Elizabeth* to theatre with a full complement of F35s onboard. It will show our adversaries we're serious. Plus, it shows we're in absolute lockstep with the Americans.'

'Forgive me,' the Foreign Secretary again, 'but I thought our only serviceable aircraft carrier was holed up in dock somewhere in the Gulf.' His brow was furrowed with doubt as he regarded the young and ambitious National Security Adviser. 'For a start, how long is it going to take to get her out to theatre?'

'Let me address that, if I may,' interjected Admiral Seaton, the First Sea Lord. 'She's currently in Jebel Ali, yes, but with a bit of elbow grease we're confident she could be under way within thirty-six hours. The Taiwan Strait is six thousand nautical miles from the Gulf, so, at a rate of twenty knots once she's in open ocean, that should have her in position in . . .' He shuffled through his notes to check his figures. '. . . fourteen days. There you are. It's fourteen days, give or take.'

'Two weeks!' It was the PM this time. 'Christ, it'll all be over by then.'

Someone down the table was clearing their throat rather deliberately. The Attorney General, Priyanka Varma, was there to provide the legal checks and balances. 'Yes, Pri?' The PM swivelled in his chair to face her. 'You wanted to add something?'

'Well, yes, I do. I'm concerned we're rather rushing into things.' She raised a perfectly sculpted eyebrow at him, a silent question mark, but when he didn't respond she went on. 'Let's look at this in the cold light of day, shall we? You are talking about ordering our flagship naval asset with, what, a ship's company of a thousand, two thousand, into a potential war zone? And we're not talking about lightly armed insurgents in the Middle East. This is China and Russia, two permanent members of the UN Security Council with a combined nuclear arsenal in excess of six thousand warheads. China alone has the largest army and the second-largest economy in the world. It's a country bristling with missiles. Have we got Parliamentary backing for this? No. Have we got the country behind us? Well, you tell me, Prime Minister.'

There was a long and meaningful silence. Priyanka Varma was almost the only member of Cabinet who could get away with speaking to the PM like that, but it was well known they had been friends at Oxford.

'Look,' she continued, softening her tone somewhat, 'I'm not quibbling with the moral dimension here. Taiwan is a pro-Western democracy that deserves our help. It's a small country, vital to our supply chain, being threatened by a big one, I get that. But going to war on the other side of the world without Parliamentary approval? I'm sorry, PM, but I think you'll have to put your case to the vote.'

Someone muttered very quietly, 'Oh, for God's sake.' It might have been the Defence Secretary; it might have been the Chief of Defence Staff. But whoever it was, the PM chose to ignore it.

'I hear you, Pri,' he said at last. 'And what if we go ahead without a vote?'

'Then I can't protect you,' she said flatly. 'I can't do my job.'

'Meaning?'

'Meaning if you decide to take this country to war with China without putting it to the House first, I will have no choice. I will have to resign.'

115

Dasyueshan Mountain Forest, Taiwan

GERMAN SHEPHERDS. LUKE couldn't be certain but he thought he recognized the sound. They could hear them through the trees, baying, barking. Still distant, but they'd be picking up their scent at any moment. Forty kilos of muscle, fur and teeth. Luke had seen one of these attack dogs bring down a man in seconds.

He shot Jenny an ominous look. Was she thinking the same as him? He had no means of telling. Not without blurting it out in front of Hannah. 'Time to move,' he said, handing the gun back to Jenny. 'Hannah?' He motioned for her to hold on to his neck as he hoisted her onto his back and took off through the undergrowth. But it was slow going, much too slow, as Luke knew it would be, weighed down as he was with an extra body. Jenny went ahead, stopping every few metres, turning round, waiting for him to catch up, the sound of dogs drawing ever closer. The voice in Luke's head was telling him: we are not going to make this.

And then, unexpectedly, another noise and close by too: a car, then another, the sound of wheels on tarmac. A road, not a rough, uneven mountain trail. Their path to freedom, if only they could reach it. Then the earth rose up and smashed Luke in the face. He'd tripped, it was a root, a branch, a hole in the forest floor, and he'd gone sprawling face-down into the dirt. He heard

371

Hannah's agonized cry as she toppled off him. Winded, Luke scrambled back to his feet but the dogs were closing in now. Two, three hundred metres at most. Decision time. He looked at Jenny and she gave him the tiniest nod. It was all he needed. This was the most terrible choice but they had to do it. They had to be ruthless. Or everything they had come here for would be lost.

Without saying a word, Jenny handed Hannah the hunting knife that she'd been carrying all this time. She shrugged in silent apology, then she and Luke turned on their heels and sprinted away through the forest, heading for the road . . . leaving Hannah to the dogs.

116

Hsiaohsuehshan Radar Station, Taiwan

MASTER SERGEANT WU CHI-MING was the first to identify the intruders. Four days had passed since the typhoon that had temporarily blinded his country's mountaintop early-warning station where he worked. Four days in which he and his team had worked double shifts, responding to constant alerts and incursions as ever larger contingents of PLA aircraft crossed the median line between Taiwan and mainland China, probing and testing his country's defences and reaction times.

But at 2.37 p.m. local time, it wasn't fighter jets, transport or refuelling planes that entered Taiwan's airspace. It was Chinese spy balloons, four of them, drifting at an altitude of two thousand metres. They were close to the strategic Ching Chuan Kang airbase at Taichung. Home to Taiwan's 3rd Tactical Fighter Wing, it also housed the country's airborne and Special Operations Command, which made it of particular interest to anyone wishing to gather intelligence on Taiwan's readiness to repel an invasion.

Master Sergeant Chi-ming duly logged the intrusion and passed the information to National Air Defence. Chinese surveillance balloons had crossed the island before and Taipei had always gone along with the diplomatic pretence that they were simply weather balloons that had somehow blown off-course.

Not this time. Master Sergeant Chi-ming was on his third cup of High Mountain oolong tea when he saw the signal from Air Force Defence Headquarters at Zhongshan. The Air Force was being ordered to engage. The spy balloons, and all their sensitive equipment, were to be shot out of the sky, irrespective of the fury this act would generate in Beijing.

117

Dasyueshan Mountain Forest, Taiwan

THE CAR COMING DOWN the road towards them was a brand new silver Toyota Corolla Cross SUV. Music blaring, windows down, kids sticking their heads out at the back. Luke and Jenny didn't hesitate. He dropped the Heckler & Koch into the undergrowth at his feet, jumped down from the forest edge and stood in the middle of the road, frantically waving his arms. The car swerved, tried to get past him but its path was blocked by Jenny.

She ran to the driver's window as the vehicle skidded to a halt. 'Please!' she implored, first in English and then in Chinese. 'You have to help us. We got lost in the forest and we need a lift back to Taipei.'

The driver looked scared. His family fell silent, and his wife in the passenger seat turned down the music. Luke realized they must look a terrible sight, his face plastered with mud from where he'd piled into the forest floor, bits of foliage sticking to their clothes, even splashes of Kreutzer's blood, which would take some explaining.

'But we have no room,' the father protested. 'See? My children are in the back.' Two chocolate-smeared faces stared back at them.

Jenny put the palms of her hands together. 'I'm begging you,' she said. 'We have to get back to Taipei at once! We can squash up in the back.'

Luke cast a nervous glance up and down the road in both directions. Bo's people must be close by. We need to get aboard this vehicle and get our heads down out of sight before we're spotted. He didn't even want to think about Hannah right now. They had done what they'd had to do.

Crammed into the back seat of the Corolla, knees halfway up to his chin, Luke dared to let out a deep breath. Jenny gave him a wan smile and sank lower in her seat. But there was no one behind them, no funereal black 4x4s chasing them down. Every few minutes he reached up and felt for the precious cargo inside his breast pocket, just to remind himself it was still there. Just to tell himself that what they had done to Hannah was justified. God, he hoped so. They didn't know what was on the flash drive. Maybe it would take days – too long – to decrypt. Maybe it would be of little value. Some already out-of-date intel on Chinese troop movements to the ports perhaps. Or some mindless petty gossip about which Politburo member is seeing which mistress. No. Luke closed his eyes. He couldn't allow himself to think like that.

'Can we borrow your phone?' he asked. 'Just a very quick call, I promise.' He glanced down at his wrist to check the time, then realized he no longer had a watch. Or a passport. Or anything at all. Bo's people had taken everything from them in that underground car park.

Silently, the driver's wife handed him her iPhone in its cherry-coloured case. She did not look happy.

Three p.m. in Taiwan. That would make it, what, 7 a.m. in London? There should be someone on the China team he could speak to. He dialled in and waited. One ring, two rings. Then it went straight to voicemail. Oh, for fuck's sake! Luke felt like screaming. He googled the number for the British trade office in Taipei, Britain's *de facto* embassy. Someone picked up.

'Can I speak to Graham Leach, please?' he said.

'He's out at the moment. Who shall I say is calling?' An English voice, calm and unruffled.

'Can you tell him his visitors from London are on their way back to Taipei? Tell him ... tell him we're bringing him the chocolates.'

'"We're bringing him the chocolates"?' Jenny parodied his words and shook her head.

'Hey, come on, I had to think of something,' he grunted, handing back the phone to the driver's wife.

They were coming into a town now, the lush green countryside giving way to a kaleidoscope of Chinese characters and shop fronts.

'What's this place called?' Jenny asked.

'Miaoli,' replied the wife. 'One more hour and fifteen minutes to Taipei.'

It occurred to Luke that they had quite possibly travelled on this exact road on the way up to the forest. Bound and gagged in the boot of a car and at the mercy of some very bad people.

The lift took them straight up to the twenty-sixth floor of Taiwan's President International Tower on Song Gao Road. Before the doors pinged open Jenny stood next to him, gently put her arms round him and held him tight. For the few seconds of their ascent neither of them spoke, yet so much still needed to be said.

'Thank Christ for that! You're back in one piece!' The lift doors opened and there was Graham Leach, SIS station chief for Taipei, and Luke found himself almost glad to see him. Almost.

'Where's Hannah?' Leach asked cheerfully. 'In your hotel, I hope, taking a well-earned rest.'

Luke and Jenny looked at each other. Such an obvious question, one they were bound to be asked. How had they not prepared for it?

'Um. She's not here,' Jenny said, stating the obvious, kicking the can down the road. This was a conversation yet to happen but right now there were other things to attend to.

'Right, then. Moving on,' said Leach, rubbing his hands. 'You've brought the goods. Well done. Impressive effort by all of you. We've brought the IT guys up from Singapore station.

Technically, they belong to Cheltenham but they're here to decrypt and assess what you've got. I don't mind telling you . . .' Leach lowered his voice, as if imparting some massive secret. '. . . there's a lot of people back in London on tenterhooks to see what's on this flash drive. Oh, yes.'

Leach spread his arms wide, the genial host, and suddenly Luke had a flashback to Bo doing the same in his temple lair.

'So,' Leach said, 'let's be having it and let's get it loaded up.'

Luke unbuttoned his breast pocket, reached in and retrieved the wad of gum containing the flash drive and held it between his thumb and forefinger. Again, that wonder at something so tiny, this innocuous-looking object, yet so much hanging on it. 'Let's hope it was all worth it,' he said, handing it over, thinking of Hannah even as he spoke those words. The dogs would have got to her just as he and Jenny were climbing into the back seat of that family's SUV. And then what? He shuddered inwardly. Luke wasn't used to guilt but he felt it now.

'Look, this may take a bit of time,' Leach said, 'you know how thorough these GCHQ types like to be. Why don't you make yourselves comfortable next door? There's a couple of soft chairs in there. Maybe get your heads down. You must be knackered. I'll come through and tell you once we've got the measure of what's on the drive. Sound good?'

118

Taipei, Taiwan

THE DOBERMAN HAD HIM by the throat, or was it a German Shepherd? It was clamping its jaws around his windpipe. Another was attacking his shoulder. Luke lashed out with both arms and sat bolt upright.

'Jesus, man! Take it easy! I was only trying to wake you up.' Leach stood back, nursing his arm where Luke's fist had collided with it. Jenny was across the room, watching him as she cradled a cup of tea.

'Sorry,' Luke said, rubbing his eyes. 'I was out for the count. Must've been having a bit of a nightmare there.'

'I can see that,' Leach replied. 'And not surprising, given what you've been through. Right. Do you want to come next door? This is pretty bloody momentous, I can tell you. Perhaps we should send a car to fetch Hannah. She deserves to hear this, at least some of it.'

Hannah Slade. The collector. The bravest person in this whole fiasco and she wasn't even a serving intelligence officer. She was a civilian, a willing volunteer from the world of academia. Luke and Jenny had had only the briefest of exchanges about her since that fateful moment when they'd abandoned her in the forest. But they couldn't put this off much longer. They were going to have to explain her absence somehow. The question was, how much should they say?

'I think we should leave Hannah where she is,' Jenny said, grasping the situation with both hands. 'There'll be classified intel on this drive and she doesn't have the right clearance. Let's go next door.'

Singapore station had sent three people. Two women, one man. They were standing almost to attention beside an array of desktop, wires and techie apparatus that Luke didn't recognize.

'It took us a bit of time to do the decryption,' one said, 'but we got there in the end.'

'And?' Luke asked.

'And it's a gold mine.' She beamed. 'It's given us everything from China's operational plans for an imminent maritime blockade of Taiwan to their cyber strategy: cutting the place off from the internet, isolating it entirely. And there are names on there too – all of Beijing's agents inside the Taiwan military, people China has on its payroll. Oh, and access codes for their ballistic missile launch sites. I mean, it's just incredible. If this checks out there's enough in here to stop any invasion in its tracks. The guy who leaked all this must be seriously pissed off with his government.'

'Was,' Luke said.

'Excuse me?'

'Was, in the past tense. He's dead.'

'Oh. I see.' Although the news didn't appear to take the wind out of her sails. 'Well, he deserves a posthumous medal, then. Anyway, we've sent it all to Cheltenham and Vauxhall and they're preparing an assessment now for Cabinet Office.' She looked at her watch. 'Should be just in time for PMQs in the Commons.'

119

Palace of Westminster, London

'THE PRIME MINISTER.' The words of the Speaker, uttered with the customary stentorian gravitas, had only a limited effect on the noisy hubbub that always accompanied the weekly Prime Minister's Questions in the House.

'Thank you, Mr Speaker,' the PM began, rising to his feet and looking around a nearly full House of Commons. 'I am pleased to inform the House that, thanks to some exceptionally skilful negotiations by our hard-working diplomats, the crisis over Taiwan has, to all intents and purposes, been averted.' He was interrupted by cheers from his own benches and the banging of hands on wood panelling, but he held up his hand for silence.

'We are not out of the woods yet. There's still a lot of work to be done. But we have conveyed to the Chinese authorities the impracticality of their position and I am pleased to say their attitude has been most cooperative. I would like to pay tribute to my Right Honourable colleagues, the Foreign Secretary and the Secretary of State for Defence, for all that they and their staff have done to avert this crisis. Ladies and gentlemen, today is a day to showcase the benefits of diplomacy. I would ask you all to join me in celebrating that there has not been one single British casualty throughout this period of tension.'

120

Vauxhall Cross, London

SHOWERED, DRESSED, RESTED, Luke Carlton felt clean on the outside, but inside the guilt was gnawing away at him. So much so that he had hardly closed his eyes on the flight back from Taipei the day before. He knew Jenny Li felt likewise. Crammed up next to each other in Economy, red-eyed and sleepless with worry, there was no chance to discuss their predicament without being overheard. Yet even on the brief refuelling stopover in Bangkok, they had barely said a word. In a single brief exchange before leaving Taipei, they had decided, on balance, to confess all once they reached Vauxhall Cross. Hannah's fate would surely have been sealed the moment they left her in that forest. She would have had no chance. The collector, they concluded, had done her duty and done it magnificently, but she was beyond saving. And the last thing either Luke or Jenny wanted was to find themselves part of a Taiwanese judicial inquiry.

So here he was, driving into Vauxhall Cross exactly eight days after they had left for Hong Kong, yet it felt like a lifetime ago. Luke searched for a space in the garage beneath the MI6 headquarters, parked his Land Rover and strode past the two Union Flags on miniature flagpoles that marked the discreet entrance for visitors who preferred not to be seen. He nodded to the black-clad security guards as the door hissed open for him. And then he was inside, walking into the circular marble atrium, and suddenly a familiar figure was rushing up to him and gripping him affectionately by the shoulders.

'Luke! Oh my God, I'm so worried about you!' It was Angela. She looked tired and stressed but then, he thought, I probably look ten years older after this week.

'Good to see you too, Angela,' he replied cheerfully. 'Sorry, what do you mean you *are* so worried? I'm back now. Hell of a trip, lots to discuss, of course.'

Angela took a step backwards, clamping her hand to her mouth. 'Oh Christ. You don't know, do you? No one's told you?'

'No one's told me what? Come on, Angela, don't be cryptic.'

She looked around and moved another step away. 'I'm so sorry, Luke. I can't say any more but you'd better get yourself up there. They're waiting for you in C's private office.'

'They? Who's they?'

A shake of the head.

'Go. Just go. Come down and see me at my desk afterwards, if they'll let you.'

Into the lift, up to the sixth floor and down the hall, then past a sign on a closed door that read 'Wellness Team', until he reached the Chief's private office. This had to be about Hannah, didn't it? But how bad could it be? He wasn't proud of what they'd done but he and Jenny had done it together and they'd done it for the Service. And the results were out there for everyone to see, even if the PM was giving all the credit to other people.

He pushed open the door. Six people, all standing. He recognized Alex Matheson, the Chief, Felix Schauer and Jenny. She looked as if she'd seen a ghost.

'Come in, Luke,' the Chief said. 'I think you've met Floyd, our Ethics Counsellor? These two people are from Legal.'

Oh God. So Jenny's told them about Hannah. She must have done. Maybe he needed a lawyer of his own.

'Look,' Luke began, hoping to regain the initiative, 'we both feel terrible about what happened to Hannah. But she didn't die in vain.'

'She didn't die at all,' retorted Felix Schauer. 'It's worse than that.' He walked over to a desktop computer, tapped a key and a grab from a newspaper filled the screen. 'Take a look at today's *South China Morning Post*. It's all over the front page.'

Luke froze.

'MI6 Left Me to Die' ran the headline. 'Dogs Ate My Face' was the line beneath it. Next to the text was a photograph of Hannah Slade, lying in a Hong Kong hospital bed. It looked as though half her face had been torn off.

'She's done an Edward Snowden,' said the Chief. 'She's gone over to the Chinese and told them everything. Everything!' She let those words hang in the air before she continued. 'So while I'm grateful for all the work you and Jenny did in retrieving that intel, I'm afraid this has blown up in our faces. Badly. Even if this is all a set-up by Beijing, and she's been coerced into it, the effect is still the same. It's nothing short of a PR disaster for the Service.'

Luke said nothing. He stood stiffly to attention, waiting for the blow to fall.

'So, Luke and Jenny, I am placing both of you on indefinite suspension pending an investigation. As from this moment, and until further notice, you no longer work for this Service as case officers. That is all.'

Epilogue

Army Command College, Nanjing, China

JUNIOR SERGEANT JIAN ZHANG was disappointed. The training for the mission he was expecting to undertake had been postponed almost as soon as it had begun. There was to be no invasion of that renegade offshore island they called Taiwan. At least, not this month.

But as he and his unit returned to barracks to await new orders their commander gathered them in to make an announcement.

As part of the ongoing and noble endeavour better to understand the malicious intentions of the capitalist imperialist powers seeking to intervene in the internal affairs of the People's Republic, the unit was to be visited at the end of the month by a special guest. That guest was a *gweilo*, a Westerner, and a former spy. But this spy had changed her behaviour and placed herself on the correct path. And Zhang's unit had much to learn from her.

The name of this guest was Dr Hannah Slade.

Acknowledgements

To Lizzie, thank you for listening patiently as I wrote this book and asking all the right questions that needed to be asked.

To my editor, Simon Taylor at Transworld Publishers, who also asks the right questions, in an ever-so-tactful way. This is our sixth book that we've worked on together.

To Julian Alexander, my equally talented agent at the Soho Agency. Thank you for all your help, encouragement and advice, especially when the pressures of too many commitments meant the inevitable pushing back of a deadline.

To Hazel Orme, my loyal and longstanding copy editor, and all those who worked on the proofreading.

To the late Royal Navy Rear Admiral John Gower for his detailed advice and expertise on naval operations, both above and below the surface, and for guidance on Whitehall procedures.

To Royal Navy Commodore (retd) Alistair Halliday for invaluable naval knowledge as well as your patience and engagement with all my many questions. It has been an absolute pleasure to learn from you.

To Ed Lucas, the ever-knowing and multi-talented author, for your advice and suggestions on some of the more technical aspects of this business.

To Richard Foster, my guide and mentor during my trip to Taiwan to research this book. Your affection for its language, culture and its people shone and you were great company throughout.

To my other friends who've served in the Royal Navy, for your patient guidance: one day I won't need to be reminded that a ship's wall is called 'a bulkhead'.

About the Author

Born in 1961, **Frank Gardner** holds a degree in Arabic and Islamic Studies. He has been the BBC's Security Correspondent since 2002. In 2004, while filming in Saudi Arabia, he and his cameraman were ambushed by terrorists. His cameraman was killed while Frank was shot multiple times and left for dead. He survived and returned to active news reporting within a year. Although paralysed in the legs, he still travels extensively, reporting from Ukraine to Colombia to Saudi Arabia. Awarded an OBE in 2005 for services to journalism, Frank published his bestselling memoir, *Blood & Sand*, in 2006. His first novel, the thriller *Crisis*, which introduced readers to SIS operative Luke Carlton, was a *Sunday Times* No.1 bestseller. The second and third Luke Carlton thrillers, *Ultimatum* and *Outbreak*, were also top 10 bestsellers.

Frank Gardner lives in London. You can follow him on Facebook and on X @FrankRGardner